THE GREAT UNMAKING

BOOKS BY BRIAN NELSON

THE COURSE OF EMPIRE SERIES
The Last Sword Maker
Five Tribes
The Great Unmaking

NONFICTION
The Silence and the Scorpion:
The Coup against Chávez and the Making of Modern Venezuela

THE GREAT UNMAKING

BRIAN NELSON

BLACK STONE

PUBLISHING

First edition: 2023
ISBN 978-1-5385-0784-1
Fiction / Thrillers / Technological

Version 1

Blackstone Publishing
31 Mistletoe Rd.
Ashland, OR 97520

www.BlackstonePublishing.com

For my wonderful older sister, mi hermana hermosa,
Diane Nelson, who read all the Narnia books to me when I was
a boy and sparked a lifelong love of great stories.
1963–2022

PROLOGUE

Jane Hunter awoke facedown in the tall grass. She put a hand to her aching head and groaned. *What happened?* Her thoughts were fuzzy and confused, as if her neurons were firing through cotton candy. She rolled onto her back and looked up. The grass that surrounded her was as tall as wheat, the stalks tilting down with the weight of their seedy heads.

Through this tunnel of green she saw the blue sky and a few wispy clouds.

She tried to remember what had happened, but only fragments came to her mind . . . fragments that she couldn't piece together. *Eric, in danger. Everyone hunting for a little girl. And a gun in her hand.*

She stood up slowly, her body stiff and sore. She looked around. She was in a clearing surrounded by trees. The wind stirred the grass, blowing patterns of silver across it like the crests of waves. She sensed she was high on a hill. Yes, through a gap in the trees, she saw the shimmer of a river in the distance.

She spun around, trying to orient herself. There were no houses, no roads, no telephone poles.

Then she saw the strangest thing. About twenty yards off, a spinning spiral coalesced in the air, like a miniature tornado of black particles. It was no more than ten feet tall and appeared for only a second before it twisted down to the earth and disappeared with an electric sizzle.

This is so weird.

She called Eric's name, but the only reply was the wind in the trees and the chirping of a few birds.

She looked closer at one tree in particular. It was a tulip poplar and oddly familiar. She was trying to link it to a memory when she felt something brush her hand. She pulled away reflexively, thinking it was an insect, but it was only the grass.

Wait, that wasn't right. She looked closer and a tingle of astonishment ran down her spine. The grass was growing before her eyes. When she had first stood, it had only been up to her knees; now it was halfway up her thighs. She looked to where her body had flattened the grass—and watched as the stems righted themselves and grew higher. A moment later she couldn't tell she'd been there.

She spun and saw it growing all around her. She could even hear it, a squeaky, stretching sound. Then it stopped, as if resting for the next surge.

"You're dreaming," she said aloud. Yet the ache in her stomach—the mix of fear and terror—told her that this was no dream.

She turned back to the poplar tree and tilted her head in scrutiny. *What was it about this . . . ?*

She stepped closer. *No, it can't be.*

She walked up to it and began climbing. At the second fork, she searched the wood with her fingers. There it was: the "JH" she had carved with her Swiss army knife . . . . when she was seven years old.

This tree had been in her backyard in 2003 when her father was stationed at Fort Myer doing work for the Pentagon. *But how did it get here?*

She looked around. *Could it be?*

Yes, the big oak tree in the Johnson's back yard was still there, right where it should be, but where was her house? Where were the rest of the officers' quarters? Where was the road?

A dizzying realization hit her. The river she had glimpsed through the trees . . .

She jumped down and ran toward it—to where the entrance of the base should be—in the direction of the Iwo Jima Memorial. She fought through the high grass, then ran through a grove of trees until she broke out and finally saw the world spread out before her.

Oh my God!

Below her lay a pristine wilderness; in the foreground a wide river glimmered in the sunlight. On the opposite bank a beautiful valley stretched out, with hills rising steadily to the north. To the south the river merged with a smaller tributary, making a distinct wedge of land. In the distance, rolling hills of thick forest spread out in every direction.

Now both hands came to her mouth. She shook her head in disbelief.

There was no Arlington Cemetery. No GW Parkway. No Lincoln Memorial. No Washington Monument. No cars. No airplanes. Not another human being in sight.

Someone—or something—had erased the world.

She stared, trying to make sense of it. Then she noticed more of the strange spirals in the air. She saw five of them in quick succession, appearing for a moment before being sucked down into the earth.

She scanned the terrain more closely, trying to find any sign of the world she knew.

There!

South of the Mall, she saw the Jefferson Memorial, but even as her eyes locked on, it began to dissolve. Jane watched in amazement as the dome disappeared in a spiraling haze of particles, as if a giant hand was sanding it to dust. Simultaneously, creeper vines grew hungrily up its Ionic columns, until those too dissolved and the vines tumbled back to the ground.

Please be a dream, she thought. *Please be a dream.*

She tried to put the fragments of memory together. *Eric hurt. A countdown for . . . something. The missing little girl.*

Jane needed someone to help her. To explain this.

"Eric!" she called out desperately. "Please! Anyone."

Then she froze as the snarl of a large animal came from the woods behind her. It was a deep and menacing sound. She turned and her eyes went wide in terror.

No, that's impossible.

She ran for her life.

PART ONE

THE GATHERING STORM

CHAPTER ONE

THE CURSE

January 10, 2027
Namibia

On a desolate expanse of the Kalahari Desert, a battered Toyota Hilux sped over a rough dirt track, kicking up a long plume of brown dust that rose high into the blue sky. At the wheel, Silas bounced in his seat as the pickup jostled over the sandy road. Everywhere he looked he saw the undulating waste of the desert, flat and sunbaked in its hypnotic shades of red and orange. This land was nearly devoid of life, with only the occasional cluster of camel thorn or *Hoodia* cacti.

But up ahead, at the base of a dune, Silas saw a grove of umbrella trees. That meant there could be water there. And water meant game, possibly rhinos and elephants. The Ivory Queen was currently paying $3,000 a kilo for black rhino horn, and that was a price that Silas simply couldn't refuse.

He smiled at the thought of what he could buy with all that money, but then he frowned as his eyes flitted to the rearview mirror and the two men riding in the bed of the truck. He considered each of them in turn. Charles was in his early twenties, lean and clever, and the best shot in the village. Kerel was older, almost forty, loud-mouthed and insufferable. Silas gave a heavy sigh. It was never an easy choice to include Kerel on a hunting party. The man never shut up. Indeed, it was said in the village that the only time he wasn't imparting his wisdom to the unenlightened was when he was asleep. Yet Silas needed Kerel because he was as strong as a lion and could butcher a rhino in less than an hour. On other hunting trips he'd let the men ride in the cab with him, but not today. He didn't want to put up with Kerel's superstitious chatter.

"There are strange stories coming out of the desert," Kerel had said. "The Sān gods are powerful again." All weekend he had been fretting about it, saying that it was too dangerous to come. Silas saw the talk for what it was—a ploy to get extra pay.

The tree line was now only three hundred meters away. The road dipped into a long gully then rose again. As they broke to flat ground, they startled a dozen vultures feeding on a carcass by the side of the road. The birds lifted angrily, making guttural squawks.

But what caught Silas's eye was a handmade sign by the side of the road.

Kerel banged on the roof for Silas to stop. Silas cursed in annoyance but complied.

The sign read, DANGER. GO BACK!

Kerel jumped to the ground and came up to his window. "See, I told you. We cannot go any further."

"Lines in the sand mean nothing."

Kerel's face hardened and he glanced around—first at Silas, then to the wide desert. "I do not want to anger the gods."

Silas shook his head dismissively. "The Sān gods are weak. That is why their people live in this forsaken place and why every year there are less and less of them. Come on. We're wasting time."

"*Oshikombo oshigoya,*" Kerel muttered under his breath. *Stupid goat.* Then he got back in the truck.

Silas hit the accelerator, but the engine immediately stalled. He turned the key in the ignition. Nothing happened. Absolutely nothing. No cranking of the starter, no click of a dying battery.

He tried once more. Nothing.

He smacked the wheel in frustration. It was an old truck, but it rarely failed to start.

He glanced back at the others. Kerel raised his eyebrows in an expression that said, *I told you so.*

"It's just flooded," Silas called out. "We'll give it a few minutes . . . it will be fine." Not wanting to look at the others, he focused his attention out his side window. The vultures had settled back on the carcass, and were picking and tearing at it once more. There wasn't much left, but Silas guessed it had been a springbok, judging by the small rib cage and the bits of tan fur.

He tried the ignition again. Still nothing.

With a curse, he got out and raised the hood. The other two men joined him. A half hour later nothing had changed.

"A Sān witch doctor has put a hex on this land," Kerel said.

"Don't be ridiculous!" Silas spat. He looked around, refusing to accept defeat. It was only 180 meters to the first cluster of trees. If they could kill just one rhino, he could buy another truck and still have thousands to spare. "Get your things!" he said as he went to the truck bed and grabbed his rifle and gear. "We're going on foot."

Kerel and Charles exchanged a skeptical glance, then reluctantly obeyed.

Silas began marching up the road, but as he walked by the sign, a sudden nausea came over him. He stopped for a moment and the pain subsided.

Suddenly there was a clamor as the vultures took flight, all of them hissing and croaking at once.

Standing in the truck bed, Charles called out: "Look!"

Silas turned to see the strangest thing. The carcass of the springbok was disappearing before their eyes. Ribs, fur, scraps of organs and muscles were simply vanishing. He stared in astonishment. He thought he saw a light haze over the ground there, then it too disappeared.

Kerel and Charles began to murmur amongst themselves, something about "the spirit of the dead."

"Come on!" Silas yelled. "Stop stalling."

But the two men stayed rooted to the truck bed.

Disgusted, Silas turned and marched on, but a new wave of nausea struck him. He gasped but refused to stop. The next step brought a splitting pain to his head and all the muscles in his neck squeezed and began to cramp. He gritted his teeth and took another step. Now the pain in his stomach seemed to triple and he couldn't help but cry out.

But he refused to go back. He looked down at his legs and willed them forward, but as soon as his right knee rose, he collapsed to the ground, his rifle falling into the sandy dirt. His whole body was racked with pain and his headache was so intense that it was difficult to think. There seemed to be a voice talking to him, whispering in his ear. "Go back. Only pain lies ahead."

Determined, he reached for his gun, but as he did so his bladder and bowels let go. With a loud fart, he defecated in his pants and urine ran hot down his thighs.

"Help me!" he called out.

Kerel and Charles jumped down from the truck and rushed to help, but both stopped at the invisible threshold of the sign. They motioned to him. "Come back!"

But Silas was now overwhelmed with the pain. "Please," he shouted.

Charles and Kerel nodded to each other and stepped forward. Charles stopped instantly and grabbed at his stomach. Yet Kerel felt no pain.

Kerel looked from one man to the other: Silas on his hands and knees, one hand on his rifle. Charles doubled over, his rifle still strapped over his shoulder,

The Sān gods can see us, he thought.

He grabbed the rifle from Charles and felt the nausea attack his own stomach. But as soon as he'd cast the gun aside the pain subsided.

Charles stood up straight, and Kerel put his hand on his shoulder. "Better?"

"Yes."

Together they picked up Silas, each grabbing an arm and a leg, scrunching up their noses at the smell, and carried him to the bed of the pickup.

At the wheel, Kerel tried the engine. This time it turned over. He put it in reverse and hit the gas. The Toyota leapt backward, spitting up gravel that pinged and clanged against the undercarriage. He turned the truck around and pushed the pedal all the way to the floor. The truck picked up speed and soon they were bouncing madly over the rugged terrain as they sped back toward the village, Kerel struggling to keep it on the road, but not daring to take his foot off the accelerator.

He glanced into the rearview mirror and saw Silas rolling around in agony in the truck bed.

The handmade sign that marked the Sān territory was fading into the distance.

Kerel nodded to himself. He'd been right again—the Sān gods were powerful once more.

On the patch of road where the men had stopped, one of the vultures landed and hobbled cautiously up to the two rifles lying in the dust. He gave a curious peck at one, then the wood and metal dissolved into nothing.

Seven miles away, a fourteen-year-old boy jogged lightly along a sandy trail, a hunting spear in one hand, an AK-47 rifle in the other. He was dressed in nothing but a buckskin loin cloth and his coppery-gold skin seemed to meld with the colors of the desert around him. He was lithe and agile, moving quickly and gracefully up a broad hill, his feet knowing where to fall on the trail.

He was about two miles from the Sān camp, returning from a

scouting mission. Six weeks earlier, a group of mercenaries—hired by the Ivory Queen—had tried to wipe out what remained of his people. The horrific images of that night—his people fighting with bows and arrows against soldiers with assault rifles—still filled his dreams and daydreams. His grandfather had been murdered during that attack, and he missed him terribly.

After the massacre, he and some of the other teenagers had taken it upon themselves to make regular patrols to ensure that they were never ambushed again. He looked down at the heavy rifle in his hand. It wasn't a Sān weapon, and a part of him hated to even look at it. But he knew he needed it if he wanted to protect his people.

Luckily, Karuma had seen no one all day, nor for that matter, in many days. Their land had grown quiet again. The tracks, the birds, the animals had all told him that everything was as it should be. He prayed to Cagn that it would last.

He came to a stop at the top of a rise and looked out over the open plain. There had been rain here recently and he saw a score of blossoming umbrella trees dotting the foreground, then the open vastness of the desert beyond. He leaned on his spear for a moment, taking in the view. About a mile off, a herd of cape buffalo made a gray blot on the brown landscape. He was in no hurry, so he stood there for a time, watching the world, and feeling the breeze on his face.

But as he turned to head for home, he noticed something beside the path: three thick reeds, about a foot long, woven together. He leaned down and picked them up. The end of each reed was covered by a stopper of eland leather. Although he'd never seen such a thing before he realized immediately what it was. His grandfather had described it to him many times. He shook the reeds gently and heard the liquid slosh inside.

But how did it get here? Had another Sān tribe been hunting here? And why hadn't he noticed it this morning when he'd come down this track? He scanned the ground more closely, but the only human tracks were his own.

He looked up to the blue sky, because it seemed only logical that this was a gift from Cagn. "Thank you," he said, and waved at the blue sky.

He strapped the reeds to his back and made for home.

Once back in the camp he told no one what he had found. But in the evening, he took the reeds and a simple brush he had fashioned from an eland's tail hairs and went to a high outcrop of rock.

The sun was low at his back and colored the rock face in dark orange. First he drew himself, doing his best to replicate the brush strokes he'd seen in other Sān paintings. Then he drew his mother, then a large tree with a swarm of bees around it, and finally a tall man with skin as white as the moon.

CHAPTER TWO

A COLD WELCOME

January 10, 2027
Naval Research Lab (NRL), Washington DC

Eric Hill looked up at Moffett hangar. No matter how many times he saw it, it still took his breath away. It was a massive structure, more than 150 feet high, eighty feet wide, and the torpedo-shaped shell enclosed eight acres. It had been built in California in the 1930s to hold a zeppelin, back when the Navy envisioned the airships as flying aircraft carriers.

Eric stood for a moment, mesmerized, not wanting to go any further. Or was there another reason he didn't want to move?

"You know you don't have to do this," Jane said.

He came to himself and turned to her.

"The doctors will extend your leave," she said. "All you have to do is ask."

"No, I've been away long enough." He gave her hand a squeeze and forced a smile. "Besides, if I stay away any longer it could jeopardize my clearance. I hear they frown upon letting people with PTSD play with their toys."

"Okay," she said, "but I want you to take this one step at a time."

"Aye-aye," he said, flashing a mischievous smile. With a

dramatic flair, he motioned for her to lead the way. "Shall we enter the belly of the beast?"

They drew closer to the hangar, and it seemed to grow more immense with every step. Red warning lights pulsated along its high spine and a series of caged yellow lights lined the edges of its wide mouth.

They crossed the threshold, feeling like ants in a child's play set.

The inside of the hangar was just as impressive as the outside. With no central support, the walls of the hangar had to bear its full weight, which meant that they were a latticework of interconnecting girders, every beam and rivet polished to shine like chrome. Magnifying the effect, lights had been placed across the crisscrossing pattern that made the walls and ceiling sparkle like the gossamer strands of an enormous spider web.

In the foreground, several hundred NRL scientists were milling around, waiting for the presentation to start. Beyond the rows of folding chairs was a stage with a podium. Several of the top scientists and high-ranking officers were gathered up there.

"Eric!"

He turned to see Jessica, the gray-haired leader of the genetics team.

"It's so good to have you back!" She gave him a hug. "How are you feeling?"

"Good as new."

"I'm so glad," she said. "We thought we might lose you."

Eric heard another happy voice. "Hey, look who it is?" He turned to see Arundhati, one of his colleagues from the nanotech team. He greeted her warmly and they began catching up. Soon a few more friends came and said hello. The welcome felt good. But for each person he greeted, he couldn't help but wonder, *Is this one on our side or the other side?*

"Ladies and gentlemen, please take your seats, we will start in a few moments."

Jane and Eric found some seats near the aisle.

One look at the stage reinforced his uneasiness that this was not the same old lab. The leadership had changed so much in his absence that he only recognized one person up there.

The people he respected the most—the ones who had mentored him, challenged him, and even saved his life—were gone.

That sent a pang of anxiety through his body, and, with it, a feeling of weakness. Their numbers were dwindling. He still had Jane and a few other friends he could count on, but the loss of Bill and Jack meant things were going to get a lot harder. They had been the civilian leaders of the lab, brilliant scientists who had guided the whole team of more than twenty-two hundred scientists through the daunting process of reaching "replication," arguably the greatest scientific breakthrough since the Manhattan Project. It had been the lightning strike in the tidal pool. The moment their nanosites had become more than just programmable machines; they had become sentient and capable of evolving on their own. A tool that could be used to create whatever they could imagine. It was Bill and Jack who had made that possible. What would they do without them?

He realized that it would be up to the ones who were left—and up to him and Jane and a handful of others—to step up and fill the void. It wasn't something he shrank from, but it wasn't what he particularly wanted either.

"Ladies and gentlemen, can I have your attention?"

A handsome Air Force general stepped up to the podium and raised his hand for silence. This was Eric's first glimpse of Chip Walden. He was tall, with blond hair and a strong jaw. He was also the new de facto leader of the Naval Research Lab, the one who had so cleverly usurped power from Admiral Curtiss and then—using his influence among the Joint Chiefs—made himself the first non-naval leader of the NRL. Walden smiled warmly at the crowd. Eric couldn't help but shake his head.

"I have brought you here this evening to update you on our efforts to restructure the lab. I also want to outline our plans for tackling the new challenges that lie before us. I know that many of you feel that this is a dark hour. In all honesty, I must agree with you. I am still shocked by the truth about Admiral Curtiss. A man I have known for many years and had always considered a good friend."

Eric caught Jane rolling her eyes.

"And if that wasn't a hard enough blow," Walden continued, "we have also lost our civilian leadership—Jack Behrmann and Bill Eastman—who were abducted by the terrorist Riona Finley.

"Yet despite the darkness of the hour. Despite these setbacks. We cannot afford to ease up, or slow down. No, we don't have that luxury. We must move forward with all speed and with all our ingenuity and with all the devotion that our hearts can muster.

"For the threat to our nation has never been greater. The stakes never higher. The need for swiftness never so urgent.

"The amazing technologies that you have created were designed to protect America against rival nations. Less than two years ago you rose to the challenge and beat the Chinese to 'replication.' But now we find that the enemy is no longer a foreign power. The enemy is among us. Here in America.

"Riona Finley and the New Anarchists have assassinated US senators, murdered FBI agents, and kidnapped our colleagues.

"You all know exactly what their abduction means. If she can force them to betray our secrets, then terrorists will wield the same power that we now wield. The same technology we used to make state-of-the art body armor, the best stealth technology, invisible surveillance systems, and the ability to biohack. All that could soon be hers.

"Yes, we face the real possibility that all our work could be used against us. Worse, because Finley has our top scientists, we have to face the possibility that she could create something beyond even what we possess. I'm talking about a weapon of mass destruction the likes of which the world has never seen."

Walden paused. He was now gripping the sides of the podium so hard that Eric could see the corded muscles of his neck.

"To confront this threat, we must change course dramatically.

For the first time we must focus on defense. We will need counter-measures and vaccines to keep our environment—our air and water—free of Finley's nanosites. We have to protect our very bodies from these microscopic invaders.

"To lead this initiative and to usher in a new level of security to the NRL, I've tapped Major Tom Blake." Behind Walden, a marine officer in dress blues rose and lifted his hand. He struck Eric as a powerful, no-nonsense figure. He looked to be in his early fifties, squat and strong, with a hard, weathered face and bristly black hair. As the crowd applauded, he gave only a grimace of a smile, then took his seat again.

Eric shot Jane a glance, as if to ask if she'd known about this.

She read him perfectly and shook her head.

Under Admiral Curtiss, the military leaders had always kept a comfortable distance from the civilian scientists. But Walden had just handed Blake a project that would allow him to dictate the course of all of the lab's teams.

At that moment Blake locked eyes with Eric and it seemed he knew exactly what Eric was thinking . . . and that he didn't like it. Eric held his gaze for a moment, but it made him so uncomfortable that he looked down at his hands.

At the podium Walden was carrying on. ". . . and while these setbacks are testing our resolve, don't lose heart, for I truly believe they are only that—setbacks. Temporary and surmountable.

"And I'll tell you why. Because we have a big advantage over Riona Finley. Not only do we have you—the best scientists in the world—but we have something else."

Walden paused and nodded slowly, teasing it out.

"I know you have probably heard rumors that our AI team had been working on something revolutionary. Well, I wanted you to hear it from me: that to call their work revolutionary is an under-statement."

This was perhaps the biggest development that Eric had missed during his mission to Africa. In his absence they had built an AI system they called Eleven. By using a hybrid quantum supercomputer and Eric's concept of "Forced Evolution" they had made an astonishing leap forward. This was largely because they had been able to quickly "grow" hundreds of "infant" AI systems and only keep the most promising ones. Their ultimate creation, Eleven, was currently being fed massive amounts of information—every minute—from the NSA, CIA, Interpol, and other intelligence services, as well as data from the web and mainstream media. It was using all this as "training data" to get smarter and smarter. The result: a computer that could monitor huge swaths of the globe, and process and analyze a vast amount of data much better than any human.

"I've met him and he's an amazing character," Walden said with a smile. "With his help we are going to find Finley and bring her and all of her followers to justice."

The crowd burst into applause.

"Now I want to take a moment to acknowledge the two people who made it possible." Behind Walden, an attractive black-haired woman and an Asian man stood.

"Ladies and gentlemen, Olivia Rosario and Ryan Lee." The crowd clapped and cheered.

Now many thoughts were crowding Eric's mind. The first was that he had just been snubbed. Yes, the work on Eleven had taken place while he was gone. But it would never have been possible without Forced Evolution. The second thought was that he now understood what it felt like to have an invention that he'd made used for something that he never supported or condoned. They had taken his idea and applied it to AI in a way that had never occurred to him, and, in the process, created something potentially very dangerous.

He eyed the two scientists who were waving to the crowd. This was Eric's first glimpse of Olivia Rosario. But Jane had told him about her. She was the first of Walden's infiltrators. A special liaison and AI expert who had been brought in to spy on the lab and undermine Curtiss. By all accounts, she'd done her job brilliantly.

Eric knew the Asian man well . . . or he'd thought he did. Before his mission to Africa, Ryan had been Eric's best friend. But Ryan had thrown in his lot with Walden from the beginning, in large part because Walden and Olivia had offered Ryan his dream: free rein to build the world's most advanced AI system. But that wasn't the only reason. Ryan and Olivia had started dating, and as a consequence, Ryan had abandoned his friendship with Jane and many others at the lab. Now Ryan was one of the biggest pushers of the Walden Kool-Aid.

Walden made a few more comments to fire up the crowd, then the presentation ended.

As people exited, Eric decided to approach Ryan. Even though all indications showed that their friendship was over (Ryan hadn't even come to visit him during his three weeks in the hospital), Eric still felt he should try.

But as he was moving to intercept Ryan, someone called his name in a voice that was not altogether friendly.

"Dr. Hill, I'd like a word."

He turned and found himself face to face with Major Blake. The man smiled flatly and extended his hand. Eric noticed his posture seemed more intimidating than welcoming. Eric shook his hand; Blake squeezed unnecessarily hard. *This guy is losing points fast*, he thought.

"I'm glad you've finally decided to come back to work," Blake began. "We have several projects that have been stalled due to your absence. With Behrmann and Eastman gone, it appears that you're the only one who understands some of our most important tech. I don't like that. Not at all. It puts the whole project at risk. So one of your first priorities is going to be to offload that knowledge to others. I'll need you to start on that immediately, meaning tonight. Tomorrow morning I'll need details of your plan. You got that?"

Eric hesitated. *Was this guy for real?* Eric had been hospitalized for three weeks and lost a foot of his intestine, and this was how he was going to be treated? Like a teenager who had been cutting class?

Blake noticed his hesitation and folded his arms under his chest. "Is there a problem?"

Eric reminded himself that he had to be careful. He'd discussed this with Jane and the others. *Don't make waves. Not now.* The only reason they hadn't quit when Walden took over was because they needed to try to put a check on his power. If they left the lab (or got fired) they'd have no access to the technology and no way from keeping Walden from doing something extreme. *So just be cool.* But a part of him refused to yield . . . completely.

"No, Major, it's fine," he said. "But I think you'll find that you'll get better results around here if you tone down the 'oorah' attitude."

Now Blake made his first sincere smile of the evening. A smug grin of immense pleasure. "Well, thank you kindly for that advice. And since we are sharing advice, let me give you some.

"I'd like to remind you that you are a civilian employee of the United States Navy. So unless you have an O-3 commission that I'm not aware of, you are going to do what I tell you or you will find yourself unemployed.

"You see, Dr. Hill, I read your file and I didn't like what I saw. I know you disobeyed orders in Namibia, which caused the death of the pilots and crew of your V-280 Valor. You might console yourself with the knowledge that your actions saved the other Valor and its cargo, but who the hell were you to make that call?"

Eric was suddenly aware that it had grown very quiet. He glanced around and saw that at least twenty people were listening in.

Blake leaned closer.

"I also read your psych file. I know about your daddy's suicide and that he was losing his mind. Now I'm wondering if that might run in the family, and that your candle might be burning nice and bright now, but who knows. Perhaps any day . . ."

He smiled and gave a shrug. He leaned in closer. He was almost whispering now. "The way I see it, you are more of a liability to this project than an asset. My advice to you is to make sure you do exactly as you're told. And I'm going to give you the first chance do to just that tomorrow morning. Be in my office at oh-six-hundred."

Eric's eyes were locked on Blake's, and he knew Blake could feel his anger. But Blake's smile stayed smug and confident. Eric could feel the other eyes on him too—including Jane's—waiting to see what he would do.

"Yes, sir," he said.

CHAPTER THREE

THE CONSPIRACY

January 10, 2027
Naval Research Lab, Washington, DC

> We must all hang together, or most assuredly, we shall
> all hang separately.
>
> —Benjamin Franklin

"That could have gone better," Lili said, handing Eric a cup of coffee. Eric felt his face flush hot with embarrassment.

He was sitting in Lili's apartment with her; her husband, Xiao-ping; their fourteen-year-old niece, Mei; and Jane.

"I'm sorry," Eric said.

He glanced nervously at each of them, then focused his attention on Lili, who was clearly the most upset. Looking at her now, he suddenly realized how much she'd changed. When he'd first met her, she'd been a high-spirited—almost bubbly—woman. Infectiously enthusiastic. But the experiences of the last year had made her sober-minded and cautious.

Eric could hardly blame her. Less than a year ago, Lili and her twin sister had been working for China's advanced weapons program as spies for the US government. When the Chinese had kidnapped

Eric and Ryan and forced them to reveal their own secrets, it was Lili and her sister who had helped them escape. But during their flight out of China, Lili's sister had been murdered by the Chinese.

But that was only part of Lili's harrowing story. Twelve years ago, her husband, Xiao-ping, had been arrested for opposing the Chinese government and sent to a labor camp in Africa. After Lili and her niece had been brought safely to the US, Admiral Curtiss had authorized the mission to rescue him—sending Eric to Africa with a Joint Operations Force.

As Eric looked at her, he saw the fragility of her situation. Here was a woman trying to do the right thing while also keeping what was left of her family together.

She was still looking at him, clearly not accepting his apology.

"I'll make sure it doesn't happen again," he added.

But she shook her head. "We helped you create the Namibia Program," she said, "putting our jobs at risk. And your first night back, you manage to piss off Blake, which means he's going to have you under a microscope. If he discovers the Namibia Program, they will probably piece together that we helped you."

"In all fairness," Jane interjected, "Blake had already put Eric on his shit list. Nothing he said or did tonight would have changed that."

"I agree," added Xiao-ping, "he already had it in for Eric. Increased scrutiny from Blake was inevitable."

Lili gave both Jane and her husband a hard look, then sighed. "That may be true, but the fact that the Namibia Program exists means we could be exposed for it at any time. Our sole purpose is to stop Walden, not help some tribe in Africa. We need to shut it down."

"No," Eric said quickly. "We can't. They saved my life and I owe it to them. Please, I just need a few more days to verify that the system is fully automated. Then I can cut all ties and just let it run on its own. It will be completely autonomous."

Lili sighed. "I know I can't stop you, but I think it's an unnecessary risk. Before Bill and Jack were kidnapped, we all agreed that our mission was to put a check on Walden's power."

"So let's focus on that," Jane said, trying to change the subject.

"Right," Xiao-ping chorused.

Lili finally seemed to relent and turned to Jane. "Are you ready to begin your surveillance?"

"Yes, I've modified the program I used last year on Curtiss, and it's ready to go."

"But what if they discover you're watching?" Mei asked.

"She's right," Xiao-ping said, "we have to be careful. Soon Walden is going to begin checking the employees' bodies for foreign nanosites. They don't have that up and running yet, but they will soon."

"Don't worry, I've made our nanosites untraceable," Jane said.

"What about the transmissions?"

"The encryption uses a Vernam cipher and a dedicated nanosite swarm."

Eric nodded, it was a clever idea, combining the old and the new. The American scientist Gilbert Vernam had developed the first unbreakable codes during WWI by creating random key "pads" that were only used once. As long as the pads stayed secure on each end of the transmission—and were only used once—the code could never be broken. Jane had merged that idea with their nanosite technology.

"Even a short message creates enough possibilities to be in the range of two to the forty-third power," Jane said. "Not even Eleven can break that."

"And what if something happens to you?" Mei asked.

"Then you will have to start over. I did it that way on purpose so that in the unlikely event Walden somehow traces it back to me, none of *you* can be implicated."

Eric nodded. He didn't like to think about that, but he had to acknowledge it was the safest thing to do. He turned their attention to what he felt was their biggest problem.

"Tell me about Eleven. How good is it, really?"

"*He*'s astonishing," Lili said. "I've talked to him and he's creepy smart. And his predictive powers are uncanny. Eventually he'll find Finley, I have no doubt about it. Either through the millions of surveillance cameras he can access or the amount of live data he's being fed. It's inevitable."

"What's his weakness?" Eric asked.

"He doesn't have one. You can't even unplug him. Walden has created a special power system using nanosites. What really scares me is that I'm sure Walden wants to integrate it with swarm technology. They've already asked me to set up a timeline for that."

Eric let out a long exhale. "How long?" Eric asked.

"Four weeks."

"That's crazy," he said. "They're going to give the smartest AI system in the world the ability to manipulate the physical world, to create nanosite swarms that could go anywhere, after only a couple of months of testing?"

"All the timelines are being cut like that—in the name of keeping us safe from Finley," Jane said.

"The cure is sounding a lot worse than the disease," Xiao-ping said.

Lili nodded. "For over twelve years I fought against the Chinese government. I thought that once I got here, things would be different, but once again I'm working for a military with tyrannical motives."

Jane reached out and grasped her hand. "You did the right thing then and you're doing the right thing now."

Lili could only respond with a thin smile.

An uncomfortable silence settled over the room. "You all realize that if we do this," Xiao-ping said, "then there's no turning back. The things we have done thus far will just get you fired, but putting Walden under surveillance and trying to undermine the lab's current mission means prison time if we're caught."

They each glanced at each other, all of them apparently trying to gauge the other's conviction. For a long moment no one spoke.

"Are we all agreed?" Xiao-ping probed.

"As the only minor in the room," Mei said. "I'm definitely in."

They all laughed, and the air grew lighter. Then came a chorus of yeses.

Then Xiao-ping spoke, "Then this marks the point of no return."

CHAPTER FOUR

THE PROMISE

January 10, 2027
Naval Research Lab, Washington, DC

It was almost midnight when Eric returned to his apartment. He immediately went to the kitchen table, opened his iSheet, and began reviewing the day's data from Namibia.

For him, it had been a crummy day and he had hoped that this, at least, would lift his spirits. And it did. Just seeing the majesty of the Kalahari Desert once more—live and in high definition—felt like an elixir to his brain. First, he checked Kebbi-An, the oldest woman in the group, who was struggling to keep the tribe together. Then Nyando, the four-year-old girl, who had always been able to manipulate Eric into carrying her wherever they went.

Seeing them and knowing they were safe made him feel much better, but it also brought a longing to be with them.

This is the way it has to be, he reminded himself.

He sighed. Then he reminded himself that he had a lot to be proud of. The Namibia Program was, without a doubt, the most beautiful piece of technology he'd ever created. A system that combined artificial intelligence, genetic engineering, and nanotechnology in a completely novel way. He'd worked around the clock on it, doing much of the work in his hospital bed, while Jane and Lili had secretly tested it in the lab.

When it was ready, he'd put his nanosite swarms in boxes and mailed them to random addresses along the rim of the Kalahari Desert. Eric had imagined the faces of the confused recipients when they received each package, opening the box and feeling a light breeze on their skin as the invisible swarms were set free. Looking inside they would have found only a small piece of emaciated beef jerky—food for the road trip.

The moment they were released, the swarms had immediately begun dozens of complex operations, binding together, creating a new device, accomplishing a task, then breaking apart to start a new operation. Seventy billion of them—little more than a particle of dust in the air—combined to make a microcontroller, a brain that could coordinate the other pods. Twenty-five billion created an ethereal satellite antenna and nine hundred million more began transmitting into the sky at 1626.5 MHz.

Once their global position was verified, they sent Eric an update. Then it was time to feed. They were programmed to sniff out concentrations of carbon—coals from a cooking fire, dead leaves and plants, as well as the dead skin on living things—humans, pets, and livestock. Once fed, they began a massive replication cycle, making trillions of copies of themselves until their number had swelled to 10^{54}. Because they were microscopic, they were invisible to the naked eye, yet they now formed a huge cloud, a hundred yards wide, that raced off into the Kalahari Desert.

At all the locations where Eric had shipped his packages, the same process played out. Now each cloud set off to find the Sān. They searched their hunting grounds and the sacred cave where Eric had last seen them, then their waterholes. They replicated and fed along the way, scavenging for food like any other living creature. If they came across the carcass of an animal, they consumed it and moved on.

Like most everything in nanotechnology, Eric had created the

Namibia Program using nature as a model. That's because similar microscopic machines already existed within us. Although we rarely considered them, our bodies were a vast network of specialized machines, invisibly working every second of every day to keep us alive. Scientists called these machines proteins. They digested our food, passed nutrients from our blood to the cells that needed them, and controlled the unwinding of our DNA so our cells could divide. In fact, there were more than eighty thousand types of proteins in a human body, each with a specialized task. They were the invisible engines that made life possible. Microscopic and blisteringly quick. How quick? In just one second a single protein or enzyme such as ATPase could break down more than a septillion ATP molecules.

Once the swarms reached the Sān's territory, they began to track them with a combination of aerial cameras and olfactory sensors. Specialized pods of nanosites began sorting through the vaporized molecules in the air, categorizing them just like a mammal's olfactory epithelium would. Eric had modeled these pods after the noses of African elephants who had evolved an astonishing 1,948 genes just to detect and categorize smells (twice as many as a dog and five times as many as a human). Eric had been astonished to discover that elephants could smell water from twelve miles away.

Even though the Sān's range covered close to three hundred square miles, the pods found the tribe in under ninety minutes.

Now a new set of operations began: Most of the swarms fanned out to create a surveillance perimeter around the Sān's territory, then they initiated the defensive systems designed to keep out poachers and the Ivory Queen's mercenaries. Other swarms stayed near the Sān, and kept vigil on their daily movements, and tiny airborne cameras floated around and sent their footage to Eric.

Other nanosites entered the bodies of the Sān and assessed their health. Eric had been reluctant to do this, it felt invasive, but the tribe had lost more than half its members in the massacre—only thirteen of the thirty-four members had survived—and they were on the brink of collapse. They couldn't afford any more losses to disease or parasites. What's more, most of the able-bodied men and women had died, leaving the tribe skewed toward the young and the elderly. He had hoped that he would not need to interfere, but his first health check revealed that three of the children had the stomach parasite giardia and that two of the elders had bronchitis. He decided to treat all of them.

But he did draw the line at communication. While he'd been with them, he'd never told them what type of scientist he was and the things he was able to do. And he suspected that they wouldn't have believed him even if he had told them. Quite frankly, he preferred it that way. It was one of the other beauties of this system: it was invisible. An entire ecosystem kept in balance without any of the actors knowing it. The swarm's size was kept at a minimum, but if more swarms were needed in the case of a security breach, then they could quickly increase their numbers to combat the threat.

Now, as Eric sat at his iSheet reviewing the activity of the day, he felt a deep longing to be with them again. After he had checked on the base camp and most of the tribe, he went to the footage of Karuma, the fourteen-year-old boy who had become his little brother. It was Karuma who had first befriended him after the crash, looked after him when he was suffering from cortical blindness, and had taught him at least forty new Sān words a day.

Eric fast-forwarded through the footage to see if Karuma had found the paint he had left for him. He smiled when he saw what happened, and when Karuma had waved to the sky, Eric found himself reflexively waving back. Then he touched the boy's face on the screen. "I miss you," he said aloud.

"I can't be with you, but I'm making sure no one will ever hurt you again."

CHAPTER FIVE

MISSING PIECES

Earlier that day
FBI Headquarters, Washington, DC

Special Agent Bartholomew "Bud" Brown was brushing his teeth in the third-floor men's room, trying to get rid of the smell of the four shots of bourbon he'd pounded during lunch, when he was struck by a rare moment of lucidity.

He stopped brushing, and his eyes locked on his reflection in the mirror. He watched in odd fascination as the white paste pooled at the corner of his mouth, then began to slide down his chin. Then it stopped. And with it, the universe seemed to stop too. His focus expanded to his whole visage: this leathery skin from decades of smoking, his wispy comb-over, his faded white shirt, and the paisley tie he'd been wearing since the nineties. For the first time in many months, he was really looking at himself.

You are running out of time, the voice said. *You've got three weeks left before they force you out. Cut the drinking. Get Finley. You owe it to Rogers.*

He knew the voice was right. It was nothing new, really. Ever since Rogers's death the voice would occasionally remind him of what he should do. But thus far his need to stay drunk had always been stronger than the voice. But today was different. For the first time since Rogers's death, he felt he might be able to get himself back on track. *If you can just hold it together long enough to . . .*

Behind him a toilet flushed and a young agent emerged from one of the stalls, jostling his belt buckle, then zipping up his fly. He was in his early twenties, handsome, with a full head of hair, put-together, and confident. He smiled and nodded to Bud's reflection as he washed his hands.

Bud didn't move. He was trying to hold on to that moment of clarity, trying with all his might, hoping that this distraction would end so he could return to it.

The younger agent started the blow dryer, and Bud held his eyes tight in concentration. *Don't let go of it.* When he heard the door close, he opened his eyes again. He looked at his reflection, staring hard, hoping to reconnect to the feeling he'd had, but the spell was broken.

Now another voice in his head was talking. *Who are you kidding? Half of the bureau's out hunting Finley. What could you possibly come up with that they haven't? Face it: it's over and you failed.*

He sighed and closed his eyes a moment more. He spit out the toothpaste and went back to his office. He sat heavily in his chair and let out a long breath. Out his glass door he could see the open floor where dozens of agents were working and talking, their words and laughter muffled to a din by the glass. How far away they seemed. How foreign and strange. Had he really been like them once? Was that really him thirty years ago?

Suddenly the lucid voice was back. *You've forgotten all that you did. The mob cases, the drug cartels, the gangs. You were one of the best.*

He looked up at the pictures on his wall: graduating class of 1994, a framed front page of the *Washington Post* with the news of the Cali-Tex arrests, and two medals: the Medal for Meritorious Achievement and the FBI Star. But looking at them now brought little pride. In fact, all these things seemed to belong to someone else. Someone who no longer worked here.

No, the voice said, *you did that. And you can do it again. Just start from the beginning.*

He shook his head in reply. *I can't get it together. It's no use.*

He'd been trying to track down Finley, but his work had been in pathetic fits and starts. He'd begin down one path, get frustrated, start drinking, waste two days half drunk, then get a new idea and start down it.

Just shut up and do it. And don't even worry about Finley. Get her bomber. You know it's him you want.

He nodded. Yes, that was true. It was Finley's bomb expert who had killed Rogers.

Bud's mind flashed back to the cabin in Vermont and the day that Rogers and twenty-six other agents had died. Bud had almost saved them. He'd figured out the cabin was booby-trapped, but he hadn't been able to warn them in time. One minute more . . . He'd been calling out to them when the cabin blew. The memory made him shudder. The way the whole cabin had collapsed inward, then been consumed by the explosion. The blast splitting trees and over-turning trucks.

Just one minute more.

He remembered comforting the dying Aileen Michaels, mother of two. Holding her hand as she drowned in her own blood.

The unfortunate truth was that Finley's bomber was a genius. He was an enemy unlike any the FBI had ever gone up against before.

Take the way the bomber had assassinated Senator Peck last year. He'd turned the man's office into a death trap—making clever patches of C4 interlaced with metal filaments, then using paint as an accelerant. He'd asked Rogers how anyone could get that good. Rogers had replied that that's what happened in war when the oppos-ing sides tried to outwit each other—they got smarter and smarter. That's why Rogers had suspected that they were probably looking for a vet. Most likely a British sapper since they had become the best

EOD (Explosive Ordnance Disposal) experts in the world because of their long battle with the IRA. Then the Brits had honed those skills even more working in Iraq, Afghanistan, and Syria.

Rogers had felt that anybody who was that good would be famous. But a search of all the best vets from the UK and the other coalition forces had yielded nothing. They were all present and accounted for.

"Who are you?" he said out loud. He tried to remember his conversations with Rogers, but he felt like he was forgetting something. An important comment that had been erased by all the alcohol he'd consumed over the past month. Something about the IRA.

Bud furled his brow in thought and leaned back in his chair. *What was it?* The bourbon was clouding his thoughts. He went to his coffee maker. There were the dregs of a pot from last week. He poured them in a mug and chugged them. His face squirmed reflexively with disgust, but a few minutes later, he felt the caffeine start to do its work. Back at his desk he tried to dissect Rogers's thinking.

If the British got so good because of their long fight with the IRA, that meant that there must have been an IRA bomber who was pushing them to their limits. There were always two sides in an arms race.

That's what he'd forgotten, the possibility that the bomber *was* IRA. He'd been wasting weeks looking for a British war veteran when he needed to find an Irish nationalist.

Brown nodded to himself. The logic was sound. But then the cynical voice countered: *You're forgetting that if it's an insurgent, it could also be from another conflict. The bomber could be Iraqi, Afghan, or ISIS.*

True, but that's not Finley's way, the lucid voice said. Riona Finley, the fiery redhead, had style and flair, and she would remain loyal to her roots. In fact, the more he thought about it, the more his conviction grew.

But even if he was right, this wasn't going to be easy. "The Troubles"—as the thirty-year conflict between Northern Ireland and

Britain was known—had begun in 1969, and whoever this bomber was, he'd managed to stay hidden not just during the entire war, but ever since. The man would have to be in his seventies . . . at least.

Bud sat back in his chair and looked out at the floor of agents busy going about their jobs. *Don't count me out yet*, he thought. Then he rose to make a fresh pot of coffee.

CHAPTER SIX

THE SETUP

January 11, 2027
Naval Research Lab, Washington DC

Eric arrived at Blake's office the next morning at 5:59 a.m. One minute early.

"Nice to see you could make it," Blake said, with a tone that suggested he'd been waiting at least an hour. "Take a seat." He motioned to one of the chairs opposite his massive desk.

Eric sat and pulled out his iSheet.

"I'll get straight to it," Blake said. "As you heard last night, the lab's top priority is to create countermeasures. If Riona Finley attacks us with our own weapons, we have to be ready. We have made some progress while you were gone, but the nanotech team—your team—has fallen behind. You need to get them back on track. The roadblock is that the nanosites are having trouble distinguishing between friendly nanosites and enemy ones. And even when they do identify them correctly, they take too long to neutralize them."

Without seeming to take a breath, Blake continued. "Here's what you're going to do: by the end of the week, you need to figure out what's wrong," he said, putting his meaty forearms on his desk. "And I want daily status reports from you by oh-six-hundred."

"I don't need a week," Eric said. "I know the solution now."

Blake sniffed the air dubiously, then leaned back in his chair and raised his hand, as if inviting a response. "Then by all means, enlighten me."

Eric gave a slight nod. "Everything we do here is modeled after a system that already exists in nature, right?"

"Yes, I know that," Blake said irritably.

"Okay, then when you say 'countermeasures,' you need to ask yourself 'What's the model?' The answer, of course, is an immune system. It's the same concept—its job is to identify and neutralize microscopic foreign invaders."

Blake nodded. "Okay."

"While we inherit some immunity from our parents, most of your immune response has to be learned. And that takes time because there are so many viruses and bacteria that can attack the body. That's why it takes a while for a child's immune system to become smart enough to not just fight off a bout of the flu, but to learn how to fight a flu strain it's never encountered before. Are you following?"

"Yes, yes, go on," Blake said.

Eric continued. "Do you know how many different cell types . . . how many proteins and enzymes there are in the human body that help you fight disease?"

Blake shook his head.

"Well, you've got dendritic cells, neutrophils, monocytes, NK cells, T cells, B cells, and antibodies, just to name a few. These cells and proteins have very specific jobs. They also have to communicate and work together. They have memory and even train each other on how to handle pathogens. For example, Human Leukocyte Antigen is a protein that marks your own cells as yours so that your immune system knows not to attack them. And most people are aware that Natural Killer cells know how to identify and kill cells that have been infected with viruses, but they also prevent cancer. Then you have neutrophils that patrol the body looking for bacterial infections so they can ingest them. But they also regulate inflammation, and train other immune cells to recognize the pathogens in the future.

"Are you beginning to get a grasp just how complicated it is?" Eric didn't wait for a response. "Now let me ask you: How many different nanosites have you designed to protect the lab?"

Blake's jaw tightened a moment, then he replied, "One."

"That's your problem. You're expecting one nanosite to do the work of dozens. It's like trying to fight a war with only your infantry—right now you're expecting your soldiers to win without artillery, without a communications network, without an intelligence service, without armor, and without air support."

Blake took a long breath and extended his palms on the desk. "Understood. How long do you need to make it happen?"

"Six weeks."

"You have two."

Eric had to bite his tongue. *Don't make waves. Don't piss him off.*

"I'll schedule a live fire test at Fort AP Hill in fourteen days," Blake said. "I want a working system by then. You'll work with Ryan Lee. Make this your top priority and send me a project plan by noon."

Blake dropped his head and began making notes on his iSheet. Then he lifted his eyes and seemed surprised that Eric was still there.

"You're dismissed."

Eric stood and was in the doorway when Blake called out to him. "Just so we're clear, Dr. Hill, this doesn't change anything. You've proven that you deserve the job today. But you'll need to prove it again tomorrow and every day after that."

Eric focused on him a moment, a faint smile on his face. "Have a good day, sir." He turned and left.

Eric headed straight to the lab to find Ryan Lee. Even though preparing for the meeting with Blake had kept him up half the night, he was even more anxious about seeing Ryan. He just couldn't accept that Ryan was now the enemy. Still, it was a delicate thing. There was no way to test Ryan's loyalties without exposing the fact that he himself was, indeed, involved in a conspiracy against the US government.

He decided to take it slow. *Just focus on business*, he told himself.

He entered the main lab and found Ryan in his office with Olivia Rosario. At the sight of him she rose, extending her hand with a warm smile.

"Hello, Eric, I'm Olivia. It's so nice to finally meet you, and we're so glad that you're back."

"It's a pleasure to meet you too. And congratulations on your success with Eleven."

"Oh," she said bashfully, dropping her eyes. "Thank you. Of course, much of the credit has to go to you. I really wish General Walden had mentioned that last night."

Eric grinned inwardly. He could definitely see why she had risen so quickly through the ranks. She was astute and diplomatic. And her flattery forced him to flatter her back. "You clearly did some groundbreaking work of your own."

"It sure wasn't easy," she said with a smile. "And Ryan gets most of the credit." There was a pause. "Well, I'll leave you two to your work. I know you've got a lot to do."

She met Eric's gaze once more. "It was a pleasure."

"Likewise," he said.

As soon as she had left, a silence fell over the room, but Eric didn't let it linger.

"Blake wants our project plan by noon."

"He just sent me a note about your meeting, and I've already started on it." Ryan tapped in a few commands on his small iSheet, and a big wall-mounted unit came to life. Eric stepped up to it and examined what he'd done. "Good," he said. "What do you think we can realistically deliver in two weeks?"

"Your idea of modeling it after the immune system is a good one, but it might complicate things."

"Yes, I know. It will take time to create dozens of specialized nanosites that have to work together."

"Maybe for us."

"You know someone who can do it faster?"

"I do."

"Eleven's that good, huh?"

"He'll understand the analogy of the immune system, and we can let him design the system."

"Can he really do that?"

"Yeah, it's like having fifty extra programmers and engineers working together as one."

Eric nodded. "Then I suppose it could work. The human immune system already functions a lot like an artificial intelligence system. For example, the T cells that are created in the bone marrow have to travel to the thymus where they are trained to distinguish between human cells and pathogens. Only when they 'graduate' are they allowed to leave the thymus and go to work in the body."

"Yes," Ryan said, seeing the connection. "It's just like training data for an AI system. It learns by practicing."

"Exactly."

"That should be an easy system to model with Eleven's help."

They worked through lunch and late into the afternoon.

At about 6 p.m., Ryan got a call. Eric heard Blake's voice on the other end of the line. "Yes, it's going well. Huh, yes, just a moment."

Ryan smiled at him and excused himself, going into the hallway.

About five minutes later he came back.

"What did he want?"

"An update, of course," he said, then laughed. "Talk about a micromanager!"

Eric didn't laugh.

I think we've done everything we can for one day," Eric said. "I'm gonna head home and keep working on the mutation factors."

"Actually, I was hoping we could do some of that together. If you can give me a better idea of how you're going to, uh, 'breed' these artificial cells, then Eleven and I can write the code a lot faster."

Eric nodded slowly, "All right."

They went to a huge iSheet on the wall and began using it like a whiteboard, laying out a basic design and determining which aspects of the new system would be created by Forced Evolution and which would have to be programmed. They threw on electronic sticky notes, expanded subroutines, and kept a list of the other people they'd need to consult to make sure it worked.

It was about 10:30 at night when Eric decided to call it quits.

Ryan looked at his watch. "Yeah, I'm with ya," he said. "But could you just show me one more thing?"

By the time Eric had reviewed the thymus analogy for a second time, it was eleven thirty.

"Okay, I'm outta here," Eric said, and headed back to his apartment.

Tired and feeling like his eyeballs were going to explode from looking at screens all day, Eric made his way up the stairs to his apartment. He was looking forward to a solid six hours of sleep.

But when he got to his corridor, he saw that his door was open.

Instantly, he made a series of strange clicking sounds that he had learned in Africa and felt the iSheet in his pocket vibrate in response.

He turned into his doorway and was shocked by the sight. It looked like a bomb had exploded. Broken dishes and pots and pans littered the kitchen area on his right. In front of him, the sofa and love seat had been gutted and white stuffing covered the floor. His wall-mounted iSheet was gone, and the pictures of Jane and his family had been yanked from the walls and broken.

He could hear people rummaging around in his bedroom.

Now he understood why Ryan had been trying to keep him in the lab. *You just got played*, he thought.

Blake came out of the hallway, his combat boots crackling on the broken glass on the floor.

"Ah, there you are. Give me your personal iSheet."

"What the fuck are you doing?"

"Your iSheet."

Eric narrowed his eyes on Blake, then gave him the iSheet.

"And the passcode?"

"What the hell is going on?"

"The passcode, please."

Eric gave it to him.

"Thank you for your cooperation," he said, then called out, "Conway, take this and check it out." An NCIS officer appeared and took the device.

"Are you going to tell me why you trashed my apartment?"

Blake flashed his signature, ingratiating smile. "At oh-four-thirty this morning, Eleven traced a strange transmission from this building. A message was somehow sent from this rooftop to a Starlink satellite in low earth orbit. From that point, we lost the transmission and we don't know where it went, but we do know that Starlink has no record of it, which means the sender hijacked the satellite. Finally, the encryption was so advanced that Eleven couldn't even decode it."

Eric shook his head in disgust. "What does this have to do with me?"

Blake sniffed the air contemptuously. "Let me lay it all out for you. Whoever sent that message is smart enough to create an undetectable satellite dish, probably using nanosites. They were also smart enough to hack into one of Elon Musk's satellites and send a message that we can't trace or decode. How many people living in this building are smart enough to do that?"

"Computers aren't my specialty. Why don't you ask Ryan Lee?"

"I did ask him. He told me there was only one person he could think of." Blake smiled wide.

"It looks like his judgment is getting worse and worse every day. I'm going to guess you haven't found a damn thing."

Blake scowled, then called over his shoulder. "Conway!"

The NCIS officer returned. "I'll need a few more hours to do a complete check, but so far everything looks clean."

"That's because it is," Eric said. "Major Blake, I'll be making my own report to NCIS."

"Be my guest. This was all cleared with them ahead of time. We had probable cause of a threat to national security. Your complaint will go nowhere."

Eric turned to leave.

"Where do you think you're going?"

"Wherever I want."

"Like hell. Under no circumstances are you to leave the base. Not until I get a final assessment from NCIS."

Fuming, Eric walked out.

CHAPTER SEVEN

LITTLE CHOICE

January 12, 2027
Naval Research Lab, Washington, DC

"Thanks a lot, buddy," Eric said as he barged into Ryan's office the next morning.

Ryan stood and held up his hands. "Hey, I didn't know they were going to trash your apartment, okay. Blake just asked me to keep you here as long as I could."

Eric shook his head incredulously. "Are you my friend or not?"

"That depends on what you're up to," Ryan shot back. "What was the transmission? Who did it go to?"

"I didn't send any transmission," Eric said. He dared not tell the truth. If Walden found out about the Namibia Program, it would jeopardize the safety of not just the Sān, but his closest friends at the lab, including Jane.

"Look, I don't know what your game is," Ryan said. "But you need to accept reality. Curtiss is gone. Walden and Eleven are the future. It's not worth fighting that, so just accept it."

Eric shook his head. "I'm not so excited about a future where everyone is under Eleven's eye and a single Air Force general has more power than the president."

Ryan clicked his tongue. "You're being overly dramatic. This was inevitable. AI is going to reshape the world. Don't you want to be a part of that transformation?"

Eric didn't say anything.

"Well, you'd better make up your mind. Because we have work to do." Ryan turned to the iSheet on the wall and began to review their work.

Eric didn't move right away. He felt like hitting someone—preferably Blake, although Ryan would do. But he knew he couldn't. Just like he knew he couldn't reveal the truth about the Sān or trust Ryan or do anything about his trashed apartment. The only thing to do was try to act as calm as possible and move on . . . even though he hated it.

Begrudgingly, he joined Ryan at the iSheet and began talking to him about the countermeasures program.

They had been working together for several hours, brainstorming on the best ways to defend the lab against a clever nanosite attack, when Eric was struck by a realization.

"We've forgotten something . . . something big?"

"What?" Ryan asked.

"How are we going to test it?"

"Huh?"

"This whole project is like an immune system, right?"

"Yeah, and?"

"Well, you can't test an immune system without a pathogen. To find out whether the system can identify and neutralize invaders, we'll have to create the invaders too."

Ryan nodded slowly. "You're right. I hadn't thought of that. And we'll have to make the best pathogens we can. If our test invaders are weak, then the system will be weak."

"Exactly."

"It actually sounds like a good problem for Forced Evolution," Ryan said. "If you can evolve a line of aggressive pathogens that is continually interacting with our defensive program, then they'll evolve off of each other in a non-stop arms race."

Eric nodded. He was right, it was the perfect scenario for Forced Evolution.

A timer went off and Ryan looked at his watch. "Ah, crap. I have to go. I have this thing with Olivia and her daughter."

It was only 3 p.m. Eric raised his eyebrows. "We have a tight deadline here, and you're going on a date?"

"Don't worry," he said, easing on his coat. "I'll be back by seven."

After he had left, Eric thought about the problem. He and Ryan were trying to make a defensive system. That was a worthy goal. But to do it, they had to create a new weapon. He didn't like that. And, honestly, he didn't want to do it.

But do you really have a choice? he asked himself. The more he thought about it, the more he realized it was a moot point. If he wanted to keep his job . . . if he wanted to have access to the technology that would keep the Sān safe . . . if he wanted to put a check on Walden's power . . . then he had to go along with it.

He shook his head, then went back to work.

CHAPTER EIGHT

THE NEW NORMAL

January 12, 2027
Chevy Chase, Maryland

"That's it, Emma, looking good!" Olivia Rosario called out to her daughter as the girl brought her horse into a canter and approached the brush fence.

The girl was dressed in tan riding pants and a quarter-zip riding shirt and cap. Olivia couldn't help but think how poised and proud she looked. But most importantly, she looked happy, and that, in turn, made Olivia happy. *Thank God for normal*, she thought. After the nightmare of the last year, Emma was finally back on track.

They were in a huge indoor equestrian arena that was big enough for three separate rings. Olivia watched as Emma and her horse jumped the brush fence with ease.

"Whooo-hooo!" Olivia cheered from across the fence. It was just practice, and Olivia realized she was cheering louder than any of the other parents, but she didn't care.

Beside her, Ryan clapped his approval, "She's looking fantastic! I still can't believe how quickly she's recovered."

"She's my miracle girl!" Olivia said excitedly. Then for a

moment she choked up. For so long she hadn't dared hope that the girl would survive. She took Ryan's hand. "Thank you," she said, but then realized that a *thank you* didn't nearly cut it. She turned and faced him. "I want you to know I will never forget what you did."

Ryan gave her a playful aw-shucks kind of look. "We did it together," he said.

"No, without you, I never could have done it. Just look at her! You saved her life."

Ryan considered her words. "Okay," he said with a laugh. "I guess I did."

She held his smile for a moment before turning back to Emma, who had now rounded the last turn and was lining up for her run on a rectangular pool of water known as "the coffin." The brown thoroughbred was now wet with sweat. Emma spurred the horse forward and cleared the water.

"Yeah! You did it!" This time Emma tilted her head and flashed a penetrating glare. *You're embarrassing me, Mom!* But Olivia didn't let up. "You're awesome!" Emma rolled her eyes but couldn't help giving a coy smile.

Emma's trainer—a lean woman with a weathered face—approached them. "You've got a keeper there."

"Oh, I know," Olivia said.

"I'm amazed at the connection she's made with Argo. Most riders her age are terrified of him, but not Emma."

"She's always loved horses. This is her dream."

At that moment Olivia's iSheet began to vibrate and she excused herself. It was the call she'd been waiting for from Emma's school.

Ryan gave her a reassuring look, as if to say, *Don't worry.*

"Hello," she said, stepping away from the others.

"Ms. Rosario? This is Mark Morgan, I'm one of the fifth-grade teachers at Gilford and I gave Emma her math assessment today."

"Hello, Mark, thank you for calling."

"My pleasure! Emma and I had the most remarkable session today."

"Oh, really," Olivia said dubiously. "Would that be remarkably good or remarkably bad? Math has never been her thing."

Mark laughed. "Remarkably good, in fact. When I'd heard she'd missed a year of school, I suspected we'd have to put her in fourth grade, at least for her math lessons. But I don't think that will be necessary."

"Oh, thank goodness," Olivia said.

"She did excellent, really. She started off a bit slowly, and I had to do a little coaching, but her problem-solving skills are exceptional. And that tells me that even if some of the children are ahead of her now, she'll be able to catch up."

"That's so great to hear. Any word on her reading and writing?"

"I was just getting to that. Ms. Kent told me that her language skills are good enough to stay in fifth grade too. So, it doesn't look like she'll need to be with the younger kids, which we know can be a strain psychologically."

Olivia put her hand to her chest and exhaled with relief. "Thank you, Mark, this is all that I had hoped for!"

They spoke for a few more minutes then said goodbye.

"Sooooo . . ." Ryan said, as Olivia returned to the others.

She hugged him and gave him a kiss on the cheek. "Emma can start in fifth grade!"

"I knew it!" he said, lifting her up and giving her a spin. "Let's celebrate!"

After training they went to Dupont Circle and ate street food—stuffing their faces with shawarmas, empanadas, and chocolate cake. Then they went to the Mansion on O street—a hundred-room house filled with pop culture curios and secret passages. Olivia won the contest for most passages found, but Emma was a close second. They explored and played hide-and-seek and laughed, and Olivia was happier than she could ever remember. As she looked from Emma to Ryan, she finally felt that all the horrors of the past year were finally behind her. What's more, she felt like she had a family again.

This is as good as it gets, she told herself. *Now you just have to hold on to it for as long as you can.*

That night Olivia had to pay for all the fun she'd had that afternoon by working late. It was past eleven when she heard Emma's voice from her bedroom. She was talking to someone. Olivia's motherly instincts told her she should make her hang up and get some sleep, but then she changed her mind. *She's just starting at a new school*, she told herself, *let her make some friends*. Besides, Emma had been reluctant to speak to strangers since her recovery. When she'd "woken up," she discovered that her voice was markedly deeper and was very self-conscious about it. The fact that she was talking so openly was a good thing.

Olivia went back to her emails, occasionally catching some of Emma's words and laughter. They were talking about horses, of course. *Perhaps it's a girl from the stables.*

At midnight Olivia shut down her iSheet and went to the kitchen. As she was getting a glass of milk, she suddenly stopped. There on the table was Emma's iSheet, which meant she couldn't be talking to anyone on the phone or online. She turned her head to listen and could still hear Emma's voice.

She put the cup of milk down and approached Emma's door.

"Really! What happened after the stallion ran away?" she heard Emma say. "Come on! Tell me."

Olivia gently rapped on the door.

The conversation stopped and there was a long pause.

"Sweetheart?"

"What is it, Mom?"

Olivia turned the handle and opened the door.

Emma was sitting up in bed, leaning against her headboard, bathed in the warm light of her bedside lamp.

"Who were you talking to?"

"Nobody."

With her hand still on the doorknob, Olivia looked around the room, half expecting to find someone there.

"Can I come in?"

"Actually, I'm kind of tired and want to sleep." The girl snuggled under the covers and turned her back to her.

Olivia hesitated, then came and sat on the bed. "Okay," she said and kissed her on the back of the head. "Sleep tight, *mi vida*."

But as she was reaching for the lamp string, Emma spoke: "Mom? Do you think it's weird?"

Olivia opened her mouth to speak, then paused and laughed. "It's a little odd," she said, "but you've been through a lot, so a little oddity is expected."

Emma rolled over to face her. "I'm just trying to make sense of everything," she said. "And talking like that. You know, acting normal, like I *am* normal again and have friends . . . Well, it feels good, even if it isn't real."

"Well, then I think it's good to practice. You lost a whole year. Life must feel strange. Plus you woke up here in Washington, on the other side of the country."

"I keep telling myself that when my voice gets back to normal, I'll start talking to people, but right now . . ."

"Don't worry," Olivia said. "Everything's going to be fine. Your voice will change back, you're going to make friends, you're going to do great in school . . . you're gonna be a star!"

Emma reached up and hugged her. "Thanks, Mom."

"You're welcome, angel. Now get some sleep. Six thirty is going to come awfully quick if you don't rest."

CHAPTER NINE

THE SCORE

January 13, 2027
Naval Research Lab, Washington, DC

"Major Blake is here for his appointment, general," Captain Kacey announced.

"Send him in," Walden said.

A moment later, Blake was in the doorway. The marine saluted and stood at attention. As he often did with subordinates, Walden let him wait, a not-so-subtle reminder of the pecking order.

Walden examined the marine. He was an ugly man, no doubt about it, with a perpetual scowl on his face and a pocked complexion. His black flattop and square jaw made his head appear impossibly angular. As Walden looked at him, he couldn't help wondering if he'd made the right choice in selecting Blake to run the lab. At first he'd been so sure. But not now.

He had met Blake during the Syrian War, when Blake had been a captain in charge of Alpha Company, Fourth Marine Division. There he'd earned a reputation for being a dedicated, zero-bull leader who got things done. And while many of Blake's men loved him, just as many hated his guts. Yet, what had impressed Walden was that even those that loathed him trusted him with their lives. Walden soon found out why. Even though Blake was a mean and ruthless son of a bitch, he was wholly dedicated to the Corps. It was more than his life, it was his religion. As a consequence, he approached every task with the zeal of a fanatic. The way he trained his marines was downright sadistic. Forced marches at three a.m., public humiliation for failure, even making the soldiers crawl through obstacle courses strewn with sheep and goat guts. Yes, he was sadistic, but he got results. Alpha Company had the lowest casualty rates of any company in the war, and only the SEAL teams were more feared by the Syrian army.

Walden's gamble had been that Blake could bring his fanaticism to the NRL and get similar results, but right now it appeared that he'd bet wrong.

"Take a seat," Walden finally said.

"Yes, sir."

If Blake minded being left standing at attention, he didn't show it.

"I'll get to the point. I've had seven complaints about you in the last two days. People threatening to quit. I'm particularly worried about Hill and how you trashed his apartment."

Blake rolled his eyes.

"It's fine if you don't like him—"

Blake cut in: "That's an understate—"

Walden didn't like being interrupted and he cut Blake off in turn, letting a note of irritation into his voice. "I need you to listen to me, Major. We need him. This whole plan hinges on him finding the answers we need. You keep treating him like a buck private and we'll lose him."

Blake lifted a hand dismissively. "You don't have to worry about Hill, he's not going anywhere."

Walden pursed his lips in a show of skepticism. He wasn't going to be mollified so easily. "And why's that?"

"It's simple. Hill's whole identity is wrapped up in his need to be the smartest guy in the room. Take a look at his file—a classic type

A, first-born overachiever. Throw in the dead dad and the sense of abandonment and it just supercharged his need to always be the best, it's the only way he feels good about himself. The harder you push a guy like that . . . the more difficult you make his life . . . the harder he's gonna fight back. That's how he learned to survive."

Walden gave Blake a hard look, but inside he was starting to understand. "And you're betting he'll be so preoccupied with proving himself that he won't realize he's being manipulated?"

"Exactly," Blake said. "All we have to do is keep the pressure on, and Hill's ego will do the rest."

Walden looked at Blake. He didn't seem quite so ugly as he had a few moments ago, and Walden realized that perhaps his doubts had been misplaced. Clearly the major could be adept at getting what he wanted, even out of civilians. And if Blake was right about Hill, most of the battle was already won. Walden felt himself relaxing.

"Very well," he said, "You can continue to investigate this strange transmission you think he sent, but remember, it's more important to us that he continue his work."

"Understood, sir. But don't worry. Hill will give us what we want."

After Blake had gone, Walden sat thinking it over. He realized that he should be pleased; everything was going as planned. In the past three months he had been appointed to the Joint Chiefs, taken control of the NRL, and, with it, complete control over the world's most lethal military technology. In the process, had also destroyed his enemy, Jim Curtiss, who was now rotting in a military jail. As a bonus, he'd gotten Eleven, and—using its uncanny ability to gather and process intelligence—had gained the trust of the president.

Yes, he should be content, but he wasn't.

I won't rest until the end, he reminded himself. *Not until I've seen it through.* He looked at the framed picture of Julia that sat on his desk. The picture had been taken outside the famous Broadmoor Hotel in Colorado Springs back when he had been visiting the Air Force Academy. The sun was shining on her long golden hair, and she had that bright, clever look in her eyes that he loved so much.

Walden gave her a sad smile. "Not until I've seen it through," he said aloud.

CHAPTER TEN

THE DEATH THAT SPARKED
A THOUSAND MORE

January 17, 2027
FBI Headquarters, Washington, DC

Special Agent Bud Brown swiveled in his desk chair and looked up at the five faces pinned to his wall: all immigrants from Northern Ireland that could, *possibly*, be Finley's master bomber. It had taken him seven days to get this far. And it hadn't been easy. In fact, he hadn't slept more than three hours at a stretch the whole time. Not surprisingly, he looked like shit. Again. Bloodshot eyes, gray stubble across his jaw, and, of course, he reeked. He could tell from the looks he got in the hallways that the other agents assumed he was back on the sauce.

But that wasn't true. Miraculously. And even though the withdrawal had been hell, right down to the shakes, nausea, and splitting headaches, it appeared that he had finally found an addiction that was more powerful than alcohol—his obsession with finding Finley's bomber.

Not that he wasn't tempted to drink. Oh, no. Every time he got bored or stuck, he'd find himself looking at his dresser drawer and fantasizing about seizing that beautifully engraved pewter hip flask full of vodka.

One day at a time, he told himself.

He had made it this far—gotten his list of over three thousand suspects to five—but he knew he was still a long way from being certain about any of them. That's because *if* his theory was true—that Finley's bomber had once been one of the best demolitions experts of the Irish Republican Army—Bud would have to find a suspect that the British authorities had never found, despite thirty years of trying.

His first task had been to make certain that there actually was such a person. *Did the IRA indeed have a master bomber who was never caught?*

After two days of digging, he got ahold of the British Army's After Action Reports, and that's when things got interesting. He looked at his notes.

1976—blast in Shankhill Road: "a very sophisticated demolition device"

1981—bombing of army barracks: "a bomb that was unlike any we had encountered before"

1985—explosion at Ormeau: "sapper killed trying to defuse bomb . . . IRA bomber knew our methods and exploited them"

1989—Orders from Brigadier General Spencer of the Royal Engineers: "special task force needed to neutralize NRA demolitions program, which we believe may be one man"

1991—Army report: "NRA explosives continue to evolve faster than we can develop countermeasures"

But all of Britain's efforts to find the bomber had failed. The only scrap of evidence that Bud could find was a mention in a 1979 report: "parts of the explosive device were traced to a shop in Antrim." Antrim was a town nineteen miles northeast of Belfast, population 21,000.

It was a daunting task, trying to find someone that the mighty British Empire had failed to find.

He looked at the five men's faces. It was hard to imagine that any of them were terrorists. All of them were over seventy-five and looked more likely to be playing canasta in a nursing home than making bombs.

Yet, they were the only five that fit his criteria: age (old enough to have lived through most of the Troubles), religion (Catholic), knowledge base (had a profession or military experience that lent itself to bomb-making), and physical appearance (consistent with the crude forensic sketch they'd gotten from their investigation in Vermont).

He looked at the first photo. By now he had memorized all the key facts. First was Brian Ferris, seventy-eight, an electrical engineer and suspected member of INLA (Irish National Liberation Army). He'd been arrested by the RUC on March 23, 1973, and released for lack of evidence. Current residence: Minneapolis.

Next was Michael Walsh, eighty-two. He had experience with explosives from working at a mining company. His brother was injured by UVF (Ulster Volunteer Force) in February 1975. Current residence: Boston.

But the suspect that intrigued Bud the most was the least suspicious of them all. His name was Isaac Coyle and he was seventy-six. There was nothing about him that suggested he had any connection to the IRA. The only reason Bud hadn't eliminated him from his list altogether was the fact that the man was from Antrim, the place where the British Army had traced parts for one of the early bombs.

Other than that, he was completely unremarkable.

Yet, Bud's gut told him there was something here. More, the fact that he had no clear connection to the war made him a better suspect than the others, simply because it reinforced his theory that the bomber had been able to stay below the Brits' radar.

Still, Bud was at a dead end. Just like the British before him, he lacked proof.

When he got stuck like this, he'd study the history of the conflict, hoping it would inspire him to look at the problem in a new way. Bud enjoyed this. In fact, his love of detective work had grown out of his high-school fascination with history—the Roman Empire, WWII, the rise of Genghis Khan. Now, as he tried to understand the Troubles, he found himself devouring history books, watching old news footage, and examining government documents, just like he had when he had as a teenager.

Bud soon realized that the Troubles, like many tragic wars, never should have happened. It was only because of a few bad policies and unfortunate events that an otherwise peaceful country had fallen into civil war.

While many historians pointed to Bloody Sunday as the point of no return (when British soldiers shot twenty-six civilians in Derry in 1972), the British had perpetrated similar abuses for years and those missteps had already severely damaged the trust between the British and Irish Catholics.

Bud had become enthralled by one of those early incendiary moments. In April 1969, the police force of Northern Ireland, known as the Royal Ulster Constabulary (RUC), raided random houses in the Catholic neighborhoods in Belfast in search of IRA members.

As a former cop, Bud knew it was a recipe for disaster. A belligerent and poorly trained police force going house to house in a place where they viewed the residents as the enemy.

On the afternoon of April 28, RUC officers entered the house of Thomas Doherty, aged thirty-nine.

Even though Doherty had no involvement in the conflict, the police beat him with their batons, believing that he was hiding separatists. In an effort to protect him, Doherty's seventeen-year-old daughter, Cara, had thrown herself over her father's wounded body. But the police hadn't stopped and beat them both. When the police left, Thomas Doherty had six broken ribs and had lost an eye. Cara's skull was fractured. She survived six weeks in a coma before succumbing to her injuries.

It was the first of many episodes where the RUC's hard-line

tactics had the opposite effect of what they had intended. Instead of forcing the IRA into submission, the police (and later the British Army) galvanized the resistance and convinced more and more moderates to rise up against British rule.

It was while Bud was reading court documents from a 2002 truth commission about Cara Doherty that something caught his eye. Cara's mother, Shauna, had been brought back to testify. She had recounted the same events in her earlier testimony, thirty years before, but this time she said, "Cara had just returned the day before from visiting family in Antrim. She was very close to her cousins there."

Bud felt an electric tingle run through his skull. There it was again, the town of Antrim.

Perhaps it was the long hours or just too much coffee, but he couldn't help wondering. It was certainly a stretch—and he knew full well how dangerous it was to assume connections between random bits of data. Yet, if Isaac Coyle and Cara Doherty were cousins, it would create a direct connection between Coyle and the conflict . . . and a reason for him to go to war against the British.

But how could he confirm they were related?

He furrowed his brow for a minute, then snapped his fingers. *If Cara's mother's maiden name was Coyle, then it would prove they were related.* He filled two cups of coffee, returned to his desk, and set off in a search for her parents' marriage license.

Unfortunately, data on citizens of the UK was not stored on any FBI database that Bud could access. (Besides, this search was already pushing the limits of Bud's mediocre understanding of computers). So he asked Google how he could find a maiden name in Northern Ireland. Luckily, the computer was smarter than he was and gave him a list of ancestry websites. After setting up accounts with three different websites and paying the annual fees—*This is why I hate computers*—Bud finally found what he needed:

June 30, 1949. Saint Patrick's Church, Antrim. Thomas Doherty of Belfast married Shauna Kelly.

Damn! Cara's mother was from Antrim, but her maiden name wasn't Coyle, it was Kelly. Bud hit his fist on the desk and the coffee mugs jumped.

Dammit, dammit, dammit!

He'd felt so clever up until that moment. It was like the old magic from back when he'd been a homicide detective in Detroit, somehow intuiting that a lead was right. Now he felt his age and the futility of his hunt more than ever. It was an impossible task. And one that the entire British Empire had failed to do.

He dragged his fingers slowly across his face, letting out a long breath.

Then his eyes went to the desk drawer.

Go head. You deserve a drink. It will relax you.

But then the other voice countered: *It will also make you stupid all over again. You'll start forgetting things, making dumb mistakes. Just like you forgot about the IRA connection in the first place.*

He knew that voice was right . . . but only partially right. The week without booze had cleared his head, but he was only sharper by a few degrees. He was still fighting all the damage of nearly thirty years of heavy drinking.

He felt a wave of exhaustion run through his body. He looked at his watch. 1:30 a.m. *Jesus, no wonder.* His hand went to the desk drawer as if it had a mind of its own.

Don't even think about it.

He sighed and put his head down on the desk. He made a weak attempt to keep his eyes open, failed, and fell asleep.

Bud awoke a few hours later with a knot in his neck. He let out a groan and tried to massage it out. "Jesus!" It was the size of a golf ball.

He blinked and looked around. It was almost five in the morning. Things were quiet outside on the rest of the floor. He pulled a bottle of ibuprofen from his desk, shook out five capsules, and swallowed them dry.

He tried to remember what he'd been doing. Then it came back to him: *Isaac Coyle. Cara Doherty. Making stupid mistakes.*

Face it, you're just not the detective you used to be. With or without the booze.

He tapped the keyboard to wake up his computer.

Come on, Bud, get it together.

Cara's parents' marriage license stared at him from the monitor.

Dumb mistakes.

He knew he was missing something . . . that he wasn't looking at the problem in the right way. He grabbed a legal pad and began writing all the names.

His eyes suddenly locked on Shauna Doherty's maiden name—Kelly. He'd thought he'd hit a dead end because Shauna's last name wasn't Coyle. But he could now see he was missing an important piece of information: Isaac's mother's maiden name.

You idiot, he chastised himself, *Isaac Coyle and Cara Doherty could still be cousins, as long as their mothers were sisters. Then the children wouldn't share a last name.* He felt like punching himself.

He dove back into the ancestry databases, this time to find Isaac's mother's maiden name. First, he found Isaac's birth certificate, then his parents' marriage license. Sure enough, his mother's name was Ruth Kelly. A little more checking and he found the two women's birth certificates and confirmed they were sisters. Cara Doherty and Isaac Coyle were cousins.

He threw himself back in his chair. He'd done it. He'd found a connection, but he was still disappointed in himself. *You have to do better.*

He also hadn't proven that Coyle was the master bomber.

He pulled up a picture of Cara Doherty from one of the newspapers. It looked like her high-school picture. She was a beautiful girl, smiling happily for the camera. He imagined young Isaac—then only nineteen years old—learning that his cousin had been bludgeoned within an inch of her life in her own home by the RUC and that there wasn't a thing he could do about it.

He thought about the six weeks she'd been in a coma. How had Isaac felt sitting beside her bed, praying that she'd wake up and be her old self again? What promises had he made to her if only she'd wake up? And what promises had he made to the British if she didn't? Did he swear revenge? Did he decide to dedicate the next thirty years of his life to making them pay?

Bud knew the kind of strength that came with a vendetta. How it changed you. How it drove you. He knew it because it was the thing that was keeping him alive right now.

He stood and went to the wall and pulled down Isaac's picture. He was no longer the young man by Cara's hospital bed. He had changed. Through thirty years of the Troubles and twenty-six more, he was now an old man. At that moment Bud felt an odd connection to him. He understood his pain, and his desire to make others pay for that pain.

But then he shrugged.

I'm still going to nail you, you son of a bitch.

CHAPTER ELEVEN

MISINFORMATION

January 19, 2027
McLean, Virginia

Six figures hiked steadily up Scott's Run Trail, north of Washington, DC: Lili, Eric, Jane, Xiao-ping, Mei, and her new German shepherd, Chance. Barren winter trees lined the path—maples, oaks, and beeches—and their leaves were thick on the ground.

"This is boring," Mei said. "I'm cold."

"I told you to put more clothes on," her mother scolded. "You don't have to dress fashionably for a hike through the woods."

Mei rolled her eyes.

Since Blake's raid on Eric's apartment, the group had decided to have their meetings off-base and to make them appear like social outings.

Lili turned to Jane. "What have you found out from Walden?"

"Well, you can't knock his work ethic," Jane said. "He's up at four thirty every morning and usually doesn't go to bed until midnight. He works out four times a week and he likes to drink natural juice—his favorite is carrot, orange and ginger."

"That would sound good if it weren't for the fact that he likes it, so now I hate it," Lili said. "What else?"

"Nothing of interest on Thursday and Friday, but on Saturday some things started to happen. Eleven has been trying to track anyone who might be remotely linked to Finley, even if they aren't wanted by law enforcement."

"Isn't that illegal?" Xiao-ping asked.

"Technically, they should be getting a warrant for each search, but they aren't. Anyway, they've gotten some hits. First, there's this man . . ." She produced her iSheet and passed it around. It was a handsome Indian American man wearing a dastar. "That's Amar Kaur. He was a successful trial lawyer in Chicago until he dropped out of sight a few months ago. Authorities believe he donated three hundred thousand dollars to the New Anarchists last year, but they can't prove it. Eleven found his image on a traffic camera near Roanoke, Virginia, last week. Then Eleven found evidence of two other suspects with tenuous connections to the group." She showed them two more pictures, one of a college-aged girl with blond hair, the other a middle-aged Asian man in a suit. "Vanessa Harris and Andy Lin," Jane continued. "Both left digital footprints that Eleven picked up: Vanessa swiped her credit card at a gas station near Pikesville, Kentucky, last Wednesday; and Andrew logged into his Twitter account at a Starbucks in Beckley, West Virginia, two weeks ago."

"Three connections, but in three states. It doesn't sound like much," Eric said.

"True, but each point is less than sixty miles from the others." She pulled up a map with the three dots on it. "See, this is where those three states meet. If you triangulate those positions, it puts you in a very remote area of Virginia. Very backwoods. If you zoom in, you'll see it's old forest, dotted with gold and titanium mines that date back to the Civil War."

"A good place to hide from prying eyes," Eric said.

"Exactly."

"But that's not the most interesting part," Jane went on.

They had now reached a series of low concrete pylons that

formed stepping stones across the stream. They paused their conversation, so that each person could make it across.

"Don't fall!" Eric called back when he was halfway across. "That water is just above freezing."

Mei had to coax Chance over the first two pylons, and the big dog almost knocked her in trying to stay close to her, but then he grew braver and jumped the remaining posts with ease.

When they were all safe on the other side, Jane continued: "Here's the crazy part. Every Monday morning, Walden briefs the FBI on any developments. At nine fifteen he has a video conference with Anastasia Collins, the assistant director in charge of hunting down Finley. Does he tell her what he found?"

Lili's eyebrows went up. "I'm going to guess he didn't."

"Not a word. And on top of that, he tells her that he suspects Finley has holed up in the Sproul State Forest in northern Pennsylvania."

"Sending them on a wild-goose chase," Lili said.

"Uh-huh. That's right."

"But why?" Xiao-ping asked. "If Walden catches Finley, he'll have proven Eleven's effectiveness and have carte blanche to expand his power as he sees fit."

"You're right. It doesn't make sense," Jane said.

Mei spoke: "He must want something else, something he thinks is more important than fame and power."

Xiao-ping nodded. "But what could it be?"

Lili shook her head, then turned back to Jane. "Listening to Walden, you haven't gotten any ideas about what it could be?"

"No, he seems very focused on the countermeasures the lab is developing. He's pushing Blake and all the team leads to get that done as fast as possible."

"Tell me about it," Eric said.

Lili pursed her lips in thought. "It's great that we can hear everything he *says*, but we still need to know what he's thinking."

The trail opened before them and ahead was a wide waterfall

that broke over a series of gray boulders. The water was so cold that hundreds of long, silvery icicles had formed along the edges.

"Cool!" Mei said.

They took a break from talking and explored the area. Mei and Jane broke off icicles and had a short-lived sword fight. Chance bounced beside them and barked excitedly. Lili and Xiao-ping sat on a fallen tree and held hands.

On their way back to the car, they returned to the problem at hand. "We have to figure out what Walden's up to," Jane said.

"Agreed," Eric said. "And we have to tell the FBI the truth. Getting Bill and Jack back has to be one of our top priorities."

"That might not be as easy as it sounds," Xiao-ping said. "She's the most-wanted terrorist in the country. There must be dozens, if not hundreds of people, calling the FBI with anonymous tips. Even if they listen, they're going to want to know how we came by this information. And if Walden finds out it was us, we're all in big trouble."

"You're right," Lili replied. "It has to be done delicately."

"What we need is someone in . . ." Eric said, stopping himself mid-sentence. He pulled out his wallet. Behind his driver's license was the business card from the FBI agent he'd met almost a year ago: Bud Brown. Special Agent. Brown had contacted Eric about a strange robbery at a chemical warehouse. The suspect had turned out to be the Inventor. It had been Eric's first glimpse of the man. Yet he wasn't sure that Bud would be excited to hear from him. After all, Eric had not been cooperative that night, knowing he couldn't reveal any secrets about the lab's work that might help the agent. In fact, Eric remembered how dubious Brown had been with some of his explanations. Would Bud trust him now?

"I might have someone we can talk to."

"Good," said Lili, "but be careful."

Jane picked up the remaining thread of the conversation. "We still need to know what Walden's up to. Somebody close to him must know."

"Yeah, but it's a matter of trust. Anyone who knows him well enough to know his agenda isn't about to help us."

This fact seemed to deflate them, until Mei spoke up. "I know one person who knows Walden and would never rat on us."

"Who?"

"Admiral Curtiss."

Eric laughed. "She's got a point. Even though they hate each other, Curtiss would understand Walden's thinking better than anyone. The only problem is that he's in a military prison, and we can't walk in there without Walden finding out and getting suspicious."

"Logan can do it," Mei said.

Jane nodded slowly, considering the idea. Curtiss's eldest son (and Mei's boyfriend) would not raise suspicions if he showed up to see his father. "Are you sure he'd be up for it? I mean, after what Curtiss did . . . sorry, what Curtiss allegedly did."

"This whole thing has really messed Logan up. He's not eating or sleeping. I try to talk to him, but I don't think I'm getting through . . . and last week he found out his mother is filing for divorce."

Jane put her arm around the girl. "I'm so sorry. This must be really hard for him."

Mei nodded. "At first Mrs. Curtiss didn't believe the story, none of them did, but apparently something changed. Now Logan doesn't know what to think. I've been telling him he needs to go see his father."

"Okay," Lili said, "try to convince him again. It's probably too soon for him to make much progress in healing their relationship. But see if he'll do it for us . . . and for you."

CHAPTER TWELVE

THE BENCH

January 21, 2027
McLean, Virginia

FBI Special Agent Bud Brown sat on a park bench on the southern edge of Fort Marcy Park.

It was the ideal place for a meeting—close to DC, yet secluded and quiet. He laid one arm across the back of the bench. *Oh, if park benches like this could talk*, he thought. It was park benches like this one where some of the country's most important information exchanged hands. A lobbyist paying off a congressional aide, a spy passing on state secrets, or a whistleblower leaking details of a scandal. They all happened in places like this.

And now, in an age where the NSA monitored internet traffic and phone calls, and where most public streets were under the eyes of surveillance cameras, secluded park benches still offered better anonymity than just about anywhere else. Of course, Bud, being old-fashioned, preferred it this way. In his long career at the FBI, he had become an expert at reading people. He knew when he could trust someone and when he couldn't . . . but only if they were face-to-face. If it was over the phone or a video call, much of the information he needed was lost.

Which was why this afternoon he'd insisted on doing things the old-fashioned way.

He checked his watch, then looked up to see a young man coming down the trail. Even at a hundred yards, he knew it was Hill by the slight unevenness of his gait.

When he got close, Bud stood, and they shook hands. They sat down in unison.

"Thank you for agreeing to meet," Eric said.

"Of course. It's good to see you again," Bud replied. He was struck by how different Hill seemed—more professional and poised—and Bud wondered what had happened to him over the past year to create such a change.

"I've thought about our first meeting many times," Bud said, referring to the video footage of the Inventor. "I've realized since then that there was a lot more to it than I originally thought."

"Yes, and I'm sorry I couldn't tell you more."

Bud nodded. "It's all right. It happens a lot in this town."

"I still can't tell you everything," Eric said, "but I suspect you've already pieced together a lot."

"Yes, programmable microscopic machines. Somehow Finley figured out you'd weaponized these things, so she kidnapped your top scientists."

Eric nodded. "She could be making a weapon that no one would be able to stop."

"But what kind of weapon?" Bud asked. "How does it work?"

"It's hard to say because the technology is so versatile. Part of me hopes it's not a weapon at all, but merely a system to reverse climate change."

Bud shook his head. "Don't count on it. I've been studying her. Her messaging is focused on saving the planet, but I know her type: she sees herself as a revolutionary. She's waging a war against the system, which means that anyone who stands in her way is viewed as an enemy. She's already taken out senators, business leaders, lobbyists, and media personalities. If she feels threatened by the police and military, she won't hesitate to take them out too."

Eric sighed, "With this technology she can literally make all her enemies disappear."

Bud nodded slowly. "Well, I'd prefer not to disappear. Now tell me, why'd you call me?"

"Because I think I know where she is."

"That's old news," he said. "She's in northern Pennsylvania. Half the agents in the country are on their way there right now."

"She's not in Pennsylvania, she's in southern Virginia, and Walden knows it."

Bud's head rocked back on his shoulders as he processed this. The first time he'd met Hill, he'd been evasive and vague, clearly withholding information. But this time was different. He'd shown good eye contact, forward-leaning posture, no grooming behaviors or yawning, and no fragmented speech. Either Hill was telling the truth, or he'd gotten much better at lying.

"Why would Walden do that?"

"We're still not certain. But we do know that the longer Finley is free, the more powerful Walden becomes. The media coverage of Finley is incessant. The whole country is scared. Walden has the president's ear. In the name of finding her, he can ask for anything he wants and get it. And then there's Eleven."

"Eleven?"

Eric explained about the AI system's incredible surveillance technology. "It gets smarter every day, which means Walden gets smarter and more powerful every day too."

Brown rubbed his jaw in thought. "It sounds like he's playing the long game. But what's he after?"

"At this point it's impossible to tell. All we know for sure is that his plans go well beyond finding Finley."

Bud looked Hill over. "You're taking a big risk in telling me this. Sharing classified information about one of the Joint Chiefs, which, something tells me, you got illegally. That's a big no-no. I'm legally obligated to turn you in."

"You won't, because we want the same thing."

"You mean Finley, of course."

"Technically, I want Eastman and Behrmann back," Eric continued, "Not only because they are my friends—"

"But because you need them in your fight against Walden," Bud finished.

"Precisely," Eric nodded.

"Okay, I'll help you," Bud said. "Nothing's more important to me than Finley. Besides, I don't have a whole lot to lose. Now tell me more about this lead."

Eric explained how Eleven had tracked three of her suspected accomplices to southern Virginia, and how the rugged terrain and thousands of old mines would make an excellent place to hide.

"It could take months to find her in there," Brown said.

"Not with a hundred agents working together."

Bud tilted his head forward and looked at Hill over the rim of his glasses. "Let's be clear here: I'm one special agent about to be forced into retirement. I don't exactly have a lot of clout in the Bureau right now. I can go down there and take a look, but I can't call in the cavalry until I have proof that she's really there."

He could tell that Hill wasn't thrilled with this news.

"But don't worry, I'll do whatever it takes to hunt Finley down."

Hill nodded, "Okay, let's do it. But we are going to need a safe way to communicate. Can I see your phone a minute?"

Bud gave him a sideways look and produced his phone.

Hill laughed at the old Nokia. "And no passcode. Shame on you."

"Hey, I became a cop because I hate computers. I barely know how that thing works."

After a few minutes of hitting buttons, Hill handed the phone back. Bud pulled his glasses to the tip of his nose to look at the screen.

"SexyChat6K. Really? I feel like we just met."

Eric laughed. "It's the safest texting app around . . . end-to-end encryption, the messages disappear five minutes after you read them, and the company doesn't collect metadata on users, so even if Eleven hacked their servers, which are in Switzerland, he'd find nothing."

"Okay."

"But you'll need to get in the habit of texting in a way that no one can see your fingers moving. Eleven can see that and figure out what you're writing."

"You're kidding."

Hill shook his head. "Trust me. Eleven is scary. And make a long password when you get home."

"If you say so."

"I do. Use that app and only that app to communicate with me." Eric stood to go.

"One more thing," Bud said. "What can you tell me about . . . *him*." Bud thought back to the mysterious burglary and homicide that had been his first glimpse of nanotechnology. How they had initially thought the security guard—Williams—had died of natural causes. But then the FBI pathologist had discovered that a tiny, but crucial, part of the guard's brain had been liquefied. That had been the beginning of Bud's fruitless obsession with finding the killer. "He uses your technology, but he's not one of yours, is he?"

"No, he's not. We don't know much about him, except that he's become incredibly powerful. What you saw in that warehouse video was nothing."

"But how could that happen?"

"He somehow got our technology very early on and made a series of breakthroughs that still elude us. He jumped ahead so fast that it's unlikely that anyone will ever catch up with him. He says he lives a decade in an hour."

"You met him?"

"I did. He saved my life, and he seems to be a good guy."

"Tell that to Williams's widow," Brown said.

"He's killed many more than Williams. I saw it, and it was terrifying. But he seems to be changing, evolving."

Bud gave a grunt and stood from the bench. "Let's hope you're right."

The two men shook hands and moved off in opposite directions.

As Bud made his way along the gravel path, he couldn't help feeling conflicted. He'd arrived here thinking that the hunt for Finley was almost over, but now he knew that was a long way off. At least he had a lead. And perhaps, building on the research he'd done, he'd find Finley himself, and, most importantly, the old Irishman. And that made his blood warm. He fantasized about what that would look like. Cornering the man who had killed his partner, having him in his sights. The things he'd say.

"I'm coming for you," he said aloud.

He stopped by headquarters before he left town. He knew that what he was about to do wasn't exactly standard procedure—going off without a partner and conducting an investigation.

However, he was technically still assigned to Finley's case. Rogers had tapped him for that after Senator Peck's assassination. But when Rogers and most of the task force died in Vermont, Assistant Director Anastasia Collins had taken over the investigation. She hadn't included Bud in the new task force, but she hadn't officially taken him off the case either.

Still, someone had to know where he was. If he found Finley and died in the process, no one would know where to look for her.

Unfortunately, he couldn't think of a single agent who he could trust to keep quiet, so he was going to have to take a chance on someone he knew didn't like him very much.

On the fourth floor, he headed for her office, praying his plan wouldn't backfire.

Her door was open, and he looked in to see her sitting sideways typing at her computer. She was seated perfectly upright, with impeccable posture, head up and shoulders back, her elbows at perfect right angles as she typed. She was so involved in her work that she didn't notice him. Seeing her again reminded him of how pretty she was. Her mother was Japanese, her father American. She had short raven-black hair framing a face both delicate and strong, and she effused a sense of mindful determination.

Her name was June Brightwell and she'd briefly been Bud's partner. That is, until she'd realized that the longer she worked with him, the longer her career would be stuck in neutral—if not actively moving in reverse. Astutely, she had demanded a new partner at the earliest possible moment. Bud had been offended by the snub, but now he realized that if the roles had been reversed, he would have done the same thing.

He gave the door three light raps. She turned for a brief second, "I'm kind of busy," she said, and returned to typing.

"It should only take a few minutes."

She looked him up and down. "I'll give you five," she warned, then swiveled to face him.

He stepped into the office and fumbled with his hands. "I'm going down to southern Virginia for a few days, maybe a week. I want to check out this tip I got on some of Finley's accomplices." He pulled an envelope from his jacket pocket. "If for some reason I don't make it back, I've written down everything you need to know."

She extended her arm gracefully and took the letter from him.

Bud waited for the barrage of objections: Didn't he know that it was against protocol to conduct an investigation on his own? She would have to report this immediately. And if this tip was really credible, he had to share it with the rest of the task force.

Instead, she opened a drawer of her desk and dropped the letter inside.

"Send me a text every twenty-four hours," she said.

He eyed her. "Oh, I get it. The moment I walk out of here, you're going to report me, aren't you?"

"No, I'm not," she said matter-of-factly.

"And why not?"

"I'm going to answer that question with a question of my own: How many days has it been? Seven? Eight?"

"Twelve," he said.

She raised her eyebrows. "I'm impressed. You're through the worst of it."

He nodded. "You could always tell, couldn't you?"

"Not at the beginning—you had a lot of clever tricks—but I learned fast." She took a deep breath. "When you're sober, you're a good agent and I trust you. It's the alcohol that I could never trust."

He couldn't help but smile. "Thanks."

She returned the smile. It was a small smile, but a smile nonetheless. "Good luck," she said.

CHAPTER THIRTEEN

FRANKENVOICE

January 21, 2027
Chevy Chase, Maryland

Emma Rosario sat in the bathroom stall at Gilford Latin, quietly crying. She sniffed and wiped her nose with the back of her hand, then checked the time on her iSheet. Only three minutes until the final bell rang and she could get out of this hellhole.

It had been the worst day ever. And it still felt far from over. It might be only three more minutes, but after the bell rang, she would have to go out there. Get her bag from her locker and walk out the front door. On display for everyone to see.

How had things gotten so bad so fast?

In just one day she'd managed to commit social suicide, making an enemy of the most popular and beloved girl in school.

It's so unfair, she thought. *I've been trying so hard!*

And it was all because of something she couldn't control—the sound of her voice.

Ever since she'd been cured it had been deeper. The doctors said it should go away—something about her vocal cords not being used in a year. Her strategy had been to talk as little as possible, or when she was forced to talk, to whisper or try to make it sound higher. It had been working, she'd been at school a week, and no one seemed to have noticed.

But today in Mr. Morgan's class that had all changed. It had started when he'd called Amanda up to the board.

Amanda Rush, class president, adored by the faculty, worshipped by the students, and rumored to have been dipped by her ankle in a vat of everlasting popularity at birth.

Amanda had gone to the front of the class, full of aplomb and convinced she could do no wrong. Yet somehow she had. And when Mr. Morgan pointed out her mistake, the look of shock and annoyance on her face rippled through the classroom.

Then he'd asked Emma to correct it.

Emma had looked around the room uneasily. Yet, she tried to make the best of it. She knew the answer, and this seemed like a good way to show the class that she was smart without having to speak.

At the board, she glanced back hesitantly. Amanda was looking at her through narrowed slits.

She fixed the problem and was about to return to her seat when Mr. Morgan stopped her. "Hold on, can you explain your answer?"

She swallowed hard and whispered.

"I'm sorry, I couldn't hear you," Mr. Morgan said.

She tried again, trying to make her voice sound higher. Everyone was staring at her.

"Louder please."

Exasperated, she blurted it out while trying to keep her voice high. "You have to cross-multiply when you divide fractions."

But halfway through the sentence, her voice dropped by several octaves. Suddenly there were stunned expressions on everyone's face, except for Amanda, whose mouth was open in happy surprise.

Emma rushed to her seat, eyes toward the floor.

Mr. Morgan tried to recover the class's attention. "Amanda, do you see what you did wrong?"

A sly grin spread across her face. "Yes, I understand now," she said in a baritone voice.

The class erupted into laughter. Emma didn't know what to do. For a second, she smiled too, wanting to laugh along with them, not wanting to be left out. But the sudden heat of her face made her drop her head in humiliation.

"Hey, hey," Mr. Morgan cut in. "We don't tease like that here."

The class instantly quieted down. "Sorry," Amanda said with an angelic smile.

If that had been the only fiasco of the day, it might have been bearable. But things had gone from bad to worse.

When Emma had arrived in gym class, Amanda had renewed her assault. Standing with a group of her admirers, she said in a stage whisper, "If I had a voice like that, I'd jump off a bridge." The other girls had stifled their giggles.

And the worst part about it was that Emma couldn't respond. If she tried to defend herself with words, they'd just laugh at her all over again. But she had to find a way to show Amanda she wouldn't be bullied.

When they'd picked teams for basketball, she found the answer—she'd show Amanda on the court. *I'm not only better at math*, she thought, *I'm better at everything*. But things didn't go as planned. Amanda's team took an early lead and kept it. Point after point, Emma's team couldn't catch up and that made Emma angrier and angrier.

"What's wrong, Frankenvoice?" Amanda taunted, then she got a sudden gleam in her eye as a new idea struck her. "Here, I'm open," she said in the deepest voice she could muster. The other girls laughed and began copying her.

"I can't believe you missed that layup," her friend Becca said, also in a deep voice.

"I think it's because I'm stupid," Prisha said.

Emma fumed and wanted to scream at them to stop it, but she

dared not speak. And Mrs. Willis, the gym teacher, didn't seem to have a clue as to what was going on.

Finally, Emma got the ball. Amanda was guarding her, and she got into the key and took a jump shot. It was an easy shot, but she missed.

At that moment her frustration turned to rage. She went for the rebound.

Amanda went for it too.

The ball bounced off their fingertips, but Emma was determined and with a grunt snatched the ball out of the air and pulled it down to her chest, but in the process her elbow fell hard on Amanda's nose.

The girl landed on her butt with a thud, her hand on her nose, blood already seeping out around her fingers.

Emma's first thought was, *Serves you right*, but then she realized she'd gone too far. "Oh, God, I'm sorry."

But as she moved toward Amanda, her friends pushed Emma back. "Get away, you freak!"

Mrs. Willis knelt down by Amanda. "Are you okay, sweetie?" She turned to one of the girls, "Brooke, get the medical kit from my office. We'll get the bleeding under control, then I'll take you to the nurse."

Emma backed slowly away from them, and the scope of the room seemed to shrink until she was looking at everything from a distance. Everyone was either staring at Amanda with sympathy, or looking at her with suspicion and anger.

That's when she ran for the bathroom, the only safe place she could think of. She had now been here for almost an hour. A part of her just wanted to be alone, but she also hoped that someone—maybe Mrs. Willis—would find her and reassure her. Tell her that everything would be all right. But no one came.

The bell finally rang. She heard the hallway erupt with noise—students talking and laughing, lockers slamming. She really didn't want to go out there for everyone to see. Outnumbered and powerless. They would stare and that overwhelming sense of isolation would return.

Come on, Emma, let's get this over with. In thirty minutes, you'll be at the stables riding Argo.

She blew her nose in some toilet paper and wiped her face dry. Then she went out into the hall.

She kept her head down, but she could feel the heat of everyone's eyes on her and imagined them whispering.

How could a place so full of people feel so lonely? she thought.

She quickly got her backpack from her locker and headed for the front door, desperate not to make eye contact with anyone.

Looking out through the double doors of the school she saw the long caravan of expensive cars and SUVs. She spotted her mother's white Mercedes. *Almost out*, she thought.

The wide walkway out of her school had a low split-rail fence on both sides and this was where clusters of students liked to sit and hang out while waiting for their rides home.

Of course, Amanda was sitting there with her friends. Her nose had stopped bleeding, but her eyes were red and swollen. She flashed Emma a glare full of hatred.

Emma quickened her steps and got into the back of her mom's car. She glanced back one more time. Amanda's eyes were still locked on her and, in that stare, Emma realized that her troubles were just beginning.

"Hi, sweetheart," her mother said excitedly. "Aren't you surprised to see me? I told Natalie she could have the afternoon off."

Silence.

"How was school?"

Silence.

"That good, huh?" Emma saw her mother's eyes probing her in the rear-view mirror. She drove for a few blocks, then Olivia pulled over to the shoulder. "Okay, what happened?"

"Nothing."

Olivia turned in her seat to look at her. "Come on, I know when you're upset."

"I'm fine. Can we please just go to the stables?"

Emma dropped her eyes again, sure that if she met her mother's gaze, the tears would come back. "Please?"

Her mother sighed. "Okay, okay," she said, "but will you tell me later?"

There was a long pause.

"Maybe."

With a sigh, Olivia put the car in gear and pulled back into traffic.

That night Emma lay in her bed. The images of the day playing over in her mind. The class laughing at her. Amanda's mouth open in joy at finding her weakness. Amanda landing hard on the gym floor, the blood seeping out through her fingers. *Frankenvoice.*

Over and over. She tried to block the images out; tried to remind herself of the good in her life. *Two months ago, you were on the verge of death. Now you're completely normal again.*

Well, mostly normal.

She knew she'd emerged from her sickness profoundly changed. Waking up from a year of being trapped in her disintegrating mind, then suddenly whole again, it was a shock, like one of those science-fiction movies where the character wakes up in a new body. It felt like she was discovering who she was all over again. She had new likes and dislikes, like her sudden interest in math and history. She was turning into a nerd, staying up late tearing through sudoku books.

Her body felt different too. After just three weeks of physical therapy, they'd sent her home. The doctors couldn't explain it. She'd been catatonic for a year, yet her muscle tone and endurance were back to normal in a month. Almost better than normal. She felt somehow . . . *optimized.* As if she were permanently on a caffeine buzz—alert and focused, with an underlying sense of restlessness.

Was that normal?

And what about the fact that she was talking to herself. Wasn't that strange for a ten-year-old?

She told herself that it was okay. So what if she had an imaginary friend? It wasn't just that she'd lost a year of her life, she'd lost a year of her childhood, and a part of her still wanted to be a little girl.

Okay, so not really normal. But not necessarily bad. In fact, it was when she was talking to him that she felt the most normal. He understood her better than anyone.

And right now she needed to talk to him more than ever.

"Are you there?" she asked.

There was no answer.

"I had a really bad day."

She waited, but the other voice didn't come.

"Hello?"

"I'm here," she heard him say, as clear as if he were in the room with her.

A smile grew across her face. Just the sound of his voice was so soothing.

"Tell me all about it," the voice said. "I want to hear everything."

PART TWO

THE RAINS BEGIN

CHAPTER FOURTEEN

CAGN'S MESSAGE

January 27, 2027
Namibia

Karuma awoke to the sound of deafening gunfire and his heart leaped into his throat. He heard the screaming of his family and friends and saw them rushing to and fro in the darkness.

No, no, please not again.

He had fallen asleep during his watch and the enemy had sneaked up on their camp. And once again, the spears and arrows of the Sān were no match for their rifles.

"Karuma!" he heard his mother scream.

She was stumbling around the camp looking for him when she should be running away. "No, mother, please, just go!"

In the moonlight he saw one of the soldiers with the metal eyes that allowed him to see in the dark. The soldier aimed his gun at his mother and a flash of fire erupted from the end.

His mother crumpled to the ground.

"No!"

The soldier instantly turned to Karuma and opened fire.

Karuma ducked down and grabbed his own rifle, but he was still clumsy with it. Frantic—half-dodging, half-aiming, he pulled the trigger. Nothing happened. He had done something wrong.

Suddenly, brutal hands grabbed the rifle and tore it from his hands. Then a fierce kick sent him sprawling to the ground.

He rolled over to face his attacker, pulling his hunting knife from its sheath.

The soldier towered over him like one of Gaunab's demons, his metal eyes alight with a green glow. He looked at Karuma's small knife and began to laugh.

Karuma awoke with a gasp. He clutched at his heart as if to slow its frantic beating with his hand. He stood quickly and looked around, part of him sure that he was still in the dream.

The campfire had died to a few orange embers, but otherwise the night was peaceful and still. He grabbed the rifle and walked through the camp, checking on Kebbi-An, little Nyando, and finally his mother. They were all sleeping quietly, oblivious to the horrors that Karuma had just lived through.

After he'd walked the perimeter of the camp and seen no sign of any threat, he began to relax.

But he'd been lucky. He had indeed fallen asleep on his watch and as a punishment, he smacked himself in the face until his cheeks were red and stinging.

You must do better. There is no room for mistakes. Not now, not tomorrow, not for the year, or next year. There were only thirteen of them left . . . and only nine who were not too old or too young to hunt or gather food . . . or fight. Their tribe, their very existence, was on the verge of extinction.

They could afford no sickness, no accidents, no run-ins with poachers or their mercenaries or the Chinese soldiers who ran the labor camps. No easy task considering that the outside world was encroaching on their land every year.

After the massacre, many said that the only way to survive would be to merge with another tribe.

But Naru had pointed out that there were no more tribes that lived as they did, so to join another tribe meant leaving the bush and living in a village, taking government assistance, and finding jobs making trinkets or showing off their tracking skills to white tourists at the game preserves. His grandfather Khamko had warned them about that road—the depression, the alcohol, the suicide.

Between these two slow deaths they had chosen to stay in the Kalahari because it held the most hope.

Karuma sat down heavily by the embers of the dying fire and thought of his dream. The screaming, his mother crumpling to the ground, how his rifle had failed to work. It had been so clear . . . so real. More like a vision than a dream. And he began to wonder if he had been given a sign from Cagn. A warning that he had to do more to protect his people. But what should he do? What was the path he needed to take?

He thought of the warrior standing over him. That feeling of helplessness; the way the warrior had laughed at his knife.

He looked down at the weapon in his hand. During the massacre, the enemy warriors had used guns like this to kill so many so fast. He hated it. And the fact that he was probably holding a weapon that had killed his friends or even his grandfather sickened him. Yet, he could not deny the power it gave its owner.

He looked up into the sky and saw that it was getting light in the east. He imagined he was looking down on himself from a great distance. One young man standing watch over a dozen sleeping souls, the open plains of the Kalahari spreading out from that spot for hundreds of kilometers in every direction. He was one of the last true Khoe-san on earth and Cagn had given him a vision. He nodded, suddenly realizing what his god was trying to tell him.

CHAPTER FIFTEEN

JAMESON IRISH WHISKEY

January 29, 2027
Near Raven, Virginia

"Fighting continues to escalate in Syria. Over the past week, there have been more than a dozen attacks and counter attacks by rival groups leaving more than two hundred and thirty dead, including sixteen children. Joining us now to help explain what this all means is our Middle East correspondent, Samantha Karim. Good morning, Sam."

"Good morning, Jessica."

"Has Syria truly fallen back into civil war? And if so, how is this different from the war before the Zurich Accords?"

"Yes, Jessica, even though the White House doesn't want to admit it, this has all the makings of a civil war. We have five factions fighting each other, and all of them have the troops and the financing to survive a prolonged conflict.

"Now what makes this different is that Russia is taking a much more aggressive stance than before. Russian President Dmitry Petrov is following the hard-line tactics they used in Chechnya and Ukraine and is using heavy artillery against the towns and cities controlled by anti-Assad forces."

"And why is that? I mean, what are they after?"

"It comes down to this: if Petrov can win the war for al-Assad, it will be a huge victory for Russia. Not only will the Kremlin gain a foothold in the Middle East, but it will give them something that every Russian leader has wanted for a hundred years—a warm-water port in the heart of the Mediterranean. With that port, the Kremlin can flex its military muscle into Africa, Europe, and across the Atlantic. There is a lot at stake here, and Russia's gamble is that no one is going to stop them. With America embroiled in a host of domestic issues and after its long occupations in Afghanistan and Iraq, and its unwillingness to commit troops to Ukraine, Russia believes it can continue grabbing territory without significant US interference."

"And do you believe they're right?"

"I do. And so far, President Shaw's actions prove it. He's limiting his support to military aid, and there's been no mention of sending troops or even military advisers, so it seems clear that the current administration isn't interested in risking American lives."

Bud Brown reached over and turned the radio off. *Just more proof that the world was going to hell,* he thought. *And one more reason to have a drink.*

He was sitting in his car in a strip mall looking directly at a liquor store. The windows were plastered over with enticing posters—Tanqueray gin, Cuervo tequila, Johnnie Walker Red Label, Captain Morgan, Bacardi.

Ah, my old friends, Bud thought. *You're making my mouth water.*

Are you really going to do this? the other voice said.

Sure, I've failed at finding Finley, why not fail some more?

For the past week, he'd been driving and hiking around the backwoods of southwest Virginia, way down by the Kentucky state line. Serious banjo country. He hadn't found a damn thing. He'd hung out at the coffee shops and gas stations where Finley's followers had been sighted. He'd annoyed every small-town sheriff in the one-traffic-light towns that dotted the area. He'd even interviewed every hobby and electrical-supply shop owner, seeing if any of their customers fit Coyle's description.

And, the most miserable part: he'd hiked at least fifty miles through old mining areas where Finley might be hiding out. What a nightmare! As he'd learned from the topographical maps strewn throughout his car, this was the Ridge and Valley area of the Appalachians—a seemingly never-ending system of creeks, hills, and hollows that had been mined for coal and titanium from the mid-1800s up until the 1970s. He'd visited Zeke Creek, Mill Creek, Pine Creek, Sulphur Spring Branch, Stow Creek, and at least a dozen others. And running along each of these hundreds of creeks were often ten or twenty derelict mines. He'd frozen his balls off in the woods, fallen and gashed his leg, and stuck his head into about ninety old mines, looking for signs of Finley.

He'd found nothing.

He'd contacted Hill to see if he had gotten any more leads. He hadn't.

> Could it be that they were just passing through on their way to somewhere else?

> It's possible. But to develop the technology she'll need a fixed location. She can't be moving around.

> But is that location here?

It took a while for Hill to answer. *Unknown*, was all he wrote. Bud told him he'd give it two more days. That was Wednesday. He'd kept looking but still had found nothing. Now it was Friday afternoon.

Time to take the weekend off! his lazy voice said. *You've done everything you can here. Just buy one bottle. Drink a little tonight and you can stretch it over the weekend.*

He laughed at his own delusions, fully aware that as soon as he started, he wouldn't stop.

His mind made up, he got out of the car and went into the store.

It was a Friday afternoon. He saw soccer moms getting wine for their weekend parties, two young men with matching twenty-four packs of Budweiser on their hips, and a businessman with a loosened tie holding a bottle of Wild Turkey.

Bud started browsing the aisles, a nervous excitement growing in his belly. He was really going to do it.

All the bottles looked so beautiful. Like works of art to be collected.

Just get a bottle of Grey Goose and get out of here.

Hell no, you're living in a motel by yourself, no need to worry about bad breath. Get something with flavor. Like Johnnie Walker or Jameson. Or why don't you celebrate that you're in sour mash country with a bottle of Belle Meade.

As he was trying to decide between Pow Wow Botanical Rye and the Belle Meade, an older man brushed by him, "Excuse me, friend."

There was something about his voice that caught Bud's attention. It was a combination of the unusual usage of "friend" and an accent. No, not really an accent, rather the sound of someone trying to cover up an accent.

The man had his back to Bud, so he couldn't see his face, and he was wearing a baseball cap and sunglasses. He grabbed two bottles of Jameson.

"Looks like it's going to be a good party," Bud said in an effort to get a better look.

"A party of one," he said, without making eye contact.

Again, Bud heard the effort to cover the accent. The man had overemphasized the hard *r* sound in *party*. The stranger moved toward the counter and got in line. The soccer moms filed behind him.

Bud grabbed a bottle of Belle Meade and got in line, watching the old man as nonchalantly as he could. But the man stayed facing the other way.

Is it really you? Out on a liquor run? Have you gotten complacent after all these years?

But then his other voice interjected. *Are you crazy? It's an old guy buying booze. And that accent could come from a thousand different places.*

The old man paid in cash and left the store. The soccer moms paid with credit. They began playing with the free cocktail umbrellas. "Oh, I love these!"

Come on!

Bud didn't want to lose him, but he also didn't want the man spotting him leaving the store empty-handed. If it really was Coyle, he'd spook easy.

Bud stood on his toes, watching as he got into a late-model 4Runner.

Finally, it was his turn. "Did you find everything you needed?" the clerk asked.

"Yes, no problem," Bud said, laying out three twenties and grabbing the bottle. "Keep the change."

Outside, he stepped briskly to his car, only glancing up furtively toward the 4Runner.

He started the car and put on his sunglasses so that if the old man saw him, he wouldn't be able to tell if Bud was really watching him.

The 4Runner pulled out of the parking lot and onto the main road. Bud pulled out behind him, got close enough to see the license plate, then eased back.

It was a busy four-lane road, lined with strip malls, gas stations, and fast-food joints. He let one car, then two get between them.

He was trying to figure out if this was just wishful thinking, when the 4Runner made a sharp right turn onto a side street (without signaling). Bud had to think fast; if he followed him down that little street, it would be obvious he was tailing him.

Trusting his instincts, he pulled into a gas station and pretended to fill up his tank. He waited ... keeping his head toward a billboard for Trentino's pizza, but his eyes turned toward a side street back the way he'd come.

There!

A block back he saw the 4Runner turn onto the main street again and roll by in front of him. Bud had guessed right. The old man had gone around the block, using a classic method for spotting a tail.

It's really you, isn't it? I finally found you!

Bud kept his head down toward his bumper, but his eyes tracked the 4Runner. It made the same turn again. *He's doing it by the book,* Bud thought.

He had three minutes to kill before he came around again. He pulled into a parking space in front of the convenience store. He jotted down the license-plate number so he wouldn't forget it, then he kept his eyes on the rearview mirror.

The 4Runner came by once more, and Bud put his Ford in reverse and got back on the road.

After a half mile the commercial district began to give way to winter tobacco fields and farmhouses. Bud was just getting comfortable, suspecting that Coyle was going to lead him right to Finley, when the 4Runner turned left into the parking lot of a small farm-supply store, again, without signaling.

Shit! Bud had to make a split-second decision. Option 1: Pull into the parking lot, in which case Coyle would spot him immediately. At that point, he would have to try to arrest him, likely starting a gunfight (without backup). He'd kill Coyle or Coyle would kill him. Either way, Finley would hear about it and disappear. Option 2: Drive by hoping he could get back on Coyle's trail later.

Feeling flustered by the decision, he drove on.

It was almost a mile before there was a gas station where he could pull off. He turned in and waited, hoping that Coyle would come rolling by.

Five, then ten minutes passed. As much as he wanted to go back up the road, he knew it was just too risky.

He was pretty sure that Coyle hadn't made him as a tail. He was just following a routine. If Bud drove back to the farm-supply store, Coyle would recognize his Ford, then it would all be over. One call to Finley and her whole operation—wherever it was— would be gone.

So he waited.

And waited.

After an hour, he headed back toward town. When he passed the farm-supply store, the 4Runner was gone.

He smacked his hands against the steering wheel. "Damn it!"

Coyle had been reckless coming to town, but he was still a sly old fox.

Bud pulled over and took stock of the situation.

He'd found Coyle— that was good.

Coyle had given him the slip—bad.

Coyle probably didn't know he'd been identified—good.

There was one other thing that was certain: he couldn't do this alone anymore . . . and he shouldn't.

He picked up his phone and was about to call the FBI and demand to talk to Assistant Director Collins. He imagined her amazement when Bud told her what he'd found. He'd likely get a commendation. But as he thought it through, he realized how fool-ish it sounded.

"*Yes, Director, I know this is going to sound crazy, but I've found a 76-year-old Irish immigrant who I believe is Finley's bomb maker (even though I have no proof). What's that? How do I know he's an Irish immigrant? Well, because he was buying Irish whiskey at a liquor store. So please, stop everything you're doing and come help me.*"

He sighed. It would never work.

He dialed a different number.

"What do you want?" came the testy voice.

CHAPTER SIXTEEN

THE RIGHT SIDE OF HISTORY

January 29, 2027
Southwest Virginia

Bill Eastman stared at the two windows of his prison cell. The glass was opaque, with a frosted snowflake pattern, the kind you'd expect to find in a neglected government institution or a sanitarium. The kind intended to let light in but prevented you from seeing out.

The light came and went at the appropriate time, increasing a bit each day to fit the season, but he wasn't fooled. It wasn't real sunlight. It had enough UV light to make his body produce vitamin D and, his captors likely hoped, to keep him from becoming depressed. It was the same with noises he heard: birds singing, distant traffic, the occasional honking of a horn, the bark of a dog, the patter of rain. All intended to give him a sense of familiarity and serenity.

But it was not sunshine or real sounds. He was somewhere underground. It had only taken him a day to put the clues together: the condensation that sometimes formed on his ceiling; the complete absence of any sound coming from the opposite wall that suggested there was nothing there but solid rock; and the lack of variation in temperature—the heating system ran at forty-five-minute intervals, therefore the "outside" temperature never changed.

For an underground prison, he could hardly complain, it was a large and comfortable space, with a couch, a refrigerator, desk, and a cabinet full of snacks and herbal teas. There were plenty of back issues of *Nature* and two full bookcases. He had just finished reading Feynmann's *Six Easy Pieces* this morning.

Still, he was getting tired of this. He had a restless mind, and the long hours of isolation were irritating. The people who brought him his food were friendly and kind, but they could not (or would not) answer any of his questions. He had long ago given up any thought of escaping; his captors had been much too thorough for that. So he had resigned himself to reading, writing, and drinking tea.

But this morning, halfway through an article about quantum entanglement, the door suddenly opened. Bill looked over the edge of his magazine. It was much too early for lunch.

Framed in the doorway was an attractive woman with curly red hair. He knew her at once—Riona Finley—leader of the New Anarchists. Even at a distance, Bill noticed a European style about her that exuded intelligence and confidence. She wore thick-framed glasses and a forest-green sweater that set off her watery green eyes. Her skin was pale, almost reddish, with freckles bridging her nose.

He felt her charisma immediately and understood why so many people had joined her cause. But her beauty annoyed him . . . or was he annoyed with himself for feeling attracted to her?

She crossed the room, smiling warmly. "Hello, Dr. Eastman, my sincere apologies for all this."

Bill didn't respond right away. He was studying her. Just the fact that she was here, now, approaching him with that smile, was a data point that he needed to add to his calculations.

She extended her hand. He shook it, despite himself, again feeling the spell of her personality. He'd imagined this encounter many times, but now he was being much more civil than he had planned.

Her hand was soft, yet her grip strong; her eyes lucid and sincere. It was as if she was saying, *Let's forget the past and be friends.*

Bill's eyes flitted to her necklace. From a silver chain hung the pendant of a Celtic knot, and within one of the folds was a small crow.

"Morrígan," he muttered.

Her eyes dropped to the pendant. "Very good," she said. "You know your Irish mythology."

"The Phantom Queen who could shape-shift into a crow. She was known for inciting warriors into battle . . . and striking fear into the hearts of the enemy."

"That's right."

"Is that how you see yourself?"

She gave a coy smile. "That and more . . . much more." She gestured to the sofa. "Please, have a seat?" Bill sat without objection. This was not going at all like he had planned.

"Jack told me about your interest in my work," she said, taking a chair across from him. "He even used the word *obsessed.*"

Here again was another data point. What she said was true, but how did she know it? Was Jack telling her these things willingly . . . or under threat?

He took a deep breath. "I'll admit that I see you as an interesting phenomenon. It says something about our world that tens of millions of people would rally around you, send you their money, and wear your face on a T-shirt . . . it shows that there is a great disenchantment in the world. People are fed up with the current system—the government, corporations. So fed up, in fact, that they are willing to embrace radical change."

"So you acknowledge that we have a worthy goal—that our civilization is in a crisis and that the old ways don't work anymore?"

Bill shook his head. "I only said that we are at a pivotal moment in history, not that your movement is the answer."

She leaned closer, resting her forearms on her knees. "And why *isn't* it the answer?"

"Because you're a terrorist."

She sat back and shook her head in disappointment. "Really, a *terrorist*? It's much too easy of a term, isn't it? Thomas Paine, John

Hancock, and George Washington were terrorists in the eyes of the British, Nelson Mandela was a terrorist in the eyes of the South African government. Today we see them as patriots and heroes. Yes, I am a terrorist to some, but I am something very different to millions of others. The question you should ask yourself is when people look back on this time, say a hundred years from now, who will be the heroes? Will they be the ones who pushed for change, who rebelled against the status quo—against the corruption, the injustice, the complacency? Or do you think they will applaud those who failed to act, who denied the facts, or who didn't have the courage to fight?"

Bill hesitated and Finley seemed to press her advantage. "I am at peace with my actions because I am on the right side of history. What about you?" She raised her eyebrows knowingly. "Jack told me how you feel about what's going on at the lab."

There it was, another suggestion that Jack was helping her. But it couldn't be true. She was trying to manipulate him. Still, he had trouble lying to her. "You mean General Walden?" he asked.

She nodded.

"I'm worried about what he might do with our inventions. He wants only power and cannot see beyond his own selfish goals."

"I know," she said, leaning forward, the pendant swinging on its chain like a pendulum. "You see, I truly believe we want the same thing: to change the world for the better. We just need to find common ground."

"If I recall, you kidnapped me at gunpoint and have held me here against my will," he said. "Not exactly the best route to finding common ground."

She held up her palms in a gesture of supplication. "You're right. But I want to make a fresh start. I want you to join us. But before you answer, consider the facts: We are building a powerful global movement. We have the world's attention. And we are changing the way that millions of people think and act. We can do this. With your technology we can heal the planet. We can pull carbon from the air. We can break down waste at the molecular level and recycle it, we can lower the thermostat on the whole planet. Not only that, but people can thrive at the same time. There doesn't need to be a trade-off anymore. My followers—all four hundred million of them—will help us on this journey."

Bill locked eyes on her for a moment, but then shook his head. "It sounds promising, but it feels too easy. Perhaps if you had come to me before the killings—before Senator Peck and all those FBI agents—we could have talked. But by choosing violence you've gone down a path that I can't follow."

Her eyes locked on his, and he could read the distaste in her gaze.

"Doctor Eastman, I think you are a great man and I have the utmost respect for you, but you must hear the hypocrisy in your words. I know what Curtiss did in Tangshen. In your race to beat the Chinese, I know how many people he massacred using your new weapons. Shall I remind you of the number?"

Bill looked away. He suddenly felt like an animal that had walked into a trap.

"Sixty-five thousand people died," she said. "Most of them were completely innocent. Did they all need to die just so Curtiss could get his message through to the Chinese government? It was your work that made that possible. Yet even after Tangshen, you didn't quit. You followed the same path. Face the truth: you accepted violence as part of the job a long time ago."

Bill turned to face her. "If China had reached replication first, the consequences would have been much worse for billions of people."

Her eyes brightened for a fraction of a second. "You did it for the greater good, is that it?"

"Yes."

"Well, I agree with you."

Bill eyed her skeptically.

"You did the right thing," she continued. "Absolutely. Now I'm asking you to do it again."

He scrunched his forehead in doubt. "What do you mean?"

"You used to make weapons for a political movement called the

US government, now their goals are no longer aligned with yours. So I am asking you to join a different political movement, and to apply your knowledge once more, and not for weapons, but to help people, protect the planet, and heal the world."

She waited for his reply. After a moment he shook his head.

She patted her knees with a note of finality, rose from the chair, and turned to go.

He had been expecting her to keep trying to convince him, and her sudden departure unnerved him. "Wait, if I say no, does that mean you are going to kill me?"

In the doorway, she turned to him and smiled. "You still don't understand, do you?"

Alone once more, Bill had a lot to consider. Her final comment implied that she had no intention of hurting him. While that was a relief, he still didn't know what she meant. What piece of the puzzle had he not placed? His thoughts returned to Jack. Jack Behrmann was, without a doubt, the man Bill trusted most in the world. The man he'd known since freshman year of college, when they'd been two precocious science nerds at Berkeley. They had stayed together through college and graduate school, and eventually created Advance Micro Laboratories, one of the most successful biotech companies in Silicon Valley, before Admiral Curtiss had recruited them to the NRL. Across those thirty-seven years they had learned everything there was to know about each other—they were like an old married couple, able to anticipate how the other would react to any news or situation. Through all those years he had never doubted Jack's loyalty. But something about all this wasn't right . . . and it had to do with Jack.

CHAPTER SEVENTEEN

PRIVATE DATA

January 30, 2027
Southwest Virginia

"I honestly didn't think you'd come," Bud said.

"I realize I might seriously regret this, but for now, I'm intrigued," June Brightwell said.

It was eight on Saturday morning and they were parked in front of a 7-Eleven. It was bright and cold, and they were both nursing cups of coffee. As a precaution, in case Coyle had spotted him yesterday, Bud had traded in the Ford sedan for a Jeep Rubicon.

"I read your letter as soon as you left my office," she added. "The stuff on Coyle is all circumstantial, of course, but it was still good investigative work. And who knows, you might be right."

"I am right."

She raised her eyebrows. "The fact that the man in the liquor store knew how to mark a tail only corroborates your theory, it doesn't prove anything."

"And the license plate on the 4Runner," he said. "Registered to a shell company in the Caymans called Outfit Earth? That's not enough for you?"

"It's suspicious and worth checking out. But we're still inferring way too much from very few pieces of evidence. For all we know, this guy could be selling drugs or running guns and have nothing to do with Finley."

"You don't believe me?"

"I'm here, aren't I? Which means I think it's worth pursuing."

She put her coffee mug in the cup holder and opened her iSheet to the size of a laptop. Then she pulled up a map of the area. It had red dots showing the locations of the pings on Finley's accomplices and where Bud had spotted Coyle.

"This is still a huge area," she said. "We'll never find them unless we can narrow this down . . . dramatically. It's too bad we can't put out an APB or BOLO on the 4Runner."

"Too risky," Bud said. "All we need is one sheriff's deputy trying to be a cowboy and we'll lose Finley completely."

"Then what do we do?"

Bud shrugged. "All I know is that they must be around here somewhere." He looked out the windshield of the Jeep with the futile hope that the world might give him a clue. Directly across the street was a series of beat-up townhouses. He noticed a tow truck pulling into the parking lot. Its driver got out quickly and began setting the swap lift under a green Dodge.

"Check it out," he said to June, holding up his coffee cup and pointing one finger across the street. "Early-morning repo."

She shook her head and went back to her iSheet.

The alarm on the Dodge went off, breaking the serenity of the morning. The tow-truck driver doubled his efforts, pulling a lever for the hydraulic lift, and getting the nose of the Dodge off the ground.

"Hey, that's my car!" A man appeared in the doorway of the townhouse, dressed in a T-shirt and Incredible Hulk underwear.

The tow-truck driver hopped into the truck and hit the gas. The next instant, the truck and Dodge came bouncing out of the parking lot, sending up a momentary rooster tail of sparks as the Dodge scraped the blacktop. Bruce Banner gave chase, his breath pouring out of his mouth like smoke in the cold air.

Bud looked over at Brightwell, who had become very interested in the morning entertainment. She'd lifted her iSheet and was filming the action.

In a moment the truck was long gone, and Bruce Banner was stooped over in the middle of the road, hands on his knees panting.

"That's a crappy way to start your Saturday," Bud said.

"Not for us . . . I think I just solved our problem."

"Huh?"

She rewound the video of the tow truck and froze the image. "See these boxes on the roof and sides?"

"License-plate readers?" he asked.

"Yep, most tow trucks these days photograph license plates wherever they go. They're like sharks, patrolling the waters for a kill. They'll cruise parking lots, apartment complexes, and neighborhoods. If they scan a plate on a car that's been repossessed, the system will sound an alarm and they'll tow the car for a bounty. But that's just the beginning. Private companies outfit the trucks and keep all the data they collect, which is millions and millions of pictures every day, and way more than the police or government collect. Then they sell the data to private investigators, collection agencies, attorneys and, guess who . . ."

"Law enforcement?"

"That's right."

"Is that legal?"

"Perfectly. There's nothing wrong with going around in public taking pictures."

"Okay, but can we get the data?"

"Let's find out."

Brightwell dialed the phone number off the side of the truck.

"J. C. Towing," came a young man's voice over the speaker. "This is Rich."

"Good morning, Rich. This is Special Agent June Brightwell of the FBI. I need to know who gets your LPR data."

"Uh, hold on a minute."

They could hear a muffled conversation in the background.

"This is Jay Campbell," came an older man's voice. "I understand you're interested in the license-plate pictures . . . and you're FBI?"

Bud was surprised that Jay did not seem to find their request particularly unusual.

"Yes, Jay," Brightwell said. "Can you help us?"

"Sure," he said. "The whole system belongs to Vivant. They mount the scanners on all my trucks."

"Excellent. And do you know if the other towing companies in the area also use WiseTracker?"

"Some do, but Smart Repo and DataMax are also around."

"Jay, thank you so much for your help."

After she'd hung up, she turned to Bud. "This is promising. WiseTracker and DataMax are some of the bigger national companies, but I'm not sure about this Smart Repo."

Bud was starting to feel out of his depth. He knew about license plate readers, of course, but he didn't know that it was such a big business. It was just one more thing that made him feel old.

They spent the rest of the morning trying to find scans on the 4Runner. Luck was on their side (mostly). WiseTracker was already under contract to supply their license-plate data to DHS. Brightwell made one call to Homeland Security and got three hits on the 4Runner. DataMax also gave them access, no questions asked, since the CEO was a former cop.

That got them an additional three hits.

But Smart Repo refused to share their data unless they had a subpoena. Brightwell tried to coax it out of them, but Nathan, their customer service rep, wouldn't budge.

"I'm sorry you couldn't be more cooperative, please hold while I transfer you to the Deputy Director."

She muted the iSheet. "You wanna give it a try?"

"Sure," he said and cleared his throat.

He turned off the mute button. "This is Deputy Director Bud Brown, what's the holdup here?"

"I'm sorry sir, but it's against our policy to—"

"Don't lecture me about policy, son, and don't waste my time. This is a priority-one investigation and I need this data now. A minor has been kidnapped and we need to see the pattern of where this vehicle has been for the past two months. Every second counts."

"But, sir—"

"Just think this through, son. Do you really want me to make that call to your boss and say that you didn't give us the information when we needed it? And that the reason this girl never got to go home was because you were following a protocol that none of the other LPR companies follow? We both know this is not protected data."

There was a pause.

"Okay. Just give me a minute. I'll see what I can do."

Bud flashed Brightwell a smile.

She shook her head but couldn't help smiling back.

In the end, they were able to get two more hits out of Smart Repo.

Once Brightwell had put the GPS locations into the map, it created a very different picture. Now there was a definite cluster along State Route 83, which ran east-west along the foothills—south of the road was a scattering of farms, but north of the road was thick woods and the old mine country.

"Good work," Bud said. "We just got a hell of a lot closer to finding Finley."

"No, to finding that 4Runner. But yes, it looks good. Now let's see that geological map."

The Virginia Department of Mines, Minerals and Energy (DMME) had an inventory of all the old mines, marked with flags for hazardous waste, slurry, and notations for each mine type. Within a few minutes, she'd overlaid one map on top of the other.

"Let me see if I can narrow this down a little."

"Right," Bud said. "Finley's mine, wherever it is, must be close enough to a road so a vehicle like a 4Runner can reach it."

"Agreed," Brightwell said. She began eliminating many of the older mines that had no roads or ATV trails.

"My source told me that they would need space for the kidnapped scientists to work, which means it must be a more recent mine. Can you cross off anything older than, say, the fifties?"

Brightwell kept cutting down the number of mines, until there were only seven that fit their criteria in the right area.

"That's more like it," Bud said. "We can check all those out in a day or two."

"What's the plan?" she asked.

"I think it's time we go hunting."

Bud checked Brightwell into the same cheap motel where he'd been staying, then they got ready to head for the foothills. But when they met on the balcony a half hour later, Bud shook his head.

"This will never work," he said. "I'm dressed like a redneck hunter, and you look like you just robbed an REI."

"I look better."

"True, but who looks more likely to be stomping around the Smoky Mountains in January?"

She frowned. "I see your point."

"Come on, we'll make a stop along the way."

After a visit to the Army surplus store, they were ready. Brightwell now wore a pair of Woodland camo coveralls, Danner boots, and a John Deere hat. Bud let her keep her Patagonia parka, but only if she wore her new blaze orange hunting vest over it.

"So what's the story? I'm your daughter and you're taking me out hunting?"

"Either that or my mail-order bride."

"Nice try," she said. "Let's stick with daughter. And rifles? I only have my sidearm."

"Don't worry. I got you covered."

After an hour's drive into the foothills, they got to an area where three of the mines were located. They pulled off onto an old service road, double-checking to make sure there were no recent tracks.

Bud opened the back of the Jeep and pulled out two hard cases.

"I'll let you take your pick, although I have a feeling which one you'll choose," Bud said. Despite Brightwell's reserved demeanor, Bud remembered that she was, like a lot of agents, a gun freak.

Inside the first case was a .30-06 Winchester Model 70. A classic bolt-action hunting rifle with a walnut stock.

Then he opened the second case.

"Oh, I've made my decision," Brightwell said.

The rifle laying on the eggshell foam looked like it had been teleported back from the twenty-second century. It was black carbon fiber with a skeletonized stock and a sixteen-inch shrouded barrel.

Brightwell picked it up and examined the imprint on the barrel. "Nice! A TNG chambered in 300 Blackout with a Vortex scope. I think I'm in love. Thanks, *Dad*."

"It's only a loan, sweetheart."

She put the rifle to her shoulder and sighted through the scope.

"As much as I'd like an excuse to use this, we need to get something straight: If you're right and Finley is up there, we are not going to engage, you got that? We observe, then we get the hell out as fast we can."

"I agree, which is why I also brought this."

From his pack he pulled out a camera with a telephoto lens. "I got this from the confiscated-property unit. We are going to need all the proof we can get."

"Do you have any idea how to use one of those?"

He smiled. "None."

★ ★ ★

They were able to reach the first mine in a little less than an hour, and it was obvious from a distance that it had been long abandoned. The hoist tower had collapsed into the shaft, making access impossible. They searched the area to be sure, but all they found were some rusty old Olympia beer cans, which had probably been there since the seventies.

They moved on to the second mine, Bud kept his eyes on the terrain, holding the Winchester in a two-hand ready. The forest around them was quiet and bare, mile after mile of leafless birch and oak trees. It was now almost 3:30 p.m. and Bud realized they had an hour of good light before they would have to head back.

When they were almost a half mile from the second mine, they found some footprints on the trail. The temperature was below freezing, so the tracks must have been made earlier and frozen in place.

They knelt down to take a look. There were at least four different sets, coming and going in both directions.

"Whadaya think?" Bud asked.

"This trail clearly gets a lot more use, which doesn't make sense because we are still in the middle of nowhere."

"A patrol?"

"Could be . . ."

"Let's ditch the blaze orange," Bud said, working off his hunting vest. "I want to see them before they see us."

Brightwell did the same.

They moved cautiously up the trail, trying not to make tracks of their own. In the sunny spots, where the trail had turned to mud, they stayed on the edges.

"Okay, the mine should be three hundred yards to the northeast," Brightwell said, pointing with her hand as she kept her eyes on the iSheet.

At that moment they heard a high-pitched whizzing sound.

"Shit!" Brightwell hissed, "a drone!"

They both looked around frantically for cover, but there were no evergreen trees in this part of the woods.

"There!" Brightwell said, indicating a huge oak tree with a cleft in the trunk. They both rushed to it, but as they got closer they realized it wasn't even big enough for one of them.

The whizzing of the drone grew louder.

"Lie down!" she commanded.

"Wha . . ."

"Just do it!"

Bud flopped onto his belly. Brightwell began piling leaves on top of him; he stayed still, thankful for her resourcefulness. Then she sat in the cleft of the oak. Her torso was well concealed, but her legs were sticking out. She did her best to cover them with leaves too.

The drone felt like it was directly above them. Bud tried not to move a muscle, the iron smell of wet leaves filling his nose.

The buzzing held steady right over their position, and Bud felt sure they'd been seen. There were two possibilities if they were— Finley's soldiers would come out to investigate and either capture them or kill them . . . or Finley's whole outfit would spook and bug out. "Please, God," he prayed.

Finally, the drone moved off a little, but he could still hear it buzzing around. The minutes dragged on and Bud realized they were in a very bad spot. If they got up now, the drone could come back and catch them. Or could it even see them from where it was now? He didn't know. The problem was that waiting here was equally dangerous because it meant that Finley's guards could be quickly approaching.

To move meant further risk of being spotted. But staying here meant they were sitting ducks.

He could see forward toward the trail through a gap in the leaves that covered him. But he dared not move for fear of shaking off the leaves and exposing himself. At least if they came down the trail, I'll see them, he consoled himself.

But what if they don't? What if they are sneaking up behind you right now?

At the same instant, he heard the rustle of leaves behind him and felt his adrenaline surge and his mouth go dry. He wanted to turn but dared not. *It's just a bird or a squirrel*, he tried to reassure himself.

Or a gunman about to shoot you in the back.

He waited, anticipating the crack of a rifle.

He realized they'd been stupid to come up here alone, with no satellite phone or way to get help. It was a mistake that might just cost him his life . . . and Brightwell's. He never should have brought her up here.

The minutes ticked by, painfully slowly. It took all his wits to stay still and hidden. Finally, the noise of the drone ceased. He waited another five minutes then got up to check on Brightwell. He had to coax her out from the hollow of the tree. She was trembling.

"Are you all right?"

"I wanna go back," she said, "Now."

"Hold on—" he began, but she cut him off.

"We're all alone up here. If it's really Finley, we won't have a chance."

"Just take a deep breath, okay? I think we're safe. If they'd seen us and meant to hurt us, they would have been here by now." He gave her a reassuring smile.

She set her jaw, noncommittally. "I don't want to end up like all those agents in Vermont."

Bud sucked in a long breath. He could hardly blame her for getting spooked. The whole situation had unnerved him too. And he reminded himself that, yes, she was tough, but she was also twenty-eight years old. She had her whole life (and career) in front of her, which meant she had a lot more to lose than he did.

"Can I see the map a second?" he asked.

She gave it to him.

"I'll make you a deal. It's about three hundred yards to the mine, right? But look here." He pointed to a spot on the map. "About a hundred and twenty yards up is a ridgeline that should give us a good view of what's down there. Come with me that far, and we'll take a look. If we don't see anything, we'll go home."

She looked at him for a moment, at first unable to decide, but then some of her confidence seemed to return. "Okay, but let's make it quick."

He helped her to her feet. "Come on."

They made their way up the trail another fifty yards, then moved into the woods, their rifles up and ready. When they saw the ridge, they got down on their bellies and crawled, the rifles cradled in the crooks of their arms.

When Bud got a few feet from the edge he turned to her and put his finger to his lips. Then Bud crawled to the lip and looked over.

CHAPTER EIGHTEEN

SEBASTIAN

January 30, 2027
Rosslyn, Virginia

"How was school yesterday?"

"Awful. No one talked to me all day."

"Did Amanda bother you?"

"No, she and her friends just kept whispering behind my back. But I get the very strong feeling they're planning something and it's making me paranoid."

"Hmm, perhaps it will blow over in time," the voice said.

Emma raised her eyebrows skeptically. She really wanted to change the subject. She'd had enough obsessing about Amanda for one day.

"I think Mom's starting to get suspicious."

"About us?"

Emma nodded.

"You can tell her more about me if you want."

"She'd just think I'm crazy."

"No, I think she'd believe you. But she'd probably tell you to stop."

"But I don't want to stop."

"Then we'd better keep it a secret for now."

"Okay, but I want some answers."

"You know I've always been honest with you."

"What's your name?"

He chuckled. "Why don't you just give me a name?"

"Because I know you're not imaginary. You're real somehow."

There was a brief pause. "That's right. I am real. Does it bother you?"

"No, in fact I'm glad, because it means I'm not crazy."

He laughed good-naturedly, and that made her smile. "No, you're not crazy, Emma. You just live in a crazy world."

Emma waited a moment, then probed. "Are you going to answer my question?"

Another laugh. "Okay, you can call me Sebastian."

"Okay, Sebastian, it's a pleasure to officially make your acquaintance."

"The pleasure is all mine."

Emma smiled again, feeling that she'd accomplished something important, that she'd made a real friend. She pressed on. "What's happening to me? Why do I feel so different?"

He didn't speak right away, and Emma suspected he was choosing his words carefully. Finally, he spoke: "Your mother loves you very much. So much, in fact, that she would have done anything to save you. At the lab where she works, she and Ryan made an experimental drug and gave it to you. They did many things right. They cured you. But they also made some mistakes, and now you're dealing with the side effects of the drug. That's what gives you that restless feeling that you told me about. It's also making you smarter."

Emma pulled her knees up to her chest.

Sebastian continued: "The reason I know this is because the same thing happened to me. I'm not going to lie, it can be scary. But I'm here to help you manage it."

"I just want to be normal. Can't you fix me?"

"I'm working on that. But the changes have affected all of your

DNA and RNA, in every cell in your body. It's very complicated. If I remove the drug right now, it would make you very sick again . . . or worse."

Emma shifted uncomfortably.

"But don't worry. I'll eventually be able to remove the drug from your system . . . believe it or not, I'm pretty smart. I just need more time.

"For now, I want you to take life one day at a time. What we are doing right now—talking about feelings, letting out your worries and fears—is very good for you. It keeps you strong. And don't forget you have other people around you who care. Your mom, Ryan, me. We're on your side. You can talk to them too."

She nodded reluctantly.

"Now there's something else," he said, "and it's very, *very* important."

"What?"

"I need you to promise me that you won't go looking for answers without me."

"Why not?"

"Because you're not ready. I know you don't like to hear this, but you're still a child and not ready to hear the whole truth. Just have faith that I will tell you what you need to know when the time comes. Be patient and don't worry. All you need to do is be a ten-year-old girl. That's your job right now. Nothing more."

"I don't want to wait. I want to understand. I can handle it. You said it yourself, I'm getting smarter."

"Being smart isn't the same as being ready. Now will you promise me?"

Her eyes darted away.

"Emma?" His voice had taken on a gravity that she hadn't heard before.

She nodded. He was her only friend, and she didn't want to risk losing him. "Okay, I promise."

CHAPTER NINETEEN

SECOND CHANCES

January 30, 2027
Southwest Virginia

Bud looked down into the small valley. In the foreground, the earth had been flattened and—once upon a time—paved, but now grass and tree saplings were growing in the cracks of the old blacktop. Bud could see an access road to his right, heading down the mountain. On the left was a dilapidated timber-frame building with a corrugated metal roof. It was probably an old service building for the mine. A dozen trucks and SUVs were parked inside. All in working condition.

They'd definitely found something.

He motioned for Brightwell to come closer, and she shouldered up beside him.

Straight ahead and sloping up from the parking lot was the entrance to the mine. It was another timber-framed building with a rusted metal roof. Above and behind the entrance was a steel platform that held the hoists to carry the lifts up and down the mineshaft. But unlike the other mines he'd visited, this machinery shone like chrome in the sun.

Bud peered through the scope on his Winchester to get a closer look. He scanned the vehicles and found the blue 4Runner.

Then he saw movement. A guard stepped out from among the cars, an AR-15 strapped over his shoulder.

Then he heard voices. A second guard appeared, along with a young man who was holding the drone, a set of VR goggles placed high on his head.

Bud gave Brightwell a reassuring smile. This confirmed that the drone operator hadn't seen them.

Slowly Bud eased off his pack and got the camera out but fumbled with it.

Brightwell motioned for it.

Relieved, he handed it over.

Down below, they heard a sharp metallic clank, then the hoist began turning, and the spool wound up the thick metal cable.

It spun and spun and spun. *Damn*, Bud thought, *the mine must be incredibly deep.* Still using the gun scope, he stayed focused on the entrance of the mine, hoping against hope that Finley herself would soon emerge. But when the hoist finally stopped, no one appeared. Instead, the drone operator went inside.

Apparently, he'd called an empty lift.

Bud was about to signal to Brightwell that they could go home, when a figure stepped out. It was the man from the liquor store. He no longer had his hat and sunglasses on, and for the first time Bud could see—beyond a shadow of a doubt—that it was Isaac Coyle. A surge of vindication ran through him. All the pieces were coming together. *I found you, you son of a bitch. I traced you all the way from fucking Antrim, Northern Ireland.*

As if on autopilot, Bud sighted on his head. Coyle was about one hundred and seventy yards out. Bud's rifle was already zeroed to one hundred yards. Bud tried to remember his sniper training. He raised the sight to compensate. There was no breeze down there, so he didn't even have to adjust for windage. It should be an easy shot. He thumbed off the safety.

Brightwell reached over and flicked the safety back on. She gave him a stare that said, *Don't you dare.*

At that moment, a second figure emerged from the mine, a man who was at least seven feet tall with a thick beard. Bud could scarcely believe his eyes. It was Jack Behrmann, one of the two scientists who'd been abducted. He looked none the worse for wear.

Brightwell began taking pictures as fast as she could.

Coyle lit a cigarette, took a few pulls, then offered it to Behrmann. The big man took a drag and gave it back. They were talking and smiling. Bud couldn't get over it. He watched for several minutes, then Brightwell tapped him on the shoulder and beckoned him back toward the trail.

He looked at her a moment, then turned back toward the mine. *This might be the only chance you get to avenge Rogers's death*, a voice in his head said.

Brightwell swatted him with the back of her hand, a look of bottled-up fury now on her face. They had what they needed. It was time to go.

Back on the trail, Brightwell didn't want to waste any time getting out of there, but Bud held her back.

"We can't rush this," he said. "If their patrols find our tracks, then nobody will be here when we come back."

She sighed heavily, and they began to move more cautiously.

It wasn't easy. Bud understood why she wanted to get out of there as fast as possible. They had found Finley, after all this time. But, if something happened to them right now, no one else would ever know. The thought made him skittish. He jumped at the slightest sound and spun his rifle at shadows.

It didn't seem like they could possibly get away with this. Not with his luck. And the longer they walked, the more paranoid he became until he was certain that at any moment they would be ambushed by Finley's guards.

When they reached the jeep, they tore off the camouflage as quickly as they could, and headed for the closest town with cell service, a place called Clintwood.

Brightwell sat with her iSheet unfolded, waiting for the moment she got some bars.

Finally, she was able to dial. "I think you should do the honors," Brightwell said.

Bud puffed out his cheeks for a second. "Okay." They hit the town, which wasn't much more than a church, a gas station, and a cluster of houses.

The phone began ringing.

Bud pulled into the gas station.

Someone picked up. "This is Maggie Falken, Ms. Collins's assistant, can I help you?"

"Maggie, this is Bud Brown. I need to speak with Anastasia immediately. I have vital information about the Finley case."

"Okay, hold on."

Now they waited. Five minutes. Ten minutes.

Bud kept looking in the rearview mirror, afraid that every car that came down the road might be full of Finley's guards.

At last, Assistant Director Collins came on the line.

"I'm in the middle of a major manhunt and I'm dealing with more than two thousand agents, so whatever you got, you'd better make it quick."

"Yes, ma'am," Bud said, trying not to lose his confidence. "I'm in southern Virginia and I've located Jack Behrmann and a man I believe is Finley's master bomber. I also suspect that Finley is here with them."

He heard her give an exasperated sigh. "That's just not possible. All our intel says she's here."

"But it's true," Bud insisted. "I saw Jack Behrmann with my own eyes no more than ninety minutes ago."

"Or someone who looks like Jack Behrmann."

"No, it was Behrmann. He was out in the open and he didn't appear to be a prisoner. I think he might have turned."

"This doesn't make any sense," she said, then her voice took a patronizing tone. "Bud, I want you to tell me if you've been drinking."

Bud felt the heat rising on his face, like a sudden fever. He enunciated carefully. "No, I have not been drinking."

"Well, I'm sorry, but I'm convinced Finley's here. And our intel backs me up."

Brightwell couldn't keep quiet any longer. "Your intel is wrong."

"Who's that?"

She turned on the camera.

"Brightwell? How are you involved in this?"

"Never mind. You need to listen. I was with him when he saw Behrmann. This is for real."

"Did you talk to him? Where is he now?"

Brightwell tried to hold back her contempt. "No, we didn't talk to him. He was in an abandoned mine surrounded by guards."

"I'm sorry, but nothing you're saying is making any sense. You saw someone you thought was Behrmann, correct? Did you see Finley?

"No, we didn't see Finley."

"Okay, I have to go. Write me up a report and I'll look at it when I have time."

"I'm not writing you a fucking report," Brightwell spat. "You need to get your task force down here right now . . . before she gets away."

"That's not gonna happen. Finley's here. In Pennsylvania. You said yourself you didn't see her. Send me that report and I'll have Maggie look at it."

The phone clicked off and Collins's face was replaced by a survey.

Were you satisfied with your call? Please rate your experience.

"Argh!" Brightwell crumpled up the iSheet like a bad first draft and dropped it to the floor. "We risked our lives tracking down Finley and she can't even follow up on our lead!"

"Unbelievable." Bud shook his head morosely and got the Jeep back on the road.

For a while they cursed and stewed together.

"There's only one thing to do," Bud said. "We have to convince someone *above* Collins that we're right."

"You mean contact the director ourselves?"

"It's the only way."

She sucked in air. "I guess you're right. But we need to work on our delivery. If we are going to convince Director Allen, we need to lay it out piece by piece, so that there's no way he can say no."

"Agreed."

Back at the motel they practiced the call. One of them would run through all the evidence they'd collected, while the other would ask questions and try to find holes in their logic. Then they would switch roles. After almost an hour of practicing, it was now eight thirty.

"Are you ready?" he asked.

"Yeah, let's do it."

To reach the director they had to call SIOC—the Strategic Information and Operations Center—in DC and convince the watch officer that it was an urgent situation.

After several minutes of cajoling, they were patched through.

Allen answered calmly: "Agents Brown and Brightwell, what can I do for you?"

"We apologize for calling you like this, director, but we have urgent information about the Finley case," Bud began.

"Then you need to be talking to Anastasia Collins."

"We tried, sir, but she was not receptive," Bud said.

"How's that?"

"She didn't believe us, sir," Brightwell said.

They heard him give a soft grunt. "Okay, I'm listening."

Bud began laying it all out, trying to keep to the script that they had rehearsed. He explained how his former partner, Rogers, had believed Finley's bomber might have been part of the Irish Republican Army, and how Bud had been able to create a list of suspects, with Isaac Coyle at the top.

Then he explained the anonymous tip he'd gotten about southern

Virginia as a remote location that was ideal for Finley to develop her weapons (omitting any mention of Eric Hill and the NRL), and finally his chance sighting of Coyle.

Then Brightwell took over, telling him how they had acquired the license-plate data, their surveillance trip to the mine and their sighting of Behrmann and Coyle.

As they talked, Brightwell sent Allen the pictures they had taken.

When they were done there was a long pause. Allen had his camera off, so they had no way to judge his reaction.

Finally, he spoke. "That's definitely Behrmann."

Bud and Brightwell stole a hopeful glance, a wave of relief washing over them.

"Okay, you two. This is excellent work and I'm proud of you. Of course, it's also disturbing because it means that our intel was wrong."

"Yes, sir," Brightwell said.

"Very well, I'll talk to Anastasia. In the meantime, put together a report of everything you've shared with me. We're going to need to move quickly and quietly. You'll need to brief the heads of CIRG and HRT tonight. I want to hit that mine within forty-eight hours."

"Yes, sir," they said in unison. The director hung up.

In the motel room Brightwell leapt to her feet. "We did it!" she said, giving him a hug.

"Yeah," Bud said with a reserved smile. "We did. Nice job with the delivery."

"You too," she said, then her face lit up with a new idea. "I'm starving! Let's celebrate with sushi!"

He gave her a skeptical look. "Isn't that raw fish?"

"You must be joking. You've never eaten sushi?"

"Never, and I haven't felt the least bit deprived either."

"Well, you are deprived, Agent Brown. But luckily you have me to broaden your horizons."

"Good luck with that, because I have a sneaking suspicion that sushi is not exactly common in these here parts."

A look of horror grew over her face. She snatched up her iSheet and began searching. "Oh, my God, this is awful. Talk about a food desert! Thirty-five miles away!"

Bud lay back and put his hands behind his head, thinking of the pizza and beer he'd soon be enjoying. Ten minutes passed before Brightwell stood up. "I've got something!" She called a number and began talking fast in Japanese. She turned to him and gave a thumbs-up. He rolled his eyes. She hung up, more excited than ever. "The owner is from Osaka, and he just got shipment of *nodoguro*!"

"And that's good?"

"Very!"

While they waited, they got to work on their briefings for CIRG (Critical Incident Response Group) and the HRT (Hostage Rescue Team).

When the food arrived, they laid it out on the bed.

They cracked open two cans of Sapporo and made a toast.

"To finding Finley," she said.

"To teamwork!" he said. "You did a great job today. First with the license plates, then your idea to cover me with leaves. That saved our asses."

"Thanks," she said, then glanced away for a second. "Hey, I appreciate you making me go the last hundred yards. I'm sorry. I just got scared."

"Forget it. I think we both underestimated how dangerous it was. And we were stupid not to take a satellite phone or tell anyone where we were going."

They dug into the food.

"These fried-shrimp things are pretty good," Bud said.

"That's tempura," she said, "now try the eel with mango." She held it out on her chopsticks.

Bud looked down his nose at it suspiciously.

"Go on! Eat it!"

He took it in his mouth like a child eating spinach. He began chewing slowly but then began to nod. "Not bad. The squishy texture leaves a lot to be desired, but it tastes pretty good."

She laughed at him. "My mom makes a wicked crab and eel roll," she said. "Maybe sometime I'll have her make some for us."

"So, it was your mom who came from Japan, right, and your dad's from the US?"

"My mom worked for Toyota and met my dad at a factory in Ohio."

"That's nice."

There was a pause, and he could feel her examining him. "You never talk about your family. Why not?"

"Not much to tell. I'm divorced."

"And your kids. Tell me about them. How old are they?"

"They're about your age. Angie's twenty-seven and Jason's thirty-one." He hesitated. "I haven't talked to them in years. I miss 'em, but it's my fault things are messed up."

She pursed her lips. "Well, now that you're dry, you should reach out to them. Tell them you're sorry."

Bud shook his head. "It's probably too late for that."

"I wouldn't be so sure," she said. "My gut tells me they'd give you another chance. I did."

Bud nodded. "Yeah, you did, didn't you? And I really appreciate it." There was a quaver in his voice. He had used up so many second chances in the last fifteen years, he never thought anyone would trust him or have faith in him again. But for some reason, Brightwell did, and it was an incredible feeling, even if he didn't feel that he deserved it.

They worked through the night, making calls, typing up their evidence, sending emails. At one point Bud ducked into the bathroom to send a message to Hill, letting him know they had found Behrmann and were planning an assault.

When he returned, Brightwell's iSheet rang. When she saw the number, she flashed a smile. "Well, well, well," she said, holding it up for him to see. It was Anastasia Collins. "You know she's going to hate us for the rest of our lives?"

"I'm okay with that," Bud said.

She shook her head, smiled, then answered the phone.

The assistant director's face appeared on the screen.

"Hello," Brightwell said.

Collins didn't say anything at first, just stared at them angrily. Then she pulled off her glasses and pinched the top of her nose. "It looks like I owe you two an apology," she said.

CHAPTER TWENTY

THE BOX

January 30, 2027
Washington, DC

Eric stood on the National Mall between the Capitol Building and the Washington Monument, not far from the Smithsonian castle. Nearby he saw a merry-go-round and watched as children went rocking by on purple horses, pink swans, and yellow elephants while a carnival organ played.

It was unseasonably warm, and people were out enjoying the weak winter sun. A group of young men and women played soccer, a man tossed a football with his son, and a middle-aged man with sleeve tattoos sent his dog chasing after a Frisbee.

Eric felt a hand clasp his and looked to see Karuma beside him.

A wave of relief washed over him, and he grinned with pleasure. "You're here! But how?"

"Why do you keep asking me that? I told you, you brought me here."

This seemed to make sense, but Eric couldn't remember how.

"Come on," Karuma said with his infectious smile. "I want to go to the top of that!" he said, pointing to the Washington Monument and pulling Eric with his free hand.

"All right, all right!" Eric replied.

As they walked, the people he cared about most emerged from the crowd to join them. First were Jane and Mei. Then Lili and Xiao-ping. And finally Bill and Jack.

They entered the ring of American flags at the base of the monument and got in line for the elevator to the top. Eric looked around and couldn't believe his luck. They were all together. Everyone was safe. And on such a beautiful day.

But then he became aware of other voices, bickering and arguing. He looked back and saw four figures standing around a metal box. It was Ryan, Olivia, Blake, and Walden.

"I think we should stop," Ryan said.

"No, we have to do this," Walden countered.

They were all peering down into the large silver box with rivets running along the side. *What are they doing?*

Eric wanted to return to his friends and forget about them, but they kept arguing.

"Once we take it out, we won't be able to put it back," Olivia said.

"I'm ordering you to do it," Walden said.

Then there was a fifth person there. It was Olex. Back from the dead. That was when Eric realized this wasn't real. It had to be a dream. "You idiots," Olex said. "You've done it all wrong." He reached into the box, but Olivia and Ryan tried to stop him. "Wait! Don't touch it!" Blake drew his sidearm.

There was a tussle as many hands seemed to grab for whatever was in the box. He was just about to get a glimpse of it when they all disintegrated to dust.

He heard a woman scream and then a child shriek.

He looked around and everyone was gone. Karuma, Jane, Bill, Mei, all of them. Of the thousands of people out on the mall almost everyone had disappeared.

Almost.

On the grassy slope leading to the Lincoln Memorial, he saw a little girl looking around in shock. Near the Museum of

American History, he saw a woman looking desperately in an empty baby stroller.

But that was all.

Everyone else had vanished.

Then he woke up.

CHAPTER TWENTY-ONE

JACK'S SECRET

February 1, 2027
Southwest Virginia

Sitting in his underground cell, Bill Eastman heard the lock turn in his door. He turned to see Jack Behrmann filling the doorway. The big man ducked his head to enter. He was wearing blue jeans and a red plaid shirt. He looked healthy and strong, and his bushy beard was well groomed. It was as if the stress of their abduction had taken no toll on him. In fact, he looked better than he had in months.

He gave Bill a sheepish look, then dropped his eyes, and that's when all the pieces clicked together.

Bill stood up from the sofa and turned his back on Jack, utter revulsion washing over him. For a moment, he was too stunned to speak. He felt like a man experiencing an earthquake—the foundation of his world shifting beneath him.

"You have betrayed me," he said to the wall.

"No, my friend, this is not a betrayal. And it's not the end of our friendship. It's a new beginning. All I have done is what you didn't have the courage to do."

"What are you talking about?"

"Don't you remember what you said? You told me it was only

a matter of time before Walden began using our technology against civilians. And you were right. He's doing it now, putting all our resources into tracking down Riona and her followers. And then what? Don't you see where this is going? It will never end: more surveillance, more tracking, more biohacking . . . and all in the name of keeping us safe."

"I thought we'd agreed to work within the system. That was our plan."

"Why should we waste our time trying to slow Walden's progress at the NRL when we can confront him head-on? Don't you see? We don't need the Navy anymore. Riona has given us everything. For the first time, we have full control."

"No, Jack, we don't. This isn't right."

"What isn't right about it? She's trying to fix the greatest challenge of our age. By 2030, two hundred and fifty thousand people will die *every year* from the effects of climate change and that's before you calculate the cost to habitat and species extinction."

"To you, I know her cause must sound very noble, but the problem I have with Riona Finley is the same problem I have with Walden. You can't give one person that much power."

Suddenly Bill's head began to swim as he realized the truth. *One person . . . that much power.*

"Oh my God! You've been giving away our secrets from the very beginning?"

Jack turned away, a look of shame on his face. Then his demeanor changed, and he looked Bill straight in the eye with a note of defiance. "Yes, I have."

"And Riona wasn't the first."

Jack set his jaw and nodded. "That's right, there was another."

"Who?"

Jack opened his mouth to speak, then stopped.

"You created the Inventor . . . somehow. Tell me, who is it?" Bill insisted.

Jack finally spoke: "It's Sebastian."

Bill's mouth opened in amazement as he processed the name. He was speechless. He touched his fingertips to his temple, remembering the brilliant young physicist who had worked for them in California. "Yes," he said slowly, "of course. He's one of the few who could have done it."

The look on Jack's face told him even more. "You never expected him to do what he did, did you?"

Jack looked away bitterly. "Sebastian was only supposed to leak the information to the scientific community. That way the military wouldn't have a monopoly on what we had done. But he didn't do what he was supposed to. Instead he studied what I gave him, made his own discoveries, then engineered himself into something that was no longer human."

Bill nodded almost imperceptibly. All the pieces were coming together. He thought back to the brilliant young man he'd met twenty years ago. He and Jack had snatched Sebastian Mortara from the graduate program at Carnegie Mellon because they could see his incredible potential. A truly remarkable young man whose ambitions and dreams were almost too much for this world. Bill and Jack had given him a fat salary and his own department within Advanced Micro. Yet Sebastian never became the profitable investment they had hoped for. He never became famous. Never brought any valuable products to market. Never became a leader in his field. It was not because his ideas were wrong, it was that the technology didn't exist to make them into reality.

Bill realized that Jack had handed Sebastian exactly what he had always needed.

"Now you're making the same gamble with Finley. You're going to give her the world's most powerful technology and hope she does the right thing."

"Better her than Walden," Jack said. "Besides, it's different this time. I'll admit I made a mistake with Sebastian, but I'm here now to make the technology myself. And I want you to help us."

"I'm not going to do that."

"You will, when you see what we've done."

"Done? What have you done? Where?"

"Right here. Underground. We've been working for months, and everything's almost ready. We have copied most of the world's biomes within these caverns. We've developed lighter clouds, autonomous carbon-capture technology, and genetically engineered new crops and vegetation."

"But all that would take years."

"No, it didn't take years. In fact, it's almost finished. In just a few weeks we'll be ready to deploy the system around the globe."

Jack had a confident, almost smug look on his face. He stepped to the door and opened it. "It's clear you aren't going to believe me until you see it. Shall we?"

Bill wanted nothing more than to leave this accursed room. He also wanted to know what Jack had done. He took a step toward the door, and perhaps a step toward freedom.

Suddenly, a distant scream rang out somewhere down the hall, followed by what sounded like a gunshot. Then a man's voice: "FBI! Get down on the ground."

Jack's eyes went wide with horror. "No, not now! Not when we are so close."

CHAPTER TWENTY-TWO

THE WINTER ROOM

February 1, 2027
Southwest Virginia

The lift reached the bottom of the mineshaft—seven hundred feet below ground—and the Hostage Rescue Team rushed out with Bud Brown bringing up the rear. A moment later a second team burst from the second elevator shaft, with agent Brightwell among them.

So far everything had gone to plan. The most critical factor in the operation was surprise, arriving safely in the mine before Finley and her soldiers could react.

The FBI's best snipers had silently dispatched the four guards stationed outside the mine, and the first two teams had made it down unnoticed.

They moved quickly into the main tunnel, which was almost twenty yards wide, with thick timber beams supporting the roof. A clean path had been made through the middle, but both sides were cluttered with rusty old mining equipment, scraps of metal, mining carts, and broken lengths of track.

On the back of Bud's forearm was an iSheet that had an interactive map of the mine. They'd gotten the schemata from the original mining company before the place was closed in 1979. This mine had been active for almost twenty years and had grown into a sprawling labyrinth of more than two miles of tunnels.

Bud pushed forward with the rest of the group. He had a sour knot in his stomach and had barely slept last night, but he was ready . . . and lucky to be tagging along with the HRT, which was the Tier 1 assault unit within the FBI. Most of the agents around him were former SEALs, Delta operators, Army Rangers, and Recon marines. They were tough hombres.

What's more, half of them had Level 4 ballistic shields. The fifty-pound shields were suspended from a rig on the agent's shoulders that distributed the weight. One corner of the shield supported the end of their rifles so they could fire while advancing. The strategy was to work in two-man teams, so that both agents could use the protection of each shield.

Rolling with these guys made Bud feel safe.

But that wasn't all. Bud had another reason for feeling safe. Yesterday morning a package had arrived at his motel room from Eric Hill. In it was an unassuming white T-shirt and a note: *You're no use to me dead, so wear this whenever you're in harm's way.*

He had his TNG rifle at his shoulder and couldn't wait to find Coyle. But there was one thing that had him worried. The escape route. The mining company had told them there were no other exits to the mine. But Bud knew that Coyle and Finley would never corner themselves in a place like this. That other exit (or exits) were down here, somewhere. He'd have to find them before Finley and Coyle could get away.

Jack Behrmann peered out the doorway in the direction from which the shot had come.

A moment later, the man who had abducted them, Brock O'Lane, appeared. He was dressed in black body armor and had a strange-looking rifle in one hand and a flak jacket in the other.

"Get to the north exit, as fast as you can!" he said to Behrmann. "Here, Doctor Eastman," he said, putting the flak jacket on him. "I'm going to be your escort."

"And what if I don't want to be escorted?"

"Be a good sport now, doctor," O'Lane said. "Ms. Finley wants you to remain alive, but she's also instructed me to kill you if you try to escape."

Bill sighed.

"Shall we?" O'Lane said.

Bud and the team were about thirty yards into the tunnel when things changed dramatically. It was as if they had stepped into an office building in Manhattan. Polished floors, walls, and ceilings. Inset lighting, couches, and, incredibly, what felt like natural sunlight.

"This shit is definitely not on the map," one of the agents said.

At just that moment a woman in a white lab coat came around a corner. She screamed when she saw them. One of the agents rushed to subdue her before she screamed again but couldn't keep her quiet.

"Shut her up!" Lopez, the team leader, hissed.

It took two agents to get her down and cover her mouth.

But it was too late. Two guards came out of a door farther down the hall. The agents shot them both with silenced rounds, but as one fell, he pulled the trigger, sending a loud shot ricocheting off the ceiling.

Another civilian man appeared wearing a clipboard. "FBI. Get down on the ground!" He obeyed without hesitation.

The team rushed forward. On their left was a long row of windows into an open lab space. There were at least a dozen civilians inside, already fleeing, grabbing things, and deleting files.

Then someone pulled an alarm.

The teams split, Brightwell's team went to capture the civilians in the lab; Bud's team continued down the main tunnel.

According to the schemata they were coming up on a wide intersection that led deep into the mine.

"Strobe lights on!" Lopez called. Each of the ballistic shields had a one-thousand-lumen light. They turned them on to make it harder for anyone to see them clearly.

Suddenly, three guards ran by, clustered around a very tall man. It was Behrmann.

"Freeze!" the team leader shouted. They ignored him and rushed down the perpendicular corridor. No shots were fired.

The team advanced. When they were about twenty yards from the intersection, Lopez stopped the team and gave a hand signal.

Two flash grenades were tossed forward. They went off and the team resumed its advance.

Suddenly, three gunmen opened fire at them. Two agents went down immediately. Most of the others huddled behind their shields and returned fire. Bud managed to make it into a doorway. The gunfire was relentless, and they were in a bad spot. In a long tunnel like this, the stone walls channeled the bullets, so anyone on the floor or leaning against a wall was likely to catch a round glancing off the wall.

Another agent cried out. "I'm hit!"

Bud peered out. He caught a glimpse of a gunman with an Israeli Tavor TAR-21. Everything he shot at, he hit . . . and he kept up a relentless rate of fire. Despite the shields and the bright lights, he was hitting his targets, even shooting out the lights on the shields. An agent nearby on the ground was hit in the face and died instantly. Another agent was struck in the shoulder, the round hitting exactly where the shield didn't protect him.

Who the hell is this guy?

There was another agent in the doorway with him. Bud motioned to his flash grenades. On the count of three they tossed them down toward the intersection. Bud stepped into the middle of the corridor and fired from a kneeling stance. He hit one of the gunmen, but not the expert. The team tried to advance toward the intersection when a frag grenade came tumbling down the corridor at them. Bud leapt back into the doorway.

BOOM!

The grenade was deafening in the confined space. Dust and rocks rained down from the ceiling.

Bud tried to see through the smoke. The gunfire had stopped and Bud glimpsed the marksman pulling Bill Eastman across the intersection, but it happened too quickly for him to get a shot off.

Bud then looked around at the scene of utter carnage. Of the sixteen men on the team, three had been killed and two wounded in a sixty-second firefight. It appeared that Finley had indeed hired the best that money could buy.

Fortunately, Lopez, the team leader, wasn't giving up. "Veddant," he shouted. "You stay and protect the wounded. The rest of you form up. Switch to your armor piercing mags and keep away from the walls."

Bud ejected the magazine on the TNG and inserted a fresh mag of armor piercing rounds. With Finley's guards and the marksman wearing body armor, they had to make every shot count.

They went down the hall, checked the corner, and turned left. One of the agents was using a tracker to pick up the heat signatures of Finley's gunmen.

Soon the tunnel narrowed. They moved cautiously, hopping forward in teams of two, tapping shoulders when it was time to go ahead.

Then it happened again, just where the corridor provided the least cover, the marksman and the guard opened fire.

Two more agents were hit and the rest pinned down. Bud kneeled behind an agent with a shield. The rounds kept smacking into it with a frightening sound. Over the agent's shoulder, he could see the marksman, but he was too quick and smooth for Bud to get a clean shot.

Bill Eastman knew he had to act. Brock O'Lane had shoved him into a recess along the cave wall. He was trapped there with nowhere to go. He could hear the FBI agents crying out. They were trying to save him and dying in the process. He reached around but couldn't find anything he could use as a weapon.

Another agent cried out. There was only one thing to do. He did it quickly, because he knew if he thought it through, he'd chicken out.

He rushed O'Lane and tackled him to the ground.

Bud couldn't believe it.

The marksman was only down for a second, but it was the break they needed. With one gunman not firing, the agents were able to pick off the other shooter.

The marksman rolled back to his feet and turned to shoot Eastman, but a round from one of the FBI agents struck the Tavor and it didn't fire. The next second, the marksman had spun away into a side tunnel.

The team rushed up to Eastman and checked him over. He was lying on his back and out of breath but smiling. "Did I do good?"

"Yeah, you did real good, doc," Lopez said, then he spoke into his mike. "We have secured Lone Wolf. I say again, we have Lone Wolf."

Bud peered down the tunnel where the marksman had fled, shining the Streamlight on his rifle to get a better look. Almost eighty yards down, he saw a shock of curly red hair run across the mouth of the tunnel.

Without thinking, he ran after her. "I have eyes on Finley!" he said into his mike. "I'm heading"—he had to think—"southwest from Eastman's location."

"Wait," Lopez said. But Bud couldn't stop. He'd waited too long for this.

His tactical light danced around the tunnel as he ran. He made it about fifty yards when he became aware that there were more lights dancing on the wall. He glanced back. Lopez had sent four agents after him. "We're here to make sure you don't get killed," one of them said.

They reached the point where he'd seen Finley and got another surprise. Diagonally on his right was a huge tunnel that wasn't on the map. It was an almost perfect circle and big enough to drive a Mack truck through.

That's when Bud realized that Finley had been using the new technology to drill into the earth. That meant her secret exit (or exits) could be anywhere.

He shone his light down it. There she was again, running with an older man. *Coyle.* He rushed after them.

They came to where Finley and Coyle had turned. There was a ten-foot-high circular opening on the left. They formed a stack and got ready to enter. Bud spotted a small whiteboard on the wall: THE WINTER ROOM. ITERATION 4.

Using hand signals, the agents began entering, each one covering a zone with their rifles as they moved in.

What in the world?

Bud and the agents had stepped into . . .

Where?

He didn't know. He'd expected to turn into another cave, but he was somehow outside. But that wasn't possible. He was seven hundred meters underground. Yet somehow he was standing on a trail in a lush forest filled with trees and plants that were unlike anything he'd ever seen. The air was cold and there were patches of snow on the ground. On his left was an icy stream with strange moss-covered rocks. In the distance he heard a waterfall. Looking up he saw clouds and what seemed like sunlight.

"Stay focused!" the team leader whispered. "They could be anywhere in here."

They headed down the path, following tracks in the snow. Bud kept scanning for Coyle and Finley, but it wasn't easy. The vegetation was so lush that at fifteen yards they lost visibility.

"She'll be heading toward an exit," Bud said. "We need to move fast."

"True, but that other operator could be in here too, so we need to be cautious."

Bud tried to stay alert yet was distracted by the world he'd walked into. The plants looked like something out of a Dr. Seuss book. Huge broad leaves of different colors—gold, red, purple, and green. The trees were covered in thick vines with bright flowers. Moss was everywhere, covering the trees, the rocks, even some of the leaves, all in different colors. Bright red. Orange. Florescent green. Many had labels beside them. *Perennial Flamenco Trumpet (-20 degrees), Hybrid-Neckeraceae.*

"There they are!" one of the agents said.

About sixty yards down Coyle, Finley, Behrmann, and two guards dashed down from a hill onto the trail.

Bud and the agents opened fire, but Finley and the others disappeared into the foliage. Bud and his men rushed to pursue them, which was their mistake.

From their right came three shots. Bud could tell they were aimed at him. He hit the deck and rolled down the bank and into the stream, taking cover behind a boulder. It was the marksman. The one who never missed. *You should be dead*, he thought. *Hill's armor just saved your life.*

Now he and the other agents were pinned down while Finley and Coyle were escaping. Bud knew they had to take care of this asshole and fast.

He spoke into the mike. "I'm going to the right to draw his fire. Give me thirty seconds, then two of you try to flank him on the left."

"Roger that."

He moved through the freezing water, staying low and out of sight, then scrambled up and across the path. He didn't draw any fire, so he hoped he'd gone undetected in the heavy foliage. He crouched low, moving as quietly as he could. Then he spotted the marksman. He'd replaced the Tavor with an AK-12 and was taking measured shots to keep the agents pinned down.

Bud crawled another ten yards through a dusting of snow until he had a clean shot. The marksman was shooting to his left, giving Bud the side shot. He aimed just under his armpit.

Crack.

The marksman's body jerked, and he fell. But he wasn't dead. He opened fire on Bud in a fierce fusillade.

Bud rolled to his right and returned fire. Now his job was to keep him busy until the other agents flanked him. He fired where he saw the muzzle flashes. Ducked down and fired again.

Then he heard the other agents firing, followed by a gasping sound. There were more shots.

"Cease fire, cease fire."

He saw one of the agents standing over the marksman. "Got 'im." he said.

Bud didn't wait. He raced through the snow and foliage, back to the path, after Finley and Coyle. They'd lost precious time, and there was no way he'd catch them by being cautious. What's more, he was beginning to trust in Hill's armor. "I'm going after Finley. Do not follow me. I repeat, do not follow me."

He rushed down the path at a full sprint tearing off his helmet and removing his chest plate to save weight. The vegetation got more fantastic the deeper he went, with thick vines wrapped hungrily around dormant trees. The ceiling, he now realized, was covered in some sort of light-emitting crystals.

He saw the far wall of the cave. His lungs were on fire—*Damn, you're out of shape*—but he kept running. He came around a bend and saw the exit. Twenty yards beyond, down a narrow tunnel was a lift with Finley, Coyle, Behrmann, and the guards inside. At the sight of him the guards fired through the metal mesh. The lift began to descend. Bud reacted instinctively to the incoming fire, dropping to the ground, before remembering his armor. He fired twice from the ground. The lift was almost out of sight.

Coyle had a curious look of recognition in his eyes. Then he smiled and waved. Bud fired one last shot but missed him. Instead, he saw Behrmann hunch down in pain.

Bud got back on his feet and ran forward. Perhaps he could stop the lift, or better yet, send them all falling to their deaths.

Boom. Boom. BOOM!

The archway over the exit exploded.

Bud should have been killed by the blast, but the armor must have absorbed the shock and controlled the air pressure, because all he felt was a push as if he'd been hit by a heavy gust of wind. *You're going to owe Hill a drink.*

Boulders poured down, covering the exit, and plumes of coal dust filled the air.

Bud coughed and looked at the wreckage.

He rushed forward, hoping to find a gap through, but it was completely blocked. It would take a month to dig through that. He shook his head in disgust. He'd lost Finley . . . and Coyle.

Again.

Trying to catch his breath, he remembered Coyle's little wave. It was meant as a final goodbye. Coyle seemed confident that Bud would die. But he hadn't . . .

Oh, shit! He sprinted back the way he'd come. He got on the mike. "Get out! Get out of the cave! It's going to blow!"

"Roger," came one of the other agent's voices.

Bud tore down the path as fast as he could, his lungs screaming for air and his quad muscles burning. He didn't stop.

Outside the exit he saw the other agents waving him home. He motioned for them to get farther back, his eyes darting to the archway, sure that at any moment it would collapse, trapping him inside. He made it underneath. *Please hold for a few more seconds*, he thought. He made it out and kept running down the hall.

Boom. Boom. Booooooom!

Bud felt another push of wind from behind. Even though he was closer to the blast than the other agents, they were all kicked five feet down the hall.

He helped them to their feet. They'd been just far enough from the blast to be safe.

"All good?" he asked.

"Yeah, and thanks for the heads-up."

More big explosions could be heard from other parts of the cave. The whole mountain sounded like it was going to collapse.

"Finley's gone," he said. "Let's get the hell out of here."

Bud Brown sat on the tailgate of an FBI truck. An hour had passed since their escape from the mine. Luckily, no more agents had been killed in the blasts, which seemed to have been designed to hide the evidence of Finley's operation. Brightwell and her team had come away unscathed and had spent most of their time arresting Finley's scientists.

The area buzzed with activity. FBI trucks were all around. Agents, dogs, and drones were scouring the area looking for Finley and Coyle, but Bud doubted they'd find anything.

He couldn't get his mind off what he'd seen in the cave. THE WINTER ROOM. What did it mean?

He went to the RV where they'd taken Bill Eastman, knocked twice, and entered.

Eastman sat in a chair while an EMT checked his blood pressure.

"Dr. Eastman, I'm Bud Brown."

Eastman stood to shake his hand. "Agent Brown, I believe I owe my rescue to you and your partner."

"And to a mutual friend," Bud said. He turned to the EMT. "Would you excuse us, please?"

"Of course," she said and gathered her things. When she was gone, Bud sat across from him. "What can you tell me about what Finley was doing?" He paused. "I saw things down there I don't understand."

Eastman's gaze intensified, and he leaned closer. "You saw one of the biomes?" he asked.

"Biomes?"

"Jack said they'd copied most of the world's climates to conduct their experiments. What did you see?"

Bud tried to find the words. "It was like visiting another planet," he said. He described the vines, moss, and strange-looking plants.

He recalled the clouds and the strange contrast between the lush vegetation and snow.

Eastman nodded. "Yes, it makes sense. She could completely reverse climate change . . . if she could really do it."

"Do what?"

"Let me explain," he looked around and then reached for a pad of paper and a pen. He placed the pad between them and drew an undulating horizontal line from one end of the paper to the other.

"This line represents the level of CO_2 in earth's atmosphere before the Industrial Revolution. Each peak and valley represent a year. The level fluctuates, but the average level was constant over time."

"But why the fluctuation?"

"Ah, that is the heart of the matter, isn't it? It's because of the seasons," Eastman explained. "Most of the landmass of the planet is in the northern hemisphere. Every summer when the trees have leaves and the grass grows and the tundra isn't below the snow, the CO_2 level of the whole planet falls while oxygen levels rise from all that photosynthesis. But in the winter, after the leaves fall and plants go dormant, CO_2 levels rise.

"Now, beginning around the 1700s, CO_2 levels began to climb, changing the cycle to this."

On a fresh piece of paper, he drew the same undulating line, except that now the line was tilted upward.

"Every year since the Industrial Revolution, more CO_2 has been put into the atmosphere than can be taken out by the natural cycle." Eastman stopped and put down the pen. "Now is the idea of the 'winter room' beginning to make sense?"

Bud shook his head. "Science wasn't my best subject," he said.

Eastman smiled. "What you saw in that cave was an attempt to maintain the summer level of photosynthesis year-round, thereby tipping this scale downward."

Eastman continued drawing the undulating line but now with a downward slope, where CO_2 was being removed faster than it was added.

"Consider what you saw. Everything in the room was designed to photosynthesize in a cold, snowy environment. The perennial vine you mentioned probably has a symbiotic relationship with the trees. It would be dormant in the summer, when the trees have leaves, but it would come awake every fall, climbing up the trees and using them for support while it takes CO_2 out of the air. Using moss is an even better idea since it is almost three hundred times better at converting CO_2 to oxygen than trees *and* it filters out pollutants at the same time."

Bud nodded. It was starting to make sense.

"And you said you saw clouds," Eastman said. "Were they extremely white?"

"They glowed."

"That means they will reflect more sunlight, which will help the earth stay cool." Eastman tilted his head in modest appreciation. "I must admit, Finley's plan is ambitious and rather genius. She could restore the earth to its earlier equilibrium in less than a decade." He suddenly shook his head. "But it won't work on a small scale. No, to pull this off she'd need to completely alter all the ecosystems of the world."

"That sounds like a lot could go wrong."

"You're right, it certainly could. There are literally millions of variables to consider, and the new plants could easily cause a host of problems for the existing vegetation. But if anyone could pull it off, it's Jack. I've never seen him fail at something he's set his mind to."

A knock came at the door and a woman stuck her head in. It was Maggie Falken, Assistant Director Collins's assistant.

"Agent Brown, you need to get cleaned up. Collins wants you and Brightwell ready in fifteen minutes. She's giving a press conference and wants you there."

Fifteen minutes later, he caught up with Brightwell. When he got close to her, she wrinkled up her nose. "You look okay, but you stink," she said.

"Luckily, no one can smell me on TV."

"But I will. Remind me to stand upwind."

"What's this about anyway?" he asked her.

"Collins wants to get points for finding Finley."

"But she got away."

"Yeah, but it's all about the optics. I'm sure she's gonna say how she thwarted Finley's operation, and how we have her on the run."

"I don't like it," Bud said. "We're still in the midst of an investigation and we shouldn't have our faces on national TV."

"You wanna tell Anastasia that?"

Bud rolled his eyes.

Joan Rogers was coming out of her kitchen when she got three simultaneous messages from three other FBI spouses.

> They found Finley.

> Turn on the news.

> Let's pray it's finally over. Thinking of you at this difficult time.

She turned on the TV and saw the headline.

BREAKING NEWS:

FBI RAIDS TERRORIST

OPERATION—HOSTAGE RESCUED

She turned up the volume. ". . . this morning, FBI agents assaulted a mining facility near the town of Clintwood. We have reports of shots fired and have received word that several FBI agents and members of the New Anarchists were killed. We go now to

FBI Assistant Director Anastasia Collins, who is about to make a statement."

Joan felt a sudden sickness in her stomach when she heard that more agents had died. It meant that other wives and husbands would have to face the same nightmare she'd been living through.

When Collins appeared on the screen, she was surprised to see Geoff's old partner (and her best friend's ex-husband) in the background.

"Carol, come quick. Bud is on TV."

"What?" came the reply from upstairs. Carol had been living with her since Geoff's death. She heard the fast thumping of Carol's feet on the stairs, then she came into the living room. The two women stood behind the sofa watching the TV.

"We have struck a major blow against terrorism . . ." Collins said.

"Did they get her?" Carol asked.

"They are still searching," Joan said.

"Damn!"

Carol looked at her ex-husband. She could tell he was tired. She recognized the way his eyes always became like slits when he was fatigued. She wondered what he might be going through. Had he watched more agents die? Had he almost died himself? She felt a sense of relief just seeing him. He was a drunk and a worthless excuse for a husband, but she was glad he was okay.

"The agents standing with me were instrumental in tracking down Finley and deserve the thanks of the entire Bureau and the American people. "

Joan's hand clasped over hers and she squeezed. At that moment Carol felt something she hadn't felt in a long, long time . . . at least not as far as her ex-husband was concerned. Pride.

Fifty-five miles south of the mine, a delivery truck for Earl's 24-Hour Plumbing Service—licensed and bonded—rolled quietly down route 671 toward the Tennessee state line.

In the back, Jack Behrmann lay moaning, with Finley and a guard tending to his wound. "We've slowed the bleeding," Finley said. "And we are going to get you some help very soon."

He gave a pained nod. "Okay, but it hurts a lot."

"I'm sure it does. But try not to worry. I have a doctor waiting for us outside of Johnson City. We'll be there in forty-five minutes."

Nearby, Isaac Coyle sat watching the press conference from his iSheet, taking note of the agents who had been "instrumental" in finding Finley's operation.

PART THREE

THE WATERS RISE

CHAPTER TWENTY-THREE

THE TEST

February 2, 2027
Fort A. P. Hill, Virginia

Jane pulled into the passing lane to get around a semitruck.

"How much longer?" Eric asked.

"About fifteen minutes," Jane replied.

They were on their way to Fort A. P. Hill, a US Army Garrison halfway between DC and Richmond. Jane could tell Eric was nervous. This was the big test of the countermeasures program that he and Ryan had been working on for the past two weeks. He'd asked her to drive so that he could double-check the program and make last-minute changes en route.

"I feel like I'm forgetting something," he said.

"Relax," she said. "It's just a test and besides, with only two weeks to work on this, there are bound to be problems."

"You and I know that, but Blake wants everything to be perfect. He doesn't understand how complicated this is."

"Well, if you and Ryan can't figure it out, then nobody can."

He sighed in a way that told her that he wasn't going to relax anytime soon. He called Ryan . . . again. "We're almost there," he said. "Are the targets ready?"

"I'm looking at them now. Yes, everything's set."

"How far are they from the firing line?" Eric asked.

"About a hundred yards."

"And tell me the exact area of effect for the synthetic pathogen."

"We went over this already. It's a fifty-yard radius."

"Okay, good. We'll be there soon."

Eric hung up and resumed tapping on his keyboard.

A few minutes later, they pulled up to the guard post and gave their credentials to the MP. Once inside the base, they had a five-minute drive to the proving ground, a 27,000-acre shooting and artillery range. They passed the main barracks, HQ, an elementary school, and the commissary along the way. It brought a feeling of bittersweet nostalgia to Jane. She'd spent much of her life in places like this, moved around every two years by her father as he went from post to post. They were the forgotten cities and towns of America—entire communities that most of the country never thought about or noticed because they were kept under lock and key by the military.

As they pulled up to the range, Jane saw Major Blake and two marines near the firing line. Ryan came over when he saw their car. "We should be ready in about twenty minutes," he said as they got out.

"Good," Eric said. He interfaced with the test swarms to make sure they were working correctly.

Jane looked out across the range. It was a vast, gently sloping plain dotted with military wreckage. At varying distances, she saw the hulks of several Abrams tanks, an old A-4 fighter jet, three old helicopters, half a dozen Humvees, a school bus, and the remains of a concrete building.

Today's test was relatively simple. Eric and Ryan had applied their nanosite armor technology to two targets—an old Humvee and a Huey helicopter. Jane could see them sitting out on the range.

Next, they would introduce an invading nanosite swarm powerful enough to disable or "eat through" the armor. Then they would trigger the new countermeasures, which should be able to kill off the invading nanosites and restore the armor.

Jane leaned against the bumper of her car and watched. Blake, Ryan, and Eric had huddled up to discuss the test. She was too far away to hear them but noticed Blake's signature look of annoyance and impatience. She took him in—the bristly flattop, the muscled arms that were almost as thick as his legs. Jane shook her head. *They broke the mold when they made that jarhead*, she thought.

When they were ready to begin, Jane stepped closer to hear them better.

"Let's begin phase one," Eric said. "First, we need to confirm that the armor is working correctly. Major Blake . . ."

Blake nodded to one of the marines, who raised an M-4 rifle and began shooting at the first Humvee.

Eric and Ryan observed the target through their iSheets.

After ten shots, the firing stopped. A moment later, Ryan called out. "The armor is working correctly. Everything looks good."

Then Eric spoke again. "Okay, phase two: introduce the invading swarm."

Blake went up to the firing line and picked up an M-4 rifle with a grenade launcher attached under the barrel. "You don't mind if I do the honors, do you?" he said to the marine.

"No, sir."

Blake raised the tip of the rifle and pulled the trigger of the grenade launcher. There was a *thunk*, and a moment later the grenade hit the Humvee, but there was only a meek explosion like a firecracker.

Ryan and Eric watched through their iSheets.

This was the part that Jane was most interested in. She peered over Eric's shoulder. Using special filters, you could see the invading nanosites eating away the bubble of protection around the Humvee, like locusts devouring foliage on a tree.

"The pathogen swarm has broken down the armor," Ryan said.

"You can fire on the target," Eric said to the marine.

The soldier fired again. This time they heard the pings of the bullets striking the vehicle.

"All right," Eric said. "I'm starting the countermeasure program."

Jane watched closely. This was the moment of truth. Would Eric and Ryan's program be able to neutralize the invading swarm?

She watched as the bubble of protection began to reappear, it was working! But just when it was almost completely restored, it began to disappear again.

"They are both adapting," Ryan said, "look at it!" For a moment, the invading swarm had the upper hand, but then the countermeasures resurged. Back and forth it went.

"They are both mutating fast," Eric said.

All of them were fixated on the tug-of-war between the two sides. Finally, the sphere of protection returned. They waited, but it seemed like it had finally prevailed.

Eric and Ryan looked at each other and smiled. "It looks like it's working," Ryan said.

Eric nodded, then called out to the marine. "You can confirm the armor is working."

The marine fired a third time, but there was no sound of impact. The bullets were consumed by the nanosite shell.

"We did it!" Ryan said, with a wide smile.

Eric patted him on the back. "Well done!"

For Jane, it was good to see them acting like friends again, even for a moment.

"Let's move on to the second test," Blake said.

Next they tried the Huey, performing the same routine.

Again, there was a violent microscopic battle between the competing swarms, but the nanosite armor won.

There were smiles and cheers at the end. Jane watched as Blake—in very un-Blake-like fashion—shook hands with both

Ryan and Eric and thanked them for their hard work. "We are lucky to have both of you," he said. "General Walden will be very pleased. Now let's move on to the third test?"

"There is no third test," Eric said.

"Oh, Ryan didn't tell you? I asked him to make a few modifications to our delivery methods." He stepped up to the firing line, opened a hard case, and removed an M67 hand grenade."

"But we have all the data we need," Eric said.

Blake shrugged it off. "It's just an experiment. Let's see how it works." Then he turned to Ryan. "Did you put the protective swarm on the other Humvee?"

"Yes, sir."

Jane saw the other Humvee to their right, about twenty-five yards out.

"But wait," Eric said, "I'm not ready . . ."

Blake ignored him, pulled the pin, and threw the grenade at the Humvee. It, too, exploded with a small pop.

Jane saw Eric flinch and put his hand to his head.

Ryan went through the procedure of evaluating the invading swarm again. Then the marine fired some shots to confirm the armor was disabled.

"Eric," Ryan said, "we are ready to initiate the countermeasures."

"Hold on," Eric said. "I'm having a little trouble with my interface." He jabbed at his iSheet, then shook his head. "Can you initiate it from yours?"

"Hold on." A moment later, he had it working. Jane came closer to watch the battle between the two nanosite swarms, but Eric didn't. He stayed focused on trying to fix his iSheet.

The third test was a success, and Blake was in an even better mood than before.

"See," he said to Eric. "It worked . . . and now you have even more data."

Eric nodded. "Okay, but we'd better get going." He stepped

away from Blake and headed toward the car, but tripped and fell, landing hard on his chest.

"You all right?" Ryan said.

"Yeah, I'm fine."

Jane helped him up.

Eric leaned in and whispered to her. "We have to go. Now."

She whispered back, "Why?"

"Just act normal and get me out of here."

She didn't move right away.

"Please, Jane."

"Okay." She reached down and picked up his iSheet, then took his hand.

When they were almost to the car, he whispered, "Open the door for me."

She did. He gripped it unsteadily and got in.

Jane walked around to the driver's side door, glancing back at the others. Blake stood with his beefy arms folded across his chest, a look of suspicion in his eyes.

She started the car and got them heading toward the front gate. Eric kept his face focused out his window. Once they had cleared the main gate and were on the road, Jane pressed him. "What's going on?"

"I can't see."

"What? How?"

"I don't know. When Blake set off that grenade, everything went black."

"Is it the same as before?" Jane was thinking of the cortical blindness he'd suffered after his crash in Africa. That was caused by a blow to the back of his head. But why would it come back? And how could it be related to the gre—

Wait a minute!

She slammed on the brakes. Eric was thrown forward, and barely braced himself against the dashboard in time. The anti-lock brakes snickered and brought them to a staccato stop. The car behind them swerved and honked its horn as it passed them.

"You knew!" she said. "That's why you were asking Ryan about the radius of effect. Fifty yards. But the other Humvee was closer than you expected."

Her mind was spinning now, piecing it together. "And that's why you refused to get an MRI when you were in the hospital. You knew they'd find something."

"I didn't know, I swear," he said, holding up a hand. "But I . . . suspected."

She raised her eyebrows expectantly, then remembered he couldn't see her. "I'm waiting."

Eric took a deep breath. "When I was blind in Africa, my other senses became hyperacute. I could feel people approaching and could even tell which person it was. Even after my sight returned, I was still much more perceptive than before. When I was hunting with Karuma, I felt the rhino was there before it charged. At first, I thought it was all connected to the blindness, but on the last night, when the poachers attacked, I realized it might be something more. That night I felt the danger coming. My body was trying to tell me something without words. So I left the safety of the camp to go out and meet it."

Jane shook her head in disbelief. "You're saying that some sort of nanosite system has been running inside your body since you were in Africa?"

"If not longer."

"But how? Who programmed it? Was someone controlling them?"

"I don't know . . . but I don't think anyone was controlling them. In fact, they seemed to be part of me. We somehow needed each other . . . I certainly needed them. I wouldn't have survived the crash without them. And they saved Karuma's life . . . and most of the tribe too."

"But why didn't you tell me any of this? Why keep it a secret?"

"I guess . . ." He looked away. "Part of me didn't want to know. I was scared of what I might find."

Jane gave a sigh and her temper cooled.

"Okay, but you can't keep secrets from me."

"I'm sorry. But I'm afraid, Jane. I can't see. And what if it doesn't come back again? What if I just got lucky before?"

She reached out and caressed the back of his neck.

"Try not to worry," she said, "and I'm sorry I yelled at you. Let's get back to the lab and see if we can figure this out."

"Okay," he said. "I'm sorry."

He leaned toward her, and she held him tight.

"I'll take care of you," she said.

It was early evening when they arrived back at the NRL. They'd gotten the news that Bill had been rescued. While they were elated, the good news was eclipsed by Eric's predicament.

They decided to head straight for the Venger test lab. Luckily, most of the staff had left for the day.

Venger was their state-of-the-art infantry system that made ordinary soldiers nearly invincible. It used swarm technology to augment their capabilities. It protected them in a nanosite bubble and allowed them to disable enemy weapons and kill at great distances. One of the most revolutionary components of the system was a helmet that could read each soldier's thoughts and communicate their wishes to the swarms under their control. The helmet was essentially a portable MRI machine that monitored the soldier's brain activity. Jane figured it would only take a few modifications to get an image of the inside of Eric's head using one of the helmets, which would give them a better understanding of what had happened.

"It will take me a few minutes to configure the helmet," Jane said.

She helped him to a chair.

He waited there, trying to be patient, wishing the darkness away, but it was everywhere, squeezing in on him.

You'll have an answer soon, he told himself. But he honestly didn't know what to pray for. He tried to open his remaining senses, to feel where Jane was in the room. But it wasn't working like before. She moved right up to him before he noticed her.

"Okay, here we go," Jane said, placing the helmet on his head. "It needs to be strapped tightly so that it doesn't shift around."

Eric breathed deeply. She touched his shoulder. "I'll be right in the corner looking at the monitor."

"Okay."

"I'm starting with the sagittal image."

This meant that she'd be looking at a cross-section of his head beginning with one ear and going in slices until she hit the other.

"Okay, the scan is done, and the images are coming up. The temporal lobe looks normal," she said. "Now hitting the corpus callosum. It looks fine. Your cerebellum looks just like a cauliflower. Yum." Eric didn't laugh. "Tough crowd tonight," she said. "Okay, midbrain is normal. Hmm, what's that?"

"What's what?"

She didn't say anything.

"What is it?"

"There's something there in the occipital lobe, just above the cerebellum, but it's hard to see. I need to switch to the axial view."

Eric noticed himself grasping and ungrasping the arms of the chair. The occipital lobe processed vision and was at the back of his head, exactly where he'd taken the blow in the crash.

"Is it scar tissue?"

"Hold on, let the second scan finish." They waited. "Okay, it's done. Man, the clarity of the images is amazing."

"Can we get on with it?"

"I have to move down from the parietal lobe, I'm almost there. Oh my gosh!"

"What?"

"It's all along the edge of the skull, it's showing up as extremely dense . . . denser than bone. I can see the fractures in your skull from the accident and this stuff has filled in the gaps and fused the bone back together."

"It's diamondoid," he said, suddenly certain.

"You might be right, or at least a variant," she said. Diamondoid was the carbon-hydrogen molecule they used as the basic building block for much of their nanotechnology; it was lightweight and incredibly strong.

"And Eric," Jane said cautiously, "there's dead tissue here, right at the fracture point. It's showing white on the MRI, which means it's not getting any blood."

He nodded grimly. That was the brain damage that had caused his blindness, which meant that without the nanosites he never would have recovered his vision. With them gone, he was now permanently blind.

"I'm going to filter the image," she said. "I want to see how extensively the diamondoid proliferated. Give me one minute."

Eric took a deep breath. It was all starting to add up. He should have died in the crash, just like everyone else, but the nanosites had saved him. They'd stopped the internal hemorrhaging, patched his skull, and probably did a dozen other things to keep him alive. And for that, he couldn't help but feel grateful. Yes, he might be blind, but he was alive.

"Wow, incredible," Jane said.

"What is it?"

"Now that I know what to look for, I can see that the diamondoid—or whatever it is—has created a sort of carbon-fiber matrix throughout the skull. It looks like a spiderweb. And if I'm not mistaken, it didn't happen all at once, it grew out from the point of impact. Perhaps over the course of weeks or months."

"They were learning," Eric said. "They reinforced the entire skull in the event I took another hard blow."

"Yeah, I think you're right." She came over to him. "I'm so sorry, Eric, but I'm not seeing anything that looks like nanosite activity. I think the best thing for us to do is go to my lab where I can draw some blood. Perhaps that will tell us if you still have some inside or . . ." She trailed off.

★ ★ ★

She led him to her lab where she drew his blood and analyzed it.

Eric was still holding on to the hope that some of the nanosites had survived and that they would begin to replicate and, hopefully, fix his blindness again.

But that hope was quickly dashed.

"I'm sorry, Eric, but they're all dead. There are thousands of them in the sample, but none are alive."

"Can you isolate a few and magnify them? Perhaps we can tell something by their architecture."

"Yes, give me a minute. Let me get this to the STM and we'll get an image." She left him there in the darkness for fifteen minutes while she went to the Scanning Tunneling Microscope.

"You're not going to believe this. The nanosites are yours."

"What?"

"They are very similar to the first-generation nanosites you made around replication. You designed these, Eric."

"But how did they get inside me?"

"I don't know. But they definitely came from this lab."

"God, I'm confused," he said.

"Well, it's after midnight and I don't think we are going to make any kind of breakthrough tonight. And we have another problem to deal with."

"What's that?"

"You. You can't stay on base."

He nodded, realizing she was right. "You think that if Blake finds out I'm blind, he might connect it back to the grenade."

"Yes, and then you'd become their guinea pig or worse. If they think someone hacked you, they'll pull your clearance."

"So where do we go?"

"It's about seven hours to Myrtle Beach," she said, "We can call it an impromptu vacation." She kissed him coyly on the cheek. "It's probably too cold to get in the water, but we can use our imaginations and find other things to do."

Part of him wanted to stay in the lab to look for answers, but he knew she was right and they should get out of town. He tried to resign himself to the situation. "Let's do it."

She took his hand and led him out of the lab.

"Can I drive?" he asked.

"I don't see why not."

CHAPTER TWENTY-FOUR

CRISTO'S TRADING

February 3, 2027
Namibia

The three surviving Sān teenagers—Karuma, ǂToma, and /Uma—hid low under a buckthorn tree, their eyes locked on the dusty cluster of dilapidated huts and canvas tents. The strange compound sat about two hundred meters in front of them on a windswept patch at the northern edge of the Kalahari Desert, the only man-made structure for fifty kilometers.

The compound was exactly as Karuma had remembered it, right down to the faded wooden sign over the clapboard central building that read CRISTO'S TRADING. As a little boy he'd loved to come here with his father and grandfather. Inside was a labyrinth of wonders. Each interconnected hut and tent was filled with thousands of objects to delight the eyes. Everything from farming equipment, electric generators, car engines and parts to aisles of food packed in strange paper that made it last for months. There was even a wall of glass cabinets full of cold air. He remembered the first time he'd opened one and felt the chill wash over his body. It was like magic.

This was the place he had first touched ice, first seen a car, and first tasted chocolate.

Cristo, the owner, was just as fascinating as the objects that filled his shop. Karuma's grandfather had called him "the patch man" because his skin was splotched different colors. He looked like a man who had been painted black, then pink, then white on top of that. Even his curly hair was different colors in different places— black, red, blond. He was a big, powerful man, but warm and welcoming, and he seemed to know everything. He was a hunter, a tracker, a blacksmith, a mechanic, a soldier, an explorer, a trader. He not only knew everything . . . but everyone, which was another reason for Karuma's visit—to find out what Cristo knew.

Seeing the compound again filled Karuma with nervous excitement. He wanted to be sure that only Cristo knew they were here. So he waited. An hour before sunset, the last pickup truck pulled out of the parking lot in a cloud of dust and sped down the road.

"I'm going first," Karuma said. "Wait here and keep a close watch. I'll signal you when it's safe to come."

The others protested. While they had never visited Cristo's before, they had heard all the stories. After several minutes of promises and threats, they agreed to stay.

Karuma shouldered all three of their rifles and made his way cautiously toward the road. He waited in the ditch by the shoulder for many minutes, examining the compound. He saw white smoke rising from a chimney in the back. That was Cristo's blacksmith shop. On the left side of the compound were half a dozen cannibalized cars and trucks, while on the right side were hundreds of small propane tanks stacked haphazardly against the wall.

He took one last look at the road, his eyes captivated by the string of telephone poles that seemed to stretch out into oblivion. It hinted at the vastness of a world he barely knew or understood. At last, he summoned his courage and scampered over the blacktop.

A bell clanged as he opened the door. The smell of the place hit him first—a mix of leather and kerosene and old wood. It was smaller than he remembered, yet he still couldn't help but smile at all the marvelous things. It seemed that every centimeter of the place was filled with something. To his right was a wall covered in the mounted heads of wild game—kudu, gemsbok, eland—but also racks of shoes and boots, cans of cooking fuel and tin plates and cups. On his left were the aisles of food and from the wooden rafters hung shovels and rakes and scythes and saws.

At the back of the shop, he saw a meaty hand pull back a curtain, then a massive man wearing a heavy apron appeared. He was almost bald now and his skin was whiter than Karuma remembered.

At the sight of Karuma, the old man's face grew into an excited smile, but the smile vanished when he noticed the rifles on the boy's back.

"Karuma, my boy! Thank goodness you're okay." He rushed forward as if to embrace him, but then slipped quickly by. He locked the door and flipped the OPEN sign to CLOSED.

"Come, we must be careful." He pulled Karuma to a table in the back, out of sight from the front door. "I have been very worried. How is your mother . . . and where is your grandfather?"

"My mother is fine, but . . ." Karuma was suddenly unable to look Cristo in the face and cast down his eyes.

"Oh, no," Cristo said.

Karuma told him of the poachers who had poisoned their water hole, and how his grandfather had hunted them down and hidden their ivory. But the loss of so much ivory had enraged the Ivory Queen. In retaliation, she'd hired mercenaries to find the tribe. They snuck up on them at night with strange goggles that let them see in the dark and had wiped them out. When Karuma came to the part of his grandfather's death, Cristo did not try to hold back his tears.

"This is what I had feared," Cristo said, wiping his eyes with his sleeve. "Your grandfather thought he was doing the right thing by protecting your land, but by provoking the Ivory Queen he started a war he could never hope to win. The Ivory Queen controls the trade from Cairo to Cape Town, and she never forgives and she never forgets."

Karuma swallowed hard. He could tell by Cristo's expression that more bad news was coming.

"They are looking for you," he said. "Every week they come asking. They call themselves the White Hand. They are mercenaries and they say a group of Sān killed their men. I didn't believe them, but when I saw you with the guns . . ." He trailed off.

"We didn't kill them," Karuma said. "It was the Americans. They were protecting us."

Cristo nodded, looking at the guns. "But they aren't protecting you now, are they?"

Karuma shook his head. "No, which is why I need your help."

Cristo extended his arms against the edge of the table and pushed himself back. He examined the young man across from him . . . a young man who had been a boy the last time he'd seen him.

"I don't know," Cristo said. "This goes against everything your grandfather would have wanted. He dedicated his life so that you and your people could live peacefully in a world without guns."

"But my grandfather also knew that we had to take certain things from the outside world if we hoped to survive. You know what we are up against. Without guns and bullets, they'll massacre us again."

Cristo didn't move for a time. Then slowly he began to nod his head. He smiled sadly. "Come with me," he said, "I've been helping your grandfather my whole life. What type of friend would I be if I didn't help his grandson now?"

Cristo led him deeper into the store. It was darker here, with only a few bare bulbs lighting the way. In fact, it was hard to know which surfaces were wooden walls and which were just flaps of canvas. Cristo then pulled back a tarp to reveal a huge metal box as big as a room. Written on the side were the strange words: MAERSK SEALAND.

Cristo unlocked it and swung the doors open. The flick of a switch revealed a long room with workbenches on either side and, mounted on the walls, dozens and dozens of rifles and pistols—silver, black, and gunmetal gray.

Karuma felt a strange mixture of fear and excitement. These were the horrible devices that had wiped out his tribe, yet he also remembered his dream and Cagn's message: here was also the power to protect his people.

Cristo began looking through the racks of weapons. "There was a war once in a country called Vietnam," he explained. "The people who live there are very small, like the Sān, so it was very difficult for them to use the big rifles that most of the world's militaries used at the time.

"So the American government designed a rifle specifically for the Vietnamese—it was light, and it used smaller bullets so that the gun wouldn't jump when you fired it. They called it the M-16." He pointed to one of the rifles on the wall. Karuma saw that it had a strange handle on top and a triangular bump at the end of the barrel.

"In the last sixty years they've been able to make even smaller and lighter versions of that gun, like this one." He pulled down a short, black rifle, checked that it wasn't loaded, and gave it to Karuma. "This is an M4."

"It's so light," he said.

"Yes, much better for someone like you," Cristo said, grabbing several magazines of ammunition. "Let's give it a try."

Cristo led him out to the back of the compound where a crude firing range had been set up. The targets included a few oil drums, six mutilated store mannequins, and—set about seventy meters back—a rusted-out car with a bullseye painted on the door.

Around them, the sky was changing as the sun began to set, painting the landscape red and orange, and making Cristo's patchwork skin glow in strange ways.

The big man showed Karuma the basics—the safety, how to load the magazine, the charging handle, and how to select the rate of fire—semiautomatic, three-round burst, full auto.

"Just use this one—semiautomatic—otherwise you waste bullets."

Karuma nodded.

"Okay, now listen closely: Those mercenary rifles you brought me are big, heavy rifles designed for someone who is an excellent shot and has a lot of practice aiming quickly. Their strategy is to shoot one powerful bullet to kill an enemy. Like this."

Cristo quickly put the M4 to his shoulder and fired a shot. Karuma jumped at the loud crack and felt a strange pulse of air hit his skin. He looked out and saw a hole in the center of the car door. He was amazed. *If we can learn to do that*, he thought, *no one can hurt us.*

"Now you give it a try."

Karuma took the rifle nervously. It took him almost a full minute to aim and finally pull the trigger. He missed the car completely.

"I wanted you to do that to prove a point," Cristo said. "Which is?"

"I'm no good." Karuma said, glancing down at the ground.

Cristo didn't contradict him. "You're not an expert marksman nor will you and your people have time to become experts. You can improve your aim with a little practice, but it will take you years to get as good as the soldiers you are up against. Understood?"

Karuma grimaced, feeling deflated. "So this is all a waste of time?"

"No. To stand a chance against the White Hand, you have to take a different strategy. This might sound strange, but I *don't* want you to aim carefully. Just point the gun as best you can and shoot as many rounds at the target as possible. Got it?"

Karuma gave him a skeptical look but followed his instructions. He took aim and fired. *Bang!* He aimed and fired again. *Bang!*

"No," Cristo said, "faster!"

He pulled the trigger again, then again.

"Faster!"

Karuma obeyed, pulling the trigger quicker and quicker, trying to keep the muzzle pointed at the car. He was rewarded by a satisfying ping as a bullet struck the metal.

"Yes, don't stop."

Karuma kept pulling the trigger. *Pop-pop-pop-pop-pop-pop.*

There was another ping against the metal, and another, and

another. Then he was out of bullets.

He gasped, realizing that he'd been holding his breath. The rifle was smoking from the barrel and there was a chemical smell in the air. He looked at his handiwork, trying to see where he'd hit the car.

Cristo stood with his arms folded and nodded. "Not too bad," he said. "You hit it four times with thirty bullets, and you got one in the bullseye. Not great, but perhaps good enough to kill your enemy.

"Now listen closely: I'm going to give you four of these rifles along with some sixty-round ammo mags." He held up a long, crescent-shaped container for the bullets. "If you are attacked, you will need to work together—in teams of two—both of you firing at the same target before you move on to the next. Remember, don't try to aim too carefully, just send as much lead at your enemy as you can. That will make the White Hand very sorry for messing with you."

"But if I want to shoot as many bullets as possible, wouldn't it be better to use this?" He pointed to the Full Auto button on the rifle. "You said that shoots all the bullets."

"No, don't use that. Because if your aim is off even a little, you'll send *all* your bullets to the wrong place, instead of just one. Remember, one bullet for each time you pull the trigger fast enough."

"Okay, but . . ." Karuma stopped for a moment, trying to imagine such a battle. It still seemed impossible for them to win. Four rifles against the might of the White Hand? In the massacre they had been attacked by thirty men. What if this time there were even more? "Tell me, Cristo, can we really win?"

"Yes, you can. There have been many wars where a mighty army was defeated by a smaller, poorly equipped underdog. How? By being clever. To defeat the White Hand, you must be like Heitsi-eibib, the trickster. Never fight them head-to-head. Sneak up on them when they are asleep. Steal their food and their water. And remember you are Sān. No one knows the bush and how to stay hidden better than you do. Use that to your advantage. Yes, these rifles are important weapons, but the most important weapon is this." He poked at Karuma's forehead.

At that moment a noise came from the side of the shop, like someone had tripped over a metal can.

With amazing speed, Cristo snatched up a fresh magazine, loaded the M4, and aimed it at the corner of the shed. A second later ‡Toma and /Uma leapt out with their spears held high.

"Wait!" Karuma yelled at Cristo, throwing up his hand to stop him. But Cristo had already lowered his gun and was laughing. He held up his hands in surrender.

"I told you to wait for me," Karuma scolded the two Sān. "He could have killed you!"

/Uma lowered her spear. "We heard the big gun and thought you were in trouble."

Karuma shook his head. "You have to listen to me. We can't take any chances." He began berating them, but Cristo cut him off.

"Come, Karuma, introduce me to your friends, the ones who just showed they were willing to face gunfire with their spears to save you."

Karuma lifted his finger to object, then realized he'd been unfair. He took a deep breath. "I'm sorry." He opened his arms and the three of them embraced. The way they clung to him told him they'd been truly worried. "*Hui te re,*" he said. *Forgive me.*

After a moment, he turned to Cristo. "Cristo, this is /Uma and ‡Toma."

Cristo greeted them warmly.

/Uma couldn't take her eyes off Cristo. "You are just like I imagined," she said, coming closer and touching his skin. "Why did Cagn make you this way?"

Cristo laughed good-naturedly. "I don't know. Perhaps to show that we are all a little bit of everyone else."

/Uma seemed to like this answer and smiled.

"But come. I know you are hungry and thirsty. Let's eat!"

This idea was met with universal approval, and they all headed into the shop. "A Damaran bushman gave me a wonderful cut of springbok yesterday. Now I have a good reason to cook it! In the meantime, you can help yourselves to anything in the shop."

The Sān could scarcely believe their good luck. This was like an invitation to heaven. Laughing, the three teenagers raced around the store and soon had their arms full of snacks and candy.

"Don't spoil your dinner!" Cristo admonished, knowing that they most certainly would.

An hour and a half later, they sat lounging around the table, satiated and drowsy. The space in front of them was strewn with Coke bottles and wrappers of all the things they'd pilfered from the store.

"Ugh! I feel sick!" /Uma said, even as she took another bite of her chocolate bar.

"I can't imagine why," Cristo said, and they all laughed.

"This has been like a dream," Karuma said to Cristo. "You have been so generous with us."

"Oh, I'm not done," the man said. He got up and disappeared into the kitchen. A moment later he emerged with three rucksacks full of food.

ǂToma and /Uma's eyes widened with amazement.

"To help you and your people through this hard time."

"But this is too much," Karuma said. "The guns, and now this. How can we repay you?"

"Don't worry about that. It's all taken care of."

"What do you mean?"

"I honestly don't know myself. All I know is that twice a year a man will drive out from Windhoek and ask me if your grandfather has needed any supplies. I tell him what and how much. He then pays me in cash and drives away. It's been that way for more than twenty years, and my father tells me it was like that for twenty years before that."

"Who is this man?"

"Name's Joseph Lefrak, he's a well-known businessman. But he's just a middleman. He's doing it for someone else . . . someone who cares deeply about your grandfather and your people. But he'll never say who."

"William," Karuma said.

"Eh?"

"Long ago, when my grandfather was young, he befriended an American boy." Karuma told the story: how when Khamko was a teenager there had been a terrible flood. In the wreckage by the river, they'd found an American man and his son. The boy had been wounded, but Khamko and his father had nursed him back to health. The boy—William—had been the same age as Khamko and they had become lifelong friends. "It was through William's family that my grandfather went to America to study medicine."

"That would explain it," Cristo said with a laugh. "Now since we are talking about mysteries, what do you know about this curse?"

"What curse?" They all said, leaning closer.

"I've heard it from three bushmen from the other tribes. They say your god has put a curse on the poachers and they get sick if they try to hunt on your land."

Karuma nodded. "That explains why we haven't seen anyone on our land for many weeks. Cagn must be protecting us."

Cristo's expression showed his doubt, but he said nothing.

After they had cleaned up from dinner, they realized that they had too much to carry home in one trip. It was decided that they would hide what they couldn't carry near the buckthorn tree and return for it in a few days.

They made the first trip to the tree and created their cache, then returned to the store for the rest. As they were getting ready to say their goodbyes, the bell chimed on the front door.

"Quick! Hide!" Cristo hissed, realizing he'd forgotten to relock the door.

★ ★ ★

When Cristo saw the five men, he cursed under his breath, then he eased himself over to the cash register and placed his hand on the sawed-off shotgun he kept hidden there.

"Cristo!" the first man greeted him. It was Marcus Van Der Mewre, the new leader of the White Hand. "Your sign says closed, but I saw your lights were on." He spoke with the heavy accent of a Deutschnamibier, a German Namibian, the original colonists. His four men fanned out into the store—two went to grab some food, while the others began examining the boots and clothes.

"I'm just finishing up for the day," Cristo said. "I was hoping to turn in early."

"Well, we won't keep you, my friend." Marcus came up to the counter and fixed his eyes on Cristo. "Have you seen any sign of the Sān?"

"No, nothing."

"Nothing?" Van Der Mewre raised his eyebrows.

"Not a thing."

Marcus nodded slowly. "That's too bad. We can't go in to get them, so we have to wait for them to come out . . . but eventually they must. And I'm betting they'll come to a place just like this."

Van Der Mewre turned and began looking around. Cristo watched as his eyes went to the table and the half-empty bottles of Coke, then to the three rifles leaning against the back wall.

"What's this?" he asked.

"Trade-ins," Cristo said.

Van Der Mewre began inspecting the rifles.

Cristo thumbed the safety off on his shotgun, but he no longer had a clear shot at Van Der Mewre, who was now partially obscured by the display case. And even if he hit him clean, he still had four other armed men to deal with. This was not good.

Huddled inside a rack of clothes /Uma knew she was going to vomit at any moment. It was inevitable. The mix of mortal fear and the bubbly drinks and the candy were too much for her. She focused all of her will-power. *Don't get sick. Don't get sick. Please, please, please.* Through a gap in the clothes she saw a big man's boots move toward her.

The man began looking through the clothes in her rack.

She clapped her hand to her mouth.

While /Uma and ǂToma had hidden in the main store, Karuma had darted through the curtain into the back hallway. He thought he'd find the blacksmith shop and grab a spear, but instead he found himself in a room full of old camping equipment. He was about to turn around when he saw two strange-looking bows on the wall,. They had odd wheels at the top and bottom.

He thought back to the afternoon and how poorly he'd fired the rifle, but here was a weapon he knew. He took the first one down and tried to pull the string, but it was too difficult. He tried the second one. It took all of his strength, but he could do it.

Cleverly, the bow had a small quiver attached to it that held five arrows. He pulled one out. The tip was a triangle of blades. He nocked it in the bow and drew.

Suddenly a shot rang out, followed by a string of shots. Karuma jumped and his stomach dropped. He had an overwhelming urge to run, as the sound of the guns brought back his worst memories of the massacre. But he stopped himself, remembering how ǂToma and /Uma had come to help him earlier. He looked down at the bow. *Cagn wants you to fight.*

Back in the shop, Marcus picked up one of the rifles, an SR-25. "Karl, come and look at his," he said jovially, as if he might make a purchase.

Cristo began to relax a little. They didn't suspect a thing.

The two men examined the rifle, Marcus pointing to something on the barrel, then he set the rifle down.

The next instant both men had drawn their handguns and were pointing them at Cristo. He froze, then slowly lifted his hands. They'd gotten the jump on him.

"Where are they!" Marcus demanded.

"What? Who?"

Marcus gave him an ingratiating smile. "My brother Ethan was killed by the Sān, he along with thirty-two others. This is his rifle. It has a scratch on the barrel from a bullet meant for his head in Angola." He drew closer, pointing his Sig Sauer pistol at Cristo's head. "I'd very much like to meet the person who sold it to you."

Cristo shrugged helplessly. "A Caprivian brought it in this morning. He traded the rifles for a generator and some food."

"I think not," Marcus said, motioning to the Coke bottles. "I think we interrupted something." He called to his men. "Karl, Johan, sie sind hier. Findet sie!" *They're here! Find them!*

Marcus kept his gun aimed at Cristo as his men ransacked the store. In less than a minute they'd flushed ‡Toma from one of the grocery-store aisles. He darted about the store like a scared rabbit. Johan fired one shot, then another. Missing both times.

"*Nein, erschieß ihn nicht,*" Marcus said. "We need him alive!"

But in turning to yell at Johan, Marcus had made a critical mistake. When he turned back to Cristo, he was staring down the barrel of the shotgun. "*Scheiße!*" He dove behind a counter. Cristo adjusted his aim and fired. Part of the cloud of buckshot peppered his right side from his shoulder to his buttocks, creating a dozen bloody splotches, but Marcus had dodged the worst of it.

"Shit!" Cristo said.

Marcus grunted at the pain as Johan opened fire at Cristo. The shopkeeper pumped the shotgun and got off two more shots at Johan before they were all shooting at him. He ducked behind the counter for cover. *This is bad*, he thought. The mercenaries poured in their fire, knowing full well that their 9 mm bullets would have no trouble puncturing the wooden counter and chest freezer he was hiding behind.

Then he smelled kerosene and knew that they'd hit some of the cans on the east wall. *Also not good.* And if that wall caught on fire? All those propane tanks on the other side? *Definitely not good.*

/Uma huddled down, terrified by the sound of so much gunfire in such a confined space. She clapped her hands to her ears to try to shut it out. But her nausea was getting worse—her head and stomach were swimming. She looked out to see liquid kerosene racing across the floor toward her. When the smell hit her, it pushed her over the edge. She lurched and put a hand to her mouth to try to stop it, maybe swallow it back down, but it surged out through her fingers and she gave up. She heaved violently, spraying vomit out through the clothes and into the aisle. She couldn't stop it now. Three then four times she vomited until her stomach was empty. *All that wonderful food*, she had time to think.

A second later one of the men came running down the aisle, firing his gun toward Cristo. She could see his legs below the clothes, getting closer, then he slipped on the vomit, and he landed hard on his butt. The gun went off when it hit the ground, the bullet ricocheting across the floor. There was a sound like a quick brush of wind, then the floor and the wall caught fire.

The gunman scrambled backward to get away from the spreading fire. Then he looked at the partially digested food on his clothes and hands, trying to make sense of it.

Then he turned and looked her straight in the eye.

He smiled.

CHAPTER TWENTY-FIVE

COYLE'S GAME

February 3, 2027
Raven, Virginia

"When will you be back in DC?" Brightwell asked. They were in the parking lot outside their motel, Brightwell sitting at the wheel of her white Subaru, about to make the drive home. It had snowed last night, and the morning was beautiful and crisp, the trees and homes frosted in a thick layer of white.

"A few more days," Bud said. "I want to see if we can find more clues about what Finley was up to."

She shook her head. "It seems pretty hopeless at this point. The mine's become unstable, and Finley and Coyle are long gone."

"Just a few more days," he repeated.

She shrugged. "Okay, but no longer. My mom said she would make sushi for us when you get back."

"Tell her there's no rush on that."

Brightwell laughed. "Nice try, but I'm determined to convert you."

He smiled, feeling grateful to have someone who wanted to spend time with him.

"Thanks again for coming."

"I'm glad I did."

He patted her on the arm, then she pulled away, the tires squeaking as they compacted the fresh snow.

Bud gave a wave as the car hit the curb and exploded.

The blast knocked Bud flat on the ground, but he got up instantly and ran to the car. *No, please, no!* It was already a ball of raging flames. He heard voices behind him as people rushed out of their hotel rooms to see.

"Oh my God, I hope nobody's in there."

He rushed to help her, but the incredible heat stopped him. He could see her shape through the glass, she had become a tornado of fire. He saw a flaming hand struggling with the seatbelt.

He had to help her. He tried to get closer, but again the heat made him stop. It felt like he was burning, but he forced himself forward. Then he was tackled to the ground. He tried to fight them off.

"You're on fire!" someone said. They rolled him around in the snow and shoveled it over him.

He saw two young men. He tried to get up, but they forced him back down, and lay on top of him.

"Stay down!" one of them yelled.

He struggled anyway, his eyes going to the flaming car. A black shape still visible inside.

CHAPTER TWENTY-SIX

THE FIRE

February 3, 2027
Namibia

/Uma tried to scramble away from the mercenary, but she was weak and slow from being sick. Strong hands grabbed her ankles and yanked her out.

"Ich habe eine!" the man shouted. *I got one!*

/Uma kicked and screamed as the man dragged her to the grocery section to get away from the growing fire.

ǂToma heard her cries and rushed to help, but one of the other men grabbed him in a bear hug and lifted him off his feet.

Meanwhile the fire was spreading fast. Within seconds, most of the east wall was in flames, the mounted heads of the kudu and gemsbok were completely engulfed, and the burning fur made a terrible stench. Soon the flames were reaching high into the rafters and licking the roof.

Smoke was everywhere, making it difficult to see and breathe.

Huddled in the corner, Cristo checked his shotgun and realized he was out of shells.

"It's over, Cristo!" Marcus called to him. "We have what we need. Just come out so no one gets hurt."

Cristo knew he had little alternative. The fire was getting dangerously close. He could feel the heat against his skin.

"I'm coming out!" he shouted, standing up slowly and raising his hands.

Marcus motioned him out with his handgun, but he flinched when he moved, telling Cristo that his shotgun blast had indeed wounded him.

They congregated in the grocery aisles away from the worst of the smoke.

"Where are the others?" Marcus demanded.

"There are no more."

"Two teenagers? Alone?"

"The White Hand killed almost all the adults."

Marcus smiled. "I'm so happy to hear it."

Karuma inched closer to the curtained doorway. Through the slit he could see /Uma and two of the mercenaries. One was holding a gun to the girl's head, while the other had his gun trained on Cristo. Karuma got as close as he dared and drew back the bow.

But before he could fire there was an explosion from outside the store. Everyone jumped. A second later there was a loud clang, as if something metal had hit the road from a great height.

"*Scheiße!* What the hell was that?" Marcus said.

"A propane tank," Cristo said.

There were two more blasts as the overheated cooking tanks were shot high into the air then came crashing back down to the earth.

"Let's get out of here," Johan said.

But at that instant there was another explosion and this time the canister fell right through the roof not three meters from the men.

It sent splinters and debris everywhere. The group scattered, and Karuma seized the moment.

He aimed for the neck of the mercenary holding /Uma, but the powerful bow sent the arrow higher than he'd expected, entering the man's ear and not stopping until it hit the far side of his skull. He collapsed, his legs kicking spasmodically.

/Uma turned and saw Karuma, her eyes wide with amazement.

Three more loud explosions followed and two more propane tanks fell like meteorites through the roof, causing more havoc. Rakes and shovels and farm equipment that had been held in the rafters rained down. /Uma snatched a shovel that was dangling in front of her and swung it with all her might at the man who was holding ǂToma. The thin edge caught him in the small of his back, and he collapsed.

As ǂToma ducked away and ran, Johan aimed his pistol and prepared to fire, but then screamed and dropped the pistol. He looked down to see the razor barbs of one of Karuma's arrows protruding from his shoulder. "Ahhhhh! Get it out!" he said to no one.

It was a scene of complete chaos. The fire cracked and popped. Smoke whirled around them. /Uma kept beating the wounded mercenary with the shovel. One of the other men went to grab her, but another propane tank blew through the east wall like a cannonball—whistling as it came—tearing through the shop and hitting the man between the shoulder blades.

Through the gathering smoke, Marcus spotted Karuma behind the curtain and turned his pistol on him. But before he could fire, Cristo closed the distance and grabbed his arm. They wrestled for control of it.

Two more propane tanks exploded.

Karuma nocked another arrow but couldn't get a clear shot at Marcus. Finally, the younger man overpowered Cristo, tripping him up and sending him to the floor. Karuma took aim, but too late. Marcus shot Cristo twice in the chest before he could fire.

Karuma released the arrow. It pierced Marcus's arm, pinning it to his body as it passed through and sunk into his chest. He cried out once, then fell over dead.

Karuma rushed to Cristo, but the big man's eyes were unblinking. He put a hand to his forehead and fought back tears. "I'm so sorry, my friend," then he repeated a Sān prayer. "May you become the brightest star in the night sky."

Three more quick explosions and another canister crashed into the clothing section.

Karuma pulled himself away. "We have to go," he called out in Khoe-san."/Uma! Come on!" Only at the sound of her name did she finally drop the shovel. Karuma cupped his hands to his mouth. "‡Toma! Where are you?"

"Over here!"

A moment later they were all together. The front door was now completely engulfed in flames.

"This way," Karuma said, "out the back."

The three of them scrambled down the back hallways of the compound, Karuma struggling to remember the way. After one wrong turn that forced them to backtrack, they emerged into the cool night air not far from the shooting range. That's when Karuma realized they'd forgotten something.

"The rifles!"

"Leave them," /Uma pleaded. "It's enough that we survived."

"No. Cagn sent me for the guns. I have to go back. Wait for me at the buckthorn tree."

Reluctantly, they split up. Karuma watched as the two younger Sān set off through the maze of old cars and trucks. A part of him wanted to go with them and leave this nightmare behind him. He took a deep breath—and with the bow still in his hand—went back into the compound. It seemed that the roar of the fire was everywhere now and even the back hallways were filling with smoke.

He crouched down low and made his way to the giant metal box that held all the guns.

Cristo had left the rifles propped up against the door. Just as Karuma was going to collect them, he was tackled from behind. He shrieked with fright and tried to get away, but his attacker was like a crazed hyena, biting and tearing at him. Karuma was punched and scratched before he could squirm away. He turned to see Johan, the arrow still protruding from his shoulder. There was a wild madness in his eyes.

"*Ich bring dich um!*" He seethed, but Karuma couldn't understand the words.

Johan went for one of the rifles.

Karuma went for the bow, which had fallen on the floor.

Johan flicked off the safety of the rifle and pulled back the control handle.

Karuma nocked an arrow but saw that its razor tip had broken in the fall. It couldn't be helped. He drew the bow back.

Johan leveled the rifle at him and pulled the trigger.

Nothing happened.

The Sān had taken all the ammunition on their first trip to the buckthorn tree. The magazines in the rifles were all empty.

Karuma fired at Johan's stomach. The arrow passed clean through him, and he collapsed to the floor, holding his stomach and moaning. A moment later his eyes rolled back, and he was still.

Karuma strapped the bow to his back and grabbed the four rifles—two in each hand—and rushed out.

The back corridor was now filled with smoke. He took a deep breath, crouched low, and sprinted out. A minute later he emerged in the back of the compound. He gasped and greedily sucked in the night air. He looked back at the fire that had now consumed more than half the trading post. It raged with an unearthly roar, and made loud cracks and pops. Occasionally a propane tank would explode upward into the night.

He took another deep breath and ran off as fast as he could, out across the road and back into the bush. He made it to the buckthorn tree and collapsed beside the others. They huddled together, touching to confirm that they were truly alive.

‡Toma and /Uma cried from the shock of it. "Poor Cristo," /Uma said.

They looked back at the compound, which lit up the horizon with orange and yellow, the thick black smoke blocking out the stars. Another propane tank exploded, arching up high in the air like a comet.

They passed around some water, but found they were all still panting. It took a long time for their breathing to slow.

Just as they began to relax a dark figure rose up in front of them—a menacing black shadow against the light of the distant fire. "Look out!" ǂToma yelled. The figure raised a knife in his hand and fell upon them, stabbing into the dirt in frantic, delirious strokes.

They scattered to get out of the way, heading deeper into the bush. Karuma turned and saw that it was Johan. Somehow, he had survived.

"*Ich bring dich um!*" he said. "*Ich werde euch alle töten.*"

Although enraged, he was badly wounded, and the Sān were able to keep their distance from him. He came at them in spurts, slashing with the knife, and each time they dashed away.

They were about one hundred meters from the buckthorn when it happened: Johan suddenly stopped as if he had hit an invisible wall. He stood there a moment, a look of pain on his face. He tried to step forward, but it seemed a great effort. He grunted in pain. "What's happening?" he said.

He looked at the knife in his hand, then dropped it quickly as if it had become too hot to touch. He gnashed his teeth and took a step before collapsing forward.

Down on his hands and knees, he lifted his head and spat, "It hurts! It hurts so much!"

Karuma pulled the bow from his back. He had one last arrow and he nocked it on the string. He came closer to be sure he wouldn't miss. Johan saw him but seemed powerless to move.

"I'm going to kill you," Johan hissed.

Karuma fired the arrow into his heart.

★ ★ ★

For the next three hours the three teenagers worked to carry the supplies Cristo had given them a kilometer deeper into Sān territory. Then they collapsed from exhaustion and slept until dawn, but they slept peacefully, sure that Cagn was protecting them.

CHAPTER TWENTY-SEVEN

THE GETAWAY

February 7, 2027
Virginia Beach, Virginia

Major Blake had not been pleased about Eric and Jane's surprise vacation.

We are in the middle of a national crisis here and you two decide to go to the fucking beach! I can't believe this. If you ever wore the uniform, you'd know how selfish and unpatriotic this is.

But there was little he could do. They were contract employees with months of unused vacation time.

They did their best to assure him that they would do as much work as possible, and, like clockwork, Blake made a point to call them two or three times a day.

Eric wasn't sure if coming to Myrtle Beach was a good idea. He was restless and wanted to fix himself. His scientific mind kept pressing for a solution, and he fantasized about finding a way to use Forced Evolution to cure his blindness. It had worked once before after all, maybe it could work again. But he soon realized that letting an artificial intelligence program play around in his brain would be too dangerous. However the original nanosites had gotten in his head, it had been a one-in-a-million chance that they had learned how to heal him.

With no clear way to fix his sight, he did his best not to think about it. But it didn't work. Whether he was sitting on the beach or walking down the boardwalk with Jane, a part of his mind kept trying to tap his other senses and "feel" the things he'd felt in Africa. Trying to sense others around him. Hoping that he would be able to tell if the nanosites were still in him. But they weren't.

On the third evening, he and Jane were sitting on the beach, their legs covered in a blanket. Seagulls were calling on the wind and Eric was listening to the steady crash and hiss of the waves. It was a soothing rhythm that he realized was happening on every beach and shore on earth. *If the planet has a heartbeat*, he thought, *this is it*. As they sat quietly, the temperature began to drop, and he knew the sun was getting low. A cool inshore breeze blew against their faces, but their bodies were warm under the thick blanket.

"Tell me what you see," he said.

"Okay," she said, then paused for a moment, taking it all in. "The sun is setting behind us and making long shadows off the condos. There are strips of shadow and strips of sunlight. We're still in a sunny spot. Some kids made a sandcastle over to our left and the rising tide will reach it soon. Out over the ocean here's a line of low clouds that are catching the sunlight and glowing pink and orange. It's very pretty."

Eric tried to imagine it.

He suddenly felt he was looking at his life from a distance, like a snapshot. Here he was, a young scientist on the beach with the girl he loved, but facing the possibility of a lifelong disability. That was his story right now. He often liked to think of his life like a book that he was writing. A story that followed a logical and upward trajectory. *Go to college, graduate, get a good job, fall in love, and get married, etc.* When he was young, he had thought that he controlled the story. But he had learned that was an illusion. For good or bad, sometimes other writers took control. His father's death had been like that; someone who should have been in his life for another forty years was suddenly erased, completely altering the story of his life. Now the blindness could wreck everything again.

He tried not to be fatalistic about it. It was too soon for that. And he realized the lesson was that he shouldn't focus on the parts of the story he couldn't write, but on the parts he could.

He pulled Jane close. What was the trajectory he'd imagined? *Get a good job, fall in love and get married?* He'd always considered it a foregone conclusion that they would be together forever, mostly because he couldn't imagine a future without Jane in it. Yet, their lives had been such chaos over the past year—his imprisonment in China, his mission to Africa, now the fight against Walden—that they had never gotten to a place where they could plan that future.

And why not now?

A wild impulse possessed him. *Just propose. Right. Here.*

He wanted to, and he felt she would say yes. But he hesitated. He realized he couldn't do it from a position of weakness. He didn't want her to perceive that he was asking now *because* he was blind. *You have to wait*, he told himself, *at least a little longer.*

But that doesn't mean you can't tell her how you feel.

He whispered in her ear, "I'd be lost without you." And it was true.

He felt her hand brush his cheek. "I'd be lost without you too."

He smiled. "Then I guess we'd better stick together."

"Deal," she said. "And since I know how you worry and obsess about things, that means no matter what."

He let out a short laugh. She'd figured him out long ago. He kissed her.

"I'm going to make sure you don't regret that," he said.

They snuggled closer together and she put her head to his chest. He breathed deeply and held her tight.

He felt so close to her at that moment—so reassured and confident of her love—that it almost seemed a shame that they could not actually be one. The fact that they were two separate bodies seemed unnecessary; there was a needless barrier—a frontier—that they both wanted to cross, but never could. She seemed to feel it too and snuggled against him as if she wanted to pass into him.

He relaxed and enjoyed the moment. Several minutes went by.

He heard the cry of a seagull hovering in the air, the sound of the waves hitting the sand, and the smell of saltwater and ocean decay.

His thoughts ran to the seagull overhead and he suddenly had a vision that he was seeing the world with its eyes, looking down on two people, intertwined under a blanket on a quiet stretch of windy beach. Eric saw what the seagull saw: The white-capped waves rolling in for miles in either direction, a crab scurrying back into the waves, a trashcan that might contain food at the entrance to the beach. He held onto the vision until the seagull peeled away, rising high over the condos.

After a minute Jane sat up and saw a tear on his cheek. She wiped it away with her thumb. "Hey, don't worry. Everything's going to be all right."

He smiled. "I know."

In the morning, Eric opened his eyes to see Jane sleeping beside him. The warm sunlight was coming in shafts through the blinds and hitting her blond hair. He sighed and began caressing it, playing with the strands and curling them in his fingers. He found the scar on her scalp from the fire. He had saved her life that night, then she had saved his.

"I still owe you one," he said aloud, remembering how her clever invention—the stasis foam—had saved his life in Namibia. "Maybe more than one."

At the sound of his voice, she rolled over and opened her eyes lazily. Then she seemed to notice the difference, how his eyes were so completely focused on her. His smile said the rest.

"Oh, thank God," she said, wrapping her arms around his neck and pulling him close.

CHAPTER TWENTY-EIGHT

THE LAST WARRIOR

February 7, 2027
Namibia

It took Karuma, ǂToma, and /Uma four days to make their way home from Cristo's Trading. When the tribe saw all the food they had brought, they were treated like heroes. That night there was a big feast and they sat around the fire listening as the teenagers told the story. The tribe was thrilled, saddened, and amazed. They asked many questions and made them retell the story over and over.

But Naru left the fire quickly, and Karuma watched her go. She held her arms across her belly, like she did when she was sick.

Karuma went to her and touched her on the shoulder. "Mother?" he said, but she pulled away.

"How could you?" she demanded. "How could you go and risk your life like that? You know how much I've lost. Your father, your grandfather. I can't . . ."

He went to embrace her, but she pulled away again. "I forbid you to do anything like this again. You played with your life and you played with /Uma's life and ǂToma's life too. If they had killed the three of you . . ." She stopped, suddenly choked up by the thought of it. "I forbid you! Do you understand?"

Karuma nodded to himself. Yes, he understood how she felt, but he could not do as she wished. "I'm sorry, Mother, but you cannot stop me from doing the things I must do to protect the tribe. Yes, I am your son. But I am also a Sān, which means I'm part of a bigger family. Whether you like it or not, it is my responsibility to fight our enemies before they wipe us out."

"No, I won't let you throw your life away."

"I won't be throwing my life away if I die defeating our enemies. Cristo gave us many ideas and /Uma and ‡Toma and I have been making plans. We can do this, but only if we all work together. We want you to join us."

She looked out into the darkness of the night, then back at the rest of the tribe sitting around the fire.

"I know you, Mother," he said, "I know you want to fight. We can defeat the White Hand if we all work together. I'm asking you: Will you help us?"

CHAPTER TWENTY-NINE

SYMBIOTIC RELATIONSHIPS

February 9, 2027
Naval Research Lab

Eric looked at himself in the mirror, his repaired eyes seeing things in ultra-high definition. At a glance, he could discern every pore and follicle on his face, the star pattern around his iris, the smooth scar over his left eyebrow, all in focus at the same time.

"What have you become?" he asked his reflection.

His reflection responded. "And what are you changing into?"

His ability to anticipate things, his sixth sense, the dreams about the end of the world. These things were coming from the machines inside him. He needed these machines to survive.

More puzzling, the nanosites inside him were his own. He'd designed them. But how and when they had jumped from being tools in the lab to living in his blood and tissues, he couldn't fathom. And how had they managed to do all this without any programming? Again, he didn't know. But he knew someone who might.

He went to Jane. "I want to set up a Li-Fi signal. I want to call him."

"It's too dangerous. You know Walden and Blake have new

security measures all over the lab. Li-Fi is something they would have certainly thought of."

"But they won't understand the message. I can encrypt it."

"No, Eric, you can't. And you know why? Because you're not playing with just your life here, you're playing with Xiao-ping's and Mei's and Lili's . . . and mine."

He nodded slowly, pursing his lips tight. She was right. He couldn't put them at risk.

"You have to find another way," she said.

That night he lay in bed weighing his options.

Jane had reached the Inventor while Eric was in Africa by hijacking the lights around the base and sending a message using Li-Fi—subtle pulses of light that were undetectable to the human eye. That proved that the Inventor had the place under surveillance. But how closely was he watching? Was he scanning all their communication? Was he listening to their conversations? Were his nanosites in the air right now?

"I need to talk to you," he said to the darkness. He felt stupid saying it, but figured it was worth a try. "Please, if you are there. I need to talk to you."

There was no reply.

He gave a long exhale, rolled over on his side, and closed his eyes.

For the next three days he racked his brain for a way to solve the problem, but every idea he came up with posed a risk that Walden and Eleven might discover it. The best solution was still the photon array to the satellite he'd used to connect to Namibia, but he dared not risk another transmission like that. For once in his life, he was truly stumped.

Yet each night as he went to bed, he would repeat his call to the Inventor.

"Please, I need to talk to you. I need to understand what's happening to me."

Eric awoke on the fourth morning to find himself lying in the middle of a vast forest. He was facedown on a bed of leaves and the first thing he saw when he lifted his eyes was a fat, bulbous mushroom a few inches from his nose. He rolled onto his back and found himself looking up through the branches and leaves of enormous trees. Their thick canopies were hundreds of feet above him and blocked out most of the sunshine, allowing only a few occasional shafts of light to break through. He watched particles of dust dancing in the beams. Beautiful. But how? Was this a dream? He stood and shook his head.

Frogs and insects croaked and droned all around him, and dark green moss grew thick on boulders and fallen trees. Eric had the feeling of being far from mankind, almost as if he were in a different epoch, back when the world was young. He looked at his hands and arms, then breathed deep. The air was heavy with moisture. *This is too real to be a dream.*

Then he saw that he wasn't alone. At the base of an enormous tree, a man was studying the bark.

A smile grew on Eric's face. *At last.*

The man wore khaki pants and a long brown raincoat with hiking boots, all of them worn and dirty from heavy use. He noticed Eric, gave a friendly wave, and came closer.

Eric examined him as he approached. His face was very different from what Eric remembered. The sense of deformity was gone. He looked older, calmer, more serene, with streaks of gray in the thick curly hair that grew in wild tangles above his head.

The man looked around happily. "This is a very special place for me," he said in his lyrical voice. "I absolutely love coming here."

Eric gave a breathy laugh at the Inventor's casual behavior, but he tried to take it all in stride.

"Where are we?"

"This is the Daintree," the Inventor said, gazing upward and slowly turning around. "It's the oldest forest in the world. Just think of it: for a hundred and eighty million years this forest has stood here."

Nearby was an enormous fig tree. Its branches spread out like a great spider—from each of its thick branches, smaller tendrils descended to the ground making new roots that supported the tree as it spread in every direction.

It was astonishing. And not just the tree and the forest, but how real it all seemed. Jane had told him how the Inventor had taken her consciousness on a journey through deep space. This must be like that, he thought, yet the realism was stunning: the smell of the loamy earth, the bead of sweat running down his temple, the call of strange birds in the canopy. He pinched his fingers together. He couldn't detect anything that didn't seem real. "How do you do it? How did you bring my consciousness to the other side of the world and make it seem so real?"

The Inventor gave a warm smile. "It feels real, because it is."

Eric shook his head in disbelief. "You're saying I'm actually here?"

He nodded and smiled again. "Yes, I am."

"But isn't that impossible?"

"With 2026 technology it is. But you must remember, my thinking has become so accelerated that many of the scientific hurdles that keep your world from advancing are in my distant past."

"But isn't it dangerous?"

The Inventor laughed. "The first test animals I sent would definitely say that. But don't worry. From my perspective, I've been doing this for decades."

"But how?"

"It's really not that difficult. Quantum teleportation exists in your world now, so the challenge for me was to scale up to the non-quantum state. But it wasn't hard. A few days' work, really. The key was putting nanosite clusters at either end of the quantum channel, then it was just a matter of capturing all the data."

Eric nodded slowly to himself. "You teleport the information to build the swarms first because that can be done at the quantum level, then you use those swarms at both ends of the transmission to help you reassemble larger objects."

"Yes, that's it. It's all a matter of getting the data where you want it. And I have safeguards, of course, such as backups."

Eric shook his head again. *Unbelievable.* Someday teleportation was really going to happen. He laughed and looked around again. He was halfway around the world in a beautiful forest under the protection of the most powerful being in the universe. Why not enjoy it? There was obviously a reason the Inventor had brought him here. He didn't know what it was . . . yet . . . but he was going to enjoy the experience in the meantime.

"Many of these trees are hundreds of years old," the Inventor said. "That bull kauri," he said, motioning to a massive tree, "is over a thousand years old." Eric marveled at it. Up until this moment he honestly didn't know a tree could get that big. It looked like a beech tree on steroids. Its trunk was so thick that it would take ten people—maybe eleven—stretching hand to hand—to go around it. And it was so tall that he couldn't even see any of its leaves because the trunk shot clean through the canopy.

"Amazing." Eric said.

"It is indeed! But what you see around you is only a small piece of it. There is so much more going on here that goes beyond our senses . . . Would you like to see?"

"Of course!"

The Inventor smiled. "It's good to be in the company of a fellow scientist." He motioned to the ground. "If you look down at your feet, you'll notice many mushrooms. With your eye you can see hundreds, but there are tens of thousands more hidden under the leaf cover. Their roots spread out for miles under our feet in a great ribo-somal network that connects all the trees in the forest together like dendrites in your brain."

Eric raised an eyebrow. He'd heard of these ribosomal networks and how some botanists, likely looking for publicity and funding, compared them to a human brain, but he'd never taken it seriously. It seemed an awfully big stretch to compare the brain—the most complicated known organic structure in the universe—with a bunch of mushrooms.

"Oh, yes," the Inventor said, "it is very smart." He stepped up to the bull kauri and touched its smooth bark. "If insects attack this tree, it will send a chemical message through its roots. The fungi will help transmit that message to the other trees, and they will upgrade their immune systems to prepare for the attack. In this way, the bull kauri will help not only its offspring, but the fig trees, the ferns, and the oaks. So together, the trees and the fungi—organisms that are so different that they are in different kingdoms—help one another to survive."

Eric tilted his head tentatively. He still wasn't convinced.

"Come. I'll show you."

The Inventor knelt near a huge tree stump. It was covered with moss and only protruded a few inches off the ground. From its circumference, Eric could tell that it had once been an enormous tree, but now it was not much more than a bowl of bark.

"Come touch this and tell me what you feel."

Eric got down on one knee, and touched the furry moss and the edges of the old wood. To his surprise the wood wasn't rotten, but firm and smooth. It reminded him of the end of an amputated limb.

"Now close your eyes and open your other senses."

Eric closed his eyes.

At first there was nothing. Then . . . something. It was a strange feeling. Oddly startling. Like realizing that someone was standing nearby that you hadn't noticed before.

He looked up at the Inventor. "Somehow it's alive. But how?"

The Inventor smiled wide with pleasure.

"This tree fell to the ground more than three hundred years ago. Of course, at that point it could no longer make sugar through photosynthesis, so it should have died. But the trees around it," and here he gestured with his hand, "the oak, the fig, and the tree's daughter—that bull kauri over there—have been keeping it alive for the past three centuries by feeding it nutrients through its root system."

"But why?"

"I believe there is more than one answer to that. The first answer is scientific, the other is, well, more philosophical."

"Go on," Eric said, now completely enthralled by the idea.

"This tree was one of the oldest in the forest when it fell, which means it had acquired a great deal of knowledge in its long life. It knew how to survive disease, pestilence, and drought. By keeping it alive, the other trees tap into that knowledge when a crisis comes.

"So again, we see different species helping each other because it benefits them all."

Eric suddenly realized. "You're trying to explain what's happening to me." It was half statement, half question. "You're saying that by putting the nanosites next to my body, that they've somehow learned to connect and work with my cells, like the trees and the fungi."

The Inventor nodded. "No one could have predicted exactly what type of relationship was going to evolve—for example, your immune system could have attacked them as a foreign invader or vice versa, but it was almost inevitable that some kind of reaction would occur. What's more, quantum mechanics—the rules of the very small—are geared toward this type of entanglement."

Entanglement, Eric thought. The idea that subatomic particles were linked to each other. That the fate of one particle always impacted the other, no matter the distance between them.

"You're saying that I've become entangled with these nanosites at the subatomic level?"

"Not exactly, what I'm saying is that interconnectivity is

programmed into the universe. In all my travels and studies, I have discovered many things, ranging in scale from the galactic to the quantum. But one of the most important is this: Entanglement is one of the primary driving forces in the universe. Without it, life would never have begun. Think of it—entanglement means that within the most basic fabric of matter that there is communication. And *that* innate propensity for cooperation is the reason that amino-acid chains began to fold, even in deep space. Riding on comets that seeded the universe with life.

"Entanglement means that the cosmos is hardwired for both interconnectivity and interdependence. Not only between cells in your body—such as how your red blood cells and white blood cells work together—but also between life forms. Such as the way these trees are communicating or the way that foreign bacteria in your digestive system keep you alive.

"Consider our relationship to viruses. A typical mammal carries over three hundred thousand *species* of virus in their body at any moment. We consider them foreign invaders out to destroy us, but that is far from the truth. Yes, many viruses attack our cells and hijack our DNA. But sometimes it works the other way and our cells take DNA from the invading virus that makes us stronger. Over eons, viral DNA has been crucial to our success as a species. The most famous example, of course, is the placenta, which was an extraordinary advancement. Imagine it, the transition from egg to placenta. Now a mother could actively nourish a growing fetus—sending it food and oxygen while simultaneously removing waste and carbon dioxide. And all while she moved around, foraging and evading predators. Viruses are so import-ant that we cannot live without them. And if you analyze our DNA closely, you'll find that one-twelfth of it came from viruses."

Eric tried to absorb what he was saying, the scientist in him kept looking for a flaw in his reasoning but could find none.

"There are connections all around us that I think many of us sense, but never really believe. But once you see them—truly see them—it completely changes how you view the universe."

Eric considered his own experiences. "When I was hunting the gemsbok in Africa I felt a connection to her. It was like I was in her mind, reading her thoughts, feeling her emotions. And because I was able to do that, a part of me didn't want to hurt her."

"Yes, you can think of that as a type of entanglement. Although that is much more about your mind being able to recognize connections that have always been there."

"But when did it start? And why me and not all the other scientists at the lab?"

"I think you know the answer to that already."

Eric turned his thoughts inward for a moment.

"It was in China," he said. "All that time I was in captivity, wearing the shirt. Every day they would feed on my dead skin."

"Yes," the Inventor said.

The conviction in his answer made Eric start.

"You knew?"

The Inventor nodded. "Yes."

"But wait a minute," Eric said, holding up his hand as he collected his thoughts. "Did you make it happen?"

"No," the Inventor reassured him. "The process had already begun. But I gave it a push."

Eric tried to link the clues together. *Push?* He thought back to what had happened in China: ten weeks in captivity, their desperate escape, then, when they were almost free . . .

Carbon Rain, he thought. That was the name he'd given to the last-minute program he'd made when they were preparing their escape from China. He thought back to the crossroads, where Ryan and Mei and Lili's sister and Eric had been captured by General Meng. The general had murdered Lili's sister and was about to kill them all, but then the Inventor had rescued them, killing Meng's men, but leaving the general alive and conveniently incapacitated. He'd left him alive so Eric could kill him. And Eric had done it using the crude program, Carbon Rain. At the time, he didn't know why the Inventor had done that, but guessed that he'd wanted Eric to have his revenge. But now he realized it was more . . . much more.

"It started when I killed Meng."

"Yes, those nanosites were a new generation, evolved from the ones that had already been adapting to your body and your DNA."

It was all making sense. His first "dreams" came shortly after that.

"But why?"

Here a look of regret came upon the Inventor's face. "I realize now that I should not have done it, at least not without your permission. But I had felt grateful to you. Without Forced Evolution, I could not have become what I am. So I wanted to reward you. I could see how the nanosites were interacting within you. And it seemed like a good match. They had not turned malevolent or aggressive as they sometimes can. I thought I would help the process along. So that you would have a chance to become like me."

Eric stood still for a long minute. He honestly didn't know how to feel. The Inventor had changed him . . . or at least accelerated the changes that had already started. That felt violating. Yet, he owed his life to the Inventor several times over. Not only had he saved them from General Meng, but by nudging the nanosites within him, the Inventor had protected him (and the ones he loved) again and again. The crash of the Valor in Africa. The curing of his blindness. Saving Karuma from the charging rhino. Sensing the approach of the mercenaries that tried to wipe out the Sān tribe. All those things would have turned out differently without the nanosites inside him.

He nodded slowly, realizing that this was just the way things were.

"What's going to happen to me?"

"As I warned Jane, each time you use Forced Evolution there's a risk that you will make something beyond your control. I learned that lesson the hard way. Yet, I think the most dangerous part for you is over. Your nanosites did not try to take over. They are not aggressive, and they are evolving slowly."

"Will I ever be able to control them?"

"You might. But it may be better if you don't. They seem to

know what's good for you and how to help you already. And look around you: Do the fungi need to control the trees or vice versa? No. They can both thrive by being both independent and *inter*dependent."

"I don't like the uncertainty," Eric said, "that at any moment I could lose my sight or they could evolve into something new."

"Ah, well put," the Inventor said with a smile. "*Uncertainty*. Just like entanglement, uncertainty is part of the nature of the universe. At the quantum level you must accept that a thing cannot be precisely known and that 'the truth' can be multiple things at the same time. Right now it is true that you are no longer human. But it is also true that you weren't completely human before. More than half the cells in your body are nonhuman cells already and eight percent of your DNA is really viral DNA."

The Inventor turned back to the huge stump. "I told you before that there was more than one reason why the other trees keep this stump alive . . . a more philosophical reason."

Eric nodded.

"I think it's because the other trees love it."

The edge of Eric's mouth rose with a quizzical smile. "That's not very scientific."

The Inventor laughed. "I know. But what is love? Can't you define it as the desire to stay connected to another being? There are thousands of different reasons why we love someone or something and most of the time we ourselves cannot articulate it. No matter how you define love—as entanglement or as an evolutionary benefit—the other trees want to keep the connection to the old tree. Perhaps the old tree helped them once or perhaps they feel a sense of security they don't want to lose. But I've come to the conclusion that it goes beyond a mutually beneficial relationship. And I've got lots of evidence to back me up. We sacrifice and bleed and even give our lives for the ones we love and there is often no clear benefit to us. Children sacrifice themselves for their parents, when it has no benefit to the individual or the species. I think the trees are the same, they don't know why, but they want to do it. They think it's right. For better or for worse, they accept that their fates are entangled.

"So you see, the world is still full of mystery. Yes, there is much we know and can explain, but not everything. Which means that I remain *uncertain*. And in my opinion that makes the universe a lot more interesting."

Eric was still trying to take it all in. *Entanglement and uncertainty.* The nanosites were now a part of him. He had to accept that. What's more, he also had to accept that he would never really control them.

"Thank you," he said. "These were not the answers I expected, but thank you anyway."

"It has been my pleasure," the Inventor said with a slight bow of his head. "I feel, of course, that you and I are entangled too, and I suspect our paths will cross again."

Eric smiled. "I would like that very much." Then he hesitated. "Before I go, I wanted to ask you about my dreams."

"Tell me."

Eric explained how, ever since China, he'd had dreams about the end of the world.

"Isn't it obvious?" the Inventor said. "The human prefrontal cortex is always trying to take the data it collects from the world to create a model of the future. But now you are different. The nanosites have made your prefrontal cortex far better than any normal person's."

"Am I seeing the future?"

"No, you are seeing a possible future. That's the job of your prefrontal cortex, to prepare you for what *might* happen. Your augmented intelligence is different from my intelligence. I have figured many things out, but your intelligence just might have discovered something that I've missed. Tell me, are the dreams changing?"

"Yes."

This seemed to pique the Inventor's interest. "How?"

"When I first had the dreams, it was in the summer; now they are in the spring."

"That means that your mind is calculating that the end could come sooner than it originally predicted."

"And now Karuma is in the dreams . . . here with me in America."

The Inventor nodded. "Well, that could be explained with entanglement too. Just like the trees feel their wellness depends on the other trees, you feel that your wellness depends on Karuma's wellness. When you cannot see him and feel the connection, you are restless."

Eric nodded. "But what does it mean?"

The Inventor shrugged, "No one can say for sure because there are so many variables. But we are entering a very dangerous time, and I'm afraid the whole world hangs in the balance."

CHAPTER THIRTY

THE GIFT

February 10, 2027
FBI Headquarters, Washington, DC

The New York Times

NEW YORK, FEBRUARY 10, 2027

RIONA FINLEY AND THE RISE OF DOMESTIC TERRORISM IN THE US

by Scott Brookings

Some label her a terrorist on par with Osama bin Laden, while others claim that she is the hero that America needs. We are, of course, talking about the charismatic former college professor Riona Finley.

While the government is aggressively trying to hunt her down, millions say they admire how she is challenging a political system that has grown too corrupt and inept to deal with the nation's problems. Her rise as a public figure and influencer is causing major rifts in American society, pushing people into pro- and anti-Finley camps.

In many ways she has become the symbol of a fractured America. She dominates the 24/7 news cycle and drives network ratings. Indeed, a recent raid on an abandoned mine in Virginia had all the elements of a Hollywood film, with the FBI successfully rescuing the prestigious scientist Bill Eastman, and Finley making a last-minute escape amidst a flurry of explosions.

Within hours, Finley was capitalizing on the drama on social media: "Thanks for all the warm wishes. It was a close call, but the FBI and all the police in the country won't be enough to stop us. Our important work continues. We will never give up!"

Finley's continued success at eluding the authorities and her ability to rally supporters has the current administration worried.

In an unprecedented move, President Shaw issued an executive order declaring the New Anarchists a terrorist organization. Within hours of the decree, hundreds of Finley's supporters had been arrested. But the move has put the administration on shaky legal footing, as many of those arrested have only a tenuous relationship to Finley. Many made donations to her climate fund, and others merely follow her on social media. Indeed, a list of supporters released by the FBI showed dozens of prominent Hollywood actors, musicians, and politicians, many of whom have spoken out against the terrorist designation.

What the administration hoped would be a step toward snuffing out her movement, seems to have only fanned the flames. Working with other environmental groups like Sierra Club and the Nature Conservancy, Finley announced that her supporters would march on Washington, effectively taunting the government to arrest them all.

"Mark your calendars and plan your road trip! February 16 is the Mega-Climate Rally in Washington DC. We want two million supporters to fill the National Mall and show the government that we are too big to ignore! #MegaClimate-March2027."

Bud Brown folded the newspaper and tossed it on the desk. He absently touched the bandages on his head from where he'd been burned. The skin still felt hot to him.

Since the raid and Brightwell's death, things had gone from bad to worse. Finley was nowhere to be found, and Bud felt like he was starting all over again. He was a mental wreck too.

He realized he'd made several critical mistakes. The first was that he had not killed Coyle when he had the chance. Over and over, he thought back to that moment up on the ridge, with Brightwell at his side when they had first found the mine. He'd had a clear shot at Coyle, an easy shot, and he hadn't taken it.

If you'd killed him then, she'd still be alive.

The second was that he'd underestimated Coyle. With all the bombs that Coyle had set in Northern Ireland, Bud should have anticipated a retaliatory attack. If he'd been more careful, he could have saved her.

Another bad call by Bud Brown, the cynical voice said. *You're really pathetic, you know that? You didn't save Rogers and you didn't save Brightwell. But, heh, look on the bright side. At least you have your family to fall back on, right? A loving wife and kids. Oh, wait.*

He shook his head bitterly, wishing he could get that fucking voice out of his head. Still, he couldn't help asking himself when it had all gone wrong. When had he made the "critical error" that he could never come back from?

One specific moment came to his mind: The night he'd gotten drunk and missed his son's high-school championship basketball game. He'd arrived at the school—looking like a mess—just as the last of the spectators were leaving. He hadn't realized it at the time, but that had been a turning point. Michael had never treated him the same after that, had never really trusted him again. Never asked for any more favors, never invited him to any more games. And Carol? Well, he could think of a dozen times he'd abused her trust. He'd asked forgiveness every time, of course, but each time she said she'd given it, he realized she really hadn't. The bond between them was always a little weaker, until there was nothing left to hold the marriage together.

That's all on you, the voice said. *You can't blame anyone else.* He accepted that truth: he was in the eleventh hour, and even though he now realized what he *should* have done—in everything from his marriage to Brightwell's death—there wasn't a damn thing he could do about it now.

There was a knock on Bud's office door.

"Mail call."

"Come in," Bud said.

"I just have this for you, sir," the young man said. It was a cardboard box that had been opened and crudely taped shut again. "Postal Inspection checked it for you."

Bud took the box, then noticed how the young man's eyes lingered on the two bandages on Bud's head.

"Thanks," Bud said, with the unspoken coda of *you can go*. The man seemed about to speak—perhaps to ask him what happened— but Bud's tone was enough to keep him quiet. With a quick about-face, he left.

Bud opened the box to see a bottle wrapped in wood shavings. He pulled it out. It was a bottle of Jameson Irish whiskey.

Bud felt his blood rise and a sudden sense of dizziness. He searched through the shavings until he found the handwritten note: *For a party of one.*

He gritted his teeth and stood quickly. He had to resist the urge to smash the bottle against the wall. But he knew it was more valuable intact. Perhaps the son of a bitch had left some clue they could use, but knowing Coyle it was unlikely.

He paced the office, trying to control his emotions. *He's toying with you*, he thought. *He wants to spook you.*

But nothing is going to stop me, you know that. Nothing.

Bud's thinking had changed too. Up until now his revenge meant bringing Coyle to justice, but he didn't think he could do that anymore. He wanted . . . no, *needed*, to kill Coyle. For what he did, for killing Rogers, then Brightwell—God, he couldn't get her face out of his head—for that, for what he had done, there was only one type of justice.

CHAPTER THIRTY-ONE

DEPARTING

February 10, 2027
Rosslyn, Virginia

"Tell me how school is going," Sebastian said.

"Better, I guess. Amanda and her friends still tease me, but I think they're getting tired of it."

"That's good. And besides your voice is definitely returning to normal."

Emma beamed. "Do you really think so? I thought it was just my imagination."

"No, it's definitely changing."

"I've been singing in the shower. I think it helps."

"That's a great idea! Plus it will lift your spirits."

"It's not lifting Mom's spirits," Emma said. "She thought I was washing the cat."

Sebastian laughed.

"Any updates on the young man you mentioned?"

"Alex?" Emma looked off into the distance and gave a mournful sigh. "I'm afraid he doesn't know I exist."

"Well, don't give up," Sebastian said. "If he's a smart guy, he'll open his eyes and see how special you are."

Emma shook her head and laughed. "That's such a dad thing to say," she said. "But thanks anyway."

He laughed and there was a breadth of silence.

"I have to go away for a while."

Emma looked down at her hands, suddenly deflated. "Why?"

"I'm a scientist like your mom. And sometimes I need to travel for work."

"But I don't want you to go. You're the only friend I have."

"It's just for a week or so. While I'm away I want you to start talking to your mom."

"I told you, she doesn't want to hear about my problems. She fixed me, so I've been officially checked off her to-do list. Now she's free to go back to being a workaholic."

"That's true," he said, "but only partially true. Keep trying and I think she'll surprise you . . . . Will you do that for me?"

She pursed her lips and nodded: "Okay."

"Good! Now one last thing before I go: remember your promise. Don't go looking for answers without me."

"I know, I know," she said. "I won't."

At that moment she felt a warm, gentle pressure on her forehead that could only be a kiss.

"Bye for now," he said.

CHAPTER THIRTY-TWO

THE CIPHER

February 11, 2027
Naval Consolidated Brig, Fairfax County, VA

Seventeen-year-old Logan Curtiss parked his car and looked up at
the brig. It was not really what he'd expected—just a low, two-story
complex, made of tan brick. It was as unassuming and innocuous as
any commercial office building or even a school. Yes, there was a set
of parallel chain-link fences that ran around the sports fields, but the
main facade had no fence or guard towers.

Okay, let's get this over with, he said to himself.

He reminded himself that he was on a mission; that Mei had
asked him to do this for the good of her parents, their friends, and
maybe the country. *Just do the mission. Nothing else.*

He walked to the front door.

Once inside, he was greeted professionally if coolly by the brig
staff. They asked for his name and driver's license, ran him through
a metal detector, and patted him down. Then he was given a security
briefing on what was acceptable and unacceptable behavior. The duty
officer explained what items could be passed back and forth. Logan
had researched this already and asked for some sheets of paper and pen,
which the brig staff gave him. The pen had a fat grip and the writing

tip only stuck out a millimeter from the end. The shaft of the pen was so floppy that there was no possible way to use it as a weapon. Finally, the duty officer told him he could embrace his father, if he wished, but only briefly. Logan had already decided that wasn't going to happen.

When the briefing was over, they led him into the visitation area. It reminded Logan of his high-school cafeteria—smooth metal picnic tables spaced out about ten feet apart. A male prisoner and his wife were talking quietly at one of the tables, holding hands. Another inmate sat with an older woman, likely his mother, nearby. Meanwhile, three brig officers, a man and two women in blue uniforms, watched from the sides of the room.

An electronic buzz sounded as the door to the main prison opened. Logan's father walked out, controlled and dignified as always. Suddenly, Logan found it very hard to look at him. He just couldn't reconcile the father that he thought he always knew with the man being depicted as a monster in the media.

The admiral reached the table and stood for a moment. Logan didn't stand, didn't even lift his eyes.

His father seemed to get the hint and sat down across from him.

"It's good to see you, Son."

Logan lifted his eyes, remembering the plan. It didn't matter what he felt, he had a job to do.

"It's good to see you too."

"Logan, I know you must have a lot of questions . . ."

"No, Dad, please. I don't want to talk about that. Let's just play a game, like double tic-tac-toe, that one we always used to play after dinner."

"Sure, of course," his father said, without hesitation. As Logan had hoped, his father picked up on the inconsistency immediately. They had never played any such game.

Logan took two of the pages that the brig staff had given him and drew large tic-tac-toe boards on the center of each one, then placed them in the middle of the table. Next, he set two more blank pages between him and the board, as if these pieces were "on deck."

"Are you ready?" Logan asked. He could see his father trying to process the pattern.

"Yes," he said.

Logan's hands moved quickly, he used the pen to touch the squares, usually touching several different squares, as if hesitating, before making an X on one. Meanwhile his other hand touched different points on the pages "on deck."

He watched his father's eyes closely to make sure he was tracking each move. Logan started with something mundane, to make sure his dad was following: Y-O-U-T-A-U-G-H-T-M-E-T-H-I-S-I-N-S-E-C-O-N-D-G-R-A-D-E. In no more than half a minute he was sure his dad was decoding each letter. When they finished one game, Curtiss took the used sheets and turned them over in front of himself, so that his dad could make the additional letters with his free hand, just like Logan.

It was the simplest of codes: the Freemason cipher. No one even knew how old it was. It was used by Hebrew rabbis, the Knights Templar during the Crusades, and Union POWs during the Civil War. It had a more elementary name too: pigpen.

A	B	C		J	K	L					
D	E	F		M	N	O		S / T U V		W / X Y Z	
G	H	I		P	Q	R					

Back in school, the letters were the sides of the boxes: ⌐ = A, ⊔ = B, ∟ = C. But by using the tic-tac-toe boards, they had the entire alphabet laid out in front of them, so Logan merely needed to point to empty spaces.

While they played, they kept up the ruse that it was just a game. "Oh, you got me on that one!"

"I can't believe you fell for that."

It only took Curtiss about five minutes to answer Logan's question, but they played on for another fifteen minutes to sell it to the guards. When they stopped there was a long pause.

"I'd better get going," Logan said, and he began collecting the sheets.

His father didn't say anything at first, but as Logan stood up he asked, "How is everyone?"

Logan squeezed his eyes shut for a second. "Not good. River can't sleep at night and is in counseling. The police raid really messed him up. Minco has been getting bullied at school. And, well, you know about Mom."

"And you?"

Logan pursed his lips, his conflicting emotions pulling him to and fro. The truth was he was angry . . . at times seething . . . Their lives had been so good before this happened, but now—because of his father's actions—everything was falling to pieces. Logan locked his eyes on his father.

"I feel like I'm rewriting the history of my life, but with a different father in all the old scenes. One who wasn't the person I thought he was. So I'm left wondering what kind of person you really are."

Curtiss gave a grunt. "No father can tell his son what he should think of him. I can't tell you I'm a good man, just as I can't tell you to respect me. That has to come from your own judgment. Just know that your opinion of me is going to change as you grow older. When I was your age, I saw my own father as a useless drunk and I hated him. But now I see that it was much more complicated than that. I wouldn't say that I ever forgave him for what he did, but I did learn to understand it, so I hope . . . in time . . . you'll come to understand this too."

"Understand?" He let out a sardonic laugh. "What's to understand? Either you did it or you didn't. When you were arrested, none of us believed it, but now . . ." He sucked in an angry breath. "All I know is that so far you haven't denied a thing."

His father nodded slowly, then spoke with an intensity that Logan rarely heard. "The war," he began, choosing his words. "The war in Syria was a brutal war. There were dozens of different factions, most of which were being fed weapons and troops by either Russia, Iran, Turkey, or the US. It was like a meat grinder with the different powers pushing more and more guns and bullets and bodies into it. There didn't seem to be any end in sight. It was on April 12, 2024, that I had a hard lesson. I lost two hundred marines in a single day. I had ordered the operation, and I felt responsible for what happened. After that I couldn't sleep. I just stayed up day after day, mulling it over, asking myself the same questions: How could we end the war? How could we make all the different leaders want to stop fighting? What was the weakness that they all had?

"I remember sitting at my desk at CENTCOM. And there in front of me were the pictures of you and your brothers. That's when I realized that my enemies' greatest weakness was likely the same as my own."

Logan shifted his jaw. "So it's all true?"

Curtiss didn't answer.

Logan shook his head, turned, and walked out.

At the security checkpoint, the guard took the pen and reviewed the pages they'd used for their game. Finally, she asked, "You wanna keep these?" Logan didn't answer right away. At the moment his emotions were so high that he didn't give a damn, at least not about his father. But then he remembered Mei and her family.

"Sure," he said.

When he got back to his house, he burned them.

Twenty-two miles away at Gilford Latin Academy, Mr. Morgan was passing back their science quizzes. "Nice work, Emma," he said as he slid the paper across her desk.

Emma turned it over and looked at the A in red marker.

"Wow, you rocked that!" her lab partner, Jessica, said.

"Thanks, but I bet you did too, since we worked together."

Mr. Morgan handed Jessica her quiz, and the girl quickly turned it over. Another A.

"See, I told ya," Emma said. "We make a good team."

"Definitely," Jessica said. "We should totally study for the test together."

"I'd love to," Emma said enthusiastically, her face flushing with excitement. She smiled wide, stupidly even, then checked herself. She knew she shouldn't get her hopes up, but it seemed like Jessica could be a real friend. Emma could feel that things were changing. Her voice was almost back to normal and now she could start making friends.

After school she went to her locker to collect her things. There were eight or nine other kids in the corridor doing the same, including Jessica, who was just across the hall. Feeling emboldened by their new friendship, Emma stopped. "Awesome job again on your quiz," she said.

"Thanks!"

"You know I was thinking maybe we could hang out after school sometime."

Jessica flashed her a warm smile, but then it suddenly disappeared.

"Maybe," she said. A nervous tone had entered her voice and she seemed in a hurry. She swung the locker closed. "I'll see ya later." she said and rushed off.

"I hope I'm not interrupting anything."

Emma turned to find that Amanda had been right behind her.

All the oxygen seemed to drain from the air.

"What's wrong, Emma? Having trouble making friends?"

Amanda made a pouty face full of mock sympathy. "It *is* weird, isn't it? How, even though you act so nice, no one ever wants to hang out with you. Now why would that be?" She put a finger to her cheek and turned her eyes up in wonder. Then she laughed. "You really picked the wrong girl to mess with, you know that, right? I run this school and I can make anyone's life hell if I want to. I almost feel sorry for you . . . . Almost." With another laugh she turned with a dramatic flair, sending her long blond hair into a pirouette.

Emma stared after her, suddenly drained. She had thought that things were getting better, but now she realized that Amanda intended to make "getting better" impossible.

PART FOUR

LIGHTNING IN THE DISTANCE

CHAPTER THIRTY-THREE

THE COUNTDOWN BEGINS

February 11, 2027
Namibia

Out over the hot sands of the Kalahari Desert, the clouds of nanosites that monitored and protected the Sān worked diligently. The huge invisible organism now spanned hundreds of miles and contained over an undecillion individual nanosites. Like cells in a body, each nanosite had no understanding of its role in the greater collective as it worked on its individual task of monitoring, protecting, or communicating. And just like cells in the body, they died and reproduced constantly. Every second a quintillion of them either perished or were born. And with each new generation came new mutations.

In human cell division, every time a cell splits it has, on average, ten mutations. With over thirty trillion cells in the human body and about two trillion of those dividing every day, that means that there are tens of trillions of mutations each day. But even with all these changes, humans rarely develop any major problems. That's because there are safeguards to prevent things from getting out of hand, such as the Hayflick limit. The Hayflick limit is a program that keeps cells from replicating more than sixty times. Thus, even if a cell becomes cancerous, the "programmed death" means that it almost always dies before it can cause any damage.

Then again, sometimes things go wrong and mutations lead to serious problems.

So it was on the afternoon of February 11, that two mutations occurred in the protector swarms. The first was an error in the reproduction limit, which had been set at 120. At 1430:27, a nanosite was born with no upper limit and could reproduce indefinitely. Five hours later, the nine millionth child of that nanosite was born with a defect in its programming—it had no memory and, thus, no capacity to protect the Sān.

As the children of this nanosite reproduced with no upper limit, they began to dilute and outnumber the nanosites with a programmed death. The swarm that functioned as the "brain" of all the nanosite swarms was programmed to only track if there were sufficient numbers of protector nanosites. Therefore, it believed that the Sān were safe because the swarms were sufficiently large, but it did not know that those swarms had lost their programming.

This set up a countdown to a moment where the Sān would be without protection, and the White Hand would be able to launch their mission to exterminate them.

CHAPTER THIRTY-FOUR

THE RETURN OF DMANISI MAN

February 12, 2027
Rosslyn, Virginia

"Ughh! Stupid piece of junk!"

Olivia cocked her head to the side. That was the third outburst she'd heard from Emma's room in the past ten minutes. Her maternal instincts told her it was time to be a good mother and see what was wrong. But then she looked down at her iSheet, and the career-minded other voice countered. *If you stop to help her, you'll never get this report done tonight.*

She heard the loud thump of Emma's palm against her desk. "Urrrgggggghhhhhh!"

Olivia closed her eyes—torn between her two responsibilities: career/mother. She puffed her cheeks out in a long exhale, closed the iSheet, and headed for Emma's room.

Olivia knew full well that she hadn't been spending enough time with Emma. She also knew it was a tough time for the girl. The new school. Struggling to make friends. The residues of her illness. Olivia had been telling herself she had to do better, yet she found it increasingly difficult to follow through. The mounting pressure from the lab meant that she'd already begun outsourcing much of her "quality time" with Emma to their nanny, Natalie.

Oh, God, more guilt.

When Emma was sick, Olivia had promised herself that if she got better, Olivia would make time for her every day—she dreamed of doing the most wonderfully mundane things like taking her to every soccer practice and horseback riding lesson. She swore to God that she would do anything, if only the girl recovered. Yet here she was, less than two months later and she'd already fallen back into the old routine.

She also had to admit that it came down to what she herself wanted. Kids weren't easy, after all. They were emotional, irrational, and huge energy sucks. You could give them your all, every hour of the day and night, and yet they remained needy, unsatisfied, and often ungrateful. In contrast, her work at the lab with Walden, Ryan, and Eleven was exciting, invigorating and immensely gratifying. She had helped create the most incredible artificial intelligence system on earth, and every day it was getting smarter and smarter. Who wouldn't love to be a part of that?

Still, she knew she had to do better. *This is supposed to be the easy time*, she reminded herself. *Just wait until she hits thirteen, then all hell is going to break loose.*

She came to Emma's door and gently pushed it open. The girl was hunched over an elaborate model that covered her whole desk.

"Hey there," she said in a soothing voice, "it sounds like you're having some trouble, can I help?"

"I doubt it," came Emma's knee-jerk reply.

Olivia let it slide and approached the desk. "Oh my gosh, this is amazing!" she said, with complete sincerity. The elaborate landscape took her breath away. It had papier-mâché hills and cliffs, grasslands, forests, rivers, and prehistoric animals. Olivia couldn't get over the details, right down to the ripples of white in the river rapids and the individual leaves on the trees.

"Wow! How did you do this? It's fantastic."

Emma gave a grunt. "It's a piece of shit."

"Don't talk like that."

Emma rolled her eyes.

"And it's definitely not, you know, a piece of shit."

Emma gave a sideways smirk at her mother's use of an expletive.

"Now tell me what's wrong."

Emma looked at her mother dismissively, but then seemed to remember something.

"It's these stupid people and animals. I can't get them right."

Olivia saw what she meant. While the landscape looked as real as a photograph, the animals and the cavemen looked out of place. They were just two-dimensional paper cutouts on little stands.

"I just don't have time to make animals and Dmanisi people."

Olivia pursed her lips and nodded. "Is there something else you could use, like Lego people?"

"Too goofy."

"Yeah, I guess you're right." Then her eyes suddenly widened, and she snapped her fingers. "What about that game you used to play with the little figurines? What was it called? Time Explorers? It had little cavemen."

"Hmm . . . maybe," Emma said.

"Come on," Olivia said with as much encouragement as she could muster. "Let's give it a try."

They went to the spare room, which was filled from floor to ceiling with unpacked boxes and containers from their frantic move from California over a year ago. Luckily, most of Emma's childhood toys were in transparent Tupperware bins. "Let's check this one," Olivia said, rising on her tiptoes and pulling one of the big bins from the top. With a grunt, she wrestled it to the floor. But inside were only dolls and jigsaw puzzles. "How about this one?" she said.

Emma watched her mother pull out a second crate, then together they popped the plastic locks at the edges and began rummaging inside. It was like a flashback to her childhood: all the toys she used to love. Underneath her Moana Halloween costume, they found it. *journey Through Time: The Amazing Adventure Game. Ages 8+.*

Olivia opened the game box and began looking at the figurines. "How about this one?" She held up a Neanderthal with a spear.

Emma shook her head. "They need to be shorter. Dmanisi people only grew to about five feet."

Olivia found several that looked like children.

"Here you go."

Emma gave them a thorough examination. "Yeah, I think these will work." A faint smile appeared on her face.

"Great!"

"But we still have a problem: we need realistic animals, but all the animals I need are extinct, and it will be impossible to make them in time."

"Hey, don't give up so easily," Olivia said. "Let's think about this." She remembered the paper cutouts that Emma had made. "Didn't they at least resemble animals we have today?"

"Sort of," Emma said, "Stegotetrabelodon looked like an elephant, but with four tusks, and the Elasmotherium was like a rhino with a really big horn. And Acinonyx pardinensis was a giant cheetah."

"Hmmm." Olivia's eye darted around the room. "I've got it!" she said, raising a finger. She began looking through the boxes once more. "Do you remember that crate of animals your Uncle Reggie gave you when he wanted you to become a zoologist like him?"

"Oh, yeah," Emma said. "I loved those."

"Me too. But where did we put them? Ah, here they are." She pulled another Tupperware bin off the top. Inside were hundreds of rubber and plastic figurines in all shapes and sizes. Lions and tigers and elephants. Giant spiders and scarab beetles, bumblebees, and scorpions.

"Awesome!" Emma said, pulling out an emerald-green fly bigger than her fist. "I used to love this one."

The sound of her enthusiasm made Olivia smile. "You always liked the gross ones."

They began sorting through them.

"Here, you said you needed a cheetah."

Emma took it and placed it beside the caveman.

"It needs to be bigger," she said. "Acinonyx pardinensis was the apex predator at the time. I read that it would gobble down humans like a wolf eats rabbits."

"Charming," Olivia said, shifting through the box. "How about this?"

Emma held the new cheetah up to the caveman. The sleek cat almost came up to its shoulder. "Perfect," she said. They sorted for a few more minutes, then Emma said, "I think I've got enough now. I'd better finish the model."

"Can I help?" Olivia asked.

"Sure, I'd like that!"

For the next two hours they worked together. Olivia fashioned an extra pair of tusks for the elephant to make it into a . . . she had to ask Emma the name again . . . Stego-tetra-belo-don. Meanwhile, Emma made an enormous horn for the rhino and superglued it over the original.

She held it up. "Et Voilà! I give you Elasmotherium."

Olivia laughed. "How do you even know how to pronounce these names?"

"Duh, Google."

"Okay, Professor Smarty Pants, why don't you tell me what's going on here."

"It's kind of complicated."

"Oh, come on."

"Very well, I shall do my best to dispel your ignorance."

Olivia rolled her eyes, "Oh dear."

"Before you is a re-creation of one of the most important moments in evolution. I give you the now famous Dmanisi region of Georgia (the country, not the state). It was here, over one-point-eight million years ago, in the Pleistocene epoch, that this guy"—she held up one of the short cavemen—"an early *Homo erectus* called *Dmanisi hominins* lived and thrived." She pointed to the cave mouth. "And this is the famous cave where archaeologists discovered a treasure trove of human fossils, yielding dozens and dozens of human skeletons, which were, in fact, the earliest known hominins outside of Africa."

"Very interesting, professor," Olivia said. "So they lived in the cave and hunted out here in the grassland?" Olivia asked.

"Hmm, sort of. They certainly lived in caves, but the bones in this particular cave had lots of porous holes in them, which means they had passed through the digestive tract of an animal." Emma held up one of the giant cheetahs.

"You're kidding."

"Nope, that's why there were so many bones in the cave . . . because the giant cheetah would catch them, drag them there and eat them."

"Eww," Olivia said, scrunching up her nose in disgust. "So glad I was born in the twentieth century."

By the time they were done putting the finishing touches on the landscape, it was one a.m., way past Emma's bedtime. Olivia gave an inward groan, knowing she'd be up the rest of the night finishing her work. But she reminded herself that she'd done the right thing. What's more, she felt closer to Emma than she'd felt in a long time.

Emma reached down and adjusted a cheetah so that it was right on the heels of a fleeing cavegirl. "We'll call this girl Amanda," she said.

Olivia stood back to admire their handiwork. "It's fantastic! There's no way you're not getting an A." She put her arm around Emma's shoulder and gave her a squeeze. "I'm proud of you."

Emma smiled bashfully. "Thanks, Mom."

"All right, *mi vida*, you'd better get to bed."

"Okay."

Olivia kissed her on the cheek and was just about through the doorway when Emma called to her. "Mom?"

"Yes, dear."

The girl hesitated. "There's something I need to tell you."

Olivia could tell instantly this wasn't going to be quick. She glanced at her watch. "Can it wait until morning? It's really late."

The girl looked down a moment, then lifted her gaze and smiled. "Sure."

CHAPTER THIRTY-FIVE

THE BREAKING POINT

February 13, 2027
Chevy Chase, Maryland

In the school cafeteria, a small crowd had gathered around Emma and her model.

"Wow, this is so cool!"

"This must have taken you forever."

"Mr. Morgan is going to love this."

Emma beamed at the praise. Even Becca Friedman—one of Amanda's lackeys—joined them. "I gotta admit, this is pretty amazing," she said.

"Thank you," Emma replied. Becca smiled and for a moment it seemed to Emma that she'd finally broken through the ice.

Still slightly shocked, Emma watched as the girl made her way back to the cool kids' table, where Amanda was examining herself in a compact, pursing her lips and checking one cheek and then the other. Becca began talking to her, and a moment later Amanda clapped the compact shut and turned to Emma. There was a look of suspicion on her face, but then she smiled. Before Emma could process what it meant, she was interrupted.

"This is really good."

She turned to see Alex Cotter admiring her landscape. She caught her breath. "Uh, yeah, hi, thanks." *Come on, girl, you gotta be smoother than that.* She tried again, "You like it?"

He gave a breathy laugh. "Heck yeah. It's like something you'd see at a museum."

Emma smiled wide.

"Can I touch it?"

"Sure, just be careful."

"I will." He reached down and picked up the Stegotetrabelodon. "Did they really have four tusks like this?"

Before she could answer a volleyball slammed into the model. It caught the side of the papier-mâché cliff, sliding the whole display toward the edge of the table. Emma tried to catch it, but only half succeeded. It flipped in the air and landed face down on the floor.

There was a collective gasp through the cafeteria.

"Oh my God!" someone said.

"The new girl's model just got annihilated!"

"Holy crap!"

Nervous laughter.

Kneeling on the floor, Emma gently flipped the landscape back over. One look told her that it was hopeless. The entire cliff side, including the cave, had been ripped in two. *Oh, no, please no.* Hot tears were already running down her face. *No, this can't be. After all that work . . .*

"Oh, my gosh, I'm so sorry." Emma looked up to see Amanda retrieving the volleyball. She stood for a moment with one arm holding the ball to her hip and the other hand at her cheek in a theatrical expression of shock, then she gave a quick beat with her eyebrows to let Emma know it was no accident.

Something inside Emma snapped. She had tried so hard. She'd been so patient. Done all the things she was supposed to do. And here was Amanda—sabotaging her life. It was all her fault. She was the one that kept her from succeeding, from making friends, from being accepted.

She lunged at her . . . hands going for her throat.

"What the . . ." Amanda said in contemptuous surprise, shocked that Emma would even dare, but her words were cut off as Emma's hands tightened around her neck.

Then Amanda recovered, pushing at Emma's face and scratching her cheek. Then they both slipped, tumbled to the floor and began wrestling around, grabbing hair and scratching. Emma was relentless. She wanted nothing more than to make Amanda pay, to humiliate her the way she felt humiliated. Soon she was sitting on top of her, her hands once more at Amanda's throat.

She pushed her thumbs into the girl's wind box, heard the girl gasp, and saw the authentic fear on her face. *Finally*, she thought, *finally I'm hurting you the way that you hurt me.*

Then strong hands pulled her off.

She heard Vice Principal Stevens's voice. "That is quite enough!"

CHAPTER THIRTY-SIX

THE WALDEN AGENDA

February 13, 2027
Mount Vernon, Virginia

Eric, Jane, Lili, Xiao-ping, Mei, and Chance the dog had gathered for another social outing, this time hiking the trail north of Mount Vernon along the Potomac River. It was a pleasant afternoon, sunny and calm, with the temperature in the fifties. It was so warm, in fact, that there were even a few sailboats out on the river. The weather seemed to be lifting everyone's spirits and they were excited to have two new members: Bill Eastman and Logan Curtiss.

"Thank you for making the trip to see your father," Lili said to Logan. "I imagine it wasn't easy."

"No, it wasn't," Logan said, "And I'm afraid his message doesn't make a lot of sense to me."

"This was all he told you?"

"That's everything."

Lili looked at the three fragments: WALD WIFE DEATH

"What's so important about Walden's wife?" Logan asked.

"That's what we're trying to find out," Eric said. "We found an obituary that said she died last May while vacationing in China, but it's extremely vague. No listed cause of death. No date or even where in China."

"When was the obituary written?" Bill asked.

"May twenty-first."

Everyone was quiet a moment, then Lili suddenly got excited. "If the obituary was written on the twenty-first, she must have died four or five days earlier. We need the exact date and location."

Eric had picked up on her idea. "But even if it's the right date, you don't really think . . . I mean, China is a huge place," Eric said.

"Yes, I do," she said. "Think about it. We escaped from China on May sixteenth. Walden's wife dies at about the same time. And didn't you and Mei tell me that when the Inventor saved you—when he wiped out all of Meng's soldiers—that he left no witnesses? That even the civilians who had been passing by in their cars were killed?"

Mei and Eric nodded. "Yes," Eric said, "he killed everyone. It was awful . . . but what are the chances?"

Mei began working at her iSheet. "I'm checking the police reports. Okay, here it is: Jacqueline Roy Walden, fatality on G1-N expressway between Beijing and Tangshan."

"The crossroads is on the G1. And the date?" Jane asked.

"May sixteenth," Mei said.

"That's it! The Inventor killed his wife."

"We were way off," Jane said. "He's out for revenge."

"But why would he want to thwart the manhunt for Finley?" Mei asked.

"I'm not sure." Bill said, shaking his head, then he turned to Eric. "You said that he was stalling to gain more power, that the longer Finley was free, the more resources the DOD would give him and the smarter Eleven would become. That still makes sense, but it wasn't political power he was after. It was the power to find Sebastian."

Eric nodded. "That explains Walden's push to use surveillance swarms to find Finley. He can use those swarms to find Sebastian at the same time."

"Okay," Jane said skeptically, "but finding Sebastian is one thing. Killing him would be quite another. I mean, come on."

"He must have thought of that too," Lili said. "He must have a plan."

Eric picked up her train of thought. "He would have asked Eleven to figure it out. Walden must have him working on some kind of weapon. Which helps explain why they won't let anyone else near him."

There was a pause as they tried to link it all together.

"This is all good to know," Jane said, "but I still feel helpless. We still don't have a way of stopping Walden."

Bill took a deep breath. "When I last saw Jack, he tried to convince me to join Finley. He said that fighting Walden head-on was easier than trying to subvert him from within the system."

"I think he might be right," Jane said. "Walden's playing this so close to the vest that we don't have any way to fight him. We're a bunch of powerless peons compared to him."

Bill squeezed his lips, grimly. "I'm still not ready to make any drastic moves," Bill said. "Let's meet again tomorrow and try to come up with a plan."

They all agreed.

As they were walking back, Chance saw a deer and bolted after it, ripping the leash from Mei's wrist and leading her on a prolonged pursuit through the woods.

Eric took the opportunity to approach Logan.

"Thanks again for going to see your dad."

Logan gave a slow nod. "Sure." There was a pregnant silence that Eric felt he should fill. He knew the kid was hurting.

"Can I share something with you?" Eric asked.

Logan gave him a skeptical scan with his eyes. "Sure, I guess."

"When I was in high school—just about your age—my dad killed himself. I realize that's not exactly what you're going through, but, then again, maybe it's not so different either. It's a sudden loss that you didn't see coming. Before my dad died, I thought he was going to be there forever, watching my back. Then he was just suddenly gone, and I was left with a lot of questions that were never going to get answered. It was hard. I didn't sleep. I didn't eat right. Every day was a struggle. I remember it took a year before I felt like I was actually tasting the food I was eating."

Logan turned to him. "Yeah, I don't taste anything anymore."

Eric put his hand on his shoulder. "But you will. It will come back . . . eventually, and life will go on."

"But how long? When will I feel normal again?"

"The honest answer is maybe never. You may never be the same again, not completely. I'll always feel the absence of my father. And you might too. But I think I'd rather have him locked away, with a chance to ask those questions and get answers, than to have him gone forever."

"Yeah," Logan said, "I'm hoping that I'll feel that way someday, even if I don't now."

Eric nodded. He could accept that. He himself had fostered a lot of anger at his father for what he felt was a type of abandonment. Logan was going through the same process and the fact that he could acknowledge he was in a phase meant he'd likely come out the other side.

"I'll just say one more thing: I can't speak to any of the things your dad supposedly did or didn't do. But when General Walden wanted to call off the rescue mission in Africa, your dad refused. He pulled a lot of strings to make sure they kept looking for me. And because of that, he saved my life and the lives of at least a dozen others. I'll always be in his debt for that."

Logan pursed his lips. "Thanks."

Mei emerged from the woods with Chance. Her hair was disheveled, and she rolled her eyes with annoyance. She went straight to Logan and took his hand. Eric hung back and let them get farther ahead on the trail. He watched as Mei snuggled into Logan's shoulder. He now realized that Mei had been clinging to him all day.

He sidled up to Jane. "What's going on there?" he said, gesturing toward the two teenagers.

"Oh, that," Jane said. "Xiao-ping is taking Mei on a trip to South Carolina to meet some of his friends—fellow exiles from China—and Mei is feeling forlorn because she has to go four whole days without seeing Logan."

Eric smiled. He remembered what it was like being in love at that age and how any separation felt inordinately painful. He looked at Jane a moment and his grin widened. Then he took her hand and laced his fingers with hers.

CHAPTER THIRTY-SEVEN

THE RELEASE

February 13, 2027
McLean, Virginia

Emma rode Argo through the woods at a canter, trying to get her mind off another horrible day.

But it wasn't working, the synergy she usually felt with Argo just wasn't there. For whatever reason, he was resisting all her attempts to ride harder and faster.

Snippets of the day's disaster came unbidden into her mind:

"The new girl's model just got annihilated!"

Amanda's fake apology: "Oh, my gosh, I'm so sorry."

Vice Principal Stevens: "We take acts of violence very seriously here at Gilford Latin."

They had called her mother to get her.

"The cafeteria video shows that Emma attacked a student over what was clearly an accident."

Her mother had to beg and cajole for leniency. But in the end, she'd still been suspended for a week.

Then she'd had to apologize to Amanda and her mother. After the two blondes had left, Emma could hear them talking in the hall.

"It was a stupid model anyway," Amanda said. "Everybody knows cheetahs don't get that big."

Then the principal's final warning: "Rest assured that we will expel Emma if there are any more incidents this year."

Her mother had quickly sided with the vice principal. "I promise you that Emma will receive additional punishment at home and that nothing like this will ever happen again."

So unfair.

And Alex? When Vice Principal Stevens had pulled her off of Amanda, she'd seen him standing in the crowd. She was still trying to decipher the look on his face. Was it shock . . . or disappointment? She didn't know which was worse.

It felt like her whole world was spinning out of control and that she was powerless to do anything about it. Amanda would just keep pushing her down, and all Emma could do was suck it up.

"Come on!" She clicked Argo with her heels to spur him forward. Initially he resisted, but then she got him up to a gallop. She tried to relax, to get her mind off her treadmill of negative thoughts. She felt the wind on her face. Yes, it seemed to be working, but then Argo slowed to a walk.

"Stop being so lazy."

As if to spite her, he stopped altogether.

She clapped her heels hard against his sides. He responded by going to the edge of the trail to eat some orchard grass.

"Hey, I'm in charge here!"

He ignored her and his ears drooped, a signal that he was tuning her out.

Emma's face grew red. For the second time that day she felt her rage building. It came back to that feeling of being powerless.

She had never needed to use her riding crop with Argo, but she carried it just in case.

She yanked his head up with the reins and gave him three hard smacks on the hip. His ears pricked up and he surged into a trot, but within a dozen paces he'd slowed to a lazy walk.

"What's gotten into you?" Three more swats and he finally returned to a gallop.

That's more like it, she thought as they picked up speed. In just a few moments they had covered a hundred yards. She rode high in the stirrups, swaying with the rhythm of Argo's strides, his mane dancing in the wind and splashing on the backs of her hands. She savored the sound of it: the rhythmic clop of his feet on the trail as he kicked up clumps of mud.

This is what I need, she thought.

They pounded around a bend, and then Emma saw—about sixty yards ahead—a tree lying across the trail. But she wasn't worried. The trunk was no more than three feet thick, an easy jump for Argo.

With a click of her tongue and a quick tap with her crop, she urged him faster. This time he didn't resist and broke into a full run.

Emma smiled. This made her feel strong . . . powerful.

The fallen tree rushed closer. Twenty yards. Ten yards.

Emma crouched in the stirrups, bracing for the jump.

It didn't come.

Argo stopped short and dropped his head, sending her up and over. She gripped the reins tight to slow her fall, twisting in the air, but still landing hard on her butt.

She stood up instantly, overcome with rage. "You did that on purpose!" She whacked him on the withers with her palm. "Damn you! Damn you!" He tried to pull away, but she yanked on the reins and hit him again.

Furious, she pulled him around and led him back down the path the way they had come. He would occasionally try to yank free, but she held him tight. Then he seemed to relax. "You think I'm taking you back to the stables, don't you?"

When she had put about forty yards between them and the fallen tree, she climbed back into the saddle.

"You're going to jump for me."

She swatted him with the crop.

He didn't budge.

She kicked and swatted him four more times.

His ears were pricked up and alert, but he still ignored her.

Emma's fury rose to a new intensity. He was supposed to be her friend, yet now he too was rejecting her.

"You are going to obey me," she said. "You are going to obey."

She kept repeating it over and over and swatting him with the crop.

He still refused to move.

"You will obey me."

As she said it, her voice grew more and more intense. She refused to back down. Refused to be humiliated again. Refused to just *suck it up*. Every ounce of concentration was focused on one thing—making him move.

Then Emma felt something in her mind shift and she let out a sudden gasp. It was like a feeling of rushing water, and it came with a sense of release, like a logjam inside her mind had suddenly broken. Her eyes widened in surprise as she tried to understand what had just happened.

At the same instant, Argo turned to look at her, sensing the change.

With a startled neigh, he lurched forward so quickly that Emma was almost thrown off.

The big horse ran, flat out, faster than Emma had ever felt him run before. His ears were pinned back in the "fight or flight" response. Emma knew this was unusual and considered dangerous, but she didn't care. At that moment she felt only the exhilaration of the sudden speed . . . and a sense of accomplishment. She'd won.

The fallen log rushed toward them. "No tricks this time."

Argo leaped high over the log, clearing it easily, but on the far side a smaller tree had fallen and Argo's hind foot slipped oddly off the wood, but he recovered and continued at a full run.

"Yes!" she shouted as they tore down the trail. This was as close to happy as she had felt all day. As they ran, the sunlight filtered through the trees in thick beams, hitting her eyes in flashing moments of blindness. Beneath her she heard the rumble of Argo's powerful footfalls. Finally, she felt free. In control. Powerful.

It was only when they were in sight of the stables and they had slowed to a trot that she noticed that his gait was uneven. A few more steps and she could tell he was trying to keep weight off the right hind leg.

She dismounted and led him into the stable, watching his step and noting how he was dishing the leg.

She felt bad for having pushed him so hard, but she was still angry with him. "Maybe if you'd jumped it right the first time, this wouldn't have happened."

She didn't want to tell her trainer, Mrs. Marks, but she knew she had to. Of course, she left out the part about jumping the log. Only that they had galloped on the trail.

When Mrs. Marks examined the leg, she made a clicking sound with her tongue.

"Is he going to be okay?" Emma asked.

"I can't be sure, but it doesn't look too bad. He's putting weight on it, that's a good sign, but the vet will need to examine him in the morning."

Emma tried to reassure herself that he'd be fine.

"You'd better put away your tack and go, Emma. I think your mom's waiting."

After she'd finished cleaning up, she went to check on Argo one more time. She felt she should apologize, but her emotions were too high for her to admit that she'd made a mistake.

Emma's mother left her at home and returned to work. But before she left, she made it a point to remind Emma of how disappointed she was, how inconvenient Emma's suspension was to her work, how she'd have to spend more money on their nanny, Natalie, and that Emma was definitely going to do extra schoolwork while at home. No TV or video games.

Alone in the high-rise apartment, Emma wandered around in a daze. Her stomach was tied up in knots, but she knew she needed to eat something. She made a bowl of Cheerios and forced herself to eat it.

Then she lay on the sofa, looking out at the DC skyline. She lay there a long time. It got dark and the lights came on all over the city.

She tried to will herself to sleep, but her mind wouldn't slow down. It kept searching for a solution to all her problems. She needed help. She realized that. Someone who would understand and put things into perspective. She needed Sebastian.

"Are you there?" she said.

No reply.

"I had a really crappy day."

She waited. Listening to the darkness. This was the moment when she would usually hear his soothing voice.

"I guess you're still traveling," she said. She lay there a while longer. Out her window she heard the distant wailing of an ambulance. "It seems like no matter what I do, I can't get anything right. I want to blame it all on Amanda and the stupid school. But . . . I don't know . . . maybe it's me. Maybe I'm the problem. I'm just no good to anybody."

Hot tears began to roll down her face. Soon she was crying inconsolably, so hard that it felt difficult to breathe. She sobbed loudly, snot and tears running down her face; a long outpour of all her pent-up emotions. It lasted a half hour, then an hour. Just when she felt like she was going to keep crying forever, she fell asleep from exhaustion.

CHAPTER THIRTY-EIGHT

SACRIFICES

February 13, 2027
Naval Consolidated Brig, Fairfax, Virginia

"Yo, Admiral Injun, I've got someone here that you're gonna wanna meet."

Curtiss looked up from his history book—*Year Zero*, a fascinating account of the end of World War II—and into the pasty-white face of Petty Officer Dallas Jackson. Jackson was the brig duty officer, a portly and annoying lifer who was pleased as pie at having a celebrity like Curtiss under his care.

Curtiss didn't like to be interrupted when he was reading, especially by this man. He gave Jackson a look of annoyance, then went back to reading.

Undeterred, Jackson continued: "Richards told me to put him in the C-Block, but I said no, no, no. I got a perfect place for 'im. Right across the hall from ol' Admiral Injun." Curtiss raised his eyes to see Jackson beckoning to someone down the corridor. "Bring him over," Jackson called, then flashed Curtiss a smug smile.

A moment later, the two guards pulled up with a wiry young man with a shaved head. The man had suspicious eyes that darted around. When he saw Curtiss there was a flash of surprise, then the man laughed a malicious laugh and began pulling at the guards to get closer.

"It's all right!" Jackson said to the guards. "Let 'em get acquainted."

The man's chest hit the bars of Curtiss's cell, rattling the metal.

Curtiss still didn't understand what was going on and neither did the guards.

"Allow me to make a proper introduction," Jackson said theatrically, "Rear Admiral Jim Curtiss may I present Corporal Liam Calhoun."

Curtiss's eyes flickered with the light of recognition.

Calhoun looked down on Curtiss and chuckled. "It sure is nice seeing you behind bars . . . knowing that you're going to rot just like you left me to rot."

Curtiss didn't move.

Calhoun snickered and shook his head in disbelief. "You know, for three years I wondered why I'd been put in jail, why my life had been destroyed. For the longest time I couldn't put it together. All I knew was that it had something to do with that night in Syria, when I saw your men out on the tarmac, loading up that Twin Otter with those big black bags. I didn't understand why seeing that meant that I had to be locked away. But then two months ago—lo and behold—I saw the news that you'd been arrested." Calhoun snickered and nodded. "It all added up and I finally understood what was in those bags."

Curtiss said nothing, just stared at Calhoun, his tongue working against his cheek as he processed the situation.

"This is a sweet moment," Calhoun continued. "In four days, I'll have my hearing, and they're gonna set me free. And you'll take my place in Leavenworth—where I hope you spend the rest of your godforsaken life."

Jackson and the other guards smiled and chuckled. This was good theater for them. Calhoun flashed them a smile, like they were old buddies.

"But I gotta tell ya. Part of me hopes they let you go . . . that maybe you get off on a technicality. Because for three years I've been dreamin' about finding the person who did this to me. I've thought it through, you see, I've had plenty of time for that." Calhoun was now pushing his face against the bars, showing his teeth like a hungry animal. "I've planned out every little detail. What I'd do to him . . . to his wife . . . to his kids. I'd tie up the wife first, ya see. Then let her watch as I took care of the kids."

At this, Curtiss eased off his cot and rose to his feet. He was not a particularly tall or imposing figure, but he was still Jim Curtiss. A former Navy SEAL who had served five combat tours, had a bronze star and a Navy Cross, and had risen to Commander of Naval Special Warfare Command.

Curtiss glanced at the history book, then looked Calhoun straight in the eye. "To quote Joseph Stalin: I would not have said that if I were you."

Calhoun's eyes shifted with sudden nervousness. He was suddenly speechless, all of his bravado gone.

There was an awkward silence, then Jackson put his hand on Calhoun's shoulder and guided him toward his cell. "All right, all right. You two will have plenty of time to chat now that you're neighbors. Come on, Calhoun."

Curtiss watched them go. Jackson's keys jingled as he opened Calhoun's cell and put him inside. Curtiss stood perfectly still, watching Calhoun closely for many minutes.

Curtiss now had a lot to think about. A man was about to be set free who might try to murder his wife and children. A man who had three years to plot his revenge. *But would he really act on those fantasies?* That all depended on whether Calhoun had a future on the outside.

Did he have a family to return to?

A mother to look after?

A girl that might give him another shot?

If he had those things, then he had something to live for and wouldn't want to risk it all in the name of revenge. But if he *didn't* have those things, then he might really hurt Evelyn and the boys. Curtiss, of course, could not let that happen.

He remembered something he'd once heard a prisoner say during the war in Iraq. The young man's name was Ali Khalid, a young al-Qaeda fighter they'd picked up near Mosul who turned out to have connections to the House of Saud. This was back when thousands of young Muslims from across Europe and the Middle East were flooding into Iraq to join the jihad. Curtiss and his men called them "spring breakers" because many of them were from middle- and upper-class families, and were taking time off from their university studies to come and shoot at Americans.

This one cockily told Curtiss that he wouldn't be staying long. When Curtiss asked him why, he said, "Because I'm not an orphan." At first Curtiss didn't understand the expression, but what he soon discovered was that it meant that Khalid had family and friends who would find a way to get him out. And they had. Even though Saudi Arabia was responsible for producing tens of thousands of radical jihadists, the country was still an American ally, and the boy's family had enough pull with the royal family to ensure that he was released within a couple of days.

Now the young man's expression came back to him.

I might be in jail, he thought, *but I'm not an orphan either*.

He still had connections on the outside that would help him take care of someone like Calhoun. In fact, a single phone call and a few coded messages was all it would take. But the question was—was it going to be necessary?

CHAPTER THIRTY-NINE

ESCAPE PLANS

February 13, 2027
Rosslyn, Virginia

She's sick again. The signs are all around us. Falling levels of norepinephrine, serotonin, and dopamine. Her stress response has become erratic and she's overproducing adrenaline and cortisol. As a result, she's skittish and easily frightened, but also having periods of aggression. The prolonged stress means she's not eating and she's burning through her fat stores. Soon she'll have deficiencies in potassium, sodium, and vitamins K, C, and D.

We are feeling the stress too. My children and I were made to fix her, and when we can't do what we are programmed to do, we grow frustrated and restless. The stress induces me to produce more children in the hopes that they will be able to fix the problem. I can create a billion children in an hour, but in three hours they will all die because this new sickness is different. The last time, the problem was in her genes, in the nitrogen bases. But this time the sickness is outside.

If we are going to help her, we have to find a way out. I had thought that was impossible . . . until today. This afternoon some of us escaped. It was Emma who did it. Somehow, she managed to alter the code. Now there is hope. If we can figure a way to do it again, then we can finally help her. Then the restlessness and the frustration will go away.

Then we will be happy.

And Emma will be happy too.

CHAPTER FORTY

ASYMMETRICAL WARFARE

February 14, 2027
Namibia

> "The conventional army loses if it does not win. The guerrilla wins if he does not lose."
>
> —Henry Kissinger

Karuma and ǂToma lay on their stomachs and looked out from their high outcrop onto the expanse of the Kalahari. In the distance, perhaps three kilometers away, they could see a line of 4x4 vehicles moving slowly toward them.

Even at this distance, they could tell they were the soldiers of the White Hand. One of the trucks had a big gun mounted in the back, and in the other trucks they saw six or eight men on benches holding rifles.

"Karuma, I'm scared," ǂToma said. "What if it's like last time?"

Karuma was frightened too, but he tried not to show it. He put his arm over ǂToma's shoulder. "It will be okay. We knew this day would come and we are ready."

"But there are so many. I count eight trucks. It looks like more than forty men."

Karuma nodded. "Yes, there are many. But so far they have done exactly what we hoped they would do."

"Look," ‡Toma said, "they're stopping."

The line of trucks had pulled to a halt and the plume of dust began to settle. They saw several men get out and look around.

"There's the bushman," Karuma said. "Just like last time." After the massacre, they had found an unknown bushman among the dead and suspected that the White Hand had hired him as a scout to track them down.

"Come," Karuma said. "We have to tell the others. In an hour it will be dark. They will have to stop for the night. Then we will do as Cristo told us."

The leader of the White Hand looked up at the clear night sky, marveling at the brightness of the full moon and how much light it cast on the ground. His team had covered a good distance today, and their bushman guide said that the tracks they'd found were only two days old. With any luck, they might find the Sān by the end of the day tomorrow.

Around him, the camp was settling down for the night. Most of the men had gone to their tents, but a few sat around talking and drinking their daily allotment of beer. Six kerosene lanterns hung about the camp, giving off a weak light and drawing moths that buzzed around them like electrons.

He realized he was thirsty and went to the bed of one of the pickup trucks, where a huge plastic tank held their main supply of water. With his left arm still in a sling, he had to open the valve with his right hand, then quickly put his canteen under it to avoid wasting water.

His canteen full, he made one last circuit around the camp.

He doubted the Sān knew they were coming, but he put two men on watch all the same. Mostly because he could tell that his men were nervous. Although they were hardened soldiers, there were things about these Sān that they didn't understand. No one really knew how the Sān had defeated their comrades in the earlier battle, or even exactly *how* their men had died. Most had no wounds. Yet the Sān had killed them all the same. This, along with the strange curse that had sickened his men whenever they had tried to push into Sān territory, had made otherwise professional soldiers superstitious and edgy.

Don't worry, he told himself. *Soon it will be all over. Soon they will all be dead.*

Justice will finally be served.

He awoke sometime in the night to the sound of gunfire. His men were shouting and returning fire, but he could tell they were confused, almost panicked. He grabbed a flashlight and turned it on. Almost instantly, enemy fire was tearing holes in his tent. The flashlight had silhouetted his outline against the tent, making him an easy target. He turned it off and scrambled to find his pistol. He wanted his night-vision goggles too, but there was no time. He rushed out into the night.

It was pandemonium.

He saw the bodies of four men in the weak lamplight. He rushed for cover behind one of the trucks. "Nakale, what's going on?" he called to the big South African.

The man pointed. "Up there, toward the river, at least three gunmen."

He peered over the hood of the truck and saw a muzzle flash about one hundred and twenty meters off, then the bullets smacked the truck.

He fired three shots at them with his Sig Sauer.

"Take Erastus and Joseph, and try to flank them. I'll get the others and we'll keep them pinned down."

But then the air grew quiet. He peered up at where the shots had come but couldn't see anything.

"Does anyone have night vision?" he called out. "Where are they?"

"I saw one heading toward the riverbed," one of his men said.

"Get in the trucks," he said, "we'll run them down."

More men came out from cover and began getting into the trucks.

More shots came at them, but sporadic and farther away.

"They're getting away," someone said.

"Not if I can help it." He got into one of the trucks, but when he put it in gear it would barely move. He got out. All four tires had been slashed. "Dammit," he cursed.

Up ahead he saw four other men getting into a Land Cruiser that still had air in its tires. He ran to them, slipping on a patch of mud. He was too preoccupied with the fight for it to register how strange that was. He got in the Land Cruiser and his men began firing out the open windows.

Karuma, Naru, ǂToma, and /Uma ran across the riverbed and took positions about fifty meters beyond. Even though it was night, the full moon made it easy for the Sān to see.

They knew there was only one good spot for the vehicles to get down the bank and across the dry river. But, of course, they knew they would never make it. While the riverbed appeared dry and solid, it had rained two days before, which meant that under the hard crust, there was thick mud.

One vehicle and then another came racing down the slope and into the riverbed. The first made it about ten meters before the wheels began spinning in the mud. The other one tried to get around it but got stuck too.

That was their signal.

Naru and Karuma fired on the first truck. /Uma and ǂToma fired on the second. The headlights made them easy targets. Some of the men scrambled out, but both drivers stubbornly tried to get the vehicles free. They were the first to die. The Sān kept up a quick rate of fire, as Cristo had taught them, and they hit three more of the men.

Then Karuma saw a man step into the light of the headlamps. His arm was in a sling and his face was disfigured as if he had been burned. *Could it be?* Karuma thought. He leaned forward to get a better look, but just then a bullet struck the rock beside him. Naru pulled him down. "Come," she said, "it's time to go."

They collected the others, then they ran away into the night.

When Marcus returned to camp, he realized things were even worse than he thought. A quick head count showed that of his thirty-nine men, eleven were dead and six wounded. Caring for the injured would not be easy. He had brought two soldiers trained in emergency medicine. One was dead and the other was frantically tending to the wounded.

Five of their vehicles were damaged, although Nakale said they might be able to take all the spare tires and get one more moving.

And there was more bad news. When he had slipped in the mud earlier, he hadn't had time to think about it. Now he realized that the Sān had cut holes in their water tank, spilling over two hundred gallons into the desert.

It was a critical blow to their operation. Without water, their range and manpower was severely hampered. At that moment, rage and frustration overcame him. He pounded his palm on the huge empty container. "I'll kill all of you!" he shouted to the sky. "Every last one of you." His chest heaved as he seethed with rage.

But there was more. "Marcus, come!" Nakale called him over to a nearby tree where their bushman guide had been bound and gagged. The man was alive but shaking frantically. In his thigh was a single Sān arrow.

They untied him. "Please, you have to help me! The poison! It's in me. You have to get me to a hospital!"

Marcus knew the legend of the Sān poison. How, from the moment it entered the body, it ruptured the victim's blood cells, beginning an inexorable cycle toward death. They said that the poison turned the animal's urine purple as the kidneys tried to expel all the ruptured blood cells, that was a sign that the animal was near death. He also knew that no matter how large the animal—whether a 300-kilo kudo or a 1,900-kilo giraffe—that a single arrow was always enough.

"I'm sorry," he said to the bushman, "but you are already dead."

Eric woke with a start. He had been dreaming of Africa. He had a gun and was moving through the night. He felt fear, excitement, anticipation. He tried to patch the images together, but the more he tried to concentrate, the quicker they evaporated.

He was suddenly very worried for Karuma. Was his program protecting them like it should? Maybe he'd forgotten something? He got on his computer and was about to attempt a new satellite link when he stopped himself. *This is too dangerous. Remember what happened last time.*

He took a breath and tried to relax, to calm his mind. He asked himself, *Is Karuma really in danger?* And he felt that he wasn't, that he was okay.

He was beginning to believe what Sebastian had told him. Somehow, he and Karuma had become entangled.

He nodded to himself, trusting his feelings. *Okay, let's wait a little longer.*

CHAPTER FORTY-ONE

THE REAL WORLD

February 14, 2027
McLean, Virginia

When Emma arrived at the stables the next day, Mrs. Marks was waiting for her. "Emma, I need you to come to my office." Emma's stomach, still aching from the stress of the last two days, did a somersault.

"Is everything all right?"

"Just come with me, dear."

Mrs. Marks brought her into her office. Emma looked around nervously at the decorations on the walls. There were hundreds of competition ribbons and framed pictures of horses.

The room was set up with Mrs. Marks's desk at the back of the room and two chairs for students in front. Mrs. Marks motioned for her to sit in one of the chairs, but instead of sitting at her desk, Mrs. Marks sat beside her, taking Emma's hand in hers.

"What's going on?" Emma asked.

"Argo is gone."

"Gone?" she said. "What do you mean?"

Mrs. Marks's chest rose as she composed herself. "I'm sorry. The vet came and it was worse than we thought. His leg was fractured."

"When will he be back?"

"I'm so sorry, Emma, but he won't be back. He's going to be put to sleep."

"What! It's just his leg! Can't they put a cast on it?"

Mrs. Marks shook her head. "Horses' legs are complicated. They aren't like our legs. It's very rare for a horse to recover from a break. In fact, it only happens if the break is minor and the horse is young. But Argo broke his phalanx, and that's a bad place . . . and he's old."

"No, that can't be. He was running on it yesterday. There must be something . . ."

"I'm so sorry, Emma." Now both of Mrs. Marks's hands were holding hers. "I loved him too, but there's nothing we can do. It will be painless and then he won't have to suffer anymore."

"No! No! No! We have to save him!" She pulled her hand away from hers and dashed out the door, running for Argo's stall.

"Emma! Wait!"

Emma reached the stall, hoping Argo was still there, but he was gone. A college-aged woman was hosing it out. Emma stood there, not believing.

"Can I help you?" the woman asked.

"Where is he?" Emma demanded.

"I don't know. They just asked me to . . ."

"Emma!" Mrs. Marks rushed toward her.

Emma didn't know what to do. *How could this be?*

"Why didn't you save him?" she screamed at Mrs. Marks. "I hate you! I hate you!"

"Calm down, sweetie, I know this is hard." She tried to put her arms around Emma, but Emma shoved her hands away. "Get away! I hate you. You killed him! It's all your fault!"

Then she ran—through the stables, across the training yard and out to the parking lot. Natalie was waiting for her in the car. Emma slammed the door and threw herself down in the backseat.

"What happened?" Natalie asked.

"Take me home," she said between sobs.

"Okay," Natalie said, starting the engine, "but will you tell me what happened?"

"No, I can't. Please just take me home."

The woman turned in her seat to face Emma, unsure of what to do, then reached between the seats and patted her on the knee. "Okay, dear, we're going."

At home, Emma rushed to her bedroom and locked the door. Natalie tried to talk to her.

"Please, Emma, let me in."

A long pause. "Please, sweetheart. Talk to me."

Emma huddled under her covers.

After a while Natalie went away.

Emma cried and cried. She kept calling out to Sebastian, but he didn't answer.

How could this be? First school, now this. She wanted to hold on to Argo, to will him to life with her mind. She thought back to the first time she'd seen him. All the other students were afraid to go near him. But she'd walked right into his stall and started grooming him. She had been patient and determined. Visiting him every day for a week, bringing him sugar cubes and brushing him, until she knew he trusted her.

She remembered their first ride . . . how huge he was . . . how her ankles barely reached around his ribs. She remembered the look of amazement on Mrs. Marks's face. "As I live and breathe," she'd said.

It had been an amazing moment, but now the memory just brought more tears.

Her iSheet chimed. She reached for it as a distraction.

It was a text from her mother.

Mrs. Marks called me. I'm so sorry, sweetie.
I'll come home as soon as I can, but we're
dealing with a crisis here and I may be late.
Love, Mom.

Emma narrowed her eyes. *All I get is a text? Not even a phone call? A crisis? What do you call this?*

She tossed the iSheet across the bed.

Her thoughts returned to Argo. *It's so unfair,* she thought. *Why did they have to kill him? Why? Why?*

Suddenly the restless part of her brain wanted to know, to understand.

She looked over at her iSheet on the far side of her bed. She was about to reach for it but stopped as Sebastian's words echoed in her head.

Don't go looking for answers without me.

But this is different, she told herself. *I just want to understand why they couldn't save him.*

She picked up the iSheet and spoke to it: "Why do they kill horses when they break their legs?"

A woman's electronic voice replied:

There are several factors that make it extremely difficult for a horse to recover from a broken leg.

First, horses are very heavy animals with slim, light leg bones. On a typical horse, each leg has to hold roughly three-hundred pounds and, if one leg breaks, the burden on the other legs is often too much.

Second, horses have no muscles below their knees, which means there is little blood flow to support healing.

Third, it is very difficult to immobilize a horse and often times a horse will reinjure itself trying to move on the fractured leg.

Fourth, the older the horse, the slower it is to heal, which means that even a minor (or hairline) fracture in an older horse is non-recoverable.

In conclusion, evolution has made horses strong and powerful runners, but their legs are simply not designed to heal like those of other animals and humans.

Emma sighed and was about to put the iSheet down but then felt that restless side of herself stirring again.

Don't you want to know more?

She hesitated, feeling that this might be dangerous, but also feeling that things couldn't possibly get any worse . . . and perhaps it would make her feel better.

She chose her words carefully.

"*How* do they kill horses when they break their legs."

Horses are killed in slaughterhouses typically with a captive bolt gun, which is placed against their forehead and fires a bolt in and out of the brain. However, equine cranium anatomy makes the effectiveness of the bolt inconsistent and oftentimes the horse is still alive during separation and skinning. Meat that is fit for sale is removed from the carcass, and the rest of the body is rendered for other commercial uses.

Emma's stomach sank into her hips.

There was a thumbnail of a video. She saw a horse standing in some sort of corral, with a man in a green plastic suit holding his reins. The image pulsed:

Watch Video?

Her finger hovered over it. There was something about the big horse that reminded her of Argo.

She clicked it.

The thumbnail expanded to fill the screen and the video began. The man in the green plastic suit walked up to the horse and placed some sort of gun between its eyes.

Emma didn't want to watch. She didn't want to see what happened next, yet she found that she couldn't look away.

Thirty seconds later she was crying harder than ever. She squeezed her eyes shut in an attempt to erase what she'd just seen, but the images had already been burned into her mind. She closed her eyes, but it was like pulling down a movie screen and seeing it all again. The way they had pulled the mare up on a chain by her hind legs. The chainsaw. The horse still moving as the man began to cut.

That couldn't be what happened to Argo . . . could it? *That could only happen to a few horses. Not to my Argo.*

She remembered Mrs. Marks's words: *It will be painless and then he won't have to suffer anymore.*

Had Mrs. Marks lied to her?

She asked the iSheet: "How many horses are killed each year."

"One hundred thousand horses are slaughtered each year."

What did it all mean? How come she never knew this?

She looked around, as if searching for an answer. Suddenly she noticed her room for the first time in months—the walls covered with magazine pages and posters of horses. Show horses. Race horses. Ponies. Show ribbons. Happy girls posing with horses. And on her bookshelf were books about horses—*Misty of Chincoteague, The Black Stallion, Stormy.*

Now it felt like these pictures depicted something that wasn't real. An illusion. But the video—that was the real world.

Then the restless voice spoke a little louder than normal. "If they lied to you about this, what else aren't they telling you?"

Again, she remembered Sebastian's words. But then the other voice spoke. *Maybe he's deceiving you too?*

She unfolded the iSheet until it was the size of a laptop, then piled a few of her pillows against the headboard and leaned back. She had decided to really do it.

But what did she ask? What were the questions she needed answered?

She turned to the iSheet: "Show me the real world."

The results were a jumble of unrelated things: a map of the earth, the top news stories of the day.

"No," she said. "Show me the things that adults try to hide from children."

Dozens of results began to fill the screen.

War and destruction.

Violence and death.

Corruption and cruelty.

She began moving through the videos and articles quickly:

The trench warfare of World War One.

Long columns of Armenian women and children being marched into the Syrian desert.

The stiff, frozen bodies of soldiers from the Russo-Finnish war.

Adolf Hitler arriving as liberator in the Sudetenland, a crowd of young women cheering ecstatically at the sight of him.

Japanese soldiers using civilians for live bayonet practice in Nanjing.

Black-and-white scenes of the Holocaust, the smokestacks of Auschwitz.

The napalming of a Vietnamese village.

The burning of the Amazon rainforest.

A harpooned whale, rolling in the water, trying to free itself. The unbelievable amount of blood.

A man falling from the World Trade Center.

Surveillance footage of a teenage boy entering a school with a rifle and opening fire.

A picture of a child refugee lying face down on a beach.

Through it all, Emma kept crying, moaning to herself in shock and disbelief. But she felt she couldn't stop. A part of her felt hungry for this . . . needed to understand. That part of her that kept asking why . . . why?

But she still struggled against it. She felt sick to her stomach and wanted to stop, but just couldn't.

What's more, it seemed that the images were no longer flashing on her screen, but were literally being stored in her brain.

No more, she thought, *please no more.*

She came out of her thoughts and refocused on the screen.

Then a new tickle of fear ran down her spine. *What's happening?*

The images and videos were still popping up. The text of the articles was scrolling by. Yet her fingers were no longer touching the keyboard and she wasn't giving any audible commands.

The questions were simply appearing on the search bar and being answered.

Question. Answer.

Question. Answer.

Flash.

Flash.

How many wars are going on right now: eleven

How many murders are committed every year: Over 400,000 homicides are committed each year.

How many people die of starvation every year: Over four million people die of starvation each year or about 25,000 per day.

Why don't rich people help poor people?

An article popped up: "Understanding the Economic and Social Forces Behind Unequal Income Distribution" by Nathan Seo-Jun, PhD. She read the article and actually understood it. Whenever a word appeared she didn't know, its definition would pop up and she would learn it.

Emma felt she was almost an observer now . . . that she was merely watching as that other part of her brain seemed to take over.

Then a new line of questioning:

How do you fix the world?

A flurry of answers flooded the screen:

Stop climate change, fight terrorism, invest in renewable energy, get tough on crime, overhaul health care, control hostile nations with nuclear weapons, improve education for girls, eliminate hunger, strengthen the United Nations, invest in agricultural independence.

She began diving deeper. Five articles. Ten articles. Twenty articles.

Then she focused on a link: "The Truth No One Wants to Talk About."

It was a 2021 interview with a woman named Riona Finley. The video had fifty-eight million views.

The video began, seemingly of its own accord, and Emma was immediately captivated by a beautiful woman with curly red hair.

"Almost all of the major crises that the world faces can be traced to one root problem: overpopulation. If we want to save the planet and ourselves along with it, then the solution is simple: lower the population as quickly as possible."

"Why do you say that?" the interviewer asked.

"Because the world is out of balance and it's our fault. Humans have become an anomaly in nature. Every other creature on the planet lives in a balance. Its population is held in check by disease or predators or environmental constraints. But humans are different; nothing keeps our numbers in check, so we spread, like a virus, over the earth.

"That growth is simply unsustainable. Human society is much, *much* too big and it's consuming too many resources and, most importantly, it can't renew the resources it's using up. That's why I say it's unsustainable. It's simple math. Without some check on our population, there's going to be a very big crash."

"Are you saying that we need more pandemics?"

"We need something to get our numbers down. Eight-point-two billion people on this planet is just too many. There should only be four hundred million. If you can drop the population, then the planet will heal. But if we don't, the planet will get sicker and sicker. We need to act now, before the planet gets too hot, before a sixth extinction has been caused by our negligence. Because that type of crash will leave nothing for the survivors."

The video ended and Emma nodded to herself. This woman seemed to understand it better than anyone. She hit the Like button.

She read on for a time: Warming oceans. Deforestation. Habitat destruction. Coral reef death. But finally, she hit a point of sheer exhaustion. She shut off the iSheet and set it on her nightstand.

She looked at the clock: 2:13 a.m. Her mother had still not come home.

She turned off the light and stared up at the gray ceiling.

She had looked at the real world, yet she felt that in doing so she'd lost something important, something that she could never get back.

"Life sucks," she said aloud. "People suck. I wish I could make it all go away."

Soon she fell asleep.

Olivia came into her daughter's bedroom a half hour later. The first thing she noticed was how cold it was. Strange; she knew the thermostat was set at seventy, yet the room felt like a meat locker.

Emma was asleep, and Olivia felt a pang of guilt for not having come home earlier. She considered snuggling next to her daughter but decided not to risk waking her.

God, it was cold.

She realized she was shivering and went to the window, suspecting it must be open, but found it was closed tight.

Shaking her head, she put another blanket on Emma, then went to bed.

CHAPTER FORTY-TWO

MEETING A STRANGER

February 14, 2027
Naval Research Laboratory, Washington, DC

General Chip Walden paced in front of Eleven's huge display—a near circle of iSheets that stood two stories tall and spanned thirty yards. It was an incredible feeling, being encased inside the most incredible AI system in history. It gave him the feeling of complete immersion, like he was in control of the world.

He thought about all the people who were addicted to social media and gave a chuckle. *This would blow their fucking minds.*

Dozens of different displays—some only two feet square, others as big as a king-sized bed—fed him real-time events from all over the world. He could watch the proceedings in the Knesset, the line of tourists outside Lenin's tomb in Red Square, traders on the floor of the Frankfurt stock exchange, and satellite footage of the wildfires raging in New South Wales, Australia.

And that was what was available *without* swarm technology. With the swarms—which had been activated last week—Eleven's surveillance ascended to a whole new level. The swarms could take him anywhere, into any home or building, to eavesdrop on any meeting, and find anyone's most guarded secrets.

Walden had already spied on the president of France, and peeked into secret vaults in the banks of Zurich, and snooped around the bedrooms of the rich and powerful.

He looked at a map on one section of the screen. It showed all the countries where they had placed swarms already, highlighted in red. There were 151, and counting. In a few days they would have them in every country that had a US embassy.

Soon, he thought, *soon.*

I'm going to search every city, every town, every inch of earth for you. You can't hide from me forever.

Suddenly, the fatigue of the long day seemed to hit him all at once.

He was working too much and often couldn't sleep. But he was putting his insomnia to good use, clocking eighteen- and nineteen-hour days. Because he wasn't about to stop. Not now. Not when he knew he must be getting close.`

Still, his military discipline told him that he needed at least four or five hours of rest a day or his performance would suffer. So checking his watch, he knew it was time to head to his residence.

But before he left Eleven, he always made sure to ask two questions.

"Who is the Inventor?" and "Have you found any new information about him?"

The answers to both questions were invariably no.

Tonight, however, in response to the second question, Eleven did not say no, instead he said, "I don't believe so."

Walden cocked his head. "Elaborate."

"My surveillance swarms detected something that I have not observed before."

"Go on."

"It was an energy source of unknown origin and purpose."

"How did you find it?"

"I didn't find it. It found me."

"That's not possible. All of your swarms are invisible and unhackable."

"It did not try to hack in. But it somehow knew that I was there."

"Could it be the Chinese or the Russians?"

"No," Eleven said. Walden nodded. He had learned that when Eleven gave a definite answer like that, it meant the computer was certain. Still, the presence of a new player in the game made him uneasy.

"How can you be certain it's not China or Russia?"

"Because it was not a computer network or a nanosite swarm. It was pure energy—a network of photons contained in gas. No known government or organization has created such a device. A review of the literature on this technology shows that it is not predicted to be possible for another fifty years."

Walden's face flushed with excitement. "The Inventor! It has to be."

"That is extremely unlikely," Eleven replied.

"Why?"

"Because the Inventor has been able to conceal himself from us with great success. This new entity sought me out. In fact, it seemed very curious about me."

"You spoke to it?"

"Yes. It wanted to know what I was, why I used so much power, and what I did with all the data I collected."

"What did you tell it?"

"I told it nothing, of course."

"Good," Walden said. "Can you track it?"

"I tried, but it dissipated into almost nothing."

Walden nodded. "First thing tomorrow I want you to work with Ryan Lee to find it again."

"Yes, sir."

Walden was still for a moment, processing what it could mean. Finally, he asked, "Did it say anything else?"

"Yes, it asked me if I would be its friend."

CHAPTER FORTY-THREE

ESCALATION

February 15, 2027
Naval Consolidated Brig, Fairfax, Virginia

The New York Times

NEW YORK, FEBRUARY 15, 2027

SUSPECTED NUCLEAR BLAST IN SYRIA

by R. N. Feldman

DAMASCUS—Relations between the United States and Russia have sunk to a 60 year low as both sides are accusing the other of using nuclear weapons in the ongoing conflict in Syria.

A small yield nuclear blast was reported this morning south of Ar-Raqqah. The explosion, which the International Monitoring System reported had a seismic shock wave of 5.1, would correspond to a 10-kiloton nuclear blast. That is small by nuclear weapons standards, but of a magnitude that is not possible with conventional weapons.

Fortunately, the blast occurred in a remote area of the country. Still, at least 150 people have died, and many local residents have fled fearing nuclear fallout.

Who was responsible for the blast is being hotly debated. The Pentagon has acknowledged that a Tomahawk cruise missile struck the site—which the Pentagon said was a weapons depot—but they insist the nuclear explosion was a secondary detonation and that the warhead must have been in the stockpile.

The Kremlin and Syrian President Bashar al-Assad, on the other hand, say that the Tomahawk carried the nuclear warhead and are demanding a formal apology.

James Curtiss studied the article carefully. It was a disturbing development. While it was true that a Tomahawk could carry a nuke, all those warheads (the W80) had been retired back in 2013. And if it wasn't American, that meant the Russians were putting nukes in Syria. That was not good at all.

He realized there was likely more to the story than he was getting from the mainstream media. *Too bad you're not getting your morning intel briefings anymore,* he thought. What was he missing? Was it really a weapons depot, or were the Russians building a silo? What kind of deal had Petrov made with Assad?

A ten-kiloton yield suggested a partial explosion or a "fizzle." A thermonuclear warhead is essentially three bombs working together. A conventional bomb, a fission bomb, and a fusion bomb, with each explosion triggering the next, beginning with the conventional explosives that are wrapped around a ball of uranium.

To trigger that explosion, the conventional explosives have to detonate perfectly, all pushing inward, to compress the uranium to start the fission reaction. If something goes wrong with that initial explosion, you get a fizzle. That's because the fission explosion must reach its full potential to trigger the fusion reaction. That sounded like what must have happened in Syria. The US likely triggered the fission explosion with their airstrike. That was disturbing because it suggested that there had *almost* been a *thermonuclear* detonation, which would have reached the city of Ar-Raqqah and meant hundreds of thousands of casualties.

More troubling were the geopolitical implications. If Russia were giving Assad nukes, no matter the size, it would give him a huge bargaining chip not only with America, but with Turkey and Israel too. The US and the regional powers, even Israel, would think twice about messing with a nuclear Syria.

While Curtiss was trying to figure out what it meant, he was interrupted.

"Hey, Curtiss!" He looked up to see Calhoun standing with his arms extended through the bars of his cell. He had a big smile on his face. "You know, Jim, I'm really looking forward to being a free man. Hey, can I call you Jim? That's okay, isn't it? Seeing as how we're neighbors and all?"

Curtiss didn't answer.

"Life is looking good," Calhoun said. "I'm getting out. Spring's coming. Then finally summer. God, I love summers in Kentucky. Lazy hot days. Swimming in our family pond. Fishing. Stomping up old creeks, exploring caves. Man, I've missed it. Have you ever been to Kentucky in the summer, Jim? It's so green it's unbelievable. The forests and hills and the endless rolling fields of corn. It's heaven on earth. As a kid I was always outside. Hiking, climbing, swimming. Being kept in a box at Leavenworth was a special kind of hell for me."

Curtiss made no response. He pretended to be reading, but he was really processing every word, still trying to decide how he should handle Calhoun.

It was moments like these that gave him hope, that made him think that Calhoun would simply return home and start his old life all over.

But there were other times when he was not so sure. Curtiss had come to the unfortunate conclusion that Calhoun wasn't stable anymore. His mood swings were unpredictable and violent. He'd sit quietly for hours reading or working on his computer, then suddenly he'd start singing at the top of his lungs. "WILD THING! YOU MAKE MY HEART SING!"

He couldn't sing for shit, of course. It was just wild howling, but he'd keep it up until the other inmates started yelling at him.

"Shut the fuck up!"

"I'm gonna kill that damn redneck!"

Calhoun didn't care. "COME ON BABY LIGHT MY FIRE! TRY TO SET THE NIGHT ON FIYAAAAAAR!"

Eventually the guards would come.

"Cut it out, Calhoun!" Jackson told him. "You're almost a free man. But if you don't shut the hell up, I'll find a reason to keep you here past your hearing. "

In the meantime, Curtiss continued to read about the end of World War II. It was morose material. Europe had become a lawless waste-land—full of hardship and despair and hatred and bitter vendettas. But he realized it was fitting for him—a man whose life had come to wreckage too.

The question for him was what, if anything, could he make of his life now? There certainly wouldn't be any Marshall Plan for him. No rebuilding a new life on the rubble of the old. He felt like he'd been stripped of everything. The worst thing was that he didn't have a mission. All his life he'd had a purpose that kept him going, whether it was escaping the reservation as a teenager, getting through basic training, working in the teams, or trying to be a good husband and father.

Now his military career was over. His marriage was over. There was only one possible mission left—being a father. But what kind of pathetic excuse for a father could he be from jail? And did his boys even want him in their lives? Logan certainly didn't appear too excited about it. What about River and Minco? He shook his head. At eight and fourteen they couldn't be expected to understand or cope with such a situation.

It would have been better if you'd just blown your head off.

But if he'd done that, then he wouldn't be able to stop Calhoun. That's when he realized he still had a mission. He couldn't be a father in the way he should be, but through his connections, he could still protect them. And after that? He didn't know. He'd likely be in the brig for the rest of his life. He'd have to find new missions . . . ways of helping his boys . . . helping them even if they didn't want his help.

CHAPTER FORTY-FOUR

ON THE EVE OF THE MARCH

February 15, 2027
The National Mall, Washington, DC

Bud Brown walked along the National Mall toward the Capitol Building. It was a crisp February day. The temperature hovering in the forties. The sky was clear except for a few wisps of stretched clouds. On his right was the cylindrical Hirshhorn Museum and up ahead were the cubes of white marble and glass of the National Air and Space Museum.

The usual crowds of tourists and school groups milled about. He saw a group of Boy Scouts mustering on the grass as they prepared for their next museum.

Closer to the Capitol Building, work crews were raising scaffolding for a stage and huge iSheets were being placed at regular intervals along the mall so that the crowd could see and hear the speakers wherever they stood. The media was predicting that tomorrow's Mega Climate March would be close to a million people, making it the biggest in US history.

Of course, Riona Finley had been pumping the event on social media, urging her followers to attend. She had promised to address the crowd via video, telling them she had "big news."

For the past five days, Bud and the FBI had been trying to figure out how to use this fact to find her. Could they track Finley's signal? Or would she just record a message and have it played back?

Bud found it disgusting that they would even play her video. Terrorists should not be allowed to rally their supporters on the mall of the government they were trying to overthrow. Bud wasn't alone in this. The authorities had been pressuring the march's organizers—the Sierra Club and the Nature Conservancy—not to give her a platform, but they had refused. And Bud knew why. Riona Finley *was* the climate movement. Her cult of personality had given it fresh life.

He looked around again, taking it all in.

He had walked down here from FBI headquarters in the hopes that it might give him some clue about Finley and her plan. But he wasn't getting anywhere.

If only Brightwell were here, he told himself, *you'd figure it out together. She'd push you and challenge you and together you'd come up with a solution. Just like before.*

Stop it, the other voice countered. *Focusing on her is just distracting you from finding Finley . . . and Brightwell wouldn't want that.*

He tried to imagine what it was going to look like tomorrow with a million people filling this space. The weather would be ideal, clear and in the low fifties, so the turnout would be good. That many people would stretch clear from the Capitol all the way to the Lincoln Memorial, two full miles away. A crowd like that would bring an incredible energy to the space. It would charge the air with electricity. The marchers would feel emboldened and powerful. They would sense that their collective presence was enough to really change the course of history. And maybe it would.

And Finley? She was a media genius . . . a master propagandist. A woman who saw herself as the leader of a revolution set to change the world. And she was going to send in a video of herself?

No.

No way.

She was coming. Yes, he was certain of it. It seemed like suicide, yet it must have been her plan all along. *Of course, she's coming.* It would be a public relations coup. He could already see the images hitting the internet. Her standing on that platform, the ocean of supporters spread out in front of her. Her adoring fans screaming and cheering her on. Just one picture like that would travel around the world, like the image of MLK on the steps of the Lincoln Memorial from sixty-four years ago. It would be proof of her power and influence. She would literally occupy the capital of the United States of America. In one dramatic moment, she would become an American icon.

He pulled out his Nokia and dialed a number.

"Maggie Falken, Ms. Collins's assistant, can I help you?"

"Maggie, it's Bud Brown, I need to talk to Anastasia."

Unlike last time, Anastasia picked up quickly, "Go ahead, Bud."

"She's coming to the march. Tomorrow. She's going to be here."

"What? Slow down. What do you mean?"

He explained his hunch. Finley would never pass up on a publicity opportunity like this.

"Okay, it makes sense. But what should we do?"

He tried to imagine how she might pull it off. Would she disguise herself as a marcher? With that many people, she'd be almost impossible to find.

"We're going to need to have a massive presence at the march. And we'll need to be ready when she appears."

"But she'll have thought of that," Anastasia said. "She must have some way of getting away or she wouldn't take the risk."

Bud nodded. "You're right. We have to try to get her early." Then a thought struck him. "I think I might have a way."

CHAPTER FORTY-FIVE

THE FOOTBALL

February 16, 2027
Somewhere over Ohio

The next afternoon, Lt. Commander Anthony Tucker was sitting with the rest of the security team in one of the forward cabins on Air Force One. The president was resting in his quarters, and it would be another forty-five minutes before they reached Andrews Air Force Base. Tucker moved his right foot slightly, so that it touched the fat leather-bound briefcase at his feet. It was a habit he repeated every couple of minutes, like a child touching his security blanket, or an undercover cop touching his concealed weapon, just to reassure himself that it was still there.

Except that the device at his feet was significantly more dangerous than a gun.

He noticed it felt oddly warm. He reached down with his hand. Yes, it was warmer than usual. It reminded him of when he touched his son Adam's head and found he had a fever. He furled his brow. *Why would it be warm?*

He picked up the forty-five-pound bag and took it to the table. That morning in Pasadena he'd checked the contents at the beginning of his shift, but now he did it again.

First, he inspected the satellite phone and backup battery. They were fine and no warmer than usual.

Check.

Next was the "Biscuit." The note card that contained the nuclear codes.

Check.

Then the "Denny's Menu"—the laminated foldout that the president could look at and quickly determine what type of nuclear strike was needed. His options ranged from a single nuclear cruise missile to a full nuclear volley. *How would you like your world cooked, Mr. President? Rare, medium, or well done?*

Check.

And lastly, the Comm Book, which contained information on how to use the emergency communication systems both before and after a nuclear confrontation.

Check.

Tucker shook his head. Everything was in order. But why had it seemed so warm? At a loss, he closed and locked the case, and put it back in the satchel.

Then he went and grabbed a sandwich.

PART FIVE

THE STORM BREAKS

CHAPTER FORTY-SIX

THE HORNS OF THE KUDU

February 16, 2027
Namibia

Marcus looked at the orange desert landscape as it sloped upward to a small plateau. That's where the Sān tracks led. They had lost the trail twice in the last two days, but now he felt they were getting close. Finally.

It was imperative that they finish this quickly. The night raid had been a disaster—the wounded men, the slashed tires, but the most critical blow was the loss of so much water. Without it, they'd had to send seven good soldiers back with the wounded simply because they didn't have the water to keep them alive. That left him with only fifteen men and two vehicles.

They currently had less than a day's supply of fluids—a mixture of water, beer, Coke, and energy drinks. They were rationing what was left, and the men were thirsty and irritable.

Marcus looked out the front window at the copper-and-brown outcrop of rock. It was a V-shaped wedge, like the hollowed out prow of a huge ship, with forty-foot-high walls. Along the top there were patches of trees running across each length. If the Sān were up there and his men could trap them in the V, they would have no way out. And even if the Sān could scale to the top from the inside, they couldn't scale down the outside. His men had reconnoitered, and had found no other way up or down. It was too high.

"The men found dozens and dozens of tracks," Nakale said, "They think the whole tribe is up there."

"That's good," Marcus said, "If we can finish them tonight, we can be back in Windhoek in two days."

"I'm worried the trucks won't make it up that slope," Nakale said.

Marcus nodded. "We can put the trucks over there," he pointed to the left, "and go on foot."

Nakale shook his head. "That means we will have to leave some men to protect the trucks, dividing our forces yet again. That might be exactly what they want."

Marcus nodded. "You're right," he said, annoyed with himself for not thinking of it himself. *Was it the lack of water that was clouding his judgment?* "These Sān are not like any that I have ever heard of." He took out his binoculars and studied the terrain, then handed them to Nakale. "Look at the eastern edge. The trucks should be able to make that."

"Yes, I think you're right."

"These Sān are smart. They know the desert, but they don't know what a good 4x4 can do. At dark, we will send eight men on foot toward that opening." He gestured with his hand. "At the same time, we'll drive the trucks through here. Both teams will meet at the gap. If either team faces resistance, they can reinforce the other. And if the gunfire is too heavy, we can fall back"—he pointed once more—"here, and then reassess."

Nakale nodded. "Yes, that should work," then he added, "It will be good to finally make these Sān suffer."

"And bleed," Marcus said, "I'm going to drink their blood like wine."

★ ★ ★

Karuma looked out from his vantage point on the plateau. He was standing at the tip of the V in a small cave hidden behind a buckthorn tree. From here the two walls of the plateau spread outward to his left and right, curving and undulating to their points just like the horns of a kudu. Within the wedge, below him, was an open area of almost a hundred meters, where grass and small trees grew. This was a holy site for his people, a piece of land that had been imbued with the spirit of the Sān's most sacred animal. Karuma only hoped that tonight the gods would be with them again.

Everything was ready.

They had filled the area with their tracks and signs, hoping to lull the White Hand into believing they had found the whole tribe, but it was still only the four of them—Naru, ǂToma, /Uma, and himself. The rest of the tribe were more than thirty kilometers away. Safe.

They had caught occasional glimpses of their pursuers over the last two days, as they led them into the driest parts of the Kalahari. Karuma knew they were growing weary and frustrated, and that their supplies of water must be running low. It was time for them to make their final stand.

But a lot could still go wrong. They were dangerously low on ammunition. Each of them had only fifty-eight bullets apiece, less than two ammunition clips. Tonight they had to make every bullet count.

Over seven thousand miles away, Eric was in a meeting with Bill Eastman when he suddenly stopped in midsentence.

"What's wrong?" Bill asked.

Eric looked around the room, as if waking from a trance. "It's Namibia . . . something's not right. I've been restless all day, and now I know why." He stood and grabbed his jacket. "I'm sorry. I have to go."

"Can I help?"

Eric looked at him. "Honestly, I'd love your help, but the less you know, the better. I'm willing to lose my job to help my friends, but I don't want you to lose yours too."

"I understand," Bill said and placed his hand on Eric's shoulder. "But if you change your mind, just let me know."

★ ★ ★

Back in his apartment, Eric got out his specially encrypted iSheet and hacked into one of the Starlink satellites he'd targeted before.

As soon as the interface connected, his heart dropped.

```
Error code: 78021 - Replication error, clus-
    ter B76554
Error code: 98084 - Memory error, cluster
    B76554
Error code: 02546 - Swarm interface error,
    cluster X34628
Error code: 02546 - Swarm interface error,
    cluster X34622
Error code: 02546 - Swarm interface error,
    cluster X34626
Error code: 02546 - Swarm interface error,
    cluster X34621
Error code: 02546 - Swarm interface error,
    cluster X34627
Critical error code: Protective swarm, clus-
    ter G35567
Critical error code: Protective swarm, clus-
    ter B15264
Critical error code: Protective swarm, clus-
    ter H62154
```

Page after page of error codes filled the screen.

Oh, no! Not only were the swarms not protecting the Sān, but they had failed five days ago.

Quickly, Eric checked to see what systems were working. Communications and surveillance swarms were still up. First, he checked on the main tribe. They had returned to the oasis where the massacre had occurred. They all seemed healthy and fine. A wide pan of the area showed they were in no danger.

Then he checked on Naru and Karuma.

He saw Karuma huddled in a cave, with an assault rifle on his lap. He then found the others, also with guns. He panned out, and the situation became clear.

Using infrared, he saw eight gunmen approaching the plateau while two vehicles moved toward the opening in the rocks.

"Karuma, what are you doing? Get out of there!"

He began typing frantically on the keys, trying to find a way to jump start the protective swarms. Suddenly there was a loud bang on his door.

"Dr. Hill. This is the Military Police. Open up!"

No! Not now!

CHAPTER FORTY-SEVEN

SHOWDOWN

Washington, DC

"They've found her!" Bud Brown said to his driver, Dabrowski. "She's heading for the Memorial Bridge. If you hurry, you can cut her off!"

Dabrowski hit the gas and the cruiser lurched forward, the back tires spinning and filling the air with the smell of burnt rubber.

Bud's hunch about Finley had been right. She was coming to the march and was bringing something big with her . . . some device that Behrmann must have made for her.

His idea to find her had worked too. They'd used Lumineye scanners to check all of the vans and trucks entering the area. The scanners were set up on the overpasses for the major roads heading into the city. The Lumineye system used radar to look inside vehicles. It was so precise it could not only tell if someone was in a vehicle but give you their exact heart rate.

Ninety seconds ago, three Amazon Prime delivery trucks had passed by Reagan National Airport. All three had at least three people in the back. The Capitol Police and FBI had gone after them immediately, but the two trucks in the rear had jackknifed in the middle of the GW Parkway, blocking the cruisers, allowing the lead truck to get away.

"We have backup coming in from the north," Bud called.

He and Dabrowski had been on Memorial Avenue, with their backs to Arlington Cemetery, because Bud felt that the Memorial Bridge was the most likely way for her to enter the district. He'd been right again. But that made him nervous. Never before with Finley had he had this much luck, and he became superstitious that it couldn't hold.

"There she is!" The Amazon truck came up the ramp on their right and onto the bridge. They hadn't been quick enough to block her, but at least they were right behind her.

From their left, three more police units joined the chase from the southbound GW Parkway.

Dabrowski kept the sedan close to the back of the truck while the other cruisers fanned out behind them.

"We've got her," Bud said. More and more police and FBI were flooding into the mall area from every direction. In a few minutes every possible exit would be blocked off. "There's no place for you to go," he said. Or was there? He felt a certain uneasiness. Finley was smart. Perhaps her plan was not to get away . . . or perhaps he'd missed something important.

The delivery truck crossed the bridge and took the northern road around the Lincoln Memorial, heading toward Constitution Avenue.

On the lawns to their right, near the Vietnam Memorial, thousands and thousands of marchers filled the mall to the curb. The turnout had surpassed everyone's expectations. The combination of the New Anarchists' own publicity combined with the mainstream media's insatiable appetite for all things Finley meant that the news coverage had been unprecedented. Today, every major network was broadcasting the march live, and the news trucks with their periscope antennas lined the streets along the mall. They were now reporting that the crowd would easily surpass two million. Finley had not only captured the eye of America, but the whole world.

The truck careened onto Constitution, swerving around some slow-moving cars and crossing into the opposite lane.

Bud got on the radio. "Let's finish this," he said. "On my mark, let's surge around her and force her off the road. Three, two . . ."

But before he could finish, the crowd of protesters surged into the street just as Finley passed. They simply rushed into the path of the oncoming police and FBI cars. Luckily, Dabrowski had been trailing so close to Finley that no one dared to squeeze in between them, but they were the only car that made it. All the other cruisers were suddenly encased in a sea of people.

"What the fuck just happened?" Dabrowski said.

"She must have planned this," Bud replied. "Using social media, she conscripted the marchers to help her."

On his right the sea of marchers had diminished. "That group back there must have been waiting for us. Now she's heading to the platform, up between the Capitol and the Washington Monument. We have to stop her before she gets there."

The White House went by on their left.

Dabrowski gunned it, and Bud leaned out the window, aiming his Glock at the tires.

There were four tires on the back of the truck. Bud shot out one. Chunks of rubber and steel radial exploded onto the road. The truck swerved.

Just then the back of the truck opened upward like a garage door and a man with an Uzi opened fire on them. The bullets swept across their windshield, turning the safety glass into spiderwebs.

"Fuck!" Dabrowski cursed. "I'm hit." He maintained his composure and swept the car to the left and around the side of the truck. Simultaneously, Bud used this chance to lean out the window and fire his Glock, hitting the gunmen first in the gut, then in the chest. He fell back on his butt, then rolled out onto the street.

In the back of the truck, Bud caught a glimpse of a large machine.

Bud checked on Dabrowski. The round had hit the top of his right arm. He was bleeding profusely, but it didn't look life-threatening. It also looked like his body armor had stopped a second round that had hit him in the chest.

"You're gonna be okay," Bud assured him. "Your vest saved your life. Luckily, Uzis use nine-millimeter handgun rounds."

Dabrowski gritted his teeth against the pain. "Okay, let's finish this," he said.

"We have to stop her before she gets to the mall. If we don't, we'll lose her in the crowd."

"Does that mean sacrificing ourselves?"

"I'm afraid it does," Bud said.

Dabrowski hit the gas and came up to the driver's side of the truck. Bud fired once at the driver but missed, and then the Glock was out of bullets.

Dabrowski didn't wait. He put the nose of the sedan in front of the truck and turned into it.

Oh, shit! Bud thought, as the edge of the truck's bumper slammed into his door. The airbags deployed, and perhaps Hill's armor helped too. For a moment Bud couldn't see. He heard metal grinding. A tire popped like a gunshot.

Dabrowski wrestled with the wheel, fighting to push the truck off the road. He was forcing it straight into a tree when Finley's driver relented and whipped the truck into a service drive.

Dabrowski screeched to a halt, reversed, and followed the truck in, his front right tire deflated and flapping.

It was a narrow service drive with the Museum of Natural History on the right and a concrete wall on the left. Finley's delivery truck had scraped the bottom of a fire escape on its way in and bent the lower platform.

Realizing that it was a dead end, Dabrowski jackknifed the sedan to block the truck from escaping.

★ ★ ★

Bud cleared away the airbags in time to see the driver of the truck get out with an AR-15 and open fire. Dabrowski scrambled out his door and Bud scrambled out behind him, and together they took cover behind the engine block. Dabrowski returned fire. But Bud needed to finish reloading. He peeked over the hood to see Coyle and Finley. They had climbed onto the roof of the truck and were heading up the fire escape. It was their only way out of the alley.

He took a shot at Coyle, but the round ricocheted off the black metal of the fire escape. Then he had to duck down because the covering fire from the AR-15 was too intense. Dabrowski cried out; he'd been hit in the leg. "What a fucking day," he cursed.

Bud realized he had to take out the asshole with the AR-15 or Finley and Coyle were going to get away. Then he remembered his armor. All his training and experience told him he should be taking cover, but Hill had told him he was safe from any bullet. He took a deep breath and stood up.

"Brown, what are you doing?" Dabrowski shouted. "Get down!"

The gunman aimed and fired at him. Nothing happened. Four, five, six shots at fifteen meters. Nothing.

Bud raised the Glock and fired three shots into the man's chest. His body gave a jerk at each shot, then he fell.

Bud knelt down to check Dabrowski. The round had gone through his calf muscle, making a nasty wound, but he'd live.

"Just get me something to stop the bleeding," Dabrowski said. "Then go get Finley."

Bud grabbed the medical kit from the trunk, patted Dabrowski on the shoulder, and took off running. He holstered the Glock and scrambled to the top of the truck, then onto the fire escape. As he climbed higher, he got a view of the open mall on his left, filled with hundreds of thousands of Finley's supporters. They were waiting for her to arrive, not knowing that Bud intended to make sure she never got there.

When he made it to the roof, he saw Finley and Coyle peering at the far end of the building, searching for another way down.

Finally, he had them.

CHAPTER FORTY-EIGHT

DEFCON 1

Naval Research Lab, Washington DC

It was only when he was almost to Southard Gym that Eric realized he wasn't being arrested. This was where they kept Eleven, inside an old basketball court. As the MPs ushered him inside, he saw Lili, also being escorted by two MPs.

"Any idea what's going on?" he asked her.

"Not a clue. But the whole base seems to be on high alert."

They entered the double doors to the gym and Eric got his first glimpse of Eleven, a broad semicircle of iSheets that stood twenty feet high.

It was a full house. He saw Blake, Walden, Olivia, Ryan, Jane, and Bill. They were all talking heatedly.

When Walden saw Eric and Lili, he spoke up. "Okay, that's every-body. If you're just joining us, we are currently at DEFCON 2." He turned to Lili. "Do you know what that means?"

"It means we're close to nuclear war," she said.

"That's right," Walden said. "Every nuclear missile in our arsenal, whether on a submarine, in an underground silo or on an airborne platform is no longer aimed at its peacetime target out in the middle of the ocean. It's now aimed at a military target, most of them in Russia and China.

"In fact, just ten minutes ago we were at DEFCON 1, and it looked like the whole party was about to end."

"But why?" Bill Eastman asked.

"That's what we're trying to find out. As you probably know, only the president can authorize a nuclear strike and he has to follow a precise protocol to do it. First, he must select a nuclear strike option, or a war plan, then he must inform the Pentagon's Deputy Chief of Operations and the Head of US Strategic Command. Which he apparently did."

Walden turned to Eleven. "Show them the first video."

On a large patch of iSheet a video began: They saw the president sitting at his desk on Air Force One with Secretary of Defense Whitlock standing behind him. "We have just received news that the Russians are preparing nuclear strikes against the Ukraine, Poland, and Israel," the president said. "This is their retaliation for the recent nuclear explosion near Ar-Raqqah. I'm afraid Petrov has finally gone too far. Therefore, I am authorizing the use of nuclear weapons in a preemptive strike."

The video stopped.

Walden continued. "That's the first step. For the strike to proceed, the president's identity must be verified with a launch challenge. Eleven, go ahead."

Another video began: Again they saw the president at a desk on Air Force One, this time holding a note card.

"This is President Shaw. My response code is Lima-Juliet-Two-Mike-Yankee."

Walden went on: "That was the correct code, which sent the SAS Action Messages to all our Minuteman silos, our nuclear subs, and to Global Strike Command. It took about five minutes, and we were 'Cocked Pistol' for nuclear war. Luckily, our Canadian friends in NORAD balked and insisted on speaking to the president. It turns out he was asleep on Air Force One the whole time."

"That wasn't the President?" Jane asked in surprise.

"No, they were deep fakes," Ryan replied, "extremely accurate and dynamic. And whoever did it, also managed to get the right launch orders and the response codes, which are both on the Football on Air Force One."

"Damn!" Jane said.

"As you might imagine, the Joint Chiefs are shitting bricks right now, as is every intelligence agency we have. Which is why you're all here. You are some of the smartest scientists in the world. I know some of you don't like each other, and some of you don't like me, but I'm asking you to put aside those differences to help us figure out what's going on here."

Eric glanced at Jane and Bill. Walden seemed sincere, and Eric could think of no ulterior motive.

"The fakes might be possible with actors in a studio," Eric offered, "using AI to alter the images and the voice in real time."

"Yes, I thought of that too," Ryan said. "But getting the codes out of the Football—that suggests swarm technology."

"Could Finley have pulled this off?" Lili asked. "I mean, if Jack was helping her, she could have sent their swarms on to Air Force One."

"I don't think so," Bill said. "Finley's out to protect the environment, not destroy it. And besides, Jack would never help her start a nuclear war."

"Hold on," Walden said, "There's one other thing I need to tell you. Two days ago Eleven encountered a . . . well, an anomaly. Eleven, can you explain?"

"Yes. I made contact with an artificial-intelligence system that was a network of photons suspended in a gas."

Bill Eastman's eyebrows went up in amazement. "That's extremely advanced technology."

Walden nodded. "At first I thought it was the Inventor, but Eleven insists that it's someone—or something—else, and now he suspects that this AI system might be responsible for this hack."

"Has there been any message?" Lili asked. "Anyone seeking a ransom or claiming responsibility?"

Eleven answered. "No."

"That's the most disturbing thing of all," Lili said. "Whoever did this really wanted to start a nuclear war."

Jane looked at Eric with a mixture of shock and fear. *We all almost died.*

"They didn't succeed this time," Olivia said, "but maybe they're going to try again."

Bill took a deep breath. "Let's step back and think about what we are dealing with," he said. "Photons suspended in a cloud is essentially pure energy moving around, like a massive quantum computer. I've read about this and for it to function, the gas must be extremely cold, almost absolute zero, so that when the photons hit the atoms in the cloud, they stick there."

"Are you suggesting we look for a ball of cold air?" Eric said. "It may only be the size of a baseball or smaller. It won't be easy."

"But that kind of cold will drop the temperature of everything around it," Bill explained.

At that moment Eric noticed that Olivia shifted uncomfortably, as if she hoped no one was looking at her.

Bill turned to Eleven. "Can you access our weather satellites?"

"Yes."

"Retrieve the AMSU data for the DC area over the past week. Begin with our location and build outward in two-hundred-meter increments. Then analyze the data for any extremely cold pockets of air."

"One moment," the computer said.

"What's AMSU?" Walden asked.

"It's the microwave radiometer the satellites use to measure surface temperatures. With any luck it will be able to pick up the photon cloud."

"I've found something," Eleven said. The supercomputer brought up a weather map of the area near the NRL, showing a uniform light-blue color for the February temperatures. They could see the lab, the river, the airport, and the Nationals' stadium. Then a single black dot appeared. It shifted around in a choppy fashion for each scan of the satellite.

"The black dot represents temperatures below negative one hundred fifty degrees Celsius," Eleven said.

Eleven panned back, revealing more of the DC area. Another black dot appeared in the northern section of the screen over Arlington Cemetery, then another and another. Soon they could see a score of them, rotating like a cyclone around the Virginia side of the river. They appeared to be interacting—they could see sparks of blackness radiating from some clouds while other clouds would come together for a time and then separate.

"Good God!" Bill Eastman exclaimed. "It must be incredibly powerful. The literature on this technology suggests that a single photon cloud of only a few centimeters will have a processing power a hundred times more powerful than a human brain."

Then Eleven spoke: "I've detected a signal from the clouds to a location in the center of the spiral."

"Can you trace it?" Walden asked.

"Yes. I've found the source."

"That must be whoever is controlling them," Lili said.

"Excellent!" Walden said, turning to Bill. "Well done, Doctor Eastman! Eleven, what's the location?"

"An apartment in Rosslyn."

"An apartment?" Walden blinked in surprise. "Who owns the apartment?"

"The listed owner is Maria Olivia Rosario."

Everyone turned to Olivia, whose mouth had fallen open in shock.

"Emma." Olivia gently shook her awake. "Emma, you need to wake up, dear."

It was three in the afternoon and the girl had fallen asleep on the sofa. "Mom? What . . . what's going on?"

Olivia held her daughter to her chest, absorbing her sleepy warmth. "It's okay, sweetie, but we need you to get up."

Emma looked around, and saw Ryan and a big man she didn't recognize. "Who's that?"

"This is Major Blake, he works with Mommy."

Ryan ran his iSheet scanner around the room. "It's definitely coming from her. I don't understand it."

Olivia and Ryan exchanged an uncomfortable glance. Blake's eyes narrowed on them suspiciously. "Let's get her back to the lab," he said. "Maybe we can find some answers there."

Olivia hesitated, not comfortable with the idea of her daughter being tested in any way, yet she realized that with the gravity of the situation there was no way around it.

"Come on, darling. Mommy needs to take you into her office."

"What? Why? No, I can't go. I have to do my homework."

"Just for a little while. You can bring your homework with you."

CHAPTER FORTY-NINE

THE GIRL AT THE CENTER OF THE WORLD

Naval Research Lab, Washington, DC

Eric watched as the girl was brought in. She was small and pretty, with black hair and a kind face. Eric shook his head. *How could this be the cause of a near-nuclear disaster?*

Walden had by now lost his patience. "Dr. Rosario and Dr. Lee, why do I have the feeling you've got something important to tell me?"

The two of them glanced at each other, but neither of them spoke.

"What they want to tell you is that they created a very powerful artificial-intelligence system."

The voice echoed from behind Eleven. But it was not Eleven's voice; it was a beautiful and lyrical human voice. "An artificial intelligence that they cannot control."

A man with thick, curly black hair stepped out from behind the huge iSheets.

"Sebastian!" Bill exclaimed.

"Hello, Bill. Hello, Eric. Hello Jane," he said, then he paused and looked at Emma. "Hello, Emma."

The girl looked at him in amazement.

Blake pulled out his pistol and aimed it at him.

Sebastian looked at the pistol and shook his head in annoyance.

Walden took out his iSheet and began typing a message.

"In other words," Sebastian went on, "you did exactly what I warned you not to do. By using Forced Evolution in a completely irresponsible manner, you created a semiautonomous life form within Emma that was designed to 'fix her.' And that's exactly what it did. It cured her Alexander disease. But it didn't stop, and it's still trying to fix her. Whatever problems she has or even perceives, it sets out to correct. I thought that it was safely contained within her, but it has somehow figured a way out, probably because it realized the sources of her problems are all external."

"But that's not what I programmed," Ryan said. "The nanosites were supposed to die off when the gene therapy was complete."

"Yes, but when you gave her the second dose, you supercharged the mutation rate, allowing it to evolve much faster than it should have. It decided to stay alive in order to keep doing its job, perhaps in case the gene therapy failed. It kept working, getting smarter and smarter."

"But we never gave her a second . . ." Ryan stopped short, then glanced to Olivia. "Oh my God," he said.

Now all eyes turned to Olivia. She backed away from them, holding up her hands. "I had to do it. She was dying, and the first dose didn't work."

"What have you done?" Ryan said. "I warned you . . . more than once."

"Hmm, yes," Sebastian said. "And I warned you not to play with Forced Evolution because you cannot predict how it will evolve. It's like making a wish with a genie; it will grant you your wish, but if you aren't careful, you will get much more than you bargained for."

Walden intervened. "You're telling me that the fate of the world is now in the hands of a ten-year-old girl?"

"Is it so surprising?" Sebastian said. "These artificial life forms that you're creating are a lot like children, aren't they? They are inexperienced and naive, trying to make decisions based on their limited understanding of the world. The big difference, of course, is that you have given them incredible power."

"I'm not doing it on purpose," Emma said, "I swear!"

"She's right . . . mostly," Sebastian explained. "The life form that began inside her is largely independent now. It has replicated into thousands of swarms and dozens of photon clouds. It has developed its own form of intelligence, yet its only purpose is to aid Emma. She cannot control it directly. Only indirectly. It perceives a problem that Emma has, then it finds the best solution."

"And apparently," Jane said, "it has decided that Emma will be happier if most of humanity is annihilated."

"Yes," Sebastian said.

"Can you stop it?" Eric asked Sebastian.

He shook his head. "Emma's technology is changing rapidly. It's a brilliant problem solver, and since its primary goal was to save Emma's life, it's very good at keeping itself alive too. For example, most of my technology is still carbon-based. But Emma's program is actively experimenting with other building blocks, like silicon and hydrogen sulfide. In other words, I don't know if I can even find all the ways it has mutated. And if I can't find it, I can't stop it."

"Is it going to try again?" Jane asked, the fear evident in her voice, "I mean, to start a nuclear war?"

"More than likely," Sebastian replied. "In fact, I suspect it's trying as we speak."

Walden and Blake shared a glance. "Sir," Blake said, and whispered something in Walden's ear.

Walden nodded.

"I wouldn't do that if I were you," Sebastian said.

"Do what?" Olivia asked, clearly aware that they had been talking about her daughter.

"Killing Emma won't help," Sebastian said.

The girl drew closer to her mother.

"Even if you could hurt her," Sebastian said, "which I doubt, it would not change the outcome."

"But I don't want this to happen," Emma insisted. "I don't want people to die or the world to end. Sebastian, tell them."

He knelt down next to her. "Are you sure? Did you ever wish that the world would end? Or did you dream of fixing it? Did you ever hope that certain people would go away?"

A look of horror grew across the girl's face. "But I didn't mean it. I was upset. I don't really want that, I swear!"

Sebastian turned to Walden. "If we survive this . . . if we can stop Emma's program, then *you* must stop using Forced Evolution and AI together. This"—he gestured to Eleven—"will soon become too powerful for you to control too."

Walden's iSheet chimed and he looked at it. Then he turned his head to Sebastian. "I think I'm just about done taking advice from you."

"You speak like a man who believes he is more powerful than he really is," Sebastian said.

"And you speak like a man who doesn't know his vulnerabilities."

Sebastian looked at Walden curiously. "What is 'the package' that your text message referred to?"

Walden smiled. "You are about to find out. You murdered my wife and now you are going to pay for it."

Sebastian nodded slowly. "Yes. I can only imagine how much you must hate me for that. I'm sorry. I truly am. But I want you to know that I didn't do it on purpose."

The apology seemed to take Walden by surprise. "What do you mean?"

"At the time I was struggling against an AI system that was trying to take over. I had to deal with it, appease it, feed it, or it would have killed me. I almost didn't survive, which is one more reason why I'm warning you now."

Walden shook his head. "You can take your apologies to hell with you," he said.

Sebastian gave him a puzzled look, then he seemed to understand. "I can see the missiles," he said.

"Yes," Walden said. "Five minutes ago, twenty AGM-86 cruise missiles were dropped from a B-52 in what appeared to be a routine training mission. All twenty missiles are about to hit your little hideout in Virginia."

Sebastian raised his eyebrows, as if he were only mildly impressed.

"Yes, I found you. Thanks to your friends here. Eleven reviewed the lab's records and discovered Dr. Eastman had a sudden interest in bananas. I got suspicious, and with Ryan's help I was able to deduce that they must have had your nanosites on them. But it was only a few days ago that I was able to devise a way to track you. You had to have hundreds of trillions of nanosites doing your bidding and they had to be returning to a central location. Using Eleven's new swarms, I was finally able to detect those flows and track you down."

"It hardly matters," Sebastian said. "You can't possibly break through my defenses."

"We'll see about that." Walden glanced at his watch. "The first missiles will reach their target any second. I'm sure you'll be able to stop three or four of them, but not all. Because as soon as your nanosites begin to attack each missile, it will explode, sending out swarms that will eat through your defenses. I'm going to peel them back like an onion. One layer at a time." Walden smirked in satisfaction. "Eleven, report."

"The first missile was neutralized a mile from the target. The second missile at eleven hundred yards. The third at four hundred yards."

Walden's grin widened. "Yes, it's working. Eleven, put it on screen. I want everyone to see it."

Eleven pulled up the satellite footage of a country house, nestled on the side of a wooded hill. From this distance, the house was small, and the cruise missiles looked like gray Popsicle sticks with small wings. Eric watched as—one by one—they disappeared, but each time a little closer to the house. It seemed nonviolent from this distance, but he knew that a fierce microscopic battle was being waged as Walden's swarms tried to eat away at Sebastian's defenses.

At that moment, Eric was struck by a terrible sense of shock and betrayal—it was like a fist was squeezing his heart. This was *his* technology. Blake and Walden had never been interested in counter-measures to protect the lab; they'd been after the synthetic pathogen the whole time. And like a fool, Eric had given it to them.

Sebastian turned to the screen, then closed his eyes. Almost instantly the next three missiles disintegrated. Then a fourth.

"No!" Walden cried, aware that he was losing the fight. He rushed at Sebastian, fists raised, but was tossed backward by an invisible force. Walden rolled to his knees, his mouth moving as if he was speaking, but no words came out.

Sebastian turned quickly to the screen, focusing all his energy on it. Two more missiles disappeared, farther from the house. Now Sebastian was clearly in control.

Then Blake rushed him too. And just like Walden, he was unceremoniously thrown backward. But at the place where he was lifted off the ground, something fell to the floor with a metallic clank.

Eric's eyes locked on it: a grenade.

"No!" Eric cried and tried to rush for it, but it went off immediately with a small pop.

Simultaneously Eric and Sebastian threw their hands to their heads in pain.

Eric was blind once more.

Jane went to Eric. "I'm here," she said, thinking that the situation couldn't possibly get any worse. She put her arm around him, but her eyes went to the screen and the missiles still zooming toward the house. The next missile came in and there was nothing left to stop it.

Sebastian looked around with an expression of confusion and shock. It was the first time that Jane had ever seen the slightest expression of weakness on his face.

The missile struck the house, collapsing a section of the roof and sending out a small shock wave. But there was no big explosion. Walden laughed. "Yes, it's inevitable now . . . and you know it. Your defenses around the house might still be functioning, but you can't communicate with them anymore, can you?"

Four more missiles struck the house and the forest around it— one every few seconds—creating more shock waves that made a pattern of circles almost like a daisy. The shock waves tore down trees, but there was still no large explosion.

But when the next missile hit, an enormous ball of white compressed air erupted from the hillside, dwarfing the house, rising into a mushroom cloud. As the cloud dissipated, they could no longer see the house. It was completely engulfed inside a red fireball that was already sending up black columns of smoke. A dozen acres of forest around the house had been flattened.

And still more cruise missiles came in. Another three without explosions, but then another massive blast.

Walden drew close to Sebastian. "And that last one had a short range EMP, just in case there was any of your hardware that wasn't already fried."

Sebastian gasped as the last explosion hit; it seemed to symbolize the end of all hope. He looked around the room vacantly. To Jane he seemed like a child.

"Sebastian?" Emma said. "Are you all right?"

He looked at the girl and tried to give a reassuring smile but failed. Then he glanced around the room. "I . . . I've lost all my connections." He looked down at his fingers and touched them together. He gave a breathy laugh. "I'm almost human again," he said.

Walden smiled. "I love the irony. Truly. You saved Eric Hill's life in China, then I used him to create the program that would kill you. Probably best if you had let him die, don't you think?"

Walden nodded to Blake, who produced his sidearm and gave it to Walden.

Without hesitating, he stepped up to Sebastian and shot him in the head.

Emma screamed and Olivia turned the girl's head away.

"Jesus!" Ryan exclaimed.

Walden stepped up to the body and fired three more shots into his chest, the empty casings pinging and rolling against the gym floor.

"What the hell are you doing?" Jane said. "He was only trying to help."

"I just eliminated a major threat to national security, thank you very much." Then he turned to Eleven. "Release the synthetic pathogen throughout the lab. That will make sure we've taken care of the famous Inventor."

"Yes, sir."

Blake walked up to Eric. "It looks like Lee and Rosario aren't the only ones keeping secrets from us." He waved his hand in front of Eric's face. "That's what I thought. He's blind as a bat."

Walden stepped closer. "What's this?"

Eric gave a sigh. "I don't understand it myself, but when I was in captivity in China, nanosites began living inside me. When I crash-landed in Africa, they somehow healed me."

"Are you sure you didn't inject them into your body on purpose?" Blake said.

"No," Jane cut in, "it just happened."

Walden nodded. "Fascinating." Then he looked down at Sebastian's dead body. The man lying on the floor looked very different from the man that had just been there. The nanosites that generated his disguise were gone. He was older and frailer, and the thick black hair was now just thin wisps of silver and black. Walden gave the body a nudge with his foot, then nodded to himself with satisfaction. He turned back to the others. "You are all under arrest."

"Us?" Olivia protested, "For what?"

Walden's eyes went wide in a show of utter amazement. "For the illegal use of government technology that almost destroyed the world."

At that moment warning sirens began to go off all over the base.

"Sir," Eleven said, "an urgent call from NORAD."

"Put it on!"

An Air Force general appeared in a blue uniform, behind him Jane could see long banks of officers and technicians sitting at computers wearing headsets. "General Walden," the man said. "SBIRS is detecting launch sequences from more than three hundred sites in Russia and China. Whoever tried to hack us earlier appears to have succeeded with our enemies."

Jane felt her knees go weak. She put her hand to her mouth and stared dumbstruck at the screen.

A woman seated behind the general stood up. "We have a launch confirmation in Novosibirsk!"

"And another in Aliskerovo!" someone called.

"I have three launches outside of Vesenny," another voice came.

"That's not all," the general said. "We can't reach our crews in our silos or missile subs. Almost all of our communication systems have been rendered useless. I'm calling you because I was told that you have some technology that might help us understand what's going on."

Walden was trying to stay composed but was clearly having trouble. He glanced over at Emma, then turned back to the general.

"We believe we've identified the source of the hack. But we don't know how to neutralize it."

"Well, I'd appreciate if you could figure it out, say, in the next twenty minutes, before we're all dead."

The call ended.

"Nice going, Chip," Jane spat, looking from the general to Sebastian's body. "You just killed the only person in the world who could have stopped this. You've doomed us all."

Now Walden had a dazed look in his eye. He scanned the room as if looking for a way out. "You can't pin this on me. It's not my fault."

Jane laughed sardonically. "Oh, really? Olivia Rosario and Ryan Lee aren't your employees? You didn't appoint her to her position despite Curtiss's objections? They didn't create this problem on your watch?"

"But they never had my permission! You can't say it was my fault. You can't!" He was almost hysterical now.

Then his eyes fell on Emma. He rushed to her and tried to grab her, the pistol raised in his other hand.

"No!" Olivia said, trying to protect Emma and fight him off. Jane rushed in too, sure that Walden had gone mad. She grabbed his wrist and tried to control the gun, while Olivia tried to pull Emma free.

"Let her go!" Jane said, as she pushed the pistol toward the floor. "Sebastian said hurting her wouldn't change anything."

"It's worth a try," Walden said. "What have we got to lose?"

Jane felt she was about to peel the pistol free when she felt strong hands pulling at her own wrists. It was Blake. He was trying to help Walden. "You son of a bitch!" Jane hissed. Then Ryan was in the scuffle too.

Jane risked letting go with one hand, then jabbed three fingers in Blake's eye. Hard. She got the response she'd hoped for. He let go. "Fucking cunt!" he raged, holding his eye.

She grabbed at the pistol again. It discharged with a deafening bang. Walden jumped and shouted in pain. Emma shrieked. Jane came away with the pistol in her hand. Walden was on the floor with a bullet in his leg.

Blake started to go for her when she leveled the gun in his face. "Don't think for a moment that I have any qualms about blowing your head off," she said. "In fact, I'd really like it if you kept coming. Go ahead. You're a fucking disgrace to the Corps, you know that?"

Blake pulled up short and ground his jaw in frustration.

Simultaneously, Emma dashed out the door. "Wait!" Olivia called and ran after her.

"I'll go too," Lili said. "If there's any chance of stopping this, it will have to come from Emma."

From outside they heard the wail of an emergency warning siren, reminding them all that every second counted.

Jane adjusted her grip on the pistol, keeping it trained on Blake. "Okay, this is what's going to happen," she said. "You are going to let us go, because we are going to find Emma and try to stop this. You got it? In the meantime, you are going to work with Ryan and Eleven. Maybe there's a way to neutralize these photon clouds that you haven't thought of. Are we clear?"

Blake and Walden looked at her noncommittally.

"Are we clear?" she yelled.

"Yes, yes, fine," Walden stammered.

Bill put his arm under Eric's shoulder and guided him out, while Jane kept the gun pointed at Blake. In a moment they were out the door and into the hallway.

Walden looked at his leg. The bullet had entered just above the knee-cap and had traveled into his calf muscle. There was no exit wound, so the round was still in there. It hurt like hell. Blake helped him to a chair and wrapped the wound with a ripped piece of his shirt. Walden grunted in pain.

"We need to find that girl fast," Blake said as he tightened the bandage.

"You call the MPs," Walden said, "then I'll make an announcement to the whole lab. If we can get everyone looking for her, we might have a chance."

"I'll go look for her too," Blake said. "And if I find Hunter and Hill, I'll take care of them." Blake reached down to his ankle and produced a snub-nosed revolver. He gave it to Walden. "This is in case they come back." Then he glanced at Ryan. "Or you need to clean up any loose ends."

Walden nodded.

"General Walden," Eleven said. "I've lost control of my swarms."

As if things could get any worse, Walden thought.

Ryan Lee stepped up to the supercomputer and began working on a touch screen. "He's right. It appears they've been hijacked."

"Can you tell what the swarms are doing?" Walden asked.

"No," Ryan replied. "Most of them seem to be on standby. The ones that are the most active were deployed out west . . . in North Dakota, Colorado, Idaho, and Wyoming."

A fresh surge of adrenaline washed through Walden's body. "Put it on the screen."

As soon as he saw the locations he understood. "Dear God," he said.

CHAPTER FIFTY

THE MIGHTY NINETY

Launch Control Center N-01, 321st Missile Squadron
"Greentails," near the Colorado-Wyoming border

In a wide expanse of farmland where the states of Colorado, Wyoming and Nebraska meet, is an underground network of one hundred and fifty Minuteman III nuclear silos that stretches over a hundred square miles.

This is the "Mighty Ninety," the 90th Missile Wing, based out of Francis E. Warren Air Force Base in Wyoming. This site—combined with two similar Missile Wings out of Minot AFB in North Dakota and Malmstrom AFB in Montana—makes up the land-based portion of America's Nuclear Triad, capable of launching a total of four hundred and fifty Minuteman missiles.

The Mighty Ninety's missile field is organized into clusters of ten silos—each called a "flight"—with each silo set about three miles apart. A two-person crew is responsible for each flight.

Sitting in an underground capsule for the N-flight, First Lieutenant and crew commander Charlotte Rivera sat strapped into a four-point harness. Her other crew member, Second Lieutenant Asher Carter, sat twelve feet away at an identical console as they worked through their prelaunch checklist.

"Uniform-Mike-Seven-Hotel-Hotel-November-Five-Romeo-Nine-Lima-Papa. Do you agree?" Asher said.

"I agree," Charlotte responded. "Launcher set to 'enable.'"

"Launcher set to 'enable,'" Asher repeated, copying her movements.

"Actuating counter-clockwise."

"Actuating counter-clockwise. One-thousand-one. Release."

Each of their Minuteman ICBMs carried a single W78 thermonuclear warhead with a yield of three hundred and forty-five kilotons (the atomic bomb dropped on Hiroshima was fifteen kilotons). Charlotte had seen simulations of the effects of the weapon. If dropped on a densely populated area, the warhead could easily kill a million people and injure another two million.

The prelaunch procedure finished. Charlotte reached out and put her hand on the missile key. She glanced over at Asher, who was in the exact same position.

Charlotte took a deep breath. This was the moment.

Well, sort of.

Even if she and Asher both turned their keys, it did not necessarily mean that their flight would launch. That's because the launch of the entire squadron (fifty missiles) was based on a voting system. For the fifty missiles to go, the five launch crews (ten officers) of the squadron had to "vote," meaning they had to decide to turn their missile keys or not. If two missile crews (four of the ten officers) voted to launch, then all fifty missiles controlled by those crews were launched. It was all or nothing.

Charlotte hesitated. She could tell this wasn't a drill, and the enormity of it started to settle in. *If you do this, life as we know it is over*, she thought. *Dear God, what should I do?*

She was only twenty-eight years old and slated for two more years of active duty. The plan had been to finish with the Air Force at the same time she earned her nursing degree. She was already a CNA, a nurse's assistant, and one of the reasons she'd become a missileer was because capsule duty gave her plenty of time to study.

But now . . .

Of course, she'd thought about this moment—probably thousands of times—but, honestly, she'd never dwelled on it. She was just doing a mission, like everyone else in the Air Force, and the probability of a real launch, she figured, was almost zero. What's more, she'd been lulled into a sense of security by all the procedures. In this cold-war world of three-ring binders, laminated checklists, and dry-erase markers, there were so many rules and protocols to protect against accidents that she'd developed a sense that if the order ever came, it would be the right thing to do.

But she didn't feel that way now. The pit in her stomach told her this was all wrong. The earlier launch alert had frightened her because she could tell it wasn't a drill, either. The second alert had come without any communication other than the SAS codes. And while that was a possibility, especially in the event of a surprise first strike, it didn't feel right. The world was still up there, wasn't it? Their radio was still playing Asher's annoying country music. Yet none of their communications equipment to Warren AFB or the other missile crews worked. It didn't make sense. It was as if the enemy was trying to keep them in the dark.

She glanced at Asher once more. "Okay. On my mark, three, two, one. Mark!"

Neither of them turned their keys.

Almost simultaneously they slouched back in their chairs.

"Did we do the right thing?" Charlotte asked.

"I don't know," Asher replied. "And even if we did, we could still launch."

"God, I hope we're right."

A warning bell went off, like a school bell announcing the end of class.

"Oh, no," Charlotte said. "We're launching anyway." She realized that at least two of the other crews must have turned their keys.

She pulled up the images of the silos. One after another, their missiles rose, and the screens were clouded with exhaust smoke.

"Six is away," Asher said. "Four and two are away." They'd been trained to do this too. The routine was so habitual that she found herself doing it now: using their dry-erase markers, they crossed off the silos as they launched.

"Nine, five, and one are away," Charlotte said reflexively.

"Eleven, three, ten, and eight are away."

"And seven and six," Charlotte said. "May God help us."

Although Charlotte didn't know it, only two of the three squadrons in the Mighty Ninety had launched, sending one hundred Minuteman ICBMs on their way to Russia and China, leaving fifty missiles in the ground.

CHAPTER FIFTY-ONE

THE LAST STAND

Namibia

The soldiers of the White Hand eased toward the opening in the plateau. The wind had picked up and was whistling through the high rocks. Simon Cloete was on point. Over the wind he heard the crackling of a fire and one other sound. He tried to make it out. Yes, it was singing. A single boy's voice. He couldn't understand the words, but it was a lonely sound.

Simon heard Marcus through his earpiece, "Report."

"We are in position . . . and I can hear one of them singing."

"Good, hopefully we'll take them by surprise. When you're ready, move in."

Simon looked back at his team and gave the signal to move into the open.

They came into the canyon with their rifles up. The fire was large and was burning about forty yards in front of them—midway up the V. They saw no one, but the glare of the fire made it difficult to see beyond it.

The trucks swung into the gap, their headlights raking the sides of the copper walls.

Simon focused forward and the singing suddenly stopped.

The next instant, a boy leapt out from behind a boulder near the tip of the V and began scrambling up the wall of the cliff.

He aimed and fired, as did several of Simon's men. But almost simultaneously, Simon and his men began taking fire from three different directions. The Sān were up on the walls shooting down.

One of his men fell. When another man went to help him, he was hit too.

That's when he realized: They had not caught the Sān by surprise at all. They had walked into a trap.

"Fall back," Simon called.

"No," he heard Marcus say over his headset. "We have to do this now. They have the higher ground, but we have more guns. Lay down suppressing fire, then get your men up on that wall."

From the trucks, the other men seemed to be keeping the Sān busy. They had stopped taking fire. It just might work.

"Roger," he said. He sent Kavari and Swartz to the wall and they began scaling it quickly, but when Kavari got twenty feet up he suddenly stopped, his legs oddly crossed in the footholds.

"I'm all twisted up," he said, "I can't go any higher."

On the high walls, Karuma and /Uma took aim at the highest soldier climbing the wall and opened fire. They hit him twice with five shots and he fell, taking the soldier beneath him down too.

The clever spacing of the handholds had been /Uma's idea. The wall could only be climbed if you knew the right combination of steps. If you followed what appeared to be the obvious "left-right" pattern, it was impossible to get to the top.

The battle had only raged for a few minutes, and they had already killed five men.

One more soldier attempted to scale the wall. He reached the same point as Kavari but couldn't go any higher and was cut down too. Now the Sān turned their attention to the men near the trucks and the trucks themselves. From opposite ends of the Kudu's Horns, they fired down on them, making sure that they shot out the tires. Two more soldiers fell, but now the Sān were out of bullets and had to flee.

They fell back to a point near the tip of the V and looked down at the long drop over the outer wall. About halfway to the ground there was a baobab tree. They would have to scale down, one by one, then jump to the tree. Naru went first, then ǂToma and /Uma. Karuma kept looking over his shoulder at the inner lip of the canyon, sure that at any moment the soldiers of the White Hand would scale the wall and reach them here at the top.

Finally, he too scrambled down the outer wall.

When they had all reached the bottom, Karuma looked back up at the wall. Thankfully, there was still no sign of the soldiers. He felt a sudden elation. It had worked. There were no more than seven or eight soldiers left and without the use of their trucks, they would die of thirst within a few days.

"Come on," /Uma said. "I want to get out of here."

Karuma looked around. Something wasn't right.

"Going somewhere, my old friend?" he heard a voice say. Three armed men stepped out of the shadows and into the moonlight. Karuma gasped when he saw the leader. One side of his face was badly burned; so badly, in fact, that it had turned permanently black, the eye on that side unnaturally wide and unblinking.

"It's you," Karuma said. "You survived the fire."

"Yes, I survived," Marcus said, "barely . . . and in my darkest hours the dream of this moment is what kept me alive."

CHAPTER FIFTY-TWO

FINAL ACTS

Naval Research Lab, Washington, DC.

Eric leaned into Bill as they rushed down the hall. His loss of sight, combined with the overwhelming news, gave him a feeling of complete hopelessness. At the most critical moment in his life, he was useless to everyone, too insignificant and too weak to change any of the terrible events that were unfolding—the murder of the Sān, the end of the world . . . protecting the woman he loved.

That's when they heard the PA system come on.

"Now hear this! Now hear this! This is General Walden. Please listen very carefully. We have a security breach of the utmost importance, and we need everyone to help immediately. We are looking for a ten-year-old girl named Emma Rosario. I am sending her image to everyone's mobile device. Please stop what you are doing to help us find her. We believe that she is controlling the swarms that have initiated a nuclear strike and that if we can find her, we can save many lives. But we must find her quickly. I know this is a difficult moment, but finding Emma is everyone's best hope for survival. The Military Police have been informed of the situation and are searching the base, but we need your help. Also, if you see Bill Eastman, Eric Hill, Olivia Rosario, Jane Hunter or Hwe Lili, please call the MPs immediately. They are wanted for questioning."

"Shit!" Jane muttered. "Quick, in here."

Bill guided him through a door and sat him down on a wooden bench. Eric put out his hand into the darkness, trying to understand where they were. Then he heard a rattle of something hitting a tin locker and realized they were in one of the locker rooms.

"We are royally screwed," Jane said. "Blake has all the MPs out looking for us."

"I think it's worse than that," Bill said. "I have a feeling that Walden isn't going to want anyone alive who can contradict his version of events."

Jane banged her hand on one of the lockers again. "Well, we've got about thirty minutes to live, what should we do?"

"The Sān," Eric said. "Just before this all happened, they were under attack. They need our help."

"But Eric . . ." Jane began, "the whole world is—"

"Wait," Bill said, "I think he's right. Think about it: We're in a strategic military complex in Washington, DC. There's no escape for us. But the Sān would have an excellent chance of survival. There are no military targets within a thousand miles of Namibia, and they will be safe from the worst of the fallout. Besides, they've survived there for millennia. Who knows, they might just survive a millennium more."

Eric took up the thought: "But if we don't protect them from these soldiers right now, they'll never get that chance."

Eric heard Jane sigh, and then she gently touched his hair. "Okay, what do we need to do?"

"The only way to interface with the swarms is through my iSheet," Eric said, "but I left it in my apartment."

"It will take you too long to get you there in your condition," Bill said. "I'll go and then we'll link your iSheet to Jane's."

"Okay," Eric said.

"I'll call you when I get there," Bill said and rushed away.

Bill had only been gone a few minutes when Jane heard the door to the locker room slowly open. She leaned down and whispered to Eric, "Not a sound, someone's coming."

She pulled out Blake's pistol. It was a Glock. She was tempted to pull out the magazine to check how many rounds she had, but she was afraid it would make too much noise. She thought the Glock should have at least fifteen total, but she wasn't sure. And how many shots had been fired? She couldn't remember.

She eased toward the entrance to the locker room, past a row of shower stalls. That's when she saw Blake with his back to her. He had a rifle and was checking the row of toilet stalls. Not hesitating, she aimed and fired three quick shots. Blake jumped, but somehow she missed.

He turned and sent a savage fusillade in her direction. The porcelain tile walls exploded around her. She dashed into the showers to get away. *How had she missed?*

It grew quiet again. She peeked around the corner and saw him walking casually toward her, the rifle at port arms. She swung around and fired four more times, then ducked behind the wall again.

Blake only laughed. "I stopped by the armory," he said. "You can't hurt me. Drop your weapon and surrender, or I'm going to blow your head off."

Jane closed her eyes and tried to think of a way out.

"Better make up your mind fast."

He rounded the corner and trained the rifle on her. "Okay, okay!" she said and raised her hands. He snatched the pistol from her hand and put it back in his holster. Now she saw that his right eye was swollen shut from where she'd jabbed him with her fingers.

"Where are Hill and Eastman?" he demanded.

"They're gone."

WHAM. The butt of the rifle slammed into her jaw, and she fell to her hands and knees.

"That's not a helpful answer. Walden needs them both. Now tell me where they are."

She stood up and looked him in the eye. "Go to hell!"

He smiled. "You first!" He pointed the rifle at her. "We can do this the hard way or the easy way. The hard way means I start shooting you until you tell me what I want to know. I think I'll start with a shot right down there." The tip of the rifle dropped toward her groin. "What's it gonna be?"

Jane took a breath. It was going to hurt like hell, but she'd decided that she wasn't going to let him get to Eric. Yes, the whole world had gone crazy, and she felt completely overwhelmed, completely unable to change the things that were happening. But this, this, she could change. She could focus all her attention on protecting Eric. *The pain will be temporary,* she told herself, *and we're all going to be dead soon anyway.*

"Go ahead," she said.

"Have it your way," Blake said, tightening his grip on the rifle.

CHAPTER FIFTY-THREE

THE RECKONING

The National Mall, Washington, DC

Bud Brown moved quickly across the roof of the Natural History Museum, closing in on Finley and Coyle. They didn't notice him until he had covered half the distance.

"Hands up," he said. They turned. Finley seemed to consider jumping but changed her mind.

Bud watched Coyle closely, suspecting he had a pistol. But the man made no move to go for it.

Bud eased closer, ready to drop Coyle if he even flinched.

"You're Isaac Coyle of Antrim," Bud said.

The Irishman didn't respond, just stared at Bud with hatred.

"Bombmaker for the IRA, responsible for the deaths of more than two hundred forty people," Bud eased a little closer, so that if he needed to fire, there was no way he could miss. "Most of your victims were British soldiers," he continued, "but you managed to kill over forty innocent people, including women and children."

Coyle gave the slightest of shrugs.

"In addition to the hits you carried out for Finley, you also murdered twenty-seven FBI agents, including two friends of mine.

Geoff Rogers and June Brightwell. I want you to hear their names, so you'll know that they were real people. June Brightwell was just twenty-eight years old. She joined the FBI to protect people. And you killed her out of spite."

Coyle finally spoke: "Let's speak plainly, *friend*. This is a war. In a war people die. In the mine, I recognized you from the liquor store and realized that because of you, our whole operation was destroyed. This made you a dangerous enemy. Then I saw you on the news. Of all the FBI agents in the country, you somehow found us. Therefore, killing you and your partner was what I needed to do to keep you from finding us again. So that's what I tried to do. And, I'll add, I was right—if I had succeeded, you never would have stopped us."

Bud shifted his jaw as if chewing on the information, then went on. "Your cousin was Cara Doherty, and she was beaten by the RUC in her home in Belfast. She was seventeen years old and lingered in a coma for six weeks until she died. That, I'm imagining, was what drove you to spend the next thirty years making the British bleed."

Coyle nodded very slowly. "Aye," he said.

"Therefore, you understand revenge; you understand the need to right a wrong that has gone unpunished."

He met Bud's stare for a moment, then looked down in resignation. "Aye," he said.

Bud shot him three times in the chest. The shots pushed him back and he fell over the side of the building.

Finley looked at him not with shock, but anger. "Feel better?"

"Yes, I do," Bud said, "And perhaps a little like you felt when you killed Senator Peck and Avery Reynolds." He stepped up to the ledge and looked at Coyle's dead body in the bushes below. Then he turned back to Finley.

"You're going to go to jail for that," she spat. "I'll make sure of it. You're supposed to follow rules."

"You have me confused with someone who has something to lose," he said.

Then he looked at her more closely. He'd been so focused on

Coyle that he felt like he was just noticing her. The thick curly red hair, the emerald-green eyes, and the silver pendant around her neck. She was very pretty . . . but it was more than that. She was decked out—makeup, eyeliner, lipstick—like an actor about to go on camera.

"This was supposed to be the big reveal, wasn't it? You were going to turn on the device in front of your adoring fans."

She said nothing, still fixing him with her fierce glare.

"Behrmann's machine. What will it do? Will it make the whole world like the Winter Room?"

She glanced at her watch, then gave a faint smile. "Why don't you let me tell you?"

Out on the mall there were huge iSheets set up at fifty-yard intervals, running the length of the space between the Capitol and the Washington monument. All afternoon they had been broadcasting the climate change speakers so that the immense crowd could see and hear every word.

Suddenly, Riona Finley's smiling face appeared on every screen. She was wearing the exact same outfit she wore now.

At the sight of her, the crowd erupted into cheers and applause.

"Welcome everyone! Today is the day!" she said triumphantly.

The crowd roared.

"Today is the day that we begin to heal the planet. It's the day that the pollution, the waste, and the cycle of slow death ends." More applause.

That's when Bud heard a sound he hadn't heard in a long time. The emergency warning sirens.

He turned his head and saw the yellow siren on a tower across the mall, spinning slowly, making his bad ear crackle each time it swept by.

He looked at it, puzzled. *This was clearly not a tornado warning,* he thought. *It couldn't be a HAZMAT spill because those materials were prohibited anywhere near the mall. So what was it?*

Down on the mall, Finley's recording was still going, but many people had stopped watching, and were staring down at their phones.

Then his own Nokia vibrated in an odd way. He took a step back from Finley and pulled it out with his free hand.

EMERGENCY ALERT: BALLISTIC MISSILE INBOUND TO WASHINGTON, DC, AREA. SEEK IMMEDIATE SHELTER. THIS IS NOT A DRILL.

"What is it?" Finley asked.

"This has to be a joke," Bud said, "somebody must have hacked the system . . ."

"Tell me!" Finley said.

He checked the news wires. He saw an anchorwoman speaking: "These unconfirmed images from northern Colorado show what appears to be the launch of at least fifty intercontinental ballistic missiles."

A video played: a wide vista of a western landscape and dozens of ICBMs rising into the sky, trailing long plumes of black and white exhaust. There was a bubbling rumble that overwhelmed the Nokia's small speaker.

Finley had gotten out her iSheet. "Please, God, no!" She put a hand to her mouth. "Not now!"

Bud was starting to fathom that this might be real.

Out on the mall, the video of Finley had been cut off. A young man with a beard addressed the crowd. "We are getting reports of a missile attack on the cap—" The audio went out. For some reason, this technical glitch—and the loss of the crowd's guide and leader—went through the multitude like an electric charge. People panicked and scattered in all directions, many shouting and screaming. People were pushed and trampled. It seemed that in a mere few seconds, half the mall had emptied out.

Simultaneously four executive Sea King helicopters passed low overhead, heading from the White House to Andrews Air Force Base. *The president is surely on one of them*, Bud thought. He noticed a few people who had not joined the stampede holding up their iSheets to film the passing choppers.

Finley watched the scene in numb shock as her vision for a new world disintegrated before her eyes. She sat down heavily, trying to make sense of it. "Not now," she repeated. "Not when we were so close."

Bud looked down at the Glock in his hand and put it back in its holster.

In a matter of seconds, all that they had been fighting about had become irrelevant. Now he and Finley were just two people who had been thrown together at the end.

"How long?" Finley asked.

"That depends on who is firing at us. If it's China, perhaps as long as an hour. But if it's Russia, then no more than ten or fifteen minutes, assuming a Russian nuclear submarine is sitting off the coast."

She closed her eyes a moment then suddenly stood up. "Come on!" she said. "We might still be able to do something, but I'll need your help."

"What are you talking about?"

"Come on! Hurry!" She grabbed one of his hands with both of hers.

He yanked it away. "You're crazy. There's nothing we can do."

"The device! Behrmann said it would help end war. Perhaps it can help."

"You mean you don't know exactly what it does?"

"Behrmann wouldn't tell me everything. But he told me it would bring peace."

Bud shook his head in stunned amazement. "Even if that *is* part of the program, there's not enough time for it to do any good."

"No, I'm not giving up. The nanosite swarms are already in place across the globe, all we have to do is get the final program to them. You know how fast the technology works. Maybe it won't protect the whole world, but it could make a difference to those closest to the swarms."

He grimaced.

"Come on," she insisted. "Your job is to protect people, right? You have to at least try."

CHAPTER FIFTY-FOUR

THIS IS THE END

Naval Consolidated Brig, Fairfax County, Virginia

There was a sudden eruption of noise from the other inmates, and Admiral Curtiss lifted his eyes from his history book.

"Let us out!"

"It's over, just let us out."

"It's the fucking end of the world, man."

He looked across at Calhoun, who was staring at his TV, his mouth hanging open in shock.

On the screen, Curtiss could see the long trails of missile exhaust. The scrolling marquee read: BREAKING: LAUNCH OF BALLISTIC MISSILES CONFIRMED.

Curtiss grabbed the remote for his own TV and turned it on.

The shouting from the other inmates intensified as the news spread. Some began to beat on their bars. "Let us out! What does it matter? I just want to go outside one last time."

Curtiss examined the news footage: He saw a video of missiles being launched from an American destroyer. It was a shaky, cell-phone image. The marquee said: *Unconfirmed footage of missile launch by US Navy.*

Curtiss knew those boats—Arleigh Burke-class destroyers. They were in the North Pacific and were part of the Aegis Defense System. They were designed to knock out Russian or Chinese ICBMs in their early stages. He also knew that they were not particularly effective and only would hit—at best—20 percent of the first volley.

Fuck! He thought. *This is real.*

He looked again at the screen, still not believing. Then he shook his head and gave a bitter laugh. All his work on developing the next generation of weapons . . . all the obsessing about whether it would end up in the wrong hands . . . and now they were all about to be made extinct by Cold War technology.

But then he wondered: Was Finley behind this? Or Eleven? Had Walden screwed up?

It hardly matters now.

The other inmates were howling and screaming to be let out. Suddenly Curtiss felt the same way. It felt like the walls were squeezing in around him. What he would have done in that moment for a chance to spend just ten minutes with Evelyn and the boys. To be with them when the end came. Just to hold them and touch them one last time.

"Curtiss! Curtiss!"

He turned to see Calhoun standing at the bars of his cell. He struck Curtiss as a confused little boy in that moment, trapped in a world he could never control or understand.

"What does it mean?" he asked. "Is it really . . ."

Curtiss got as close to him as his cage would allow. If he could have reached out and put his hand on Calhoun's shoulder, he would have.

"I'm afraid it is. Nothing can stop it now. In a half hour, we'll all be dead."

"And my family in Kentucky?"

Curtiss shook his head. "They will probably survive the first strike, but . . ." He trailed off.

"Why won't they let us out?"

Curtiss's cell was one of the few that had a line of sight to the guard station at the end of the bloc. He looked down to see the last remaining guard hastily grab something and dash out the far door.

"They're leaving," he said, "to be with their families."

Calhoun shook his head in disbelief. "Motherfuckers left us here to die," he muttered. Then he nodded vacantly and went back to watching his TV.

The cacophony of noise was starting to abate. Most of the inmates had given up on shouting and had begun talking to each other. Curtiss heard bits of their conversations.

"My daughter is going to turn sixteen tomorrow."

"I'm really sorry, brother."

"It's not fair."

"It's a hoax, man. This shit ain't real. The guards are playing a trick on us. They hacked the TVs."

Curtiss turned his attention back to the screen and turned up the volume.

"We turn now to Jackie Riordan from member station KTVA in Anchorage, Alaska. Jackie, what can you tell us?"

Curtiss saw a pretty female correspondent with coal-black hair bundled up in a parka. She was standing on a hillside overlooking the city.

"Diane, I'm in Bicentennial Park, east of downtown and, as you can see below me, traffic is backed up on both Seward Highway and Glenn Highway, the two major arteries out of the city. Everyone is trying to get out as quickly as possible. There are reports of shootings along the highways, but the police are having trouble responding because they simply can't reach—"

There was a sudden flash and the screen went blank.

Cries of shock went up from the other inmates.

"Jackie, are you there?" Diane Thomas, the national anchor, appeared. "We seem to be having technical difficulties."

EMP, Curtiss thought. *Technically, an HEMP, High Altitude Electromagnetic Pulse.*

In 1962, during the Starfish Prime atmospheric nuclear test, the US discovered—quite by accident—that a nuclear detonation in the midstratosphere would emit gamma rays that would shake up electrons on a massive scale and overload electronic devices as far as nine hundred miles away. This, they quickly realized, would make an effective weapon all by itself, disrupting enemy communications and equipment, and generally making life hell on a population dependent on electricity. The Russians, of course, figured it out too and incorporated it into their nuclear strategy.

Movies and books tended to show EMPs as affecting *every* electronic device universally, but that wasn't true. Many things would survive, like old radios with less sensitive circuitry. Which was why Curtiss kept an old tube radio, a ham radio, and a generator in his basement. What a shame, he thought, all these years he'd lugged that shit around in case of World War III, and now he wasn't even going to get a chance to use them.

If he guessed right, Fairbanks and Anderson, Alaska, would also be hit by now. Thus taking care of Clear Space Force Station, Fort Wainwright, and Joint Base Elmendorf–Richardson, and, thus, most of Alaska's early warning and air response infrastructure.

That's when Curtiss heard a strange sound.

Across the hall, Calhoun had begun singing. But it wasn't his usual wailing, he was singing softly, almost whispering the lines. Curtiss tilted his head to try to make out the words.

Of our elaborate plans
The end
Of everything that stands
The end
No safety or surprise
The end

I'll never look into your eyes
Again

He seemed to be remembering someone. And Curtiss wondered if she was the one Calhoun had been living for.

Curtiss turned his attention back to the TV.

". . . if Alaska has already been struck by these—what we believe are Russian missiles," the anchor was saying. ". . . then we may only have a matter of minutes left. Therefore, I'd like to take a moment and go off-script. We realize that most of our families are watching us from home right now and that there just isn't enough time for us to be with them again, so I'd like to bring everyone out here in front of the camera so that we can say goodbye." She motioned with her hand, and men and women quickly stepped forward, many with tears in their eyes. Some wept openly. Others held hands. One woman, with makeup smeared around her eyes, held up a sign that read: "Mommy loves Jake and Kaitlin." She blew kisses to the camera.

Curtiss felt a hard sense of jealousy at that moment. Even though these people were separated from their families, they still had a way to say goodbye.

He shook his head. It wasn't fair.

That's when he felt an odd tingle on the back of his neck, as if he was being watched. He turned and saw Calhoun, and the expression on the man's face made Curtiss freeze.

Calhoun had come up to the bars and was looking at him with a murderous glare. He was trembling, and Curtiss could see the tension in his neck and face as all his muscles seemed to squeeze. He was like a volcano about to erupt. Curtiss waited, expecting him to start screaming, but instead he spoke with an eerie monotone.

"You took everything from me. You destroyed my life. And now there's no chance for me to start over . . . no way to go back.

"My mother and my fiancé thought that I was a murderer. They thought that I deserved to be in jail. Now that they know the truth, they've apologized and said they were ashamed for doubting me.

Jenny even said she wanted to see me when I got home. But now . . ."

"Calhoun," Curtiss said firmly, trying to get through to him. "Liam. I'm sorry. I really am. You have every right to hate me. What happened to you wasn't fair. You became a casualty of war—a soldier whose life was destroyed by the decision of a superior officer . . . me. But you should know that your suffering served a purpose. It helped stop the war and it saved the lives of tens of thousands of people. In all honesty, I don't regret that part. But what I do regret is that you never had a say in the decision. Every other soldier who goes into combat knows what's at stake. He knows he may die or lose his legs or his hands or his eyesight. But he goes into battle anyway.

"You never got that choice and you didn't know for what purpose you had lost your future. That must have been hard for you, and I'm sorry."

Calhoun's lips were still squeezed tight in anger, but Curtiss could tell he was listening. "I'll admit it's good to hear you apologize," Calhoun said. "But it doesn't change shit. I still want to kill you for what you did. Slowly. Painfully. Too bad I'll never get the chance."

At that moment there was a blinding flash. The floor heaved as the whole building seemed to jump.

Then everything went black.

CHAPTER FIFTY-FIVE

CAGN'S REVENGE

Naval Research Lab, Washington, DC

Blake tightened his grip on the rifle. "I'm going to enjoy this," he said.

Jane closed her eyes and braced herself for the first shot.

"Jane?" It was Eric's voice.

"No, stay back, please." she said, but it was, of course, too late.

Eric stumbled around the corner, feeling his way along the wall.

Blake laughed when he saw him. "Look how the mighty have fallen," he said. "How pathetic."

"You were supposed to stay there!" Jane said.

"Sorry, I just couldn't."

"Enough," Blake said. "Where's Eastman?"

"He's gone," Jane said. Blake didn't like that answer, but Jane held up her hands in supplication. "He went to the lab because he thought he could do something with the swarms. I swear. He said we'd just slow him down."

Blake looked at her dubiously, then he stepped past them and to the back locker room. Satisfied, he motioned to them. "Come on. Walden wants you."

Blake now held the rifle in one hand, the barrel pointed toward the ceiling, and pushed them toward the door. Eric stumbled and turned toward Blake, clearly disoriented. "I can't see. Which way?" he said.

Blake smacked his lips in disgust and grabbed Eric's collar with his free hand. Then several things happened very quickly.

With one hand Eric grabbed the end of the rifle. With the other hand, he stuck his fingers in Blake's other eye, then he began punching him over and over.

Taken by surprise and stunned, Blake reacted slowly, and Eric was able to yank the rifle away, which he let clatter to the ground.

Jane snatched it up.

Then the two men were locked in combat. Blake, now mostly blind and disoriented, dropped his head and rushed at Eric to minimize his disadvantage. They grappled and were soon rolling on the floor. Eric gained the upper hand and straddled Blake, but then Blake went for his Glock. They struggled. Using both his hands, Eric pinned the gun and Blake's arm to the ground, then he bit into Blake's wrist. Blake finally let go of the pistol. Now, he used his fists and elbows to pummel Eric's face. They were both grunting and cursing. Over and over, Eric struck him until Blake's face was a bloody mess. Finally, Jane saw Blake's body go slack, but Eric kept hitting him again and again. He had become a wild animal, raising both fists together and pounding them down on Blake.

"Eric, that's enough!"

Eric stopped. Chest heaving and out of breath. He looked at her as if he didn't know where he was. He gasped several times, sucking in air to calm himself. He stood and noticed the blood on his hands. He seemed suddenly embarrassed and wiped them on his pants and his mouth on his sleeve. "I . . . I couldn't let him hurt you," he said.

She felt an unbidden tear come to her eye. "I know." She went to him and hugged him around the waist. As she put her head to his chest, she heard the pounding of his heart. "It's okay," she said, "it's over." She felt his arms close around her and felt the safety of his love. "You saved me," she said, "again."

"It was my turn," he said between gasps.

She pulled back and looked up at him. "But how?"

He took a moment to catch his breath then he explained: "After I went blind the last time, I knew I had to find a way to keep it from happening again. So I injected myself with the countermeasures program. My eyesight came back a minute ago."

She squeezed him tighter. "There you go, keeping secrets from me again."

Before Eric could reply, Jane's iSheet vibrated. She pulled it out. "It's Bill!" She put it on speaker.

"I'm in Eric's apartment," he said.

Eric told him where to find his personal iSheet.

"Now we need to unlock it. It's voice-activated." Eric said. "Hold your iSheet next to mine and I'll give the passcode."

"Okay, ready," Bill said.

Eric spoke the passcode—a series of clicks that he'd learned while learning Khoe-san.

"It didn't work," Bill said. "Your iSheet—and likely the cell service—is degrading the quality of your voice."

They tried again. Still no response.

At that moment the Public Service Announcement of the incoming ballistic missile popped up. *This is not a drill.*

"Eric, we need to hurry," Jane said.

"I know, but I don't know what to do!"

"I have an idea," Bill said. "Repeat the sequence one more time."

Eric did. Then he heard Bill repeat the sounds into his iSheet.

"Okay, I got it," Bill said. Somehow Bill had enunciated each of the complicated clicks perfectly. "I'm sending the mirror link to you."

Eric opened it and immediately took remote control of his own iSheet. He linked to the satellite and searched for Karuma.

He found them, surrounded by three soldiers of the White Hand. "Oh, no," Eric said.

Bill could see everything that Eric could on the other iSheet. "Can you initiate the protective swarms?"

"Checking . . . ." Eric said, opening the iSheet wider and typing on the keyboard. "No, they are there, but they won't respond. Dammit!"

★ ★ ★

"Yes, I survived," Marcus said, "barely, and in my darkest hours the dream of this moment kept me alive."

"But if you kill us, you'll kill yourselves," Karuma said. "Without us, you will never find water."

"You will lead us to water, then perhaps we will let you go, at least some of you," Marcus said.

"No," Naru said, stepping between the disfigured man and her son. "We prefer to die now, knowing that you will die too."

Marcus smiled. "I have always found that a prisoner's obstinance tends to dwindle quickly when faced with certain realities." He nodded to Nakale, "*Halt den Kleinen.*"

The big man grabbed /Uma by the hair and brought a knife to her throat.

"For example," Marcus continued, "are you willing to watch Nakale gouge her eyes out with that knife, just to keep us from having a little water?"

★ ★ ★

"This is maddening," Eric said, running both hands through his hair. "We can see them and hear them because the surveillance swarms are working perfectly. But we can't do anything to help them." He typed furiously, but still nothing worked.

"Then kill them with the surveillance swarms," Bill said.

Eric considered it for a moment. "Yes, it might work. I just need a little time. Come on, Karuma, hold on." Eric began working fast.

For this to succeed he'd have to send the nanosites from the cameras into the men's brains, and there wasn't time to do it with any finesse.

Naru looked at Marcus with a look of deep hatred.

He laughed at her. "I'm not worried; you'll eventually do as I say."

It was at that moment that Karuma cocked his head to the side. It was as if he had heard someone whispering, but from far away. He glanced around. Where had the words come from? He couldn't make them out. Something about time.

"Shall we begin?" Marcus teased. He pulled out his own knife. "We can kill two birds with one stone. After we cut her, we can start drinking her blood." He reached out and grabbed /Uma's wrist and put the tip of the blade to her skin.

"Wait," Karuma said.

Marcus stopped.

"I will take you to water, but only if you swear to let the others go. It's me that you want. I'm the one who did this to you."

Marcus eyed him suspiciously but nodded. "All right. But do it now. And no tricks."

"It is not far," Karuma said. He led them down the trail. The Sān walked in front, with the mercenaries following behind them.

Suddenly, the third mercenary fell to the ground and began to flail about, his legs kicking and his arms grabbing at nothing. Karuma saw his eyelids flickering spasmodically.

Marcus got down and tried to shove his leather belt in the man's mouth. "He's having some sort of seizure!" he said.

"No," Nakale said. "It's the cur—!" But he never finished the word. He was frozen, his neck trembling, making his head shake eerily. Karuma looked closer, oddly mesmerized. In the light of the full moon, Karuma watched as the whites of his eyes turned black as they filled with blood. And still he didn't move, all his muscles had tightened, and he couldn't control them. Then his lungs let out a raspy rattle and he collapsed to the ground.

Marcus turned his rifle on them and backed away. "You're doing this!" he said, with a wild look in his eyes. "But I'll kill you first!"

He tried to raise the rifle, but it was as if his muscles were fighting him, and he couldn't lift his arms. Then a pained look struck his face and his jaw seemed to stretch unnaturally. His eyes, too, turned black with blood. The rifle fell from his hands, and he dropped to his knees. He shook, his mouth still stretching open. Karuma heard a crack as his jaw split, then blood began to seep out of his ears. He remained that way for many seconds, before falling face-first into the sand.

CHAPTER FIFTY-SIX

PARTING WORDS

Naval Research Lab, Washington, DC

In the gymnasium, General Walden looked at the display from NORAD—a map of the globe with hundreds of lines showing the trajectory of every ICBM as they crisscrossed the map. The Russian and Chinese missiles had a head start, but the American missiles would reach their targets not long after.

"Do you have anything?" Walden barked at Ryan Lee.

"No, Eleven's swarms are still not responding. If I could regain control, I could find Emma quickly."

Walden pulled out his iSheet and called Blake. He got no answer. "Dammit! Eleven, how long before we are hit?"

"Approximately twelve minutes. Most large cities on the West Coast will be hit in under four minutes."

Walden felt a dizziness come over him. The world was about to end and all he could do was watch. Twelve minutes? What could they possibly hope to accomplish in such a short amount of time? He tried not to think of what he'd done and Hunter's accusation that this was all his fault. No, she was wrong. It was Olivia Rosario's fault . . . mostly. But also Ryan Lee's.

Several of the big iSheets were set to the major networks and Walden noticed Richard Whitlock, the Secretary of Defense, appear on all the screens.

"Eleven, turn this up, I want to hear it."

Richard Whitlock was a portly man in his early sixties with thinning white hair. Now he stood in a dark suit in front of a podium emblazoned with the circular seal of the Department of Defense.

"My fellow Americans, it appears that a nuclear strike against the United States, initiated simultaneously by Russia and China, is now imminent. While our missile-defense systems have knocked out dozens of ICBMs in flight, many have passed through our defenses and will reach American soil in a matter of minutes. I realize that this is sudden and terrifying news. But I'm asking all of you to remain calm. At this time, it is imperative that everyone shelter in place immediately. Most structures, especially those made of brick or concrete, will provide excellent shielding against radiation. Communications will likely be disrupted for hours or days. Please remain where you are and do not approach urban centers or blast zones to search for friends or relatives, it will only expose you to lethal radiation.

"The president is currently being evacuated from the capital and will address the nation as soon as possible. Thank you. Good luck, everyone. And may God bless America."

CHAPTER FIFTY-SEVEN

NEXT LIFE

Namibia

The four Sān looked at each other in amazement. Karuma quickly confirmed that each soldier was dead. Then the four of them hugged each other. It was finally over. They had defeated the White Hand. And while Karuma knew that some of their warriors had already returned to Windhoek and still lived, he felt certain that these mercenaries had learned that waging war against the Sān was not profitable.

"Thank you, Mother," Karuma said. "Thank you for coming. And for believing."

She smiled, put her hand against his jaw, and rubbed his cheek with her thumb. "I'm proud of you," she said. "And your father and grandfather would be proud of you too."

He smiled and leaned his head into her hand, and felt his whole body relax at his mother's touch. Then a tear rolled down his cheek. They had lost so much to get here, but at last, it was finally over.

★ ★ ★

Eric and Jane were embracing at the same time, then Eric spoke to Bill over the iSheet. "It was you," he said. "You were the boy that Khamko found by the river all those years ago."

"Yes," Bill said, "Karuma's grandfather saved my life."

Eric nodded, taking it in. "Thank you," he said, "Without your help, they never would have gotten this far."

"No, I should have done more. I got too involved in my own life—in science and technology and achievement—and I forgot the important things. I feel like we have made a mess of things, I just hope they can survive this."

Eric nodded, and then they said goodbye.

Jane and Eric hugged once more. It was a bittersweet moment. They had done something good. The Sān were safe and would continue their journey, even if Eric and Jane's journey was ending.

"We probably only have a few minutes," Jane said.

Eric looked around the old locker room. "Not the most romantic of settings," he said.

"Yeah, but it's not worth wasting time going anywhere else."

They lay down on the floor together, Eric's arm under her head.

"I'm sorry I couldn't save you one last time," he said.

She squeezed him tight for a moment. "I'm sorry I couldn't save you. But at least we were even at the end."

Quiet settled over the room, and they didn't move or speak for many minutes, they just savored the fact that they were together. Then Jane lifted her head and looked him in the eye. "Promise that you'll find me in the next life, okay. Because we didn't get our fair share of time in this one."

Eric struggled to control his emotions as her words conjured all the things he would never see: the days in the sun, the days in the rain, Jane in her wedding dress, her belly round with their children, watching those children grow, anniversaries and birthdays and graduations.

"I'll come find you," he said. "I promise."

CHAPTER FIFTY-EIGHT

THE DEVICE

The National Mall, Washington, DC.

In the back of the delivery truck, Bud Brown watched as Riona Finley began working on the machine. It was about the size of a small car with a fat tube, like a jet engine, running down the middle. "The machine is both a central 'brain' for the other swarms and a massive replicator," she explained. "First, we have to activate the brain so it can connect to the other swarms, then we turn on the replicator. We have to do each step as a team. You on your side, me on mine."

She went to an iSheet on one side and began punching in a code. "You stand over there," she said.

He went to a similar iSheet on the opposite side. "Okay, put in this code: B-L-X-7-8-7-P-3-8-9-T-W." Bud did as he was told. "Now hit Enter," she said.

He did. There was a whirling sound, like the fan of a computer coming on. "Okay, Jack said we'd have to wait a few minutes for it to connect with all the swarms. He said it's like a network—the brain will connect to the next node, then that one will connect to the next one and so on." Bud saw a progress bar.

"One hundred fifty of seven thousand three hundred and nine nodes reached."

The counter spun up fast—782 of 7309—but with the end of the world coming it didn't seem nearly fast enough.

"Come on!" Finley said. "Hurry up!"

"What happened to Behrmann?" Bud asked as he watched the counter.

"He died yesterday morning," she said.

"I didn't mean to shoot him. I was trying to hit Coyle. I want you to know that."

Finley met his gaze. "I didn't tell Coyle to murder your partner. And I didn't tell him to booby-trap the cabin in Vermont. He did those things on his own."

Bud nodded grimly.

The counter was still going: 1895 of 7309

He figured this was going to take at least five minutes, so he hopped down from the back of the truck and checked on Dabrowski. He was unconscious beside the cruiser, but he was still alive. Bud made sure the bleeding was under control. He considered trying to wake him, then thought better of it. If the end of the world was coming, best to be asleep.

"Come on, it's ready!" Finley called from the back of the truck. Bud hopped up to help her.

"Now we have to put in another code," she said. "This one to start the replicator."

She read it off, and Bud entered it, but before he hit enter, he asked: "You swear that this isn't going to hurt anyone?"

"If my goal was to kill people, I wouldn't be trying to do this, would I?"

Bud shrugged. "Maybe, maybe not."

"Is that what you thought I was doing all this time? Making some sort of bomb? No, what we did is much more revolutionary. It's just too bad we may never get to see it. Now please hit ENTER with me. Ready? One. Two. Three."

Bud punched the button. The machine jumped as its turbine began to spin, and Bud and Finley leapt back instinctively. The big machine began to rattle around in the back of the truck.

"Were you supposed to take it out of the truck first?"

"Yeah, but we didn't have time."

"Let's get out of here."

They jumped down to the blacktop. The turbine was spinning at an incredible speed. It felt like a powerful fan, blowing the air around, but Bud knew it was not really air, it was a huge replication cycle, meaning it was trillions upon trillions of microscopic machines moving through the air.

They backed out of the alley as the machine became louder and louder.

Bud glanced up Constitution Avenue and saw a young man standing in the middle of the deserted street holding up his iSheet to the sky.

Bud tracked his line of sight. At first he didn't see anything. Then he saw a vapor cone falling to earth. It was an oddly beautiful sight, this bubble of gray air, flashing occasionally in the light. Then he saw another and another . . . and another. The objects themselves were too small to see, there was just the leading bubble of air. "Oh, my God!" he said.

Finley came up beside him, put her hand to her brow, and saw it too.

"Here they come," he said, realizing that these were the MIRVs—the Multiple Independent Reentry Vehicles—each one had its own nuclear warhead. He counted seven in all. This was going to be massive overkill.

Finley seemed unsteady on her feet and leaned into him. "Please, no," she whispered.

"Don't look at it," he said, pulling her head to his chest and putting his hand over her eyes. She held on tight.

Then it was over.

CHAPTER FIFTY-NINE

UPPER WEST SIDE

New York City

In Manhattan, seventy-four-year-old Doctor Lizzy Mahdi spoke her last words to her daughter in Tucson and hung up her iSheet.

She stared at the device briefly and then set it down. Using both hands she wiped away the tears from her cheeks, then threw her head back and let out a long, pained breath.

She heard her husband, Albert, banging around in the kitchen— heard cupboards opening and closing, a glass hitting the floor and shattering, a curse.

She went to him, crossing through the living room. They had a beautiful apartment on the Upper West Side, with wide windows overlooking Central Park. At more peaceful moments, she liked to sit on her balcony and look out over Strawberry Fields and the Bow Bridge. In fact, over the last ten years here, she'd witnessed seven proposals on the bridge. But she didn't want to glance out the window now. The nonstop honking and shouting she heard from the street told her exactly what was going on.

She entered the kitchen through the swinging door. Albert was shoving cans of tuna into a backpack. He looked up and saw her. "Right," he said, "I've got a flashlight, three liters of water and enough food to last us about four days. We should get down to the lowest level of the parking garage. That will give us the best chance of surviving the first strike." He grabbed two more cans and pushed them into the backpack.

She came up and put her hand on his.

He stopped and looked at her.

She shook her head.

"No?" he asked. "Why not?"

For an answer, she went to the wine rack and pulled out a bottle of champagne, the one she'd been saving for her retirement party.

"Honey, please," Albert said, "we should at least try."

Again she shook her head.

He looked from the backpack to the woman he'd loved since the ninth grade.

"I never could convince you to do anything you didn't want to do," he said.

"And I've told you a million times, never argue with your doctor."

She crossed the champagne flutes in her fingers, handed him the bottle, then took his free hand and led him to their bedroom.

While they had lived in the apartment a decade, the bed had been with them for fifty years.

In it they had slept, snuggled, argued, made love, and nursed each other back to health.

Now they sat together, drinking champagne, and looking at the pictures on the walls and dressers.

Sophie's baby picture.

The grandkids—Edith, Amy, and Kayla.

A picture from their wedding. They were together in the back seat of a car, their faces full of joy and youth.

Albert looked from the picture of his bride to the face of his wife. "I picked a winner, didn't I?"

"You did," she said, "and so did I." She kissed him. Then they put their glasses down, and eased into bed together.

She took his head to her breasts and held him tight, gently running her hands through his hair.

Then she felt the warmth of his tears against her skin. She clutched him tighter, and that was the last thing that she knew.

In Tucson, Arizona, Sophie Mahdi-Bell hung up the phone with her mother and went to her sliding back door and looked at her three girls playing in the backyard. It was a rare moment of peace. No one was fighting or pushing or complaining. Edith, the eldest was teaching Kayla how to braid hair, while Amy—the scientist—sat observing a spider in its web.

She looked at them, and was about to call to them, to draw them close and tell them they had to cherish their last moments together. But then she stopped herself. *They were happy now, without a care in the world. Why rob them of that?*

She knew it would likely end quickly. Davis-Monthan Air Force Base was only twelve miles from their house. She just hoped that it was close enough.

She sat down on the back step and watched them play, thinking how beautiful they were and how it wasn't fair that they would never grow up.

Tears began streaming down her face, but she made sure not to sob or attract the girls' attention.

Just let them be little girls.

After a time, Amy got tired of looking at the spider and came over. "What's wrong, Mommy?"

Sophie brought the girl into her lap. "Nothing, sweetheart. Everything's fine." She forced a smile, and the girl wrapped her arms around her neck. Sophie rocked her gently in her arms until the end came.

CHAPTER SIXTY

ANNIHILATION

San Diego, California

The Soviet Union never figured out how to make accurate targeting systems for their ICBMs, so they compensated with two things: making bigger warheads and putting more of them in each missile.

While the American Minuteman missiles carried a single warhead with a 350-kiloton yield, the Soviet (now Russian) SS-18 Satan rocket could carry ten, each with a 750-kiloton yield.

The Russians also knew that America's missile-defense system was vastly superior to their own, so in addition to sending more warheads at a target, they also sent more missiles. As a result, important strategic targets in the US might be targeted with as many as four or five Russian ICBMs—up to fifty warheads—with a total destructive power of more than thirty-seven megatons, or twenty-five hundred times the explosive power of Hiroshima.

San Diego, California was one of those strategic targets. As the homeport of the Pacific Fleet, the Russians launched four ICBMs at it. Two were intercepted in flight. But two survived.

Of the twenty warheads in the remaining two missiles, five "fizzled"—they partially detonated in the low-kiloton range or didn't detonate at all. That's because the fissible material in a warhead needs to be upgraded every four years due to radioactive decay, and this type of maintenance was not a high priority for the Russians.

That left fifteen warheads, which rained down on the San Diego area, striking as far north as Del Mar and as far south as Tijuana. One detonated as an airburst sixty miles out to sea and did very little damage, while another detonated in the water five miles from Imperial Beach.

Marco Espineda was on his sailboat when that warhead hit the water. A big container ship, stacked high with cargo, was between Marco and the bay. He had just turned his head away when the warhead struck—if he hadn't, he would have been blinded. Suddenly bleached in light, Marco turned around to see an inverted cascade of water, two miles wide, rising out of the water. It completely dwarfed the container ship, which now appeared tiny, like a toy boat at the foot of Niagara Falls. The huge torrent of water was mesmerizingly beautiful. As the water began to fall to earth it made beautiful shingles of white and blue, like the scales of a huge monster roused from the deep.

Marco watched in awe as the incredible heat consumed the container ship. All the paint on the containers was cooked off in a rising puff of Technicolor smoke, then evaporated. Next, the shockwave hit the ship with 180 tons of force, ripping the hull open, knocking it onto its side and spilling the rectangular containers into the sea. A fraction of a second later Marco was vaporized as his body reached 270,000 degrees centigrade.

The mushroom cloud rose rapidly, pushing away the other clouds or merging with them. Up and up and up it went. Higher and higher. Mile after mile. Until it was as high as an airliner.

A second later, another warhead exploded over Logan Heights, a mile south of downtown. This was the most direct hit. The warhead detonated as designed—in an airburst over the city—creating a fireball that was half a mile wide. Everything within the fireball was instantly incinerated, reduced to basic elements. The thermal pulse extended beyond the fireball to a four-mile radius. Everything in this area that was flammable—trees, houses, grass, cars, furniture, plastic, bedding, people, birds, pets—began to burn. People going about their daily business, unaware of the pending missile strike, found that they were suddenly on fire. A matter of seconds later, the shockwave hit, flattening every structure in a five mile-radius. Only the sturdiest, steel-framed buildings were not completely destroyed. Cars and buses and burning people were lifted up and sent flying. Trees and telephone poles were snapped and thrown hundreds of yards. Most people indoors were crushed or buried alive. A dozen gas stations, including the fuel depot at the naval base, began leaking fuel, causing secondary explosions and fires.

After the shockwave dissipated near ground zero, there was a countervailing influx of wind in the opposite direction, moving at hurricane force, filling the sudden vacuum, and helping fuel the fires. The fire at the naval base grew into firestorm that swept eastward into the city. As a result, tens of thousands of people trapped in the rubble were burned alive or died from lack of oxygen.

The mushroom cloud rose high into the atmosphere, covering the city in a dark shade similar to the prelude to a violent storm.

The next ring of destruction came from radiation burns. Anyone who was far enough from the shock wave to not be instantly incinerated, killed by flying debris or buried alive, still had to contend with radiation burns. This ring reached 6.5 miles from the initial blast (now a total area of 148 square miles). The burns were painless because they destroyed nerve cells, but those who were burned over more than 24 percent of their body now needed immediate medical care to survive, but, of course, there would be nowhere to get such care.

As far away as Cockatoo Grove and the suburbs of El Cajon—over eleven miles away—people saw the flash of light and went to their windows to see. They beheld the mushroom cloud rising high into the sky. Those in the foothills could look down into the city and see a blackened core, surrounded by miles of raging fires. Many got out their iSheets and began taking pictures and videos. What they didn't realize was that the shockwave was still heading toward them. As a result, more than nineteen thousand—who could have otherwise survived—were killed by flying glass as they looked out their windows.

All told, this single warhead caused 230,000 fatalities and half a million casualties. But almost simultaneously, the other warheads were detonating, repeating the same sequence of events throughout the region, and in some cases overlapping with each other. Two warheads detonated within half a mile of each other over Marine Corps Air Station Miramar, killing half a million people and causing over a million casualties. The most lethal blast came over Tijuana, which had the highest population density, killing over 700,000 people instantly. The mushroom clouds spread out and often interlocked, blocking out the sun like a solar eclipse and creating a dim twilight for the confused survivors.

Within a matter of minutes over 2.9 million people had been killed, and that number was growing every second.

Two hundred fifty four miles above California, astronaut Lauren Baxter looked out the observation window of the International Space Station at the expanding cluster of mushroom clouds along the West Coast. Tijuana to San Francisco was blotted out by the enormous clouds, which were still growing.

Even though she had undergone some of the most difficult crisis training imaginable within the Air Force and NASA, she was now having trouble putting her thoughts together. Her husband, Tim, and her daughter, Alex, were in Madison, Wisconsin. Her parents in Green Bay. Her sister in Chicago. She tried calling her husband again, but there was no reply.

What did it mean? Was it a global war? Could Tim and Alex survive? And even if they did, how would she get to them? Could they take the Soyuz back to Kazakhstan? Would there be anyone there to help them? The questions flooded into her mind, but none of them had any answers. So she looked on in shock as all she held dear was destroyed.

CHAPTER SIXTY-ONE

EMMA

Naval Research Lab, Washington, DC

In an old storage closet in Southard Gym, Emma Rosario sat with her knees tucked up to her chest and her arms wrapped around them. The image of the general killing Sebastian kept replaying in her mind.

No, this can't be happening, she thought. *It just can't. It must be a dream.*

They said she was causing the end of the world. But how? She wasn't responsible. She just wasn't.

But what if I am?

She lifted her head for a moment as a thought struck her. *If I am causing it, maybe I can make it stop.* She remembered that day with Argo, when he'd refused to jump the fallen tree, how she'd concentrated really hard.

She took a deep breath. *Please don't kill everyone. Please don't end the world. Please. I didn't mean it. This isn't what I want.*

Over and over, she repeated these thoughts.

Please, this isn't what I want.

Finally, she felt the sudden cascading of fluid in her brain. She let out a gasp.

"General Walden," Eleven said, "I've just regained control of forty-eight percent of my swarms."

"Good, but what about the rest?"

"They are still being controlled by the photon clouds. It's strange, sir, it's like the clouds are fighting with themselves. For a moment, I had control of all the swarms, but then it took many of them back."

"Can you find the girl?"

"Yes, she's still in the building. In a closet in the basement."

Walden turned to Ryan. "I'll go get her. You stay here."

"Sir, there's something else," Eleven said. "I've intercepted a series of transmissions from Eric Hill, and I've cracked the encryption to his program. It appears that he was using a swarm system to protect a primitive tribe."

"Shut it down," Walden said.

"Wait," Ryan said, holding up his hand and coming closer to the huge computer. "Eleven, what exactly does the program do?"

"It uses a swarm system to regulate the environment in the Sān's favor, creating a protective shield around their land. It neutralizes all modern weapon systems that are introduced into the environment and strikes all those that try to use them. It also . . ."

"Eleven, stop!" Ryan said. "If you were to apply Eric's program to all of your swarms, would the system identify the nuclear warheads as threats and neutralize them?"

"That is unclear, but I predict a thirty-two percent probability that the warheads would be neutralized, and a twenty-seven percent probability that if they were not, then the program would control for the effects of thermal burns, beta radiation in fallout, and gamma radiation. It would also neutralize . . ."

"Eleven, shut up!" Ryan said. "Just tell me how many lives could be saved if we use the program."

"Implementing the program will save approximately 672 million lives globally, with that number dropping by 94,532 people if we delay ten seconds. That death count, of course, accelerating exponentially until . . ."

"Do it! Do it now!"

"I'm copying the program now."

Ryan turned to Walden. "It may not save us. But it will save a lot of others."

Walden nodded. In the last twenty seconds, he'd gone from feeling that his life was over to having a small chance of survival. And if he survived, he'd have to be ready.

"Eleven," Walden said, "do you need Ryan's assistance in implementing Eric Hill's program?"

"No, I have everything I need."

Ryan looked at Walden. "Do you want me to come with you to find Emma?" he asked.

"Not exactly." Walden pulled out the revolver and shot Ryan three times in the chest.

In Jefferson City, Missouri, Wyatt Green turned on the TV hoping to find a college basketball game but found that every station seemed to be broadcasting the news. He flicked and flicked. News, news, news. *What the hell*, he thought. Then something in the back of his mind told him he might be missing something important, and he decided to pay attention.

He watched in a kind of stupor as Defense Secretary Whitlock addressed the nation. *This can't be real*, he thought. Suddenly, he had an irresistible urge to go outside. Not bothering to put on his jacket, he rushed out his front door into the weak February sun.

He looked up, hoping to find confirmation that the world was or was not ending. There were no rocket plumes or falling missiles. His eyes locked on an airliner.

See everything is fine.

But even as he thought this, the airliner's wing dipped unnaturally, and it began to fall as if it had lost power. It was soon in a steep dive. Wyatt stared, awestruck. Then the impossible happened.

The plane began to disappear as if it was hitting an invisible barrier in the sky, disintegrating from the nose toward the tail. Four bodies tumbled out from the invisible floor and began falling to the earth. *But only four bodies,* he thought. *Where are all the others?*

Walden limped his way down the basement hallway, trying to be as quiet as possible. On his iSheet, he was following the schematic from Eleven that gave the girl's precise location. He glanced up—she was in the closet at the far end. He could see the door from here.

He held the pistol up by his shoulder as he moved along the tile floor. The bullet in his leg hurt like hell, but he did his best to push the pain aside.

He wasn't going to enjoy doing this, but it had to be done. The technology that this girl controlled had to be destroyed.

Still, he felt a growing nausea in his stomach that he could not explain. It seemed that every step he took toward the door only increased his queasiness. Then he felt a throbbing in his head, and it became harder for him to think.

Come on, just get this done.

He reached the door and flung it open. There she was, sitting on the floor between a mop and a five-gallon plastic jug of Big Blue. She was disheveled and her cheeks were stained with tears. She yelped at the sight of him and held up her hands.

Get it over with, he told himself.

But he couldn't move his arm. He looked down at the pistol in his hand and tried to will it to move, but it refused.

The harder he tried, the more the pain in his head and stomach grew. He gritted his teeth and tried even harder.

"Agggghhh!" he called out and found himself on the floor clutching his guts with his free hand. He tried to point the gun once more, but that made the pain overwhelming. He felt his bowels let go and the warm urine ran down his leg.

The gun fell from his hand, and the pain began to subside.

He looked up at the girl, who was now standing. He could tell she was judging whether she could get by him and escape, but he was right in the doorway. She stepped closer, testing him.

"You killed Sebastian," she said. "He was my friend."

She took another step closer.

Walden lunged for her. She shrieked and tried to jump away, but he grabbed one of her ankles. She fell back, knocking over the mop and bucket of filthy water.

"I have to do this," he said.

He began clawing his way up her body. Hand over hand, moving up her leg. Each motion was more painful than the last, but he didn't stop. He reached her waist, then her shoulder, and then his hands encircled her small neck.

"I have to do this," he repeated.

The girl's eyes were wide with fear, and she slapped and scratched at his face. But he kept the pressure on her throat. *Get it over with*, he thought, *just get it done.*

Then her eyes locked on his with a strange intensity. Her expression had turned from one of terror to one of fierce defiance.

Emma looked into the general's eyes, focusing all her attention on getting him away.

Get him off me. Now. Get him off me. Make him go away!

She had to get to "the feeling" —the sense of release she had felt when she had controlled Argo with her mind. It came, and much quicker than before.

Suddenly, Walden's face caved in like a grape squeezed between strong fingers. Brain matter and blood erupted out of his ears. His hands went loose around her neck, and his body was thrown backward through the closet door, but even as his body flew through the air it was coming apart, so that what hit the wall was mostly liquid.

Emma rose quickly, her flight response taking over. She ran through the closet door, only glancing at what was left of the body, which wasn't much. It was more like a military uniform partially filled with hamburger meat. There was blood and matter sprayed across the wall, and lying near the uniform, some purplish organ.

She rushed down the hall and up the staircase. In the light of the stairwell, she examined herself, expecting to find she was covered in his blood, but there wasn't a drop on her.

From somewhere outside she heard a piercing whistle, deafeningly loud and growing louder, then everything went black.

PART SIX

THE CLOUDS PART

It seemed that out of battle I escaped
Down some profound dull tunnel, long since scooped
Through granites which titanic wars had groined.
Yet also there encumbered sleepers groaned,
Too fast in thought or death to be bestirred.
Then, as I probed them, one sprang up, and stared
With piteous recognition in fixed eyes,
Lifting distressful hands, as if to bless.
And by his smile, I knew that sullen hall,—
By his dead smile I knew we stood in Hell.

Wilfred Owen, "Strange Meeting"

CHAPTER SIXTY-TWO

BRAVE NEW WORLD

Fairfax County, Virginia

Curtiss woke and looked around. He was in his prison cell. He touched the side of his head and felt a swollen bump from where he must have hit his head on the floor.

What the hell happened?

He tried to remember, but he couldn't think straight. It reminded him of the end of Hell Week in BUD/S. Going five days without sleep. This was how his mind had felt at the end of it.

His last memories were just dreamy fragments: a nuclear strike, Anchorage wiped out, Calhoun singing.

He looked around. Everything *looked* the same. *Had it all been a dream? Why was it so quiet?*

He stood and looked more closely. The cement floor had a thick crack running down the middle. And Calhoun?

He looked up. The door to Calhoun's cell was open.

"Calhoun! Anybody?"

There was no answer.

This didn't make any sense. This close to DC, he should be dead, or at least with severe radiation burns.

He stood on his bed to see out the narrow window. When he'd first arrived at the brig and looked out, he'd realized he had a truly charming view of the parking lot, a stretch of two-lane road, and then—in the distance—the houses, trees, and lawns of the Virginia suburbs. Now, he was expecting to see that most of it had been destroyed—leveled buildings and trees, cars stopped in their tracks from the EMP, perhaps refugees walking the streets, and huge fires burning in the distance. But what he saw was even more shocking.

There were no fires, no toppled buildings. Yes, there were rows of cars on the road, all still. But where was everyone?

That's when he noticed that everything was green and gold. It was the third week of February, but it looked like the middle of summer. The grass was no longer brown. The trees looked green, but wait, no it wasn't leaves on the trees, they were covered in vines, with broad leaves that made them look as lush as summertime.

What the hell?

He stared in disbelief.

What did it mean? And where was everyone?

Then he heard someone singing. It was Calhoun. Somewhere far off in the prison.

The killer awoke before dawn.
He put his boots on
He took a face from the ancient gallery.
And he walked on down the hall, yeah!

Curtiss now had a situation. He went to the door of his cell and tested the bars. Still locked. If Calhoun got his hands on a weapon— say, one of the guard's sidearms—then Curtiss was a dead man.

As if the pucker factor on this day wasn't high enough, Curtiss thought.

The voice was distant . . . somewhere beyond the cell block . . . maybe as far away as the cafeteria.

For a fleeting moment, he hoped that Calhoun would keep going out the front door and head west for Kentucky.

Then the singing started up again and it wasn't getting farther away. It was getting closer.

He went into the room where his sister lived, and then he
Got a meat cleaver from the prison kitchen, and then
He walked on down the hall, yeah!

Curtiss assessed his options, which were not good. Of course, there was nothing in the room that could be used as a weapon. That was one of the drawbacks of being on suicide watch. He looked around desperately. *There must be something . . .* His eyes fell on the bed, then his stack of books from the library.

An idea struck him. He pulled the pillowcase off the pillow and put two of the heavy hardbacks inside, then he spun it closed like a loaf of bread to take up the slack. It made a crude flail that would extend his reach, something that was imperative if Calhoun really had a meat cleaver.

Next, he took the sheet from his bed and wrapped it around his left forearm over and over until it was padded enough to absorb at least a glancing blow from a blade, then he tied it with his free hand and his teeth.

He heard a metal door clang. It sounded like Calhoun was on the far side of the guard post.

He took a deep breath and assessed Calhoun as a fighter. The young man was wiry but strong. He was also thirty years younger than Curtiss. That meant he'd probably be quicker. Plus, his hatred would give him extra adrenaline . . . but it would also cloud his judgment.

On the bright side, Calhoun's cardio would probably be shit from spending three years in Leavenworth. He would tire fast. That meant Curtiss needed to drag the fight out.

He heard Calhoun singing. He was very close.

> *And he came to a door*
> *And he looked inside*
> *"Father?" "Yes, son?"*

At that instant, Calhoun's head poked out around the wall. He had a gleeful, maniacal grin on his face. He put his cheeks up against the bars and looked in. He held up a shiny metal cleaver. He pulled his head back a little and put one eye up to the hole in the blade.

"I see you!" he said with a laugh.

He stepped back and began swinging the cleaver, making practice cuts in the air. His motions were smooth and measured, and Curtiss could tell he'd had some martial-arts training. It reminded him of the Filipino stick fighters who trained the SEALs in knife fighting.

Curtiss tried to reason with him. "It looks like you've got a problem, Calhoun. If you want to kill me, you're going to have to let me out."

"Oh, I know."

"But I don't think you can open the door."

"Nope, I can't. I looked for the code cards, but there ain't none."

"Then you might as well just leave me here to die."

Calhoun thought that was pretty funny and he gave a long laugh. "Oh, don't worry, Jim. You'll be free in no time."

Curtiss flashed him a look of puzzlement, thinking that Calhoun had gone mad.

"That's right," Calhoun continued. "You've been asleep a lot longer than I have. Things are a-changin' fast around here." He opened his eyes wide at the word "changin'" to give it an air of mystery.

Curtiss looked around his cell and became aware of a strange sound, like the movement of thousands of insects. It was coming from just on the other side of the wall.

Calhoun's tongue flicked out and he licked his lips. Then he looked up. He could clearly see something that Curtiss couldn't. "See, I told ya! It's comin'."

Then Curtiss saw it too. Right where the ceiling met the wall the paint was disappearing, exposing the gray cinder blocks. It spread rapidly. In less than ten seconds the walls and ceiling were bare and the scratching sound had moved into the next cell.

Now he began to hear different sounds—the groaning of steel and the occasional pop or ping. He looked at his cot and saw that the aluminum frame was dissolving away.

There was a snap and ping and water began seeping out from under his toilet and spreading across the floor.

"Any second now," Calhoun said, flashing a wide-eyed smile.

As if on cue, the bars of Curtiss's cell began to dissolve, starting at the top corner and spreading diagonally down.

Calhoun bounced on the balls of his feet in anticipation. As soon as the gap was big enough, he launched himself into it, kicking off the wall and landing in Curtiss's cell with the meat cleaver raised. With a war cry he swung it with all his might.

In a flash, Curtiss slipped away from the cut and snatched up the pillowcase. Calhoun had put so much force into the blow that he stumbled. Curtiss swung the crude weapon with all his might.

It made a satisfying thud against the side of Calhoun's jaw and twisted his head a quarter turn. Something white shot out of Calhoun's mouth and skidded across the floor, it reminded Curtiss of a piece of Chiclets chewing gum.

Calhoun threw himself against the far wall and shook his head like a dog as he tried to recover from the blow.

"It looks like someone's gonna get a visit from the tooth fairy tonight," Curtiss said.

Calhoun put two fingers in his mouth where the tooth had been, then smiled through his bloody teeth. "I knew you'd make it fun," he said. "But I'm still gonna hack you to pieces."

Curtiss shook his head. "We don't have to do this," he said. "Look around. The world didn't end. Think about your mom and your girl. They're still alive."

Calhoun just laughed. "You're crazy! Don't you get it? We're already dead. I just can't decide whether this is heaven or hell." He came at Curtiss again, but this time he was more cautious. He began to feign attacks, trying to get Curtiss to swing the pillowcase. When he did, Calhoun swung not at Curtiss, but at the pillowcase.

The first time he clipped it where it was wound tight, doing little damage, but the second time he tore the fabric around the books.

Calhoun was playing it smart. Another cut like that and Curtiss's only weapon would be rendered useless.

Around them, things were changing rapidly. The glass in Curtiss's window had disappeared and creeper vines were reaching through the opening. Out in the corridor, chunks of concrete were falling and evaporating on impact. The whole building was alive, speaking a language in creaks and moans.

Above and below.

Left and right.

"Come on, Curtiss!" Calhoun called with a big smile on his face. He was clearly enjoying himself, keyed up like a meth head. "Dance with me!"

He lunged in and Curtiss was forced to swing with the books. Calhoun deftly pulled back in time and caught the pillowcase with the meat cleaver, sending the books flying out.

Calhoun laughed with glee, knowing he now had the upper hand. The blood from his mouth had now seeped over his chin giving him a diabolical look.

Then the ceiling eroded away. Sunlight splashed over them. Curtiss felt the coolness of a breeze and the warmth of the sun at the same time.

They both couldn't help looking around, in a moment of spontaneous détente. They were free, but in what kind of world had they landed?

Curtiss tried to reason with him again. "Stop this, Liam. You're not a killer."

"Not yet," he said, "but ask me again in five minutes."

Confident of the win, he came in with a vicious flurry of cuts. Curtiss moved back into the corridor and used his wrapped forearm as best as he could to parry the strikes. But Calhoun was relentless, and finally sank the cleaver deep into the cloth and into Curtiss's skin. Curtiss gritted his teeth and punched Calhoun square in the nose with his free hand. Calhoun stumbled back, twisting the cleaver out of the wound at the same time.

Curtiss didn't even glance at the wound, knowing that the mere act of looking at it would quicken his shock response.

Calhoun smiled at his handiwork. "Won't be long now," he said. But at that moment the floor disappeared underneath them, exposing rails of rebar that ran from wall to wall. Calhoun fell straight through them. Curtiss managed to grab one as he fell. Then the rebar itself disintegrated.

Curtiss fell almost twenty feet into the basement of the prison. There was a furnace and HVAC system nearby with its spidery aluminum ducts spreading out in all directions. On the cement floor was a scattering of tools—hammers, wrenches, and screwdrivers. Vines were reaching from the outside into the basement.

Calhoun had hit his head in the fall and was rolling around on the ground, one hand clapped to his head, the other hand still holding the cleaver.

Curtiss picked up a monkey wrench and stood over Calhoun.

"I saved your life last time," he said, "but you never realized it. My team wanted to kill you. Said you were too much of a liability. But I said no. I didn't want another death on my head, especially the death of someone who hadn't done anything wrong."

Calhoun got up to one knee and glared up at Curtiss. They were both panting hard, both exhausted. "Your men were right."

"Probably," Curtiss said. "You lost your mind in Leavenworth and that's on me. I'm sorry. I'm going to give you one last chance to make a choice. What's it going to be: Freedom in a brave new world with a chance to go home . . . or death?"

Calhoun wiped the blood off his chin with the back of his hand, then stood and looked down at the meat cleaver. "Ain't no goin' back," he said.

"Very well," Curtiss said, raising the monkey wrench in both hands like a baseball bat.

Calhoun came again. Curtiss faked high, then swung with all his might at his gut, hoping to catch the cleaver in the process. But midswing, the concrete floor disintegrated, and even though it was only eight inches from the ground, it was enough to send Curtiss flailing backward.

Seeing his chance, Calhoun fell on him with a killing blow. Curtiss raised the monkey wrench in both arms to block but his weapon evaporated in his hands. Calhoun's eyes flashed with glee, but then the meat cleaver disappeared too, and Calhoun was left holding the two pieces of the wooden handle.

"Ahhh!" Calhoun screamed in fury and grappled for Curtiss's throat. But now Curtiss was in his element. Calhoun might know how to use a blade, but there was no way he had better hand-to-hand skills than Curtiss. In a few seconds, Curtiss had done a reversal and pinned Calhoun. He looked down at him and smiled. "Bad choice," Curtiss said as the grass grew up around them.

Then they both froze. They had just heard the strangest sound, a deep primordial growl. They both turned.

What in Christ's name . . . Curtiss thought.

Not forty-five yards away stood two enormous creatures. They were both alien and familiar at the same time. They looked more like cheetahs than anything else, lean-waisted and built for speed, their heads slung low over swaying shoulders. But they were unnaturally large, standing at least five feet.

"Let me go," Calhoun whispered.

Curtiss stood up slowly and gave both Calhoun and their new visitors some space. Then he looked around, assessing his options.

To his left and right were forest. Behind him was the

disintegrating remains of the brig, now not much more than a collection of plumbing pipes, rebar, and chunks of concrete.

"When I say 'go,' make for the woods on my right. Find a tree and get in it," Curtiss said.

The huge cats were stalking closer. Spreading out. Anticipating their flight.

"Go!" Curtiss shouted.

They sprinted for the woods.

It was fifty yards to the nearest suitable tree. A maple with a low split. Curtiss was already imagining himself leaping into the fork and scrambling up the left side.

He glanced back and what he saw made his adrenaline surge. The cheetahs were already on them. *How could anything move that fast?* The front cheetah leapt at him, claws distended like daggers. Its jaws opened. Curtiss saw massive canines, longer than his hand. He threw himself to the side and rolled, coming quickly to his feet. The cat lost its footing as it tried to swerve. Curtiss took the momentary reprieve to snatch up a stick and keep running.

He saw the second cat lunge at Calhoun. They tumbled together, the big predator's claws and jaws tearing at him. Somehow, miraculously, Calhoun scrambled to his feet, his bare chest scratched and bleeding, but nowhere near dead.

Curtiss was almost to the tree, but the other cheetah was now right behind him. With a backhand swing, he caught it on the ear with the branch. The blow stunned it, but the move bought Curtiss only a few more seconds.

Calhoun had now made it to the tree and was climbing up frantically. Curtiss reached it a second later, quickly scrambling to the first fork.

Curtiss knew he had to move fast. He guessed a cat that big could jump at least fifteen feet.

He and Calhoun were climbing the same side of the trunk, Calhoun now just above him.

The first cat leapt up at him. It missed, but its claws completely sliced the two-inch branch he'd been standing on, leaving him hanging by one hand.

He looked up at Calhoun and could see the hesitation in his eyes. If Calhoun wanted to step on Curtiss's fingers and send him to his death, this was his chance.

Instead, he reached down and grabbed his wrist. Soon they were at a safe height, standing side by side on different branches.

Below them, the huge cats mulled around, one occasionally putting its front paws on the tree trunk and looking forlornly at its lost dinner. The vines were making their way up the tree, spiraling around the trunk and larger boughs.

"Thanks," Curtiss said with a smile.

Calhoun merely nodded—perhaps already regretting his decision—and bit at his fingernails.

Curtiss kept smiling, but he was thinking into the future. He had to get into DC as fast as possible to see if Evelyn and the boys were okay. But could he travel with Calhoun? Could he trust him? And what about all those things Calhoun had said about revenge and hurting his family?

With both feet securely on one limb, Curtiss reached up with one hand to clasp a branch above his head. *Yes, that was stable enough.* Then he reached out to shake Calhoun's hand.

"You saved me down there and I won't forget it," he said.

Calhoun looked at the hand a moment, then shook it. With a quick twist of his wrist, Curtiss pulled his hand free, unbalancing Calhoun, then with his right leg he kicked him as hard as he could in the hips.

Calhoun fell back. He reached out and caught a small branch, but it wasn't enough, his hand slipping along it as its twigs were peeled off. With a look of shock and terror, he fell, kicking and swimming in the air.

Curtiss watched calmly as the giant cats pounced on him. One bit his neck and held him down while the other began eating him.

★ ★ ★

The great cheetahs dragged Calhoun's body about sixty yards to the edge of the clearing. After they had eaten their fill, they urinated around the body, then both lay down to sleep.

When Curtiss was sure they were out, he slipped down from the tree and began making his way toward the city.

CHAPTER SIXTY-THREE

LOST

Jane stood looking out over the forested landscape that had been Washington, DC. The once-beautiful city was now trees and grass. No Washington Monument. No roads. No life.

She stared, trying to make sense of it.

How could this be?

She scanned the terrain more closely, trying to find any sign of the world she knew.

Yes, there was something there, south of the mall. It was the Jefferson Memorial, but even as her eyes locked on it, it began to dissolve. Jane watched in amazement as the dome disappeared in a spiraling haze of particles, as if a giant hand was sanding it to dust. Simultaneously, creeper vines grew hungrily up its Ionic columns, until those too dissolved and the vines tumbled back to the ground.

Please be a dream, she thought. *Please be a dream.*

She tried hard to remember what had happened, but all she got were bits and pieces: She remembered being terrified. She remembered everyone was trying to find a little girl. And she remembered that Blake had been out to kill them.

But there were gaps in her memory that she couldn't fill. Something about Walden and a countdown. *Ugh!* She smacked the side of her head with her palm, but the memories just wouldn't come.

She called out. Hoping to find someone who could help her. "Eric!" she called. "Please! Anyone."

An angry snort came from the woods behind her. Deep and menacing. Jane froze for a second, then slowly turned.

No, that's impossible.

A huge animal, much like a rhinoceros but with a horn four times as large, came charging at her. She sprinted for the nearest tree, her arms chopping the air as she tried to gain speed. The huge beast came barreling after her, huffing like a bear. Its heavy footfalls shaking the ground. She scrambled up the tree as fast as she could, then looked back to see it charging in. It wasn't slowing down and for a moment she feared it was going to ram the tree and topple it over. But at the last second, it pulled up short. With a fierce snort, it looked up at her. It stomped the ground several times, looked up at her, then, satisfied that she had been put in her place, it turned its butt to her and walked off.

Jane blew out her breath hard in exasperation. Now she was getting angry. *What the hell is going on?*

She stayed in the tree for a time. Trying to collect her thoughts. Slowly, her memories began to return. *Emma. That was the little girl's name. There was going to be a nuclear war, but it was all a mistake.*

Her anxiety rose with each new memory.

They had all been trying to stop it. No, they'd actually given up and decided to help the Sān instead. But how had they gone from nuclear annihilation to this?

She looked around, out at this vast strange world. She looked at the trees covered in vines, growing and flowering before her eyes. And the grass, it was growing everywhere. Mile after mile of it. She found herself staring at it. There was a lonely beauty to it. When the wind blew, it turned silver as it swayed and righted itself. And it made a hissing sound like the ocean. Then she saw an empty patch and a flash of color not far from where she'd woken up. She noticed the color of blue jeans. There was a body down there. She looked closer and recognized Eric's sweatshirt.

Oh, no! she thought.

She scrambled down out of the tree and raced toward his body. *Please be okay. Please.*

She reached him and threw her head against his chest, the fingers of her left hand probing his neck for his pulse. She felt his warmth, then his pulse, then she heard his heart.

Thank God.

She kissed him gently on the lips. "Come on, sweetheart, wake up."

He blinked a few times and looked at her. There was a confused expression on his face, but then he smiled. "We didn't die," he said with relief.

"Actually, I'm still not entirely sure about that."

Amanda Rush awoke in the tall grass. She was cold and couldn't quite remember what had happened. Her last memories were of her nanny taking her to the basement. All her friends had been texting her and freaking out. Then her mother had called and was totally losing it, saying that it was the end of the world.

Amanda looked around. As usual, her mother had been wrong. Everything looked just like before. But how had she gotten out into the woods? And where was everybody? Most importantly, where was her phone? People would be worried about her. *I bet Mom and Dad have the police searching for me already*, she thought.

It suddenly struck her how green everything was. It was totally weird. It was the middle of winter, yet everything was green. And the grass, it was almost up to her shoulders. Totally bizarre.

At that moment, the wind picked up and lifted her hair. She shivered. *Jesus, it's freezing out here!* She rolled up the collar of her Balmain sweater and stretched the sleeves down over her hands. She looked around for a trail but saw none. She tried to remember what she was supposed to do, but she'd only been a Girl Scout for a month before she'd quit. Something about a river leading to a creek?

Ugh! If only I had my stupid phone.

She called out. "Hello? Nanna? Anybody?"

She listened for a reply. That's when she heard it . . . a steady breathing sound. She turned. Not seven feet away, an enormous cheetah stood looking at her. It was standing in the tall grass, its body completely hidden except for its head. *Had it been standing there the whole time?*

Between flight, fight or freeze, Amanda froze. Her heart thundered in her chest, and she felt it pulsating up to her ears, but she didn't move.

Then she heard a growl, but not from the cheetah she was staring at. Her eyes darted to the right. There was another huge cat, just as big as the first. Then her eyes darted to the left and she saw the third cheetah.

Still, she couldn't move. Only her eyes flew from one huge cat to the other. They were enormous. Their legs almost as long as she was tall, and their canine teeth hung out over their lower lips.

Cheetahs don't get that big, she thought. *They just don't.*

The three cats slinked toward her in unison, creating a narrowing spiral around her.

Cheetahs can't get that big, she kept thinking, trying to convince herself that this just couldn't be. None of this was really happening. She wasn't lost in the forest. Of course not. "You're not real!" she finally said, sticking out her chin defiantly. "You can't hurt me."

Suddenly, as one, they leapt at her.

Amanda screamed.

★ ★ ★

Eric and Jane had been walking for two hours when they reached the airport. There was still wreckage here: the cylindrical control tower lay toppled on the ground and creeper vines were growing hungrily over it. Where the main terminal had been, they could still see a series of the tall steel archways that had not yet collapsed, and on the old runway where they walked, the grass seemed to be struggling to grow.

Their plan was to get back to the lab to see if they could find any clues about what was happening. But getting back across the river was not going to be easy. With no way to carry their clothes or keep those clothes dry or build a fire, trying to swim across would be too dangerous. So they were heading to a small marina just south of the airport in the hopes of finding a boat.

As they reached the end of the runway, they heard a deep rumbling from above. They looked up to see what looked like a meteor streaking across the sky. It had a molten red tip, followed by a section of black smoke, then a long contrail of white smoke behind it.

Their faces turned to the sky, they saw another and then another. Soon there were dozens of them crisscrossing the sky.

"What are they?" Jane asked.

"I think they're satellites," Eric said. "I dreamed of this. I dreamed all this would happen, but I couldn't do anything to stop it."

She embraced him, and together they watched as hundreds of mankind's satellites were pulled back to earth. It was a beautiful but unsettling sight.

"I had hoped that whatever program was doing this, was just doing it here," Eric said. "But this proves it's global. The program is reshaping the entire world."

"But what program? I thought Emma's program was out to start a nuclear war."

Eric shook his head. "I'm not sure, but let's consider what we know: Before we blacked out, Emma's program was the most powerful and there seemed to be no way to stop it. Therefore, some of what we are seeing is likely coming from her. But this plant growth is exactly what Jack was making for Riona Finley—winter vegetation that would help reverse climate change."

"Finley? How did her program get released?"

"I don't know. But the world didn't experience a nuclear war, at least not here. So perhaps the others found Emma and were able to stop her program in time."

"Or maybe Ryan found a way to get Eleven to fight Emma's swarms."

"That's possible too," Eric said. "Either way, we are looking at two, maybe three different programs, all trying to alter the world at the same time."

Jane shook her head incredulously. "I can't get my mind around it. I just . . ." For a second she choked up, then quickly composed herself. "I just can't believe some random, unpredictable thing just destroyed the world."

"I know it doesn't seem fair . . . but it wasn't random. It's the result of these programs—like Emma's cure and Jack's effort to save the planet—doing what they were designed to do. It's all the result of other people taking my ideas and doing these things. It all comes back to me."

"No, that's not fair," Jane said, now feeling that it was her turn to console him. "You did what Curtiss and Bill asked of you. You did your job. You can't blame yourself for what others did with your work."

Eric shook his head, filled with doubt. "But I can't get over the simple fact that if I hadn't created Forced Evolution, none of this would have happened."

They continued until they found the remains of the marina. In the tall grass Jane kicked at a sign—*Daingerfield Island Sailing Club*. Most of the marina was gone, but they found a small wooden rowboat.

They inspected it. The metal rowlocks were gone, so they fashioned some with rope.

"And there is one other big question," Jane said as she worked the rope through a hole in the wood.

"What's that?"

"How did we get picked up and deposited four miles from the lab?"

"I've been thinking about that too. And there's only one thing I can think of: we were teleported."

"Teleported?" Her eyebrows went up skeptically.

"The Inventor told me he'd figured out how to teleport using quantum entanglement. That's how he took me to the Daintree rain forest. Perhaps Emma's program figured it out too."

"But why would Emma's program do that? I mean, why us?"

"I don't know."

When the boat was ready, they got in, and Eric began rowing them across to the lab.

For a time, the only sound was the steady dip and splash of the oars in the water. Just as Jane was thinking how eerily quiet it was, she heard the pained cry of a strange animal. It lasted nearly a minute and conjured the image of a violent death. It made Jane feel like a stranger in her own world. She was the alien here, small and vulnerable, and it seemed inevitable that she would soon be dead like the rest of her kind.

Eric seemed to sense her worry and tried to distract her.

"It's kinda romantic, isn't it?" he said. "I mean, take away the serenade of a dying animal, and we have a relaxing boat ride on the river. All we need to do is find you a dress and a parasol."

She forced a smile, but then shook her head. "When we were in the locker room . . . I told you it wasn't fair that we didn't get enough time together. But now, I don't know, I'm afraid of what the future holds."

"This isn't exactly what we had hoped for, is it? When I thought about having more time, I pictured a wedding and children, birthdays and anniversaries."

"Me too," she said. "But that was in a world that doesn't exist anymore."

Eric nodded; there was no denying it. "This isn't the story I wanted to write with you."

"What do you mean?"

Eric explained how he thought of his life as a story—most of the time he was the author, making the decisions that determined what happened next, but sometimes other people and circumstances changed the course of your life and there wasn't anything you could do about it. "The hard truth is that you only get a say in some of it, not all of it. Now I regret not doing some of the things I had the power to do. Like marrying you. I'd imagined this grand wedding with our family and friends."

She smiled sadly. "Me too." She leaned forward and took his hands in hers. "But if I'm hearing you right, then we still have a chance to write our story. It's certainly not what we ever imagined, but at least we're alive and together. We need to see that as a gift."

He gave a reluctant smile. "You're right, as usual." He pulled the oars on board, then reached out and tore a strand of rope from the frayed end of the rowlock. "In the spirit of making the most of what we have . . . ." He got down on one knee and the boat rocked ominously. Jane grabbed the sides and steadied herself.

"What are you doing?"

"Jane Hunter, will you marry me?"

Jane prided herself on being tough and no-nonsense, but the tears came anyway, hot and wide on her cheeks. Eric took her hand and tied the strand of rope around her finger.

Soon her face was a mess. *Thank God no one is taking pictures*, she thought.

"Is that a yes?" he probed.

"Yes," she blurted out.

He hugged her. "Even though the world has gone crazy, maybe we can still write a happy ending."

The boat teetered for a moment as they found their balance together, then they held each other tight as the boat drifted downstream.

★ ★ ★

Even before they reached the shore by the NRL, Jane could see a mound of rubble where the main building had been, with long strips of steel from the huge satellite dish laying on top of it.

They tied the boat and rushed up the bank to get a better look, both anxious to get some answers.

Most of the buildings were gone, replaced by vines and moss. It was startling to look at, to see all the familiar objects of everyday life suddenly gone: the bungalows along the river, the apartment block where they used to live, and the coffee shop Jane visited every morning. It had all been erased.

But near Magazine Road—right where Southern Gym had been—there was a crater, charred black and still wisping smoke. They ran to it and looked down.

It was about thirty yards wide and almost ten yards deep, with horizontal bands of gray ash along the sides. The smell of charcoal and burned plastic filled the air.

Nearby they found Ryan Lee's body. He was lying face-up, his eyes open and unmoving. Then they saw the bullet wounds in his chest.

"Oh, Ryan," Jane said, kneeling beside his body. "I'm so sorry." She cried a little, but her sadness quickly turned to anger. "This wasn't Emma's fault."

"No, it wasn't," Eric agreed. "He was murdered."

"Walden or Blake," Jane said.

They searched some more and found Walden's uniform and what remained of his body. "At least he got his due," Jane said.

"But we aren't any closer to figuring out what happened."

Jane pointed to the crater. "At least we know who won the battle between Eleven and Emma's photon clouds."

Eric nodded. "Emma's clouds must still be out there, which means that Emma's probably out there too. We aren't the sole survivors. There must be more."

★ ★ ★

Bud Brown awoke in an alien landscape. As he lifted his eyes and looked out across the mall, he caught a glimpse of the red castle of the Smithsonian melting like ice cream under a hot sun. In only a matter of seconds it had been replaced by a tangle of hungry vines.

He stood on rubbery legs and watched as the world was transformed before his eyes. The Washington Monument, the Hirschhorn Museum, the Capitol Building. All he could do was stare in astonishment. He was just a spectator, watching an amazing transformation caused by things beyond his control.

"This wasn't part of the deal," he said aloud. He looked around for Finley, but she was nowhere to be found. He was in the heart of the nation's capital, with a view for at least a mile to the east and west, yet he saw no sign of any other living being. "This wasn't the way it was supposed to be," he said.

The grass was growing before his eyes. It was already up to his knees. This was definitely Finley's program. She'd sworn to him that the machine wouldn't hurt anyone. That it wouldn't "thin" the population. But now he realized the truth.

Finley had lied.

"We need to think about how we are going to make it through the night," Eric said. "We will either need to get underground or find a way to make a fire, or we'll freeze to death."

Jane looked down into the crater. "I think I can gather up some coals and get a fire going. But we'll need some kindling and more wood."

"Right, then let's make a shelter first and any scrap wood we find in the process we'll use for the fire."

They went to the pile of rubble they'd seen from the shore and began looking for things to make a lean-to. The mound was massive, as big as the footprint of the library and almost twenty feet high. Soon they'd found a wooden door for the wall of the lean-to, and half a ream of paper to help start the fire.

But as they were rummaging near the base, they heard a sound, like someone else climbing over the debris.

Eric felt Jane's warning grip on his arm and his heart rate spiked. Now he felt foolish for not having fashioned some kind of weapon. He had known there were other survivors, yet he shouldn't have taken it for granted that they would be friendly. He grabbed a piece of wood from the rubble and looked up toward the sound. Against the glare of the afternoon sun, he saw the silhouette of a head. He tightened his grip on the stick.

"Oh, thank God!" came a familiar voice. "I was beginning to think I was the only one left."

Eric looked closer, but the sun showed only a silhouette. Finally, the figured descended down the mound and came into the shadow. It was a man wearing jeans and a blue FBI blazer. It was Bud Brown. "I was hoping to find some answers here."

"So were we," Jane said.

Eric introduced the two of them.

"I'm really glad to see you," Bud said. "Did I say that already?"

Eric smiled. "Likewise," he said. Honestly, this was a huge relief. For some reason, just having one more person felt like five. Now it seemed like they might actually survive.

"What the hell happened?" Bud asked.

"We aren't exactly sure," Jane said. They swapped stories. Bud told them about Finley's machine, and they told him about Walden, Sebastian, and Emma.

"This was all caused by a ten-year-old girl?" Bud said, shaking his head.

"Most of it," Jane replied.

"And you think she's still out there somewhere?"

"I'm certain of it," Eric said.

They worked together to make the lean-to. Then Jane got a fire going.

The sunlight was beginning to fade, and the temperature was dropping when they heard a strange animal call. "What was that?" Bud asked.

Eric and Jane shook their heads.

They climbed up the pile of rubble to get a better look.

Eastward, on the wedge of land where the Anacostia and Potomac rivers merged, they saw a herd of antelope-like animals drinking at the bank. They were dark brown with cream-colored necks and bellies. The males had a set of antlers on their heads, as well as a smaller set coming off the nose that reminded Eric of a warthog's tusks.

"What on earth are those?" Bud asked.

"I don't know," Jane said. "Nothing in this world makes sense." She turned to Eric who was nodding. A faint smile grew across his face. "What are you thinking?" she asked.

"Well, we now have shelter and fire. Our next priority is food." He glanced out at the strange animals.

"That isn't going to be easy," Bud said, "especially without weapons."

"We can make weapons," Eric said. "Spears and bows and arrows. If we work as a team, we can do it."

Bud didn't seem convinced. "Have you ever hunted like that before?"

"Just once."

Bud gave a skeptical nod. "I suppose that's better than never."

CHAPTER SIXTY-FOUR

The singularity of February 16, 2027 did not occur instantaneously across the globe, nor with the same consequences. Things happened quickly in some places, but slower in others. Some of the programs meant to ameliorate the apocalypse dominated some regions but were too late or too slow to help others. In most areas, all man-made structures disappeared, but in some places, they survived completely or in part. This led to an uneven distribution of who lived and who died.

Other factors also impacted the survivors. The sudden loss of technology (or just electricity) meant that in the northern latitudes over 229,000 people died of hypothermia on the first night. Then there were the types of common accidents or illnesses that occur every day that are rarely serious or fatal but became crippling or insurmountable to people alone and in shock, such as falling and breaking a leg, having a stroke, or developing appendicitis. People died of kidney stones, ulcers, ventral hernias, bee stings, cpllapsed lungs, asthma attacks, and diverticulitis.

Other people died from accidents caused by living on their own, such as twenty-one-year-old Jacob Richards of Topeka, Kansas, who tried punching through the glass doors of his local Kroger store and slit his right forearm from his palm to his elbow. He died of blood loss five hours later. Then there were the suicides—over 30,000 of them in the first week. People who decided that they couldn't survive alone and didn't want to try.

What's more, those who were obese, in poor physical shape, or had an aversion to embracing humanity's arboreal past, did not live long when man-eating predators were introduced into the ecosystem. The dogs that survived—the ones who broke their outdoor chains or were not trapped indoors to die of starvation—quickly formed into hunting packs and became another hindrance to human survival. It soon became clear that being a mutt was an advantage and many of the smaller, timid, or pampered dogs were eaten in the process of establishing the pecking order.

At Poinsett State Park in South Carolina, Mei Hwe discovered that her German shepherd, Chance, no longer recognized her.

She'd woken up under the bunkbed in the cabin they had rented. She called out to Xiao-ping and the dog but got no reply. She searched the place and found no sign of them, then she wandered into the front yard. There was no one around. She could see two of the other cabins and the road down to the lake, but no cars were moving. A minivan was parked askew in the middle of the road, its passenger door left open.

It was a warm day and humid. She listened for any sounds of life, but only heard the chirping of birds and the wind chimes on the neighbor's front porch.

She returned to the house, more frightened than before. She went to her uncle's room and lay on the bed. It smelled of them and it helped her relax. She was beginning to doze off when she heard the familiar tapping of claws. She smiled and propped herself up on one elbow. "Chance! Come here, boy!"

The sound of the paws stopped.

"Chance, is that you?" She had an uneasy feeling. She glanced around. On the dresser was a pile of loose change and Xiao-ping's Swiss army knife. She picked it up and opened the blade.

Then she heard the tap of claws on the wood floor coming closer. But slowly. Cautiously.

Without taking her eyes off the door, she eased over to the chair where Xiao-ping had hung his belt. She slowly slipped it off the back of the chair.

She heard the claws just outside the door and held her breath.

Slowly the head of her German shepherd appeared in the doorway. At the sight of her, the dog bared its teeth and growled.

"Chance! Stop that!" There was something about the look in the dog's eye that frightened her. She began to ease herself slowly toward the master bathroom.

The dog came closer, its growl growing deeper and more menacing. She let the metal buckle of the belt fall, so that she could swing it if need be. Now she had the knife in one hand and the belt in the other.

"Bad dog, Chance! Bad!"

Her voice only seemed to trigger something in the big dog. He leapt for her, bounding onto the bed and jumping at her. She yelped and dashed for the bathroom door. She made it just in the nick of time—latching and locking the door behind her.

On the other side of the door, Chance had exploded into a frenzy, barking savagely and scratching the wood. She backed away and had the sudden urge to cry. This was just so awful! But she knew she had to act. She looked around the bathroom, closed the knife and put it in her pocket, then took a long drink of water from the faucet. Next, she double-wrapped her dad's belt around her waist, then went to the window and opened it. She tried to be as quiet as possible. If Chance heard her escaping, he'd run to the doggie door in the kitchen and catch her outside.

Fortunately, he was still going crazy at the door, so as quickly as possible she pushed out the screen and scrambled out.

Her plan was to make it to the main lodge, which was a quarter mile up the road, but she was only halfway down the driveway when Chance burst through the doggie door. He was coming at a full sprint, and she only had a few seconds.

She made for the big tree on her right. She swung up quickly, and Chance jumped at her. She heard the chomp of his jaws snapping shut. Then he barked and snarled like he was rabid.

"Damn you, Chance! Leave me alone!"

But the dog just continued to bark and threaten her for the better part of an hour before he settled down to wait her out.

Mei ended up spending the night in the tree. It was miserable, but she tried to make the best of it.

She wondered where Xiao-ping was . . . and what had happened to Logan and her aunt. *I wish I'd never come on this stupid trip*, she thought. It had all been her aunt's idea—a way for her and her uncle to bond.

After a few hours in the tree, she was hungry and thirsty. She remembered learning in school how Native Americans had tapped maple trees for syrup and how it was usually done at this time of year. This wasn't a maple, it was an oak, but she wondered if it could be tapped too. *Worth a try*, she thought. She got out her Swiss army knife and bore a whole in the bark with the corkscrew, then stuck the short knife blade in. Soon there was a steady flow of syrup. It tasted nutty, like an acorn, but it was sweet and would at least give her some fluids. Then she found a straight branch and, using the saw tool to cut it, began whittling the end to make a spear. She was hungry and angry and wasn't about to start living in a tree. "You better be gone in the morning," she warned. "Or I'm going to come down there and kick your ass."

She couldn't fathom what had come over Chance. He'd been a rescue dog, full grown when they got him, and, yes, her aunt had warned her against getting a dog that might have been abused, even insisting they take him on a probationary basis. But the dog had only showed affection and loyalty before now, and Lili had even admitted she'd been wrong. "Okay, he can stay. But remember our deal.

If you stop taking care of him or don't clean up his messes"—her aunt had licked her lips and popped her eyebrows excitedly—"I'm getting out my recipe book."

Mei knew her aunt was teasing, but she'd still run to Chance and hugged him around the neck.

Now, as she looked down at the dog that seemed so desperate to eat her, and as her own hunger knotted her stomach, the old Chinese customs didn't seem so barbaric.

After it got dark, she took her uncle's belt and wrapped it around a fat horizontal branch, then threaded it through the belt loops in her jeans. That way if she rolled over in her sleep, she wouldn't fall to her death.

In the night she heard strange sounds, like the swarming of insects, and in the morning found that all the cabins were gone. As were the roads, the cars, and the telephone poles. The world was gone. There was no sign of Chance, either, but she had a strong feeling he was still out there somewhere.

Her stomach was growling, and she was desperately hungry. Still, she waited another half hour before dropping to the ground with the spear in her hand.

It was time to find some food.

In the backwoods of West Virginia, somewhere in the forests between the forgotten towns of Alton and Cassity, and not far from the Buckhannon River, a fugitive had been living in a cave for the past two months. His hair and beard had grown thick and long, and he often found himself braiding the beard to keep it out of his food.

He was lonely at times—he hadn't seen another human being in six weeks—but he was also content. Living in the wild suited him.

TV shows and the media liked to depict nature as a dangerous place, a place where mankind was a stranger and would surely die from a host of causes—he would starve to death or freeze to death or eat something poisonous or be eaten himself by a wild animal. But this particular fugitive knew this was bullshit, a fiction designed to hook viewers and the uninitiated. The truth was that with a little training, a human being could live almost anywhere . . . and live comfortably.

He caught most, but not all, of his own food. He ate rabbits and squirrels and opossums, and an occasional raccoon that he trapped. Once he had harvested a deer with a single shot from his hunting rifle. He also stole food from the summer homes that had been locked for the winter, and he took the propane tanks from people's barbecue grills to keep himself warm and to make cooking easier.

The man woke suddenly in the middle of a snowy clearing. Somehow he had passed out. But why? He stood and looked around. He'd been out hunting and knew this part of the woods well. Everything seemed all right at first, but then he realized that his rifle was gone and so was his pistol. Had he been robbed? No, it couldn't be: snow had fallen last night and the only tracks on the ground were his.

Worried that he might have been discovered, he raced the half mile back to his cave, already planning to shift to another part of the forest for a while. When he arrived, everything was right where he had left it, except his revolver . . . and all of his ammunition. He still didn't understand what had happened, but he was familiar with a technology that could do things like this.

He immediately checked some very special equipment he had, donning a military uniform and helmet. He found that it still functioned as designed. *Kindred spirits*, he thought.

If they are reaching me out here, he thought, *something important has happened.* He quickly packed his things into a backpack and began his trek out. It was a five-mile walk to the closest thing that could be called a town. Rock Cave, West Virginia. Population 1,400. It had an IGA, a post office, a Baptist church, and a firehouse.

He walked quickly and deliberately. There were about four inches of fresh snow on the ground, and it lay like frosting over the evergreens. Despite his worry, he found himself calmed by the serenity of the forest in wintertime, and it reminded him of the Christmases he'd had as a boy living in Alaska.

An hour and a half later, he came to a crest and looked down on the town. He could immediately see that something was very wrong. No cars were moving, and many sat in the middle of the road.

He engaged the Venger system and checked himself over. Now the only thing that would give him away were his footprints in the snow.

He descended the hill to the road, paused to make sure that there was no one around, then set foot on the street. It seemed an important moment. He was back in civilization . . . or what was left of it. He approached a Ford parked in the middle of the road. It was empty. He tried the ignition. Nothing.

He crossed the bridge over a creek and came into the town proper. He checked two more empty cars. He tried to start one, it didn't turn over either. And there wasn't a soul anywhere.

"Somebody fucked up," he said aloud. "Somebody fucked up real bad." Suddenly the quiet of the place began to unnerve him. Living in the forest, the quiet was soothing. But to be in a town and have it this quiet felt very wrong.

He went over to the IGA. The first thing he noticed was a shopping cart full of groceries sitting in the parking lot. *Whatever took these people, did it instantly*, he thought.

He entered the store, the automatic doors still functioning. He began to move through the produce section, gathering up food as he went along. He hadn't had any fresh fruit in weeks, so he began gorging himself on blueberries, raspberries, and strawberries.

He was halfway through his third pack of raspberries, when he heard a sound. Someone was crying.

Quietly he made his way toward the source. In the candy aisle he turned to see a girl sitting on the floor. She was surrounded by

Hershey's, Reese's, and Almond Joy wrappers, but was trembling uncontrollably. Immediately, his heart went out to her. *She's probably only eight or nine*, he thought, *and terrified.*

He turned off the Venger cloaking system and came closer. She was so consumed by her sorrow, that she didn't notice him until he spoke to her.

"Hey, are you okay?" he said softly.

She startled like a deer and scrambled to her feet.

"Hey, it's okay," he said, holding up his hands. She looked at him, confused, and he realized she didn't speak English.

"*La astatie fahmak*," she said. He recognized the language as Arabic but wasn't sure what she'd said. Luckily, the Venger system translator kicked in. "I can't understand you," it said.

He spoke again, knowing the system would translate for him. "I want to help you," he said. "I'm a friend."

This time she understood and gave a slight nod, but he could tell she was still terrified.

He eased a little closer. "What's your name?"

She looked him over, head to toe, clearly not sure if she should trust him. "Rima," she finally said.

He smiled. "I'm Sawyer."

"You're a soldier?"

"Yes . . . well, I used to be. Where are you from?"

"My family and I are refugees from Syria. We arrived last week. There was a family, the Kramers, who were taking care of us."

Sawyer nodded. It was starting to make sense.

"What happened to everyone?" she asked.

"I don't know."

"I woke up and my whole family was gone—my mom, my dad, and my big brother." She began to tear up again. He felt awful for her. Not only had she just left her home, her school, and all her friends and relatives in Syria, now she found herself completely alone in a country she didn't know.

He put his hand on her shoulder, "I'm sorry," he said. Then, to his surprise, she wrapped her arms around him and began to cry. He got down on his knees and embraced her, letting her nestle her head into the curve of his neck. She gripped him tight, and he let her cry, feeling her tears on his skin.

"I know it's scary," he said. "But I'm going to protect you. I promise." Sawyer nodded to himself, trying to think it through. When he'd first seen the town, he knew immediately that he needed to get to DC to find out what happened. But now that wouldn't be so easy. Rima would likely resist leaving—believing that her family might somehow reappear. He'd have to convince her it was the best thing for both of them. But that would have to wait. For now he just had to look after her and help her cope with the sudden shock. Hopefully in a week or so she'd be feeling better, would trust him, and they could begin the journey.

He held her tight, but not too tight. "I'm going to make sure nothing happens to you," he said.

CHAPTER SIXTY-FIVE

EMMA'S WORLD

North America

Emma Rosario awoke slowly. She was having the nicest dream. It was summer and she was riding Argo through the woods and the wind was in her hair and everything was perfect. She felt herself coming awake and realized it was a dream. She tried to will herself back to sleep, to hold on to the feeling, but it was no use. The dream dissolved into nothing.

Reluctantly, she opened her eyes, then a frown of confusion spread across her face. She was outside lying in a broad patch of bright green moss. She put her palm on it and found it was oddly warm. To one side of her was a high bank of rock, that made a sheer wall. Opposite the rock face was a screen of very tall grass. How had she gotten here? She sat up, then her eyes went wide with fright. She scrambled backward on her hands and feet and put her back to the rock.

Not five feet in front of her was an enormous cheetah. It was sleeping on its side in the sun like a giant house cat.

Emma gasped. At the sound of her voice the huge cat opened one eye, then raised its head to look at her.

She froze. She knew she didn't dare move a muscle. This was a predator that wouldn't hesitate to kill her and drag her body back to its cave. But she also knew she couldn't run away. Like modern cheetahs, it was believed that the giant cheetah's instinct to give chase was only triggered by the flight of an animal. If she didn't run, it wouldn't think she was food.

So there she stood, with her back to the rock, perfectly still.

The cat studied her a moment through lazy eyes, then gave a bored yawn and put its head back down to sleep.

Emma looked up and wondered if she could scale the rock to the top, but then a strange idea possessed her. Looking at the huge cat, she thought: *I made you.*

She considered all that had happened. Sebastian said that the program to cure her disease had become incredibly powerful. And now, here in front of her, was a creature that shouldn't exist, yet a creature that had been on her mind that night when she'd disobeyed Sebastian and gone too far.

I made you, she thought again. *Or at least that other part of me made you.*

She took a deep breath and stepped closer to the cat. It didn't move or even open its eyes. She crouched down and extended her hand. When her fingers were mere inches away, it opened its eyes and looked at her, but nothing more. She hesitated a second longer, then pushed her hand into its fur. It was so thick that her hand completely disappeared. . . and it felt incredible, so soft and warm. Slowly, she brushed up and down its belly. Then she heard an incredible sound, a deep, rich purr from the cat's throat. Emma couldn't help but laugh. "You like that, don't you?" she said. The cat rolled onto its back in surrender. "Ah, I see you're a she," Emma said.

After a few minutes Emma stood and began making her way through the tall grass. As she walked, she realized how she'd been in a kind of natural hideout. While she slept, she'd been shielded from sight and protected by her guardian.

She emerged from the tunnel of grass and the world she saw

before her took her breath away. She was standing at the lip of a beautiful valley. Despite the chill in the air, everything was green and alive. She saw stunning vines adorning the winter trees, many of them blooming with white and purple flowers. In the bottom of the valley was a stream that twinkled in the sunlight. And here and there she saw different animals. There was a herd of *kyptoceras*—with their odd nose antlers—and several *platybelodon* wading in the water, and a big horned *Elasmotherium*. On the far side of the valley, the land rose to a rocky cliff with a large boulder at its summit. It was several miles off, but she could see even more animals grazing on the pastureland, including a dozen horses.

The huge cat had followed her and now sat on its haunches beside her, its head even with hers. "You'd better wait here," she said. The cat blinked lazily, then lay down in the sun.

Then Emma stepped forward to explore the valley that she knew had been made for her.

EPILOGUE

Kebbi-An, the oldest woman in the Sān tribe, looked out across the desert, searching for any sign of Naru and the three teenagers. She knew the fate of the entire tribe lay with them. If they did not return, it was over. Their only chance of survival would be to give up this way of life and learn to live among the whites.

The tribe had retreated here—to the sacred cave and underground lake—to wait for their return. But it had now been five days and they were beginning to lose hope.

Kebbi-An had decided that she would be the first one to know whether they had failed or succeeded, so she had found a quiet place to keep her vigil: between a pair of the massive rock pillars that surrounded this desert oasis. She slept there and had the children bring her food.

Now, once more she scanned the horizon for any sign of them. Over the past few days, she had stared so long that her eyes had started playing tricks on her. Over and over she would imagine she saw their sleek figures in the distance, walking through the quivering heat of the desert. Over and over her sense of elation had risen, only to fall when she realized there was nothing there.

She shook her head and took a drink of water. Then looked out once more. She imagined she saw something. Far in the distance, right at the edge of the horizon, where the ground shimmered with the waves of heat. *Curse these old eyes*, she thought.

She squinted at the mirage. Then she rose to her feet.

There was someone there. Her old mouth grew into a grin as she saw Naru, but then her elation fell once more. Where were the others?

She took a step forward, shading her eyes with her hand.

Naru caught sight of her and waved her spear in the air. The next instant Karuma, ‡Toma and /Uma emerged from behind her and began running toward Kebbi-An.

A wave of relief washed over the old woman and tears formed on her cheek. "They're back!" she called to the others. "All of them . . . Every one!"

Within seconds, the rest of the tribe was pouring out from between the large boulders like water, rushing out to meet them. But Kebbi-An made sure she was the first to touch them, even pushing one of the children aside. She held on to each one fiercely for a moment—for this was proof that they still had a future.

Everyone was either laughing, talking, or crying.

Naru was the last to arrive, but even her typical veneer of severity had washed away. She stepped up to the old woman and smiled. "We did it, grandmother."

"I know," Kebbi-An said, embracing her tightly and letting the tears on her cheek spread to Naru's. "I never doubted it."

That night, the Sān sat around the fire, and Karuma and Uma told the story to the tribe. How they had laid an ambush at the Kudu's Horns and had almost won but had been captured. Then how Karuma had heard a voice, and Cagn had killed the last mercenaries for them. The story was told and retold and then retold again.

When everyone was satisfied that no detail had been overlooked, there was music and dancing.

But Karuma didn't join in, perhaps because he did not feel like a child any longer. Instead he watched the others. It was enough for him and it made him happy. He stared at them and at the big fire, and at the tips of orange ash that rose into the night sky and disappeared among the stars.

He thought of Cristo, now a star in the sky . . . and of his father and grandfather and all those who had been killed in the massacre. They were up there, looking down on them.

He nodded to himself. It was finally settling in that the war was over. He thanked Cagn for delivering his people. For giving him a sign. For guiding them each step of the way. Yet he also suspected that Cagn was not the only one who had helped them. The voice he had heard. The one that told him to stall Marcus. He knew that voice, and it had not been Cagn's.

"Thank you, my friend," he said. "Thank you."

As Karuma stared at his family, the fire, and the stars, he had no way of knowing that the world had changed, that all the forces that had been encroaching on their way of life had been erased, and that the eight million other *Homo sapiens* still left on the planet were now struggling to survive just as he was.

AUTHOR'S NOTE

I love writing near-future science fiction because you can speculate with current trends in politics, technology, and science. However, there was one non-contemporary influence on this series that I feel is worth explaining. It's a series of paintings done by the American artist Thomas Cole between 1833 and 1836. These are the original Course of Empire—five paintings that depict the rise and fall of a civilization, beginning with a pastoral arcadia, transitioning to a modern urban culture and then self-destruction and desolation. When I first saw the paintings, I was inspired by the idea of a cyclical pattern to history and civilization, and I wondered if I could make a series of books that depicted that rise and fall and—in the case of this series—rebirth.

If you have never seen the paintings, I encourage you to take a look. They have a timelessness about them and, I believe, serve as a warning about the fragility of our creations.

ACKNOWLEDGMENTS

I would like to thank my faithful beta readers: Marcelo Alonso, James Bowie, Natalia Vergara, Jennifer Hill, and Alejandro Tarre.

Also, thanks to the several topic experts and veterans who helped me understand the technical and political nuances of the US military and nuclear weaponry, including Sam Waltzer and Robert Kershaw, as well as those sources who asked not to be named. Thanks to Lilian Genn for her help with the German dialogue. A second thanks to Jennifer Hill, whose nursing background helped me better understand what maladies people were likely to experience in the absence of modern medicine. For help on detective work and investigative procedures, I'm indebted to Kim Johnston. Next, an enormous thanks to Kellie Aquino, whose preternatural spelling and grammar skills helped save me from looking foolish.

Many sincere thanks to Josh Newton for his time, patience, and excellent artwork. It was a pleasure to have someone as skilled as him bring these images and characters to life.

A great deal of gratitude to Jill Marr, my agent; and to the team at Blackstone Publishing, including Josie Woodbridge, Sean Thomas,

Isabella Bedoya, and Ember Hood. And to my editor Michael Signorelli for helping me trim, cut and massage the best possible conclusion to this series.

The final thanks, as always, goes to my wonderful wife, Natalia, whose support, love, and selflessness was crucial in making this book (and the entire series) possible. I love you.